THE SEMONOV IMPULSE

DUNCAN KYLE was born in Bradford, Yorkshire, a few hundred yards from the house where J. B. Priestley grew up.

He started his career as a junior reporter on the *Bradford Telegraph and Argus*, later going on to the *Leicester Mercury* and the *Yorkshire Post*. In the mid-fifties he joined *John Bull* magazine – which later became *Today* – in London and from there went on to become editorial director at Odhams where he wrote his first novel, *A Cage of Ice*.

It was the success of this book which persuaded him to become a full-time writer and to fulfil his long-held ambition to live deep in the country. He now lives in Suffolk with his wife and three children.

DUNCAN KYLE

The Semonov Impulse

FONTANA/Collins

First published in Great Britain by Weidenfeld and
Nicolson under the pseudonym James Meldrum 1975
First issued in Fontana Paperbacks 1983

Copyright © Rupert Crew Ltd 1975

Made and printed in Great Britain by
William Collins Sons & Co. Ltd, Glasgow

The debt is to Shirley and John

CHAPTER ONE

In the early part of 1972, following several attempts to hijack Aeroflot aircraft on scheduled flights within the Communist bloc, attempts which were made mainly by East European dissidents wishing to escape to the West, the Soviet aviation authorities put into practice a carefully devised method of defeating hijackers. The method was based upon conclusions reached in a long report, the committee which submitted the report having examined in as much detail as possible every hijacking reported at that time anywhere in the world.

Prolonged study by the committee had revealed that hijackers followed, in general, a more or less fixed pattern of behaviour. A hijack demanded control of the aircraft's flight deck. With that control alone, a successful hijack could be achieved, and when hijacks were carried out by a single individual, as had happened many times in the United States, the man invariably made a sudden entry through the flight-deck door, armed with pistol or grenade, and simply ordered the pilot to fly him to his chosen destination. Hijacks *had* been achieved without an intruder on the flight deck, but such a behaviour pattern was rare and had *never* been followed, so far as the committee could ascertain, when more than one individual was involved. Groups of two or more hijackers *invariably* stationed one man (or woman) on the flight deck.

The behaviour of hijackers within the aircraft cabin was also examined in minute detail. Where a single individual decided to take over an aircraft from the cabin, his usual weapon was a grenade, though pistols and machine pistols had been used. Where the flight-deck hijacker threatened the life of pilot and co-pilot, the cabin hijacker threatened the aircraft itself. Do as I say, he said in effect, or I destroy the plane and everybody in it. The method used was almost always the same. The cabin hijacker stationed himself in the tail, where the explosion of a grenade would be most dangerous, and gave his orders to the flight deck via the aircraft crew's communication link, usually consisting of a microphone/loudspeaker package on a bulkhead.

Where two hijackers were involved, one was on the flight deck, the second either at the front of the passenger cabin, or, more commonly, at the rear, from which he/she could watch the backs of the seated passengers' heads. Since hijackers invariably kept passengers in their seats, the hijacker at the tail was at a considerable advantage. If three invaders took over the aircraft, it was usual for one to be on the flight deck, one at the front of the cabin facing the passengers, and one at the rear.

There was also a clear pattern to their subsequent behaviour. Hijackers *in* the cabin tended to stand in the middle of the aisle, not to either side, in order to maintain the maximum field of surveillance. They did not often move from these chosen positions unnecessarily, or walk up and down the aisle.

Four or more hijackers provided an entirely different set of behaviour patterns and the committee concluded with reluctance that it was impossible to move successfully against larger groups without endangering aircraft and passengers to an unacceptable degree.

The problem, therefore, was so to construct the crew's and the aircraft's defences that observed patterns of behaviour could be used against the hijackers. If the intruders took up predictable tactical positions, then they could be counter-attacked by predicted, tactical means. In formulating their plans, the Soviet officials, unlike their Western counterparts, were not inhibited by any need to be seen to deal humanely with the hijackers. In Soviet eyes the hijacker, by his act of piracy, sentenced himself to death.

The attack upon Bulgarian Airlines TU 154 flight 109 from Varna to Rome was carried out by two men travelling together on Canadian passports. They revealed themselves as the aircraft crossed the Adriatic, little more than half an hour from Rome, and the flight-deck crew became aware of them only when a man came swiftly through the door, shouted for their attention and ordered the pilot at pistol point to make for Ciampino, *not* Leonardo da Vinci. The hijacker ordered the captain to announce to Rome Air Traffic Control that he was proceeding to a landing at Ciampino, then to make no further radio contact. Nor must the captain respond to any further air traffic control radio instructions. The hijacker demanded earphones and stood listening as the message was passed and as Rome District responded first with puzzlement, then with firm orders to proceed to Leonardo da Vinci. Everyone on the flight deck understood that when no acknowledgement of the order was received from Bulgarian Airlines flight 109, the Ciampino approach would be cleared.

In the rear of the passenger cabin, one of the TU 154's three stewardesses took her seat, as ordered by the second hijacker. The seat was one of six which had been specially fitted with a tiny transceiver concealed beneath the headrest padding. She then felt beneath the seat and moved the switch activating the microphone circuit and spoke softly into the concealed mike: 'One in the cabin, one on the flight deck.'

'Remove your headphones,' the intruder on the flight deck ordered the pilot and co-pilot.

The captain turned in his seat, glanced at the man, and complied. He noted the hijacker's position and that the door leading from the flight deck out to the cabin was held open by the hijacker's body. Then he reached up to the control panel above his head and moved a switch which activated a small, specially installed electric motor. He waited.

The motor was connected to the door's spring-closing mechanism and its effect was simply to increase the effort required to hold the door open. A few moments later, the captain again turned the solenoid switch, further increasing the engine's output. In a small mirror built into the lower control panel, he watched the effect. The electric motor was able to deliver one horse-power, but to use its full power was to defeat its purpose, which was to use the door to separate the hijackers. Full power would reveal what was happening, i.e. that the crew was taking counter-action. He glanced over his shoulder.

'Face forward,' the man ordered sharply.

The captain complied, but he had seen what he wanted to see: the man's body was braced against the door and he was having to exert considerable strength to keep it open.

Again he adjusted the solenoid switch, keeping his eyes on the mirror. A minute passed in silence then he heard the man move and the click as the door closed. It was time for stage two. The captain checked the hijacker's position again. The man stood with his back to the door, feet slightly apart, pistol held at waist level. The captain smiled to himself at the accuracy of the predicted behaviour pattern, and activated a second switch built into his seat beside his left hand.

The hiss was inaudible from where he was sitting, but the instantly-following choking noise he heard clearly and he was already rising from his seat as the hijacker's body fell. The switch had been, in effect, an electrical trigger, operating a gas gun built into the bulkhead by the door. When the gun had fired, it had directed a lethal jet of hydrocyanic gas directly into the hi-

9

jacker's face. One breath was enough; hydrocyanic gas is the perfect close-quarters killer. Simultaneously with the firing of the gas gun, another gas was discharged from four other points on the flight deck: oxygen into which had been mixed certain substances to neutralise hydrocyanic gas. As the hijacker died, the crew remained safe, and within seconds the ventilation system had removed all trace of the gases from the flight deck.

The captain examined the hijacker, satisfied himself the man was dead, and resumed his headphones.

'Still one man in the cabin?' he asked.

The hostess's voice came back softly. 'One man.'

'His position?'

'Front row window seat, starboard side.'

'Standing?'

'Yes.'

'How is he armed?'

'Machine pistol.'

The captain frowned. This second man was not acting as predicted. 'Has he moved at all?'

'No.'

He rotated the solenoid switch anti-clockwise, turning off the power to the door mechanism, then removed his headphones again. The flight engineer helped him to drag the hijacker's body away from the door. Then the flight engineer opened a small locker and took out a pistol, long barrelled for accuracy. After that he removed a circular plug about two inches in diameter from the middle of the door, just above waist height. The far side of the door, visible from the passenger cabin, was decorated in a pattern of black circles, so that the absence of the plug would be scarcely noticeable.

The TU 154's captain took off his jacket and hung it up, and in trousers and shirt-sleeves only, to show he was unarmed, opened the door and stepped into the three-metre-long corridor. He saw seventy-odd pairs of eyes swivel to watch him and knew the armed hijacker would have seen them too. It didn't matter. He was unarmed and had no hope of either surprising or disarming the man. Instead he said loudly, 'I am the captain. I must speak to you.'

A pause. Then, 'Come forward slowly.'

He took three paces forward into the small, squarish space by the forward exit door and turned to look at the hijacker.

'Well?'

'There is fog at Ciampino.'

10

The hijacker frowned. Then he said, 'You take orders from the man on the flight deck.'

'He told me to say,' the captain said, 'that he wishes to speak to you.' He watched with pleasure the flicker of doubt and indecision on the hijacker's face. 'Apparently it is urgent.'

The hijacker looked at him appraisingly, and the captain knew what was passing through his mind. The hijack had been carefully planned and the plan was now destroyed.

The captain turned the screw a little. 'It is a question of where to divert.'

'Tell him, Lod Airport, Tel Aviv.'

'I am afraid,' the captain said, 'that we have insufficient fuel. I have informed him of that. He now wishes to confer with you.'

The man hesitated, looking for alternatives and finding none. He would be thinking, the captain knew, that his friend dared not leave the flight deck because alarm messages would be radioed instantly and it was clear that the imposed radio silence had been part of the hijack plan.

The hijacker hesitated, then nodded. 'Very well. I will come. But do not attempt any action against us.'

'I am concerned only with the safety of my aircraft and the people aboard,' the captain said soothingly. 'Nothing else.'

He watched as the hijacker moved sideways past the three seats, saw him look for a moment along the cabin, then step into the short corridor. The soft-nosed bullet almost amputated the man's arm at the shoulder. Its charge had been specially reduced to minimise the risk to the aircraft structure, but at ten feet the bullet's effect was terrifying, smashing the man backwards on to the cabin floor.

Almost casually, the captain bent to pick up the machine pistol. A second later the flight-deck door opened and the engineer came forward. Together they dragged the badly wounded man on to the flight deck. He was whimpering with the pain of his shattered arm and broken ribs and bright arterial blood flowed freely from the arm. If the bleeding were not stopped, the man would die, which was not important in itself, except that he must not die before he could be made to talk, made to reveal the detail and purpose of the hijack plan.

On all overseas flights from Soviet bloc countries, one of the aircraft's crew is a member of the *Komitat Gosudarstvennoi Bezopastnosti* or its equivalent in the satellite country concerned. On this flight the engineer was, in fact, Russian, a KGB man. The captain watched him at work with the medical kit, clamping off the severed artery before beginning to interrogate and almost certainly to torture, the prisoner.

'Captain!' The co-pilot's voice made him turn.

'What is it?'

'Twelve minutes from touchdown.'

The captain swore, slid into his seat, put on his headset, called Rome District, identified his aircraft and asked for instructions for landing at Leonardo da Vinci.

'Negative,' the air traffic controller's voice came flatly back. 'Your Ciampino landing confirmed.'

The captain knew what must have happened. The traffic pattern had already been changed to allow him into Ciampino. It would have been assumed that his silence had been the result of radio trouble. Now, with the new pattern fixed and perhaps dozens of aircraft involved in timing changes, it was too late and even a little risky to change the traffic pattern again.

'Confirm Ciampino,' he said.

'Ten degrees left. Down to eight thousand feet.'

The captain moved the controls obediently.

'Okay. You are now on the centre line –'

The captain concentrated now upon the complexities of the landing. He had to concentrate hard and it was more difficult than usual because a sound tore at his concentration. The hijacker had begun to scream...

CHAPTER TWO

It began every two minutes or so, away to the west, a thin sound at first, held back and diminished by the wind, but growing louder with every second. For a few moments it remained merely a whistle, but then other noises joined in and grew louder too. A distant, low growl became a muted roar; displaced air whooshed in accompaniment. Budzinski turned his head to stare through narrowed eyes down the approach path. He was half-dazzled by the noon sun, so not until the aeroplane was half a mile short of touchdown, until its black shadow was discernible in swift undulations over the scrub, could he see enough of the onrushing jet. When he could, his lips thinned in impatience. Maybe the next. Maybe the one after that. Maybe something had gone wrong. Somewhere a grey goose walked across his grave and the involuntary shudder made him angry with himself.

He glanced quickly towards the van half a mile away, wishing he could hear the terminal loudspeaker, even though it was not necessary for him to hear. In drawing up the disposition plan, he had known that and placed himself deliberately nearer to the Learjet. The others would hear and act accordingly; all Budzinski had to do was watch the van. When the van finally moved towards him, then and only then would his own role begin. Methodically his mind went over the operation again, searching for weaknesses even though every detail had been examined and re-examined. He knew the waiting was going for his nerves and resented it. Tension before an operation was normal, natural, even encouraging, because it was now so familiar. This, though, was not normal tension. Budzinski was experiencing a creator's doubt. Because the plan was his, because he had conceived it in secret, because for the first time he had been unable to discuss it with the subtle minds of the Mossad, he carried the whole responsibility, and not just of command but the more burdensome responsibility of initiation.

The whistle began again. Budzinski looked for the aircraft, watched its approach, picked out the words Trans-Meridian as it floated down over his head. The big Boeing touched and its sudden reverse thrust blasted violent sound at him. He swore softly to himself and tried consciously to relax. Two more minutes.

Two minutes of waiting, of build-up, then another plane that could be anything. Soon, if all had gone well, one of the swooping silver shapes would be the right one. If all had gone well, his men would be aboard. And Schmidt.

Schmidt.

Joachim Schmidt, alive still, sixty-six years old, coming at last to...

Budzinski looked again towards the van and wondered how the others were standing the strain. He smiled briefly, knowing the answer. Moise would be forcing himself to relax, making himself stare blankly at some fixed point so that his alert black eyes would not be darting everywhere. Moise's slim body would be tense, but under harsh control. When the moment came, Moise would almost flick into movement. Unlike Shimshon. Shimshon would *be* relaxed, coiled lazily somewhere, blinking amiably. He always blinked amiably. He'd even blinked amiably when the unbelievable news first arrived in a letter from, of all places, Schenectady, New York...

The letter had lain unopened for three days, and there was irony in that. Irony, indeed, in the fact that it had been forwarded at all. Budzinski had been in Tel Aviv for those three days at the deathbed and at the funeral of Manfred Ritter, his last living relative. Manfred, who had been in France in September 1939 and so had escaped the holocaust, escaped Layerhausen where the rest of them had died.

On his return after the funeral, Budzinski, a man always alone, felt loneliness too. He had walked for an hour in the citrus groves and watched the children play as dusk came, seeking to balance his mind again, before returning to the kibbutz office where the letter was waiting, one among several. He'd read two others first, letters addressed in familiar handwriting. The blue airmail letter came last, almost an explosion at the end of a sad, quiet day. Even after he'd opened it, glanced at the address at the top, frowned at the signature at the bottom, he had had no inkling. He had begun to read it almost casually, with only half his mind, because the rest was taken up by memories and the residue of grief.

> 1735 Cedarwood Drive, Inlet Park,
> Schenectady, NEW YORK.

Dear Major Budzinski,

You may remember, though I doubt it, that we met at the home of Dr Michael Edelmann some ten years ago. There is no reason why you should remember me. But I remember you, and I am writing to you in the hope that, unlike the government of our land, you have not abandoned the cause of retribution. There is no-one else for me to approach because I know no others. I do not even know where to send this letter, so am addressing it to army headquarters in the hope that it will be forwarded unopened.

I know how tenuous this line is. Major Budzinski may be dead, may have responsibilities which prevent his taking action, may have come to agree with the government's policy. I fervently pray that none of these is true. Hopefully, therefore, I am sending this information to you.

It is very simple. Three weeks ago I saw Joachim Schmidt. I can imagine that you will not believe this easily, so it is necessary to give you both my credentials and my evidence.

Like you I am an Ashkenazy Jew, born in Poznan. Also I am one of the survivors of Layerhausen. When I was taken there in 1943, I was thirteen years old and would have gone like most of the others to the gas chambers. The reason I did not, the entire reason for my survival, is that I am a musician, a pianist. At nine I was regarded as a prodigy and my name was known. Schmidt had the impulse to hear me play. After that, he kept me as a servant, also as a kind of pet. You will know that Schmidt was a violinist of a good standard. You may know also that there existed at Layerhausen a chamber ensemble. I was made the pianist in that ensemble.

For more than a year I lived in Schmidt's quarters at the compound so I knew him well. I was there when, in late 1944, in the kitchen, he accidentally sliced away the pad of flesh at the tip of the little finger of his left hand. He was drunk and cutting sausage. When the finger healed, he was left with a flat, inclined plane at the tip of the finger.

Three weeks ago I was in Bulgaria. I am now a professional accompanist on the piano and I was visiting the country with Madame Laurette Stallo, an American soprano of whom you may know. Madame Stallo appeared twice with the opera company in the Black Sea port of Varna and also gave several recitals, in one of which she sang with the Varna chamber orchestra. One of the members of the orchestra was Joachim Schmidt.

I did not recognise him at first and I do not believe he knew me at all. Since I was a fifteen-year-old boy when he saw me last, that is scarcely surprising. But I saw the finger and recognition followed.

You will ask yourself, and ask me if we meet, whether the finger is sufficient evidence. I know it is not. It is probable that many thousands of people inflict similar injuries upon themselves every year. Also he has changed. He is fat and what hair he has is now white. He wears a moustache, also white, and heavy glasses.

For additional evidence I can offer my own recognition of his face. You may think that not enough, for in thirty years he is much changed, as we all are. But there is one other thing, a movement of the left hand in abrupt transition from a low to a high note on the violin. The movement is fast and must be accurate to a remarkable degree. Schmidt was always proud of his glissades and I saw it many hundreds of times. His own hand movement was highly idiosyncratic, involving a sudden straightening of the thumb and forefinger. That same movement is made by the violinist I saw in Varna. I have seen many hundreds of violinists. That movement of thumb and forefinger is Schmidt's alone.

Major Budzinski, this can only be an assurance. Joachim Schmidt *is* alive and in Varna, Bulgaria. I do not merely believe this is the man; I *know* him.

I know also what this man did. But so do you, so I will not weary you by restating it.

But as Eichmann was brought to trial, so too should Schmidt be brought to trial. If Israel has turned her back on revenge, I believe not all Jews have done so. If Israel no longer wishes to pursue, to capture and to try the remaining criminals, then individual Jews must surely be free to act in the name of the dead millions. If Schmidt cannot be tried, he should in justice be executed by a Jewish hand – an Ashkenazy hand.

I know in my heart that you believe this too.

William Gold
(Wilhelm Goldman)

Budzinski had lain awake all through that night. At intervals he had switched on the light beside his bed to read the letter again, absorbing its quiet certainty. After Mengele and Bormann, Schmidt was perhaps the most important, certainly the most hated, of the remaining major war criminals still at large. It was not the numbers of his victims that had generated the particularity of the hatred – far fewer people had perished at Layerhausen than at Auschwitz, Treblinka or Dachau – but it was impossible to forget the refined and deliberate cruelties that Schmidt had inflicted. He would summon people from inside the gas chamber itself, tell them they were to be released, help them into a waiting car. Then, when the camp gates opened, the car would go outside, merely to turn round and return. The victims would go back into the chamber. Schmidt watched their expressions as hope flared and died again. He thought it funny.

There were many stories about Schmidt; Budzinski lay in the night remembering them. Schmidt the violinist once played Bach beside the oven crematoria, giggling, announcing that he fiddled while Jewry burned. Budzinski's own parents had probably died – he had never been able to find out with certainty – in Layerhausen. He knew how Gold, the letter-writer, felt; all Jews to whom Layerhausen was a matter of personal history cherished for Schmidt a special kind of detestation, a special anxiety for justice, which meant revenge, and that was justice after all.

Somehow, as the darkness faded and morning came, Budzinski's mind came out of the past into the future. It now dwelt not on the still surprising knowledge that Schmidt was alive, that after a quarter of a century he had finally been found, but on the severe practicalities of action. Gold's closing words had stirred again the deep and powerful determination for revenge that had motivated Budzinski through the long years of seek-and-capture and seek-and-destroy.

He poured cold orange juice into a glass and sat bare-chested on the balcony, looking across the citrus groves to the desert beyond. It was six years since Golda Meir's edict had disbanded the action squads; was he now fit enough to face the demands of action, or sharp enough mentally? At forty-three he was on the edge of middle age, his reflexes a little slower, his muscles less vigorous. He stretched out his legs, pointing the toes, feeling muscles move and tighten. Even sitting as he was, his belly was flat and hard. Not bad for forty-three, he thought, but scarcely the bundle of strength and energy he'd been at thirty in Argentina, when they found Eichmann's trail and caught him and then just missed grabbing Mengele six months later. There were persistent rumours now that Mengele was dead. Probably put about, Budzinski thought sourly, by Mengele's own people. There'd been enough rumours that Schmidt was dead, too, but Schmidt wasn't dead. Schmidt was playing his damned violin in a chamber orchestra. He thought again of Gold's words: '... individual Jews must surely be free to act in the name of the dead millions. If Schmidt cannot be tried, he should in justice be executed by a Jewish hand – an Ashkenazy hand. I know in my heart that you believe this, too.'

Budzinski nodded as the words ran through his mind. The edict had been specific, calling off the hunt absolutely. The Arabs and the uncertain future now demanded all of Israel's attention; the past should be remembered but not acted upon. *But*, 'individual Jews must surely be free...' As his eyes strayed contemplatively over the lemon trees, he made his first decision.

The following day he travelled again to Tel Aviv, telephoned his old boss Chaim Lissak and suggested lunch. They had remained in touch, so that invitation was not unusual. Lissak, former commander of the action squads and now a brigadier on the army staff, would know how the land lay. Budzinski, however, approached his subject with care. Chaim Lissak would not countenance flagrant disobedience of major policy. For all his secret exploits, Lissak remained a copybook soldier. Budzinski wanted to discover whether the policy was engraved on stones, or whether perhaps it could become flexible, given suitable circumstances. Towards the end of the lunch, after some reliving of old events, he began to slap his thighs irritably and sigh a few times and contrived a kind of plastered-over irritability.

'Your trouble, Josef,' Chaim Lissak said, 'is that you want still to be a young man. You should marry and divert your attention. It's not too late. Settle.'

'Settle!'

Lissak grinned at him. 'Build better machines. You serve Israel that way, too.'

'I got my diploma in nineteen forty-nine,' Budzinski said. 'I'm out of date. In those days it was wool and cotton weaving. Nylon was a great novelty then. I'm an apology for a textile engineer nowadays. Boys of twenty know more!'

'So be humble. Learn it all again.'

'I liked it once, but the world intervened. It's hard to go back.'

Lissak said, 'The past is for conversation; the distant past for study and philosophy. The future is for action.'

'Action is ruled out.'

'There are other kinds, Josef. Positive action –'

'We were positive enough!'

Lissak sighed. 'Constructive, I should have said. Build things. Make things. Serve the living. They need it.'

'We should not have given up,' Budzinski said. 'Not while so many are free. It's a betrayal.'

'No, Josef. Millions were killed. The real betrayal was to lose more in the search. How many men have we lost searching for Mengele? Do you know?'

'A few.' Budzinski shrugged. 'I don't know the figure.'

'Twenty-three. Sons, brothers, husbands. We can't spare them, Josef.'

'He's still walking about. Perhaps Bormann too, whatever the Germans say about that skull they found. Others too. Schmidt maybe...'

Lissak said, 'Old men. We should worry now about a few old men?'

'I do.'

Lissak sighed. 'So do I. But it's foolish and I should not.'

'What would happen,' Budzinski asked, 'if one of the big ones was found?'

'No hypotheses. No ifs.'

'No, listen. Suppose, just suppose, that somebody located, say, Mengele, or Bormann. What then?'

'I don't know.'

'We'd leave them, would we? Walking, living. Leading their lives!'

'It's an unlikely hypothesis and you know it. Twenty years we looked. More. You and I, we both searched, then again we searched.'

'All right. It's a hypothesis. What would the government do?'

'Leave them, or seek extradition.'

'And the man would vanish again. With Eichmann,' Budzinski said, 'we knew these things would happen. That's why he was brought here and put on trial. Trial, Chaim! Justice!'

Lissak grinned. 'Find Mengele here, in Tel Aviv, and justice you'd get. All the trials you want. But we don't look any more in Buenos Aires or Paraguay.'

'Even if Mengele were located?'

'A positive identification? You got Mengele?'

'No. Just tell me what you'd do.'

'Go to Golda,' Lissak said. 'Maybe she'd say yes, but I don't believe it. They made the decision. No – that's what Golda would say.'

'Unless he was in Tel Aviv.'

'In that unlikely circumstance, Josef, a point would be stretched.'

Budzinski said, 'Lod Airport is in Tel Aviv.'

Lissak said suddenly, harshly, 'What is it you have?'

19

Budzinski told the lie quickly, flatly, without vehemence. 'Nothing. But the point is bloody interesting.'

'If you have something,' Lissak said, 'forget it. The orders are clear. No action against war criminals on foreign soil.'

'The penalty?'

'We can't afford it, Josef. Not now. Fly Mengele into Tel Aviv and maybe they'd cheer you. Fail in public and there is nowhere to go. Israel would disown you. You couldn't even come back. If you did, a lifetime in prison. We are a law-abiding country. Think, Josef. Think what is needed. Remember the planning, the resources we used, to get Eichmann out of Argentina. Forget it.'

Budzinski said, 'There's nothing to forget. I'm just interested. I have strong feelings about this.' He stretched arms and legs, made himself smile. 'But I'm a textile engineer now, as you remind me.'

Lissak said, 'Take my advice. Marry. Have children. Children focus the eyes on the future.'

'Change babies? At my age?' Budzinski laughed.

'Do you good. You were wrapped up in the hunt too long. You need to be wrapped in something else.'

'Not dirty nappies.'

Lissak said, 'You dirtied a few yourself. How's Shimshon?'

'He blinks amiably at the lemons.'

'And works, yes?'

'He works.'

Shimshon was working when Budzinski returned to the kibbutz, shovelling sand and gravel and ballast into a concrete mixer. In the last three months he'd built several chess boards of concrete to stand in the open air. Now, more ambitiously, it was ping-pong tables for the children. Shimshon had spent weeks building the wooden moulds; now he was ready to cast the first table top.

'Will you be long?' Budzinski asked.

'Half as long, if *you* get a shovel.'

They worked two hours, mixing, pouring and packing, positioning rods and mesh in the liquid concrete. When the work was finally completed, Budzinski said, 'Where's the table going?'

'In front of the gymnasium.'

'How do you move it two hundred metres?'

Shimshon smiled. 'Wheels, Mr Engineer.'

'And how do you get it up on wheels?'

'Levers, Mr Engineer.'

'Good, Shimshon. You're learning.'

20

'Or maybe,' Shimshon said, 'I get the mobile crane over. You want coffee?'

'I want beer.'

'And to talk.'

'How do you know?'

Shimshon said, 'Telepathy maybe. Or the look on your face. Where?'

'Somewhere quiet.'

He handed Shimshon the letter and watched him read it. Finally Shimshon said, 'So? You know the rules.'

'I know them.'

'You think they'd be bent, do you? For Schmidt?'

'No,' Budzinski said, 'they won't.'

'You've tried?'

'I talked to Chaim Lissak in Tel Aviv yesterday.'

'That wasn't clever, Josef.'

'I didn't tell him.'

'You don't need to. He guesses.'

'No, Shimshon. I pretended I'm bored. Looking for action. Just asked him "what if?"'

'What if what?'

'If a big one were found. Bormann, Mengele, Schmidt. He said if they were found in Tel Aviv, okay. Anywhere else, the Government proceeds through official international channels. Which means he would escape of course.'

Shimshon looked at him for a moment, blinking. 'You're going after him anyway.'

'Yes.'

'You want me?'

Budzinski said, 'If we fail we're finished. We get no assistance, no government support. If we don't bring Schmidt back here, we can't come back at all.'

Shimshon nodded, rose, sipped his beer. 'For Schmidt it's worth risking. How do we do it?'

Budzinski said, 'I have an idea, but it's only that. We'd need help and money. And a lot of work.'

'And secrecy, Josef. That won't be easy.'

'I know.'

Nor had it been easy. The network of people anxious to assist in the process of retribution was six years unused and therefore difficult to reactivate. Also there were risks attached to using it. Communication had always needed to be clandestine, but a well-

21

organised and secret information system had existed, centred upon the office of the Israeli secret service, the Mossad. Now all contacts had to be doubly clandestine, for the Mossad itself must at all costs be kept in ignorance of what was going on.

The two advantages Budzinski and Shimshon had were derived from their own experience. Firstly, both had been involved in retributive operations of varying kinds in many countries so they knew with precision the requirements and disciplines involved. Secondly, in the course of their activities they had made numbers of very valuable contacts in a variety of places, people who could be trusted for the most powerful of all reasons: that they too had lost families in the camps. The war and its aftermath had scattered these people widely, and a kind of value lay in that, because that second, post-war dispersion had resulted in many new, first-generation Jewish Americans, French, British and others. People with passports and deep scars. People like Gold.

The first thing was to check Gold's identification. This was finally done by a Viennese-born plastic surgeon now practising in Los Angeles, who went with his wife on holiday to the Black Sea and compared the face of the Varna violinist, feature by feature, with the two surviving photographs of Joachim Schmidt. His report confirmed Gold's.

Once that report had been received, the shape of the operation could be planned. Its aim was to produce Schmidt on Israeli soil. If that proved impossible, the secondary aim was the execution, *in situ*, of Joachim Schmidt.

Because their target lay on the other side of the Iron Curtain it was clearly impracticable to seek to snatch Schmidt from his home, or in the street, since it would be nearly impossible to remove him subsequently from Bulgaria. With enormous luck, it could just conceivably have been achieved, but luck was not a calculable factor. They had to find another way.

The occupation of one of their contacts raised a possibility. Budzinski wrote to one of the directors of an Italian recording company, setting out his requirements. A few days later the Italian also took his wife to a Black Sea vacation resort and contrived to attend a performance by the Varna Chamber Orchestra. Afterwards he introduced himself to the orchestral manager, expressed delight at what he had heard, then attended several more concerts, expressing ever greater enthusiasm after each. Following the last concert, for which he had travelled to Sofia, he issued an invitation to the orchestra to make a series of recordings in Rome. He was referred to the Ministry of Culture where he sold the idea vigorously and learned two days later that the Minister would be delighted to allow the excellence of the Varna Chamber Orchestra to be demonstrated abroad. Discussions concerning royalties and a possible concert or two followed, were satisfactorily resolved, and the Italian returned home to make the necessary arrangements. He reported to Budzinski that he had discussed the personnel of the orchestra, man by man, with both the orchestral manager and the senior official of the Culture Ministry who had been given responsibility for the tour, and that neither had shown any special reaction to mention of the elderly violinist who was now known as Istvan Kodes. The Italian said he wondered whether in fact the Bulgarians knew who the man was. He had, it seemed, been a member of the orchestra for eleven years.

Budzinski pondered this question at length. If the Bulgarians did not know, then Istvan Kodes/Joachim Schmidt would presumably travel to Rome with the rest of the orchestra. If they knew, it was virtually certain he would not. It was important that the question be resolved.

Meanwhile planning continued. When the date upon which the orchestra would travel to Italy had been fixed and the flight number was known, two members of Budzinski's small team arranged a holiday in Bulgaria, booking well in advance to travel out again to Rome on the same Bulgarian Airlines TU 154 flight. The two men were to travel on Canadian passports which, though forged, would be of high quality and unlikely to be too closely examined, since their destination was the Black Sea riviera, to which the Bulgarians made access deliberately easy because it was a low security area and their need for foreign currency was considerable.

There remained two other areas of difficulty, apart from the problem of whether Istvan Kodes/Joachim Schmidt would make the trip at all. Both concerned his swift removal from Rome. For many years the principal airport of the eternal city was Ciampino, but in the sixties a completely new and modern airport, named after Leonardo da Vinci, had been constructed. International scheduled services now used Leonardo da Vinci airport. Charter and private flights used the more antiquated Ciampino. The best time to seize Schmidt was immediately upon landing and the best means of transporting him to Israel once he'd been seized was in a jet aircraft. If the operation had been Government approved, an aircraft of El Al, Israel's national airline, might have been used, as one had been used to remove Eichmann from Argentina. But that was out. Instead, Budzinski and Shimshon decided that a small private jet, an 'executive' machine, should be used. The problem therefore was: either to transport Schmidt from Leonardo da Vinci to Ciampino, or to divert the Bulgarian TU 154 to Ciampino.

So, although the outline of the operation was clear, various thickets of difficulty obscured vital details. Additionally, cash was required. The American-Jewish plastic surgeon and the Italian-Jewish recording company director had made their necessary reconnaissances at their own expense and been both eager to do so and able to defray the cost. Provision of the two Canadian passports required cost nothing, because they had been obtained administratively, rather than on the black market. But now real cost began to enter into the calculation, cost greater than the private commando could bear. To raise it, Shimshon flew to Zurich, ostensibly on holiday, in fact to approach a prominent Jewish banker in the Swiss financial centre. The banker was frosty at first, but his German cousins had died in Ravensbrück and Shimshon's appeal was not lost upon him. At first he agreed only to make approaches to several wealthy friends, but something in the nature of the venture began to appeal to him and ultimately he also made possible the provision of a Learjet 24D executive aircraft whose performance was fully up to that of the fighter aircraft of little more than a decade earlier. Shimshon returned with the assurance that adequate cash was available and with news of the Learjet, to find that there had been no progress in discovering whether Schmidt would be in the party which flew to Rome. This problem was proving intractable. The Bulgarians had agreed that the full orchestra would make the trip, but that did not exclude the possibility that one violinist might be substituted for another. The Italian Foreign Ministry, whose consular department issued visas to Iron Curtain visitors, had proved impenetrable. No doubt the Mossad would have its methods but the Mossad could not be approached. Budzinski, who was determined by now that the operation should proceed, finally decided to go ahead on the assumption that Schmidt *would* go to Italy. If, on the day, Schmidt did not turn up, then he would be executed later, in Bulgaria. Budzinski preferred that justice should be seen to be done and as publicly as possible; all the same, if it could not be done in public, then it would be done in private.

This decision was made more hurriedly than he would have wished because other needs were pressing him. Somebody had to fly the Learjet, and since Budzinski himself had had training on jet fighters, he was the obvious candidate. The problem here was that it meant a trip to the United States, and if Lissak learned that Budzinski was going to America to learn to fly a twin-jet passenger plane, the operation would be blown.

'Didn't Chaim Lissak tell you,' Shimshon asked Budzinski, 'to get married?'

'I'm not –'

'Shhh, Josef. And listen. If he hears you're involved with a nice Jewish girl, what will he say?'

'He'll laugh.'

'And congratulate you. And believe, because he *wants* to believe, that Josef Hothead is settling down. Furthermore, when you alerted him during that not-very-discreet conversation –'

'I didn't alert him!'

'No. You were delicate, of course. Subtle. Casual. You forgot his wires. Touch him and bells ring. But he's not without vanity, who is? So – advice he gives to Josef Hothead. Josef Hothead takes this advice. Vanity is tickled. He says, look at my sensible Josef, eh? I tell him to find a girl and what does he do? He finds a girl. Lissak says you're a wise man and your hands are full and turns his attention elsewhere.'

'He's not even thinking about me.'

'No? Not with one little corner of his mind? He's thinking, Josef. You know Lissak. But let him see you holding hands with a nice girl and sighing a bit and he'll respect your privacy and look the other way.'

Budzinski grinned. 'So find me a nice girl, matchmaker. About twenty-two, maybe, five feet six, thirty-six, twenty-two, thirty-six. Big dowry too, of course. Magnificent cook.'

'Better yet,' Shimshon said, blinking at him. 'Miriam Maisels.'

'Shalom. We'll talk when you're sane again.' Budzinski rose and headed for the door.

'What's wrong with Miriam?'

'Nothing,' Budzinski said. 'Except she's fat.'

'Plump. Only plump.'

'And has five children.'

'Beautiful children. A ready-made family.'

'I'm not spending the rest of my life jumping when Miriam growls. That's what killed David.'

'He was hit by a truck.'

25

'On his wedding day he was hit by the truck. After ten years with Miriam he was too dazed to keep his eyes opened crossing the road.'

'She has a strong character, certainly. But think about Miriam. Think clearly. And not about marriage.'

'An affair, you mean?'

Shimshon laughed. 'Think another way. Suppose you were compiling a dossier on her.'

'All right. Eyes black – and glittering. Weight, a hundred and eighty –'

'I'm serious, Josef. The dossier. Background, to start with.'

Budzinski looked at him. 'All right. Third generation American. Idealist. Came to Israel to grab a husband.'

'Wrong, Josef. Why did she come here?'

'All right. To work. She came to work.'

'And she works. With her hands, Josef, and not because she has to.'

'I know. Okay, Miriam Maisels. Sober assessment. She's a Zionist fanatic.'

'Right. Her attitude to Mengele, say, or Bormann?'

Budzinski nodded suddenly. 'Or *Schmidt!* She'd kill them with her bare hands.'

'Without too much difficulty,' Shimshon said, smiling. 'And Miriam's an activist. So let's look at the lady again. Widow with five children. If you were going to marry Miriam, *then* Lissak would know you were safely tied down. She's rich. Her parents are also rich and live in America. Very orthodox. If you were going to marry Miriam, what would happen?'

Now Budzinski was smiling, too. 'She'd take me by the arm – or the throat! – and drag me to America for parental examination.'

'And what would Lissak think?'

'He'd be glad it wasn't him! But he'd believe it. He'd certainly believe it.'

'They'd have a band to see you off, Josef.'

'There's this little thing,' Budzinski said. 'When she found out, she'd tear off my arms and legs, several at a time.'

'No. In advance she knows.'

'Bring her in?'

'For this one purpose, yes. Invite Lissak to the betrothal.'

'She's –'

'She's *secure*. Keep your mind on that.'

Budzinski and Miriam parted company at JFK International Airport, New York, she to fly on to visit her parents in Chicago, he heading on to Wichita, Kansas, to take lessons on the Learjet 24D. Ostensibly he merely accompanied the pilot as passenger; in fact, once the fast little executive jet was in the air, he flew it. In six days, he logged twenty-two hours, though logged is perhaps the wrong word, since the hours were entered in his instructor's log. By the time he returned to Israel with Miriam Maisels, he was well capable of the one necessary flight.

Behind him then, as he stood in the shadow of a hangar at Ciampino, the chartered Learjet waited on the concrete apron assigned to private aircraft. The Learjet's pilot, who had flown it from Geneva, with Budzinski as his sole passenger, now lay unconscious, safely drugged, across the rear two seats of the small passenger cabin. Half a mile away, close to the passenger terminal, the van stood empty, with Moise and Shimshon close by, ready to move when the Bulgarian Airlines TU 154 taxied to a stop. Budzinski nodded to himself. Everything was as ready as they could make it.

Now, once again, the sky began to whistle. He turned to stare along the approach path. Here was another aircraft in its landing sequence. He raised his hand to shield his eyes as it dropped closer. A jet, certainly. He noticed the clean wing with no engine pods. As it swept over him he saw the high tailplane, the three rear-mounted engines. Now he could pick out the livery colours, the green and red horizontal stripes on the tail, the blue fuselage stripe.

Tension released itself in a little shudder. The waiting and the weariness were over, and quite suddenly Budzinski felt calm and cool, intent now upon success.

Joachim Schmidt was coming to Rome!

Budzinski watched as, half a mile away, two figures walked towards the parked van. If confirmation had been needed, this was it. Budzinski turned his head to watch the touchdown, listened to the diminishing whine followed by the savage blast of reverse jet thrust, saw the big plane slowing, turning, braking, following the bat-man's signals, coming to rest.

The van moved towards it, but slowly. Budzinski nodded to himself. No sense in being too early. There'd have to be clearance from the tower before the doors opened and the ladder trucks were not yet in position. The van must arrive as the first passengers appeared at the nose door: there should be three passengers, one of them Joachim Schmidt! Budzinski glanced quickly, pointlessly, over his shoulder at the parked Learjet. How many minutes now before they were all safely inside it and howling away to Israel?

Two dark spaces appeared in the side of the TU 154's fuselage and widened as the doors swung inward. The stair trucks moved in close, into position. Was Schmidt aboard? Was all well? In a moment he'd know. His fingernails dug unnoticed into the palms of his hands as the little grey van rolled to a stop at the bottom of the forward stair. He saw Moise slip quickly out of the passenger seat and open the van's rear door. Then move towards the stair.

And crumple.

Though the sound of the shots took two full seconds to reach Budzinski, he had already seen the muzzle flash and knew it was over. Sickeningly he knew it must have been over before the landing. Somewhere between Sofia and Ciampino, when they'd made their bid, they'd been beaten, overpowered. *And made to talk!* The shooting from the TU 154 had been immediate, the targets known. They *must* have been made to talk! Staring helplessly, he saw the van door open and something fall slowly out. Shimshon!

Budzinski stared in despair at the two bodies, small, black punctuations on the wide tarmac. Then, suddenly, there were sirens and revolving lights as airport security raced to blanket the TU 154. In moments the van was surrounded. For long seconds Budzinski stood frozen, overwhelmed by failure and grief. Two men lost on the aircraft, Moise shot dead as he approached it. Then *Shimshon*. He doubted whether any of them were alive. And even if the two men in the aircraft had survived, they would not be returned, probably not even handed over to the Italians. His eyes tightened against the flaring grief but he remembered and made himself reach into his pocket for the tiny transmitter. He blinked away tears and looked again at the big Bulgarian jet. No-one had yet started down the ladder. Crew, passengers, his own two men, and maybe Schmidt – all were still in the plane.

Briefly he hesitated. He'd prayed it wouldn't come to this. But he'd known, they'd all known, that it might. The others had done their duty, and failed. Now he must do his. His thumb lingered a second, no more, before coming down firmly on the button, and he watched in anger, without satisfaction, as the TU 154's tail assembly was blasted to the tarmac. At least the bomb had been planted successfully. At least, for a few hours, everybody aboard the TU 154 was stuck in Rome.

But now he must move. And now the waiting Learjet was useless. By the time he could take off, even without formal clearance... by the time he reached Israel, word would have gone ahead. There'd be no mercy awaiting him there and there was nowhere else to fly. Budzinski dropped the tiny transmitter into the perimeter grass, ground it with his heel and hurried away. He hadn't long; the airport's entrances and exits would already have been closed, the shots had already brutally demonstrated that. The plan was known. They might even be looking, not just for another member of the hijack gang, but for Josef Budzinski.

There remained one more thing to do. He raced to the private aircraft maintenance hangar, slowed to a walk, and entered quietly. Two men were working on an Aztec at the far end, heads down under the lifted cowling. Budzinski went quietly into the grubby lavatory, pulled an oil-stained white boiler suit and blue baseball cap from behind a rusty cistern and slipped them on. The exits would be blocked but he didn't need to reach the exits.

Two minutes later, hurrying, he reached the baggage shed in the terminal, stepped inside, lit a cigarette and made himself stroll casually towards the door. The terminal concourse, when he reached it, was full of movement. Officials hurried rapidly to and fro and voices everywhere chattered in excitement. Over the loudspeaker a girl spoke soothingly, appealing for calm, saying there had been an accident and that delays, while inevitable, should not last long. She repeated the announcement in Italian, then began again in English.

Budzinski moved towards the Interair desk, paused as he came close, glanced quickly at the guards at the concourse doors. He dropped his cigarette on to the floor, stubbed it out and placed an envelope quietly on the counter. The Interair girl was looking the other way and as far as he could tell, no-one had noticed him. He moved away, aimless now, knowing there was no way out. He might not be picked up at once, but it couldn't be long...

'We regret to announce,' the loudspeaker system said suddenly, 'that it is forbidden to enter or leave the terminal. This is a police order. We ask for your co-operation. Repeat, it is forbidden to enter or leave the terminal.'

Well, he wasn't going to make it easy for them. He glanced back at the Interair desk. The girl still hadn't seen the envelope, but she would, soon enough. Budzinski went into a lavatory, stripped off his overall and baseball cap and returned to the concourse He wondered how many years he'd get, how long it would be before he saw Israel again. If ever. He forced himself not to think of the four friends who would never see their homeland again, never see anything again; instead he concentrated on one small fact; *Schmidt* had been aboard the plane. If he had not, the hijack would not have been tried. That meant Schmidt was now in Rome. They hadn't captured him, but he was here. He'd be somewhere out on the tarmac now, well protected, with his violin case and his white hair and his sensitive hands – those blood-stained, sensitive hands! The whole system was now mobilised to protect Joachim Schmidt, butcher of Layerhausen, butcher of Budzinskis, as it was simultaneously mobilised to hunt down Budzinski himself. Soon Schmidt would be whisked away, a drink in his hand, a comfortable cushion under his bottom, while Budzinski stared at cell walls and Shimshon and Moise and Guyon and Manfred were placed in boxes, lids nailed down, gone to join the families Schmidt had murdered long ago.

Budzinski saw the girl at the Interair desk move along the counter, notice the envelope and frown. She reached for the telephone and spoke into it quickly. Budzinski strolled closer. A few moments later, a youngish man came hurrying towards the Interair desk, took the envelope, opened it and read the message. Was he an Interair executive, or a newspaperman? The envelope had been addressed to the Airport News Service. Budzinski saw the quick flicker of a smile on the man's face and nodded to himself. A newsman recognising a story. Good! Soon it would be on the agency tapes, uncomfortable, embarrassing, awkward for the Bulgarians to handle.

Satisfied, he glanced quietly round the concourse. Police were moving forward now, in a long line, examining passports. But they were still some distance from him. He retreated a few paces, taking cover among a largish group of passengers who stood quietly waiting, innocent but irritated. Behind him somebody turned, bumped against him and apologised.

'It's all right.' Budzinski, turning and nodding, suddenly noticed a glint of gold at the man's stomach. A watch chain across an old-fashioned waistcoat and dangling from it a tiny gold star. Budzinski said, 'Shalom.'

The man smiled. He was, Budzinski thought, probably in his middle sixties, sad-eyed, very bald. He said, 'Shalom. A nuisance, this.'

'Worse than that,' Budzinski said quietly.

The man blinked at him and the blink brought thoughts of Shimshon. Budzinski felt tears prickle at his eyes.

'Are you all right?'

There was a strong trace of accent still. Budzinski said, 'Polish?'

A nod. 'British now. But yes, from Poznan. I've been in England a long time. Textiles. Sam Cohen, from Manchester.'

Budzinski hesitated only a moment because there was nothing to lose. He said, 'Joachim Schmidt was on the plane.'

'Joachim –' The man's voice faded in surprise.

'Of Layerhausen,' Budzinski said.

Cohen blinked again, several times. 'Is he dead?'

Budzinski said, 'No. We were trying to capture him. Take him back for trial. Four of *us* are dead.'

Cohen glanced round, quickly, almost furtively. 'So what happens? To you?'

Budzinski gave a little nod in the direction of the line of advancing policemen. 'They'll pick me up in a few minutes.'

There was deep pity in Cohen's eyes. Budzinski said quickly, 'I'm sorry. It was wrong to speak to you. You must not be involved in this.' He turned to go.

'Wait,' Cohen said sharply. 'Maybe we can help.'

'There's no helping me now.'

'No, listen. Maybe we *can* help. There are seventy-four of us. Bridge players. It's private charter. Listen, the way you speak English, where are you from?'

Budzinski said, 'The way I speak? I went to school in Yorkshire. I thought I'd lost the accent.'

Cohen turned, took two steps and tapped the shoulder of a small, middle-aged man in a black overcoat. Budzinski saw him whisper and take the little man's arm. The two of them came over.

'This boy,' Cohen said, 'he tried to arrest Joachim Schmidt. Schmidt of Layerhausen. He was on a plane.'

The little man stared at him. 'That's why all this?' A little gesture took in the scene around them.

Budzinski nodded.

Cohen said, 'They tried. This boy and four others. The others are dead. Can we get him out?'

The little man's eyes searched Budzinski's face. They were hard eyes, small and very dark. Budzinski stared back at him. He felt drained and helpless. He realised the little man was holding out his hand. He shook it. 'Albert Castle,' the little man

31

said. 'Formerly Schloss. I'm British now. British Jewish.'

'Jewish British,' Cohen said. 'Listen, Albert. If you have all the passports together. You're the secretary –'

'No good. They're British passports, Sam. His is Israeli, eh?' Budzinski said, 'Unfortunately.'

'You see.' Then Castle smiled suddenly. 'We can do better, maybe?'

'How?'

'Crew room. Don't forget where we chartered the plane!'

'Hey, you're right, Albert. Where is he?'

'Over there.' Castle looked Budzinski up and down, assessing him. He said, 'Dark pants he's wearing. That's good.' He moved away quickly.

It couldn't happen, couldn't possibly happen! But Budzinski felt a little flare of hope as a pilot approached, as he watched people whispering urgently and a few of the bridge players moved into a circle around him to shield him as he put on the pilot's jacket with the gold wings on the left breast. The pilot put on a raincoat over his shirt-sleeves, smiled a little, and said, 'At airports they only look at the uniform.'

'What a fit, the cap,' Cohen said.

'Wear it, yet,' Schloss said. 'And give me your passport. I'll keep it for you.'

The pilot pointed to the entrance to the crew rooms. 'Don't hurry,' he advised. 'And you look tired enough to be genuine.'

He had no documents. The pilot looked nothing like Budzinski and either passport or licence would be a giveaway. Budzinski walked steadily towards aircrew territory, holding his breath as he passed the advancing line of airport police. On the other side of the line were people who'd already been checked. If he could only get past!

One of the policemen glanced up as he approached. Right in his way. *Damn!* Budzinski made himself stop beside the policeman. 'How long do you think it will take?'

The man shrugged.

'I'd better check the bloody met again. Excuse me.' He nodded and walked away, his spine crawling, expecting any instant the sudden, shouted 'Halt' which would be the end. Nothing happened and he walked on.

In the aircrew quarters he sat in an armchair, closed his eyes and pretended to doze. One or two others were doing the same, airline pilots to whom delay was part of life. For an interminable hour he stayed still, almost trembling with the effort of stillness, his nerves jangling, hot prickling tears forming in his eyes. But at last there were footsteps, a slap on the shoulder, a genial voice saying, 'Wakey, wakey. Time for off.'

Budzinski rose and followed the pilot. After a few steps, he said, 'What happened?'

'They're still looking but we're clear to fly. You're all right.'

Later, on the aircraft, he felt somebody shake his arm and looked round, a little dazed.

Cohen said, 'You didn't hear?'

'No, I –'

'You were asleep,' Cohen said gently.

'Asleep! I can't have been.' But he had.

'Do you good, boy. Listen, there's fog at Manchester. At Gatwick we're landing soon. You know where that is?'

'No.'

'South of London. A train ride only. Listen, we're going to wait there. They say maybe the weather will improve. What about you? You could come to Manchester.'

Budzinski thought for a moment. 'Will they let me through? London's better for me.'

'The pilot says it's not so easy going in. Coming out of Rome, coming out of anywhere, who cares? But going in, it's different.'

'I'll have to use my own passport?'

'That's right.'

Budzinski glanced at his watch. They'd left Rome nearly two hours ago. He was certain his name was known there. But in Britain? Had an international alarm been put out? He said, 'I'll have to risk it.'

'Good luck, boy. You'll need luggage or it's suspicious. Here – it's the best we can do.' On the aisle seat beside Cohen rested a large shoulder bag. 'Dirty shirts. Some socks, a pair of shoes. All we have here, boy, the baggage is in the hold. We've got a raincoat for you too.'

He waited with them in the transit area until a suitable scheduled flight was announced. It was from Malta. When the passengers came in and began trooping towards immigration, he joined them quietly. He had a little more than three hundred pounds in his pocket, a gift he'd tried to refuse, the product of a whip-round among the Jewish bridge players.

His whole body began to tremble as he handed his passport to the immigration officer. He must stop it somehow! He stamped his foot hard and said to the raised eyebrows, 'My bloody foot's gone to sleep.'

'I see. Here on business, sir?'

He'd stamped hard and his foot hurt, but at least the trembling had stopped. 'Just to see some friends. I was at school here.'

'How long will you stay?'

'A few days. Three or four.' It was unbelievable! If there was an international call out, it wasn't for Josef Budzinski by name. When Guyon and Manfred had been made to talk, they must have kept his name back somehow! Or perhaps he'd got here too quickly, before –

'Enjoy your holiday, sir.' The man was holding out his passport, with a little, formal smile.

'Thanks.'

He was through. Through immigration, anyway, and customs should hold no terrors. Nor did they. A couple of minutes later he was standing in the big hall at Gatwick, looking round him almost in a daze. He had money and he was in England. Of all places – England, where nobody ever checked anybody's papers. England, where he could travel as he pleased. Not, he realised suddenly, reality cutting harshly into the brief euphoria, that he had anywhere to go. He swallowed. It was safety, but perhaps a very temporary safety.

He crossed the big, tiled floor to the railway station entrance and bought a ticket for London. During the forty-minute journey, he tried to decide what to do next, where to go to ground. But his mind didn't seem to be working. Reaction had set in and the scene on the concrete apron at Ciampino was running endlessly through his mind like a loop of film. Again and again he could see Moise move forward and fall, then the slow opening of the van door and Shimshon's body sliding out. The train came into Victoria almost before he knew it and nothing had resolved itself. He left the train and went through the barrier and thought of Aaron. Was Aaron still in London? A year ago he'd still been there, but diplomats moved about. Aaron could be anywhere now.

Budzinski looked for a telephone and could not see one. He stopped somebody and asked. The big sign was pointed out to him and he hurried across the station towards the telephone hall, fumbling in his pocket as he walked. He'd been looking for the old familiar red telephone boxes, but clearly things had changed. It must be twenty years, no, more than twenty, since he'd been in Britain. Of *course* things had changed. He looked at the telephone and found that that had changed, too. He remembered the old boxes with Button A and Button B and the operator who said 'Number, please'. He pulled out of his pocket the change he'd been given when he'd bought his rail ticket at Gatwick, and found that the coinage, too, had changed. A notice labelled 'Dialling Instructions' helped him to understand. Then he looked up the number.

'Embassy of Israel,' a girl's voice said.

'Mr Aaron Bloom, please.'

Budzinski waited. Aaron was knowledgeable and had contacts. A voice in his ear said, 'Second Secretary.'

'Mr Bloom, please.'

'Speaking.'

The movement was almost unconscious. Budzinski hung up quickly, without identifying himself. He stood still for a moment or two thinking. What *would* Aaron do? Aaron was tough and intelligent, loyal and resourceful, he'd demonstrated all those things often enough. Once, in Spain, he'd saved Budzinski's life and until a moment earlier, Budzinski had simply *assumed* that he could rely on Aaron. But could he? Aaron was official now; Aaron was Government! Aaron's duty was clearly to the state of Israel, not to his friends, especially not to friends whose activities that state had expressly forbidden. What *would* Aaron do? It was a difficult question. There was a strong individualistic streak in Aaron. Gaiety too, and recklessness. But also strong commitment.

Budzinski walked away from the telephone, found the taxi rank and told the driver to go to the Israeli Embassy. Aaron was the best contact he had; the risk must be taken. But if he'd identified himself, and if the Embassy knew, as they must, about the fiasco at Ciampino, then Aaron might have other people waiting with him. No, he'd do it this way.

He paid off the taxi awkwardly in the unfamiliar coinage. At the entrance, as at all Israeli Embassies nowadays, was an electronic gate. A sign read 'State your business.' He pressed the button and spoke into the microphone grille: 'Sidney Conan, The Hebrew University appeal.' The gate swung open. He smiled and went through the Embassy gate towards the front door, taking in the scene and deciding quickly how to use it. He smiled and nodded at the commissionaire, winked at the girl at the reception desk, and went straight up the staircase. On the next floor he stopped and waited until a girl came down a corridor and said, 'Mr Bloom's office?'

She directed him to the second floor, clearly assuming as he'd hoped, that he'd been sent upstairs and was merely lost. He found the door with the words Second Secretary on it and walked without hesitation into the room.

35

CHAPTER THREE

News of the hijack of the Bulgarian airliner first reached Tel Aviv in a series of Associated Press flashes from Rome. The first was merely brief news of a gun battle on the apron at Ciampino and said several men were reported to have died. Except in newspaper offices, little notice was taken. The second AP message, four minutes later, said, 'Speculation here that hijackers were Israeli. Four men reported dead.' That information was passed immediately to the Prime Minister's office, from where a *most immediate* signal was despatched to the Israeli Embassy in Rome, demanding immediate investigation of the situation. The First Secretary, Moshe Amit, immediately set off by car for the airport.

The third AP message said, 'Unconfirmed report that Joachim Schmidt, former commandant of the Layerhausen concentration camp, was aboard the aircraft. Bulgarian Embassy will not comment. Hijackers almost certainly Israeli.'

Within twenty minutes, a statement was issued from the office of the Prime Minister of Israel publicly regretting that individual Jews, acting in direct contravention of standing Government instructions, should have attempted an act of air piracy of a type condemned many times by the Government of Israel. The statement added, with a characteristic touch of defiance amid the sackcloth and ashes, that any government which chose to give asylum to mass murderers like Joachim Schmidt, could not be considered free of guilt, and must bear some responsibility for the incident. Nonetheless, Israel wished to express its sorrow at this breach, by Israelis, of accepted international standards of behaviour.

By the time that statement was being issued, the head of the Mossad, Israel's highly efficient intelligence service, was waiting in the ante-room to the Prime Minister's office. When he entered the office a few minutes later, he was asked one question: 'Who did it?'

He replied that he had already given instructions for the fullest investigation, that the five arms of the intelligence service were making immediate and urgent enquiries as to the whereabouts of former members of the now-disbanded seek-and-capture squads and that it should soon be possible to put names to the people involved. The head of the Mossad was abruptly instructed to remain by the ante-room telephone until he had the information.

Gradually more detail came through from Rome. Two of the four dead men had been shot as they waited at the bottom of the aircraft steps, presumably for disembarking passengers, among whom may have been Joachim Schmidt. Two more, according to a statement by the Bulgarian Embassy in Rome, had been killed aboard the aircraft. The Bulgarian statement denied the presence of Joachim Schmidt aboard the TU 154 and the Embassy even went so far as to issue a list of all the Bulgarian passengers aboard the flight. A few minutes later, Reuter reported that the Bulgarian passengers had been taken by coach from the airport to the Embassy for their own protection. Then, from AP, came the news that a Learjet had been found on the private aircraft section of the airport. Its Swiss pilot had been left tied up in the back of the passenger cabin.

One of the first calls made by the Mossad had been to Brigadier Chaim Lissak, formerly controller of the retributive action groups. Lissak, however, was out of the country. In fact, he was in France, at the Toulouse headquarters of the Sud- Aviation company, discussing the spares position of the Super-Frelon heavy-duty helicopters used by the Israeli army. The head of the Mossad swore when he heard the news, because most of the information about the complex and highly- clandestine activities of the men he had commanded, which might have identified the hijackers quickly, was in Lissak's head, and nobody else's. As it happened however, the frantic checking of files, the programme of telephone calls and house visits already embarked upon, became in part unnecessary when the First Secretary of the Rome Embassy, Moshe Amit, managed to persuade Ciampino security officials to allow him to visit the mortuary and look at the bodies of the four dead men. Asked if he knew any of them, he shook his head, thanked them, and left. As soon as he could do so discreetly, he went to a telephone and informed the Embassy that he had recognised one of the bodies. The signal from Rome, received in Tel Aviv, said that one of the men involved had been Shimshon Talmon.

The Mossad now had a focus. They also had further and explicit instructions from the Prime Minister herself. 'If there were more than four,' she said, with forbidding calm, 'and almost certainly there *were* more than four, the others are to be

37

discovered and placed under immediate arrest. If they are abroad, they are to be found and brought to Israel. Is that clear?'

The head of the Mossad said it was very clear and received the Prime Minister's permission to return to his own headquarters in order to take personal command. Within minutes, a Mossad agent was in a helicopter on a ninety-mile trip to a kibbutz on the edge of the Negev. Ironically, as he ducked clear of the machine's spinning rotorblades and ran towards the kibbutz office, he passed two concrete table tennis tables at which children were playing.

'Where,' he demanded of the chairman of the kibbutz, 'is Shimshon Talmon?'

'Who are you?'

'I represent the government and the matter is urgent. Where is he?'

'Not here.'

'Then where?'

'On holiday.'

The long history of self-management among the kibbutzim made them resentful of outside, and particularly, governmental investigations. The Mossad man sighed to himself and tried another tack. He said, 'Shimshon Talmon is dead.'

'Dead?' The chairman's face sagged briefly.

'He was killed at an airport in Rome, less than two hours ago, trying to hijack an aircraft.'

'Then why did you ask?'

'Because I must know who was with him.'

'From here? No-one. Shimshon went alone. I grieve that he is dead. Leave him at peace.'

The Mossad man groaned to himself. Every word would have to be quarried. He said, 'Let me explain. Our people and our aircraft have been attacked, usually by Palestinian terrorists, in many places. We have always condemned this activity. As a nation we live by the law and to you, surely, the law must come before everything.'

'If you speak of rabbinical law, yes.'

The Mossad man tried again. 'We are a nation in danger –'

'The Jewish people have been in danger for four thousand years.'

'Never greater than now.'

'I do not agree. The existing state perhaps, not the Jewish people.'

The Mossad man tried to keep hold of his temper. 'Tell me, *please*. It is very important.'

'I have told you. Shimshon went alone.'

'Then tell me who his friends are.'

The kibbutz chairman's face did not alter, but his tone was contemptuous. 'You should be ashamed to ask.'

'Nevertheless, I ask.'

'In Russia the Cheka, the OGPU, the MVD, *they* demand names of friends. In Germany the Gestapo, *they* ask too. And ask and ask. With rubber truncheons. Does Israel come to this?'

It was pointless to continue.

The Mossad man rose. 'Shalom.'

'Shalom.'

He went outside, into the heat again, and looked around. Somewhere here there would be young men, army reservists, whose loyalty was differently constructed and who would answer his questions. He found one in the tractor shed, bent over a running machine, and tapped him on the shoulder. The man looked up enquiringly.

'I want to talk to you,' the Mossad man shouted.

The man shrugged, frowning. The agent walked round the tractor and switched off the engine and the young man scowled. Perhaps, the agent thought wryly, it had not been easy to start.

'My identification.' He held out the Defence Ministry card bearing his photograph. 'I need answers to some questions.'

'Okay.'

'Good.' Briefly the Mossad man thought how much easier things would be when the older generations, with their gentle stubbornness and the closed-in philosophy developed in oppression, had moved on and the young were in full control. 'Where is Shimshon Talmon?'

'On holiday.'

'With whom?'

'So far as I know, alone.'

'His friends, then. Who are his friends?'

'Here?'

'Yes, here.'

The young man grinned. 'Here everyone is Shimshon's friend.'

'Now, look –'

'It's true. You know him?'

'No. Give me names. Maybe I'll know some of the names.'

'All right.' The young man began speaking names, a lot of them. None meant anything to the Mossad agent, but he listened carefully. For a while he thought he was being given a roll call of the whole kibbutz, but then –

'Did you say Josef Budzinski?' He could hear his own incredulity.

'Yes. Josef is a friend of –'

'Where *is* he?'

'I do not know. But he is newly betrothed.' The young man grinned. 'Soon he is to marry Miriam Maisels, a lady with five children.'

'And where is she?'

'With him, I think.'

'But not here. Not at the kibbutz?'

'No.'

'Thanks.' The Mossad man left him and hurried back to the helicopter. Budzinski! He should have known; everybody should have known. Or at least guessed. As the helicopter lifted off, he was already on the radio.

From the Soviet Embassy in Rome, the KGB officer who had been flight engineer aboard the TU 154 airliner on which the hijack had been attempted, was reporting to the headquarters of the First Chief Directorate of the KGB in Dzerzhinsky Square in Moscow. The procedure was slow and difficult because of the need to encipher each sentence and then to decipher each response. He was warned, too, that there might be anger in Moscow because he had allowed the captured Israeli to die. He had obeyed the standing orders, certainly, in extracting the maximum information relevant to the airliner's safety. All the same...

The teleprinter chattered again. Two five-letter groups. He deciphered quickly. *Repeat fifth name.* Josef Budzinski's name had fourteen characters. He added the dummy character to the end of the first group and sent off the three five-letter groups. They'd asked him to repeat every name.

A pause and the KGB man waited. When the machine chattered again he tore off the slip and went to work. The deciphered message was faintly disappointing. He'd hoped to learn something about the man the airliner was supposed to have carried, the war criminal of long ago. But the order said merely, *Report KGB rezident Rome for assignment.* It looked as though Moscow wasn't particularly excited.

Moscow, however, *was* angry. Hijack attempts upon Eastern bloc aircraft had not been as frequent as in the West, but they had still been too frequent for comfort. Moscow did not much care what happened to British Airways, Lufthansa or Pan Am (except when they were in Soviet airspace) but cared a great deal about hijacks within the Soviet bloc. The decision now made by General K. R. Virillin, head of the First Chief Directorate, paralleled exactly that made by the Israeli Prime Minister. He gave priority orders that any hijackers remaining alive were to be found, apprehended and taken to the Soviet Union for public trial and private punishment, *pour encourager les autres*. The KGB knew five names. Four men were dead, one free. Others might be involved, but to discover other names, it was first necessary to find the one who had got away.

The Great Archive, begun by the Secret Police in the days of the Czars and meticulously maintained ever since by the Committee of State Security, was searched. In the Great Archive were files on eleven hundred million people, more than two thirds already dead. There were files on three of the five men and these were extracted. The KGB computers searched for cross references: Were friends of the five known? Had they relatives in the Soviet bloc countries? Where had they lived? Who else had lived there? It took time, but the system was thorough and the vastness of the body of information it contained made almost any search productive.

The file on Josef Budzinski was substantial. It recorded his career from the date his promotion to commissioned rank in the Israeli army had been promulgated and listed his subsequent promotions. It recorded the date upon which he had been seconded to retributive activities against war criminals. It included two photographs of Budzinski, one ten years old, one seven. And it listed the seek-and-arrest or seek-and-destroy tasks upon which he had worked. The information was detailed because for eleven years from 1948 the KBG had a man successfully infiltrated into the Israeli intelligence machinery. Supplements to the Budzinski file listed names of people with whom he was known to have worked, including contacts and hard-line Israeli sympathisers in cities Budzinski was known to have visited.

A summary of what the Great Archive produced on Josef Budzinski was promptly put on the diplomatic wire circuits to all KBG Residents in Europe, North America and in several countries in South America, with instructions that the search for Budzinski should begin immediately and that all necessary men and resources be utilised. The summary, however, like the file, was empty of one significant factor in the life of Josef Budzinski. It listed his birthplace in Poznan, Poland, and the fact that his parents had probably died in Layerhausen. It named the school he attended to the age of nine. The next chronological entry was for his arrival in Israel in 1949/50.

During the hours immediately following the attempted kidnapping of Joachim Schmidt, therefore, the fact that Josef Budzinski was a member of the Israeli action group became known to, and was disseminated within their own organisation by, the foreign intelligence services of Israel and the Soviet Union. Deliberately, neither nation released his name because each wished to lay its hands upon him. Had Interpol been informed, Budzinski would have been arrested, or at least held in custody, upon his arrival at Gatwick Airport, London.

But Budzinski was not apprehended and moments after six pm he entered the offices of Aaron Bloom, Second Secretary of the Israeli Embassy in London.

He watched Bloom look up, saw the slight widening of the eyes in recognition, the quick return of the habitual blandness. 'Hello, Aaron.'

'Joe.' The tone was flat, devoid either of surprise or welcome. Budzinski moved fast across the room, pre-emptively, round the desk, to stand half behind Aaron's chair.

'You know, then?'

Bloom nodded, half-turning in his chair to look up. 'Yes, I know.'

'I need help.'

'You do indeed.'

'And?'

'You shouldn't have done it, Joe.'

'It's like that?' He must watch Aaron closely, now, for already it was clear that this too had gone wrong. As if to emphasise the fact he heard the bang from below as the Embassy's front door closed for the night. The sound made him think of a cell door closing.

'How else can it be? What you've done, Joe – you know the law now.'

'Yes, I know. It's against state law, Knesset law. But there's another. An eye for an eye –'

Bloom gave a tiny sigh. He said, 'I'm a dinosaur myself, but I restrain it.'

'Schmidt, Aaron. It was Schmidt.'

'I know, Joe.' Budzinski wondered whether there might be a pistol somewhere in Aaron's desk and watched his hands, but Aaron was composed, almost unnaturally still. Aaron, however, had always been honest nearly to the point of lunacy, unless the recent years of diplomacy had stamped it out of him.

Budzinski watched his eyes and asked quickly, 'Have you pressed a button, Aaron?'

Bloom smiled.'No.'

'Is the Embassy alerted?'

Bloom's eyes were steady. There was sympathy in them somewhere but it was well suppressed. He said, 'Every Embassy is alerted. The Mossad wants you. Golda's orders. You're to be returned to Israel for trial.'

Budzinski remembered Aaron at other times, cool, self-contained, resourceful. They had always, until now, been on the same side. Never friends, perhaps, but comrades-in-arms, ready to trust, *needing* to trust each other.

'All right. There's a general alert. But specifically, Aaron, did you expect me here?'

'Why should we?'

'Because –' Budzinski hesitated and watched Bloom's face carefully. Was it possible Aaron didn't know? Surely he must. When had they met first? Fifty-eight? Then it *was* possible Aaron didn't know.

'Because *what*, Joe?'

'Because *you* are here.' It was lame, but it covered the question.

Bloom said, 'Hardly that.'

'So you haven't got two tough youngsters ready to burst in?'

'No. But you are an Israeli citizen on Israeli territory. You are subject to the laws of the state.'

'Ah.'

'As a representative of the government, I must order you to place yourself voluntarily in custody, Joe. You will remain here until arrangements have been made to return you to Israel.'

'No help, then?'

'Understand, Joe. This is necessary. You know the reasons.'

Budzinski said, 'A few years ago, you'd have been with me.'

'Before the Six Day War I'd have been with you. We have to live in *this* world now, Joe. And it's changed.'

'And you've changed with it?'

'Yes, I have. When the hunt was ended, I accepted it. I wanted it to continue, but that was private and emotional. I could see the decision was a good one. You don't.'

'No, Aaron. But let me ask you: if we'd got Schmidt, if we were at Lod Airport now, this minute, with Joachim Schmidt, instead of here in this office, what would you think?'

43

'I'd disapprove officially and give a little private cheer.'

'So?'

'But you *failed,* Joe.' Bloom said it in a soft, even tone that made Budzinski wince. Then he said formally, 'Have I your word that you will not try to escape? That you –'

Budzinski hit him below the ear with the side of his hand and Bloom collapsed across the desk. He had tried to make the blow only as hard as was necessary, but it was a lethally dangerous strike and he could have killed him. He checked anxiously that Bloom was still breathing and then, relieved, looked round for means of securing him. Bloom's tie was silk, made from a square; it secured his hands. There was a cotton raincoat in a wardrobe and he tied the arms tightly round Bloom's feet. Two handkerchiefs, one from a trouser pocket, the other from the breast pocket, made a gag and held it in place. Budzinski picked Bloom up, put him in the wardrobe, closed the door, turned the key and put it in his pocket. Once Aaron came to, he would soon free himself, but Budzinski needed time enough to get clear of the Embassy. How, though, with the front door closed and certainly locked? Mirthlessly he remembered one of Lissak's favourite maxims: always use the front door if you can.

He picked up one of the two phones and waited for the switchboard, then realised that with the Embassy closed, the switchboard would be closed too, leaving only one or two lines open. The phone in his hand buzzed continuously in the same way the phone at Victoria had buzzed. Probably an outside line. He replaced it and picked up the other, an obvious internal phone with labelled buttons. He pressed the button marked *'Reception Office'* and waited, wondering how Bloom would speak. When Budzinski had telephoned, Bloom had answered not with his name but with the words 'Second Secretary'.

'Commissionaire,' a voice said in his ear.

Budzinski said, 'Second Secretary speaking. My visitor is leaving now.' He kept his voice soft and unemphatic and waited tensely. If the man knew Bloom's voice...!

'Yes, sir. I'll wait at the door.'

Budzinski went out quickly, still tense and anxious. Embassies were careful places; the commissionaire might well have realised it was *not* Aaron and be using the intervening minute to get help, or arm himself. He went down the stairs quickly, swinging his bag apparently cheerfully and ready to hurl it, if necessary, in the face of anybody who looked dangerous.

But the commissionaire was alone, patient, his hand on the

key. As Budzinski approached he turned it, then bent to slide back the bolt.

'Thank you. Good night,' Budzinski said.

'Night, sir.'

Behind him the big solid door banged and Budzinski drew a deep breath of relief, then turned and hurried quickly away. The old habits came easily. Don't hang about, it's always suspicious. Even if you've nowhere to go, always *look* as though you have. Walk purposefully. He moved briskly along the street, round the corner. Where now? Where *was* there? He knew only one other person in London and it was probable that Sidney Conan was the wrong man to approach. He brooded about Conan as he walked, recalling their two meetings in recent years and the sharp contrast with the earlier acquaintanceship, the acquaintanceship of a quarter of a century ago.

Conan had been an ordinary boy then. Fairly bright, a doctor's son; pleasant but undistinguished, one among a crowd of boys at a grammar school in a provincial city. They'd known each other fairly well, then, coming together each morning with the others of the school's small Jewish population to say the *Shema* while the school *en masse* held morning prayers according to the customs of the church of England. Most of the Jewish boys were refugees from Europe, from Poland, Germany, Austria. But Conan's family was how many generations English? Four or five, anyway. The family must have connections, too, and beneath the ordinariness of the young Conan an unsuspected but deep ambition must have burned, because the change in his circumstances had been large and dramatic. Conan had gone to Oxford, to Balliol, and read law and had by now practised as a barrister for many years. But, and far more important, he had married not merely well but supremely well, at least in financial terms and possibly others too. When he had married, Budzinski knew, Conan's father-in-law had been well-to-do, the owner of a small hotel in West London. But during the long British property boom, he had made one brilliant gambit after another, until he was now a millionaire several times over. After that, like wealthy Jews the world over, Conan's father-in-law had made frequent and generous donations to a variety of projects in the growing Israeli state, including one of two and a half million pounds to found a school of architecture. So the twice Joe Budzinski and Sidney Conan had met had been in Israel, with Conan accompanying his father-in-law. Conan looked well fed, almost to the point of being florid. He was mannered, too, always behaving, it

45

seemed to Budzinski, as though he were in a court of law. Not that he was unpleasant, far from it; the Sidney Conan with forty years of life behind him was both affable and expansive, but he'd selected his posture years earlier and adopted it with thoroughness.

Could he now, Budzinski asked himself, seek help from Sidney Conan, with his rich man's contacts in the upper levels of Israeli society? Or would Conan (like Aaron Bloom, but perhaps for different and possibly social reasons) believe it either wrong, or imprudent, to help a fugitive from the Israeli state? He thought about it for a few minutes, getting nowhere. The amiable boy might have been helpful, but the amiable boy had long disappeared and the man's attitude could not be predicted. On the other hand, there was nowhere else to turn. What was the phrase? He tried unsuccessfully for a moment to remember. Then he recalled a play, long ago; he'd seen it with a friend whose parents kept a shop and hung a theatre poster in the window and so got half-price tickets. *Hobson's Choice!* A play about a shoemaker called Hobson. Budzinski almost smiled, remembering Hobson's choice was no choice at all. Only one option. Since he had no-one else to go to, he must go to Sidney Conan.

He began to look for a telephone, but with a sense of futility. If Sidney took him in, hid him somewhere for a few days, where did that get him? He'd still be a fugitive; he'd be a fugitive for the rest of his life, that was already clear. But to surrender tamely, to go to trial for the offence – offence indeed! – of trying to capture Joachim Schmidt, went hard against the grain. The Mossad would probably be after him, too. Well, if the Mossad caught him, so be it; but they'd have to find him first. Meanwhile Schmidt remained at liberty and in various parts of the world there were still Jews who regarded retribution and punishment as a continuing duty. With help, if he could reach help now, he could still continue the hunt for Schmidt. With new papers, a new identity, he could perhaps even pursue Schmidt into Bulgaria and kill him there. Suicidal, maybe; no, suicidal certainly! But worth it, for Schmidt.

He saw one of the old red telephone boxes and headed towards it. Perhaps it was only on railway stations and the like that they'd disappeared. He opened the dog-eared A – D directory and looked for the name and found two entries: *Conan, Sidney, Barrister at law (Chambers); Conan, S J L, 436 Chester Square SW1.* Budzinski cast his mind back, but the word chambers

46

meant only the large comic pots the British kept unhygienically beneath their beds for use during the night. All the same, the first entry in the directory, with its use of the first name, and the listing of his profession, must be a business number. Privately, too, the English had a curious disposition to use initials, rather than first names. Budzinski made a mental note of the Chester Square address and went in search of a taxi.

It was a tall house on the square, Georgian, with black iron railings. He went up the half-dozen steps to the front door and saw the brass panel of engraved names, each with its bell-push. Budzinski pushed Conan's bell and waited. Mechanically the squawk-box said, 'Who is it?'

'Budzinski.'

'Joe Budzinski?' Surprise and the box distorted Conan's voice.

'Yes.'

'Then come on up, dear boy.' *Dear boy,* indeed. Once upon a time it would have been, 'Come in, lad'; but Conan had probably not used the expression in as many years as Budzinski himself.

The lock clicked. Budzinski pushed the door open and climbed the thickly-carpeted stairs. Sidney Conan waited at the top, smiling, hand outstretched.

'Hello, Sidney,' Budzinski said, shaking hands.

'How very nice, Joe! Come in, come in.' Conan led the way into the flat, turning to close the door. 'I must say this is a pleasant surprise.'

'It's good to see you, too.'

'What'll you drink? Sit down, old chap.' Conan gestured towards a chair.

'Have you whisky?'

'Of course.' Conan poured pale fluid from a crystal decanter on a silver tray. 'Water, ice?'

'As it is, thanks.'

Conan handed him the drink. The tumbler was fine crystal, too. 'Joe, I'm going to apologise.'

'For what?'

'Because I can't stay, damn it. You caught me at a bad moment.'

'Oh?' From the moment he'd come up the stairs, Budzinski had been alert for nuances. But the genuineness of Conan's greeting had been reassuring; he'd been fairly sure Conan didn't know. But now... greeting and then departure?

'Tyranny of the profession, Joe. I only got in ten minutes ago. Conference with some rascally solicitors. And I'm in court in Exeter tomorrow so I'm travelling down tonight. I was just packing a bag.'

'I see. Pity.'

'It is, isn't it! The devil of it is, old chap, that I'm going from there to spend a long weekend in Bournemouth and I can't cry off because it's my nephew's bar mitzvah. Ruth and the children are there already.'

Budzinski sipped the silk-smooth single malt whisky and made himself smile. 'Pity. Still, it's a good time, the bar mitzvah.'

'Oh, we'll have a party!' Conan said. 'But how long will you be here, Joe? What brings you? How are things on the kibbutz?' He laughed. 'Questions, questions. I ask questions for a living but it's a bad social habit!'

Conan *didn't* know; now Budzinski was certain of it and the knowledge relaxed him. He wondered whether to tell Conan and decided against it. Conan would know soon enough, but meanwhile his ignorance kept the atmosphere easy. In any case, he could no longer hope for sanctuary here. He said, 'I came on impulse, really. It's a long time since I was in England.'

'You're going nostalgically north?' Conan asked. 'See the boys?'

'Maybe. Do you keep in touch?'

'Not a lot now, old chap. I occasionally see old Greenfield in Cambridge. My parents are both dead so there's hardly any reason to go up to Yorkshire now. But I hear occasionally. Once upon a time somebody took a tenner off me for a life member-ship of the Old Boys' Association, so I still get the school magazine three times a year. Matter of fact –' he collected Budzinski's glass and refilled it as he spoke, 'matter of fact, it's only up there I feel my age. One's contemporaries have bald heads, fat tums, and six kids, you know. But you'll find any number of people you know in Dewhurst's coffee shop any day of the week. Talking wool, of course. I'd go, if I were you. Go see Doc Dörflinger, too, he'd be glad to see you.'

'He's still alive?'

'Still the same. I still stand in awe of him somehow. At our age it's absurd, of course. But I still expect him to say "Be kvy-et!"'

'And does he?'

'Sometimes I think he wants to, but he seems to restrain himself, albeit with a certain difficulty. And now, Joe, I'm sorry, but I really must get ready. Awful, I know, but…'

Budzinski heard himself say, quite suddenly, surprising himself, 'Have you heard the news, Sidney?'

'No. What…?'

Wondering why and not knowing, Budzinski went on; it was as though somebody else had switched him on.

'We hijacked a Bulgarian airliner to Rome today.' Why, when he'd decided on silence, was he telling Conan after all? He didn't understand the impulse but it was very strong and somehow he had an inexplicable conviction of its rightness.

'You *what*!' Conan turned and stared.

'We were badly shot up. I got away.' His voice sounded flat and metallic in his own ears. He watched Conan recover quickly from the surprise; poise was part of Conan's stock in trade.

After a moment, 'Why, Joe? What was the purpose?'

'Joachim Schmidt was on the plane.'

'*Was* he, indeed!'

'It was slaughter. Dreadful. Four of our people were killed.'

Conan's eyes closed tightly for a moment. Then he asked quietly, 'Was it authorised?'

The barrister again, Budzinski thought. He said wearily, 'No. But it *was* Schmidt.'

'Of course. It's different. Schmidt, Mengele, Bormann if he's still alive. I know how you feel, Joe. What happened?'

'The two on the plane must have lost control. When it landed they were ready for us. Guns. Everything. It wasn't even a battle.'

'And Schmidt?'

'I don't know. We had a bomb on the plane, just in case. When I exploded it the tail section blew off. Schmidt is probably still in Rome. At the Bulgarian Embassy, or maybe the Russian.'

'Till they get him out,' Conan said softly.

'Yes. Till they get Schmidt to safety.'

'Do they know about you, Joe?'

Budzinski shrugged. 'Bound to know. If not yet, quite soon.'

Conan took Budzinski's empty glass. 'Another?'

'No.'

'I'll help if I can, of course.'

Budzinski nodded. 'I'm grateful.'

'They'll be hopping mad, won't they? Golda, Eban, even Dayan won't like a hijack.'

Budzinski said, 'I'm finished. I know it. I'll even accept it. But not today, Sidney.' He felt tears prickle at his eyes. 'Tomorrow, maybe, or the day after, it may be easier.'

'What will you do?'

'Give myself up. Go to the Embassy. But not tonight.'

Conan gave a strained little laugh. 'I doubt if you could if you tried. They close the shop. But when you do, what do you suppose will happen?'

'They'll put me on trial. Court martial. I'm a reservist major so that's the way it has to happen. I know all the arguments. But it's ironic, you'll admit.'

'To try you for an attempt on Schmidt? Yes, ironic *is* the word. Or – well, tragic.' He added suddenly, 'Stay here, Joe.'

Budzinski looked up quickly. 'You'd be in trouble, Sidney, if –'

'I shan't *be* here, old chap. Not for three days. No, four. It will be lonely, but you'll be safe. Nobody will find you. There's food and drink. It gives you time to decide. Depending on what you *do* decide, it also gives me time to drum up some help, work something out.'

Budzinski said, 'It's still a risk for you. You're rich, Jewish and you can be connected with me. And, anyway, your Israeli connections aren't exactly a secret.'

Conan smiled. 'I'm highly respectable, Joe. I get Treasury and Home Office briefs. Look, have you everything you need?'

'I imagine so, I don't need much.'

'Well, if you do need anything, or if you have to get out, you can help yourself to what's here.'

'Thanks.'

Conan left the room and reappeared a moment or two later in a dark, velvet-collared overcoat, carrying a small suitcase in one hand and a bowler hat in the other. 'Have you any money?'

'Nearly three hundred.'

'Should do for four days, dear boy. I'll telephone when I can. Make sure you're all right. Be careful and try to relax, Joe.'

'I will. Thanks.'

Conan headed for the door, then stopped. 'I'm an idiot. You'll need the keys. Here!' He tossed a leather key case across the room. 'The two little ones are for the car. Use it if you like.'

'I doubt if –'

'All the same, it's there. The garage is at the back. Car's a Jensen, not exactly inconspicuous but –'

'Don't you need it?'

'I'm going by train. That way I can work for a couple of hours. Good luck and don't be hasty.'

'I won't.'

Budzinski heard the flat door close, then the street door. Another whisky? Four days of drunkenness to drive the Rome scene from his mind? No. He rose from his chair and paced the comfortable, high drawing room for a while, nerves and muscles refusing to untense. After a bit he began to explore the flat, not intrusively, simply to do something. There was a study, a library almost, four or five thousand books and an exquisite antique desk. Once two boys had sat in the same classroom. No, not once, a thousand, two thousand times; two Jewish boys in a Yorkshire grammar school, growing up together. So much the same in those days; now so different. Conan's father-in-law had given away two and a half million. Two and a half million! It was a long way from Exchange Place, Leefield, to Chester Square. And a damn sight further to hijacks and slaughter at Ciampino.

The evening paper lay unopened on Conan's desk and Budzinski picked it up. There was a brief stop-press item about the hijack. Rome would be fodder for tomorrow's newspapers. He sat at the desk and tried to read the *Evening Standard*, but though his eyes moved along the lines, his mind was impervious to the sense of what he read. He began to turn the pages impatiently, skimming, but the paper seemed full of inconsequence. What did a one-day strike in Birmingham matter with four friends dead?

He almost missed it. If there hadn't been a picture, he'd have turned the page and things would have been different. But he absorbed the headline and the picture together, recognising her despite the harsh, contrasting tones of the flash picture. He'd seen her once at the Munich Olympics before the disaster. He read the diary note, casually at first, then again quickly as the sudden impulse cut into his mind. He glanced quickly at his watch, checking the times. Then he pushed the paper away and tried to think logically.

After a moment he knew logic scarcely came into it. There was no time to plan, hardly time even to think.

But there was time, *just* time, to act.

He examined the entrances and exits first, went down to the garage and unlocked the door, leaving it ready to swing open, then returned upstairs. There were things he needed, but didn't have. He'd have to improvise, adapt, take Conan at more than his word. He started in the big bedroom. No wardrobe; doors instead. Conan had a dressing room, of course. Correction: *two* dressing rooms, the first Budzinski entered belonged clearly to Ruth. Halfway through the door, seeing the dressing table, the make-up bottles, he half turned to leave, thought better of it and began to look at her clothes. He looked at a fur coat. Mink, naturally; plenty of it too, though Ruth Conan was small. He slipped it off the hanger, switched off the light and put the coat on the bed.

In Sidney's dressing room he looked at clothes. Conan had become a bit of a dandy, but there were several plain, dark suits among the finery. He tried one on quickly and found it baggy, a bit short in the sleeve, but possible. What about the trousers? Without braces, Sidney Conan's trousers would fall off him. Damn it, he had to have *braces!* He ransacked drawers till he found them, then a shirt, collar an inch too big. It would have to do. He began to dress quickly, looking among a hundred ties for a sober one.

Now shoes. Sidney's shoes were no good; a size too small. He'd have to wear his own, black admittedly, but kicked, scuffed and dusty now. He wasted precious moments searching in the kitchen for shoe polish and brushes and, hurrying too much, got a streak of black wax on his shirt cuff.

In the mirror he looked reasonable. Dark clothes hid imperfections of fit.

Now the other things. Transferring his pistol to the suit pocket, he felt grateful the jacket was so loose. But the gun wasn't necessarily enough. He looked in the medicine chest in the bathroom. Cough syrup, deodorant, travel-sickness pills, after-shave, razor blades: none any use. But he cut two strips from a wide roll of adhesive plaster. Back to the bedroom, hurrying; time slipping away, Sidney's side first. The bedside cabinet held cigarettes, writing paper, a couple of books. Ruth's side, then. Surely they didn't *both* sleep perfectly, always. He grabbed at the bottle. Pheno-barbitone. Now – what else? He thought quickly. More ties. He took four from the rack in Sidney's dressing room, pocketing them. Silk and expensive.

In the drawing room he stood still for a moment, looking round. Ruth would get fat if she wasn't careful. He took three big chocolate creams from the box and wrapped them in a twist of paper.

The raincoat was fine, but the bowler hat fell over his ears. He tore a strip of lavatory paper and packed the hatband until it fitted.

That was it, then. He ought to stop and think, but if he did... no – it was better not to think.

He looked at his watch. It had taken twenty minutes. Out! Out, while the impulse was in flood.

In the street he looked for a cab. No luck, the square quiet, the cars private. Which way, then? He didn't even know the area, had no idea where taxis could be found. He walked, then ran when he saw moving traffic. A minute waiting, then a cab came.

Budzinski told the driver where he wanted to go and sat back tensely. Damn it, he hadn't a cigarette! His fingers drummed in irritation on his knees. The cigarette would have relaxed and concentrated him, instead the craving fractured his concentration. He could stop, perhaps. Buy some. No, he couldn't; there wasn't time.

He watched London going by: fat, sleek London with its shining cars and prosperous shops. He slid back the partition. 'How heavy will the traffic be?'

'Round there? Murder, guv.'

Budzinski said, 'I don't want to be long and I don't want to get stuck.' He took a pound note from his pocket, added another. 'Here. Can you do anything?'

'Thanks, guv. I can try. There's a little street across the road from one of the entrances. I can stop at the top. Should be okay there.'

'How far away?'

'Seventy yards. Eighty maybe.'

'I want you to wait.' It was too far, in the open. But he wasn't stopping now.

'The law'll be there, moving us on.'

Budzinski said, 'I'm in a hurry. It's important. Five pounds?'

'Fiver? I'll manage it, guv!'

Budzinski wondered if the man was Jewish. It was possible; the accent, the profile suggested... No! It would be an absurd risk. Operate alone.

'How long will you be, guv?'

Budzinski thought. He said, 'I'm not quite sure. Depends when it's over. I hope it won't take long.' He looked out of the window, recognizing nothing. It was more than twenty years since he'd been in London and then only for a few days. He saw the words Brompton Road high on a building, but the street was unfamiliar. For a moment he felt a flash of panic at the thought that he was operating, blind and unprepared, on territory he didn't know and hadn't reconnoitred. He fought it down and sat back, aching for the cigarette.

The taxi swung left, past lighted shop fronts, then sharply left again. As it slowed he caught a glimpse to his left of lights and a small ocean of waiting cars, then the cab stopped.

'Down there, guv.' The driver pointed.

Budzinski froze for a moment, then made himself speak. 'You'll wait here?'

'Okay, guv. I may have to move a bit. But I'll be here. Or over there.' Budzinski followed the pointing finger, eyes taking in the scene.

'If you can, be *here*.'

He got out, took a couple of deep, deliberate breaths to calm himself, and marched towards the Royal Albert Hall. Then he began to work his way round the building, looking for an artists' entrance. When he found it, he looked once, with concentration, inside, trying to make a mental photograph of the scene. There were more people than he'd hoped, and a barrier guarded against intruders. No chance, then, of going in; the whole thing would have to be done on the pavement outside where the lights were bright and a few people lurked to waylay any arriving celebrities. Not that there would be many celebrities tonight, he imagined.

He watched the traffic moving round the one-way system. That helped; her car could only approach from one direction. He stood with his back to the wall, waiting, the fur coat over his arm but virtually useless now. A few cars arrived and he examined each one carefully, realising now that he had an extra difficulty. It was a tiny matter, but critical: some light from the Hall shone into each car, but not enough; it was not until the light went on inside the car, automatically as the door opened, that he was able to see with any clarity who was inside. It meant he would have to move very fast when the moment came, taking a far greater risk of failure than he had hoped. There would be a mere second or two, while the door was open and the people inside prepared to get out. In those few seconds he had to act. As in Rome that morning – was it only that morning? It seemed an eternity, now – he watched the vehicles that were not his targets as they passed, as they halted, as passengers climbed out. Over and over, the words of the *Evening Standard*'s brief story went through his mind.

Miss Semonov will be escorted by Sir Robert Speight, president of the British Gymnastic Federation. Sir Robert stands almost six feet four and Miss Semonov a mere five feet so he will tower over her as Miss Semonov towers over her gymnastic contemporaries. Her remarkable prowess, seen by hundreds of millions at the Olympic Games

54

and since, is almost solely responsible for a near-explosion of interest in gymnastics in Britain. Tonight is also quite a coup for Sir Robert. In his presidential year, he has lured the world's most celebrated girl gymnast to London merely to present the annual championship awards.

Budzinski wondered whether the man's title presaged a Rolls and chauffeur, perhaps even a glass partition to make things trickier. He toyed with the question for a moment, then forced it from his mind. Speculation was useless; only hard, fast, unexpected action would give him a chance of getting away with it.

A car came suddenly, a black Rover, polished and shining, sliding to a halt. Damn, there *was* a chauffeur! Budzinski saw the man lean to put on the handbrake and stepped forward, eyes peering sharply into the rear seat and saw the small familiar face with its cropped blonde hair peer up at him. He reached for the door handle, pulled it open and barged rapidly inside, hurling the fur coat over Sir Robert and Katya Semonov, then slid to the floor with his back to the far door so that the two passengers could see the pistol in his hand. To the chauffeur he said quickly, 'Drive on, or I will shoot Sir Robert.' He wasn't in the best of positions, and it could have gone wrong, but he jammed the pistol against Speight's chest and said, 'Tell him.'

'He's armed,' Speight said quietly. 'Better do as he says.'

The car moved away with a little resentful jerk and Budzinski assessed the situation quickly. It was unlikely now that he could successfully get the girl away from the two men and into a taxi, as he'd hoped. He might conceivably manage it, but instinct said no and he believed in the instinct.

'Where are you taking us?' Robert Speight demanded.

Budzinski, busy thinking, ignored him.

'Well at least tell the driver where to go!'

'Listen to me,' Budzinski said then. 'There's a mews on the north side of Chester Square. Go down it. Stop at the far end.'

'Shall I, sir?' The chauffeur sought confirmation from Speight.

'Do as he says.' Speight's voice, it seemed to Budzinski, was weary, almost bored. The lack of fear was disconcerting. He must be careful.

'Move over,' Budzinski ordered. 'I will sit on the seat.' The two edged across and Budzinski felt more comfortable now that he could see satisfactorily. He demanded more speed, well aware that fast though he'd moved, somebody outside the Albert Hall might have seen the pistol and informed the police. And taken the number. It was possible that police patrol cars were already on the lookout for the black Rover.

There was another factor he disliked and had to take on trust – he hadn't the remotest idea of the way to Chester Square. Would the driver be clever enough to test him by going the wrong way, driving direct to a police station? There was no way of knowing and he dared not reveal his ignorance. He must hope his orders to drive to the mews had convinced the chauffeur that he knew his London.

Speight said suddenly, 'Why not go via Marlborough Street, Sutton?'

Chancing it, Budzinski said, 'Don't be stupid. I told him to go direct. If he doesn't there'll be casualties. I'll shoot if I have to.' He glanced across at Katya Semonov who sat, tiny as a child, in the far corner. She was staring straight ahead, face set.

Minutes brought them to Chester Square. Budzinski directed the chauffeur until the Rover halted at last in the shadows of the mews. 'Switch off the engine and hand me the keys.' He pocketed them as the chauffeur handed them back over his shoulder. 'Now. I shall get out first. Then the chauffeur. Then Miss Semonov and finally you, Sir Robert. Is that clear?'

'Perfectly,' Speight said. Budzinski was momentarily surprised to hear him break into Russian, translating for Katya Semonov, but he realised Speight's fluent Russian was probably the reason why the girl had no other Russian with her, no KGB interpreter. That in itself was a bit of luck.

He picked up the fur and climbed out of the car, using the coat to mask the pistol as he stood waiting. As the chauffeur emerged he made him stand with his back to the door. Katya Semonov followed, tiny and taut, a red ribbon in her hair like a schoolgirl. Then Sir Robert Speight.

'Now walk back along the mews,' Budzinski said. 'Sir Robert and the chauffeur first, side by side. Miss Semonov will walk with me. If there's any nonsense, *she* is the one who will get hurt. Clear?'

Speight said quietly, 'I wonder if you realise? Miss Semonov is a Soviet citizen of great distinction. A lot of people will be looking for you, not all of them British, I imagine.'

'Walk.' As they moved Budzinski stayed half a pace behind Katya Semonov. She glanced at him only once, a little nervously perhaps, but no more than that. Considering her youth – he knew she was nineteen, though she looked about fourteen – she was very self-possessed in this situation. Speight strolled along in

56

front, tall, thin and elegant, the chunky chauffeur beside him. Budzinski had already decided that if any of them made a break, he'd shoot, though not, as he'd said, at Semonov. He wouldn't shoot to kill, but he wouldn't hesitate either.

But there was no break. When they reached the garage door, he made the chauffeur open it and had them move slowly inside. He closed and locked the door himself, and followed them up the stairs into the flat. The first task now was to immobilise them. He took one of Conan's ties from his pocket, gave it to the chauffeur and ordered him to tie Sir Robert's hands behind his back with it. He then made Speight lie face-down on the floor and ordered the girl, in Russian, to tie the chauffeur's hands. With the chauffeur also face-down on the carpet he breathed more easily. The girl's hands he tied himself. Then, taking her with him as a hostage, went quickly into Conan's dressing room and collected more ties and bound the feet of the two men. Next he made them wriggle close to a big leather chesterfield settee and lie side by side in front of it. When they were in position, Budzinski bent and lifted the back of the heavy settee so that it tilted over on top of them. They'd be uncomfortable, but they could breathe. He stopped then and looked at the girl. She watched him calmly and in silence.

'Sit down,' he said, pointing to a deep, soft armchair. She went and perched obediently on the edge. Budzinski shook his head. 'Sit *in* the chair. I want you sitting with your bottom right at the back.' Seated like that among the squashy velvet cushions, her feet were off the floor.

So far, so good. Now it was time to think. The first part of the operation had gone well, astonishingly well considering it had been entirely *ad hoc*, played wholly by ear. But that had been the easy part. From here, it became more difficult. And one thing he didn't like at all: the Rover car abandoned in the mews outside. While it might not be found for a little while, the moment it *was* found, it would certainly be identified rapidly as Speight's. And that would give the police hunt, which he must regard by now as under way, a solid point of focus.

But had anything *else* gone wrong? It was important to know. He made himself go back over the whole thing. Was there anything he'd done, or not done, that would leave a trail? There was the taxi, certainly, but he expected that the driver would merely have become tired of waiting and driven away. And everything he'd taken with him, the ties, the plaster, the pheno-barbitone, the chocolates, had been in his pockets. He checked quickly and everything except the ties was still there. Okay, so far.

It was then that he remembered the hat and felt a sudden panic. He recalled the red silk lining, the metal initials SJLC on the soft leather band inside, the hatter's imprint in gold. He'd left that damned hat in the taxi. And it would perhaps be traceable to Conan. No, not *perhaps*. He must regard the tracing as a certainty. Even if it might take time, he must behave as though the tracing would be virtually immediate. And *that* meant abandoning the flat, abandoning the one haven he had.

CHAPTER FOUR

In Rome, the remains of the TU 154 had by now been towed away from the concrete apron in front of the terminal and the airport was operating normally. But in the minutes immediately following the explosion which had severed the tailplane from the fuselage, a nervous conference had taken place between airline officials and the TU 154's captain and flight engineer. The immediate problem was what to do with the hundred-plus passengers now stranded and standing exposed on the tarmac. The Bulgarian captain and the Russian flight engineer believed that the danger was now past, but they could not be sure and the explosion that had wrecked the aircraft had demonstrated that the one remaining member of the hijack group was not without resources. They did not know, and certainly dared not assume, that the explosion had been the hijack group's only remaining gambit Two single-deck buses were hurriedly brought. With the passengers loaded the buses were driven to a distant part of the airfield and there guarded by airport police, while the captain and flight engineer returned to the terminal to make more permanent arrangements.

Italian officials, naturally, were anxious to give all possible assistance and it was not long before they came forward with the offer of an Alitalia DC8 to transport all passengers who wished to return to Bulgaria. They were thanked, but informed that a decision was awaited from the Bulgarian Embassy. The Bulgarian Ambassador had already travelled to the Soviet Embassy to discuss the problem and the Soviet Ambassador was awaiting Moscow's decision. The discussions between the Soviet Union and its satellite produced several decisions, the first quickly, others following later.

Accordingly, the Italian police were asked to provide a car and motor-cycle escort for the two coaches for the journey into Rome, where the passengers were to be taken temporarily to a large house owned by and close to the Soviet Embassy and normally used to house VIP visitors. The house, a detached Roman villa, stood in its own grounds and there was a standing plan to guard it, frequently employed and known to be efficient. Captain and crew travelled with the passengers and, once in the villa, began to make their formal reports on the attempted hijack and the events following it.

In the course of the afternoon, the various non-Soviet bloc passengers – assorted Africans, Arabs and European and American tourists – were interrogated to make sure they had not been involved in the plot, and then released to go their separate ways. A few others, Bulgarian and Soviet officials on approved missions abroad, also proceeded on their way. The members of the Varna Chamber Orchestra, including Istvan Kodes/Joachim Schmidt, remained in the villa until a decision could be made as to whether the proposed recording and concert programme could now be allowed to continue.

It appeared that everything was proceeding smoothly until, in mid-afternoon, copies of the Rome evening newspapers arrived at the two Embassies. Soviet and Bulgarian diplomats were then disconcerted to read a report that the much-wanted World War II mass-murderer Joachim Schmidt had been among the passengers. They were even more disconcerted, shortly afterwards, when the streets surrounding the villa began to fill with people, some of whom even carried hastily-prepared placards which demanded that the Russians hand over Joachim Schmidt to face trial for his hideous crimes against humanity and reminding them that there was no statute of limitations on war criminals.

When the first demonstrators began to assemble, whilst their numbers still remained small, it would have been possible, indeed simple, to smuggle Schmidt out of the villa in a van or on the floor or in the boot of a car. But the crowd grew swiftly and the Soviet Ambassador's first reaction, that the Italian police would quickly disperse a few Jews, was soon shown to be wide of the mark. In any case, orders had been specific. The members of the Varna Chamber Orchestra were to remain in the villa pending the decision reached between Moscow and Sofia. Furthermore, as the crowd grew, it became increasingly clear that its members were not all Jewish. There were Jews in it, certainly, and they were vociferous, but the crowd was made up of a wide variety of people, including a great many youthful international tourists and large numbers of ordinary Italian working men, many of them middle-aged, who would remember German behaviour in Italy after the Italian surrender and still feel strongly about it.

The facts of the situation were duly reported home by the two ambassadors and instructions were given that the press report be vigorously denied and that a list of the names of members of the

Varna Chamber Orchestra be issued. The list must include the name of Istvan Kodes and either the Bulgarian or the Russian Embassies must find among their staff a man who was both young and a violinist. For him a passport must be prepared in the name of Istvan Kodes. In due course, if the crowd did not disperse of its own accord, a few chosen members of the international press corps in Rome must be invited into the villa to meet the orchestra members, including the new Istvan Kodes. *But*, the orders warned, sufficient time must be allowed to elapse for the new Kodes to be given a suitably detailed fictional biography, and to learn it. He must not make any kind of slip if it became necessary for him to meet the press.

Unfortunately for the Russians, the crowd did not disperse. In fact, as the afternoon wore on, it grew in numbers. Worse, despite a Soviet protest to the Italian Government, no steps were taken by the *carabinieri* to disperse the crowd, partly because Interior Ministry reports indicated the international nature of the crowd. Only by bringing in water-cannon and gas would there have been any hope of dispersal and the Italian Government had no desire to turn hoses and tear-gas on hundreds of young visitors and hundreds more of their own people, particularly since the crowd was, so far at any rate, behaving itself.

Not that everybody in the crowd was behaving well. Whenever large numbers of people are gathered for a purpose that can even indirectly be interpreted as political, agitators are to be found. Some of the agitators were Jewish, determined upon retribution against Schmidt, but far more were young Italian Trotskyites, anxious to provoke trouble in the general cause. So the Italian police appeal to disperse and go home, issued repeatedly over a loudspeaker from a police Lancia, was promptly answered by shouts of 'Lies' and 'Get Schmidt out!' from dozens of voices.

The crowd stood its ground.

When things begin to go wrong, it is often true that they go on getting worse. And so it was with the public relations exercise the Soviet Embassy in Rome was compelled to conduct at about 6 pm. The Embassy always endeavoured, as a matter of routine, to keep on file as much information as possible about leading press men in the city. But the press corps was not a constant thing; foreign newspapers switched their men from one capital to another, often after quite a short period, replacing them with new men or women. The Russians were better informed, naturally, about the Italian press, but there were so many of them that it was impossible to know them all.

In addition, the embassy could not always issue specific invitations to individuals whose sympathy (or stupidity) might be known. It had to decide in many cases which papers and agencies to invite and then hope that the right men turned up. To do anything else would be to destroy the effectiveness of the exercise before it even began.

They were unlucky, in that they did not know that one of the *Chicago Tribune*'s Rome men had gone off on holiday the day before and been replaced by the number-two-stringer from the paper's Paris bureau. The *Tribune* man had been invited for two reasons: first that though he was of great probity and widely respected, he was usually the worse for liquor by early evening; and secondly because his file showed that he had once told a Tass agency man at a concert given in honour of the visiting American vice-president that he had a tin ear and didn't know Beethoven from the Beatles. It was the worst of bad luck, then, that the second-stringer from Paris, whose name was Paul Giraud, was the son of a French professional musician who had emigrated to America in the late nineteen-forties to join the Chicago Symphony Orchestra. Though Giraud was not himself a particularly talented performer, he had been steeped in the orchestral music world from childhood.

Giraud was not the only unexpected arrival among the party of visiting press men but, though the Russians did not know it, he was the dangerous one. Like the others, he was greeted with a smile and a handshake by the Soviet press attaché, and given, like the others, a large and very cold glass of vodka. Like the others, he obeyed the custom and drank it quickly. Unlike most of the rest, however, he declined to take a second. Giraud was not suspicious, or at least not abnormally so; like most newspapermen he was mildly sceptical about most things, more so of political matters and inclined to profound disbelief when a government source felt itself obliged to offer explanations. Governments, he held, explained only when somebody had goofed and explanations could not be avoided; hence most explanations could be held to be evasions at the least and downright lies a lot of the time. However, he was not on his own ground and his Italian was not particularly good. When the conference began, he was prepared to leave the questioning to the dozen or so experienced resident correspondents who were in the room with him.

He watched as the members of the Varna Orchestra were led in, entering the spotlight a little nervously and with no similar previous experience to sustain them. The press attaché then made a brief, formal statement ridiculing the idea that any member of the orchestra could conceivably be a war criminal. Both the Soviet and Bulgarian governments had, as was well-known, been unceasing and tireless in their efforts to trace such monsters. When they were found they were always brought to public trial. The long record of trials spoke for itself. No, what was present here today, the press attaché insisted, was an orchestra. Its members were all Bulgarian and were all artists who had played together for many years. To prove it he intended to ask the orchestra to play one of the most difficult Mozart chamber pieces without its conductor. No orchestra could do *that* satisfactorily, surely, he said, unless it were entirely genuine.

Time magazine's Rome bureau chief rose and asked that Istvan Kodes identify himself. A young man stood up. He was perhaps twenty-five, fair-haired and bespectacled; he was blushing slightly.

'Where were you born, Mr Kodes?' the *Time* man asked. He waited while the question was translated.

The young man replied and the interpreter translated. 'Constanza, on the Black Sea.'

The young man remained standing while the press corps inspected him. Then a woman from *Die Welt* asked him the colour of the upholstery on the TU 154.

Unless the woman knew the answer, Giraud thought, the question had been foolish; and clearly she didn't know, for when Kodes, after a moment's thought, said he wasn't good at these things, but he thought it had been red, she could only nod and resume her seat. Other questions followed, but in Giraud's ears they sounded weak. If the Istvan Kodes on the plane were not the Istvan Kodes standing before them, then he would not be exposed this way.

A minute or two later, Giraud said, 'Perhaps we may hear the orchestra play now?'

'Of course,' the press attaché said, with a smile. 'I was waiting until your questions were finished.'

Giraud watched and listened carefully as the Mozart was played. In particular he watched first Kodes, then the other members of the violin section. The press attaché sat rapt, throughout, as though lost in the music; a man without a care in the world. When the final chord sounded and died, he blinked a little as though returning to reality from some far-off and wonderful land. *Bullshit*, Giraud thought to himself. The press conference hadn't been called because everybody was happy with the music, but because *somebody* was very unhappy indeed at the story that had somehow got out.

He stood up. 'The diminuendo passage in the second movement; I should like to hear it again.'

'Of course,' the press attaché said. 'It is important that you realise we have nothing whatever to hide.'

'Thank you.' Giraud resumed his seat. The press attaché, at any rate, was no musician. But the leader of the Varna Chamber Orchestra was sweating. *He* knew.

What neither the press attaché nor the other reporters present were aware of, was that in the slow diminuendo passage of about fourteen bars, the five violins played alone. As they played it became quickly obvious, at least to Giraud's educated eye, that while four bows moved in unison, the bow of Istvan Kodes was not one of them. Giraud glanced round at the other press men as the music went on, and wondered if they had noticed that Kodes' transition from upstroke to downstroke failed to match the others'.

At the end, he rose and said, 'Thank you. May I ask how long Mr Kodes has been a member of the orchestra?'

'Six years.'

'Thank you.'

No-one else, apparently, had noticed. There was more questioning but it was desultory. Giraud began to believe he had a scoop on his hands and did no more to damage it. He nodded deliberately, as though in approval, when the press attaché wound up by thanking the press men, saying he felt sure the conference and demonstration must have convinced them and adding, with a smile, that more vodka and some canapés were already waiting for them. Giraud did not stay for the vodka and inevitable caviare the Soviets always used on their careful public relations exercises. Leaving the rest of them to it, he left the villa. As he did so, various people in the crowd outside demanded to know whether he had seen Kodes and what he believed. He replied each time that he had indeed seen Kodes and that Kodes was certainly a musician of accomplishment but beyond that it was impossible to be sure.

He was followed through the crowd by a man from the Soviet villa staff who watched Giraud hail a taxi and immediately called up a waiting car and followed Giraud to the building which housed the offices of the *Chicago Tribune*. There he watched Giraud go inside. He reported by telephone that the American reporter had returned to his office and was told to remain there, on watch, in case Giraud came out again quickly.

But Giraud didn't. Instead he went directly to his office and called for the Rome telephone directory. The first statement issued by the Bulgarians, soon after the damaged aircraft's passengers had been removed from Ciampino to the villa, had said the orchestra was visiting Rome at the invitation of the Tiber Recording Company. Giraud intended to find out who, at Tiber Records, had issued the invitation. Because he was on unfamiliar territory, and because by that hour of the night the Tiber Records offices were closed, he found it temporarily impossible to get in touch with anybody who might give him the answer. He was not defeated. Every newspaper bureau has local freelances on retainer to assist its staffers with local obscurities. Giraud called Alfredo Stefano on the telephone and asked him to come at once to the *Trib* office. When Stefano arrived, Giraud told him exactly what he wanted and was assured that the information could be procured, and quickly.

At approximately the same time that Joe Budzinski was impulsively leaving the Chester Square apartment in London with the intension of kidnapping Katya Semonov, Giraud finally got through by telephone to Alessandro di Angelis of Tiber Records.

A few minutes earlier, in London, Pável Mikhailovich Kropotkin, a KGB captain officially member of the staff of the cultural attaché at the Soviet Embassy in London, was waiting beyond the barrier of the artists' entrance at the Royal Albert Hall to greet Katya Semonov when she arrived with Sir Robert Speight. Normally it was a matter of practice that Soviet athletes and artists of all kinds went nowhere in the West without a KGB escort. There had been too many defections and every defection by a celebrated Russian was a severe propaganda blow, as Rudolf Nureyev and Olga Marasova, among others, had proved. Certain exceptions, however, were made. Msistlav Rostropovich, Igor Oistrakh and Rikhter, for example, were customarily unescorted. So were other people, on occasion, and in the case of Katya Semonov, who had been to visit a children's orthopaedic hospital in the afternoon and was to be escorted both there and to the gymnastics championships by a former British ambassador to the Soviet Union, it was felt that the presence in the inevitable photographs of men with bulging armpits would be indiscreet. When she left the Royal Albert Hall, Kropotkin would take her back to the Embassy hostel.

He waited, smoking a cigarette and wearing a dinner jacket cut to conceal the small, flat, Czech automatic he always carried, holding a polite but inconsequential conversation with the stage-door-keeper about the unpredictable ways of celebrated artists and meanwhile watching, through the rectangle of the open door, for the arrival of the black Rover carrying Katya Semonov and Sir Robert Speight. Finally he saw the black and chrome of the Rover's distinctive bonnet slide past, slowing to a stop. It halted with the doors out of Kropotkin's vision. He said, 'Excuse me,' to the doorkeeper and stepped towards the open entrance, just in time to see the rear door of the Rover slam to. A moment later the big car moved forward.

Kropotkin took two fast strides after it but he was too late; as the car slid away he could see two heads against the rear window and the outline of the chauffeur's cap in front. Kropotkin didn't pause to speculate, to ask himself futile questions he couldn't answer: this was a departure from the approved itinerary and his precise duty was to prevent (or, if he could not prevent it, to monitor) any such departure. He looked round for a taxi and was lucky enough to find one. He signalled, jumped in quickly, pointed to the disappearing tail-lights of the Rover and said, 'My friend has forgotten something. Will you follow his car, please.'

'The Rover, guv?'

'Yes, the Rover.'

The taxi moved off and Kropotkin sat anxiously on the edge of the seat watching the two red tail-lights almost unblinkingly.

The cab driver slid back the glass partition. 'Where's he going?'

'That's the trouble,' Kropotkin said. 'I don't know. But it's a document and he's got to have it first thing in the morning.'

'Happens all the time,' the cabby said. 'The things people leave behind. You wouldn't believe it. Other day I found a box in the cab. Guess what was in it!'

'I don't know.' Nor did Kropotkin care, but he was totally dependent on the cabby's efficiency and his goodwill. 'What was it?'

'Bloody snake, mate. Took the lid off and there it was. This geezer, I'd picked him up at the bleeding Cumberland Hotel and taken him to the Overseas League –'

'He's turning!' Kropotkin said urgently.

'Don't worry, mate. I won't lose him. But what's a feller doing with a bleedin' snake? Not as if I'd taken him to a strip club, eh?'

Kropotkin made himself laugh, but his eyes remained fixed on the back of the Rover. It would be so easy to lose sight of it and, once its lights were lost among all the other pairs of red rear-lights, it would almost certainly be impossible to re-establish contact.

'Will he be going far, guv?'

'I told you, I don't know.'

'But you want me to follow him wherever –'

'Yes.'

'You see, this way he could be going anywhere, heading west like he is.'

'Don't worry. You'll be paid.'

'No offence, guv. Just like to have the instructions clear. Go along Knightsbridge, you see, and before you know where you are, the next stop's bleedin' Bristol. Done that more than once, I tell you, and some of these bleeders haven't a pound in their pockets.'

In front of them the Rover made another turn, then a second.

'Chester Square, I reckon,' the cabby said. 'You get an instinct, like.'

'Good.'

'No, he's not. He's turning out again... oh, I see. There's a mews there, guv. Dead end. Want me to go down there?'

'A dead end, you say?'

'S'right.'

'Then don't bother.' Kropotkin got out and pushed two pound notes into the cabby's hand. 'Thank you. You did well. Keep it.'

'Ta, guv.'

As the taxi slid away, Kropotkin turned up the collar of his dinner jacket to hide the white of his shirt and slipped quietly along the mews and into a recess in the wall where the shadows hid him. At the end of the mews the Rover had halted. After a moment its lights were extinguished. There wasn't much light, but enough for Kropotkin to see a man get out first, then three others. The tall figure was Speight, the tiny one was Semonov, the man in the hat was the chauffeur. But who was the third man, carrying something bulky?

Kropotkin remained where he was in the shadows. He could not be sure that anything was wrong, though instinct suggested it was. All the same, it was possible that Speight lived there, that they had all called here for some innocent purpose and would soon return to the Albert Hall. His duty, however, was clear; he must maintain his watch discreetly unless he was sure something was wrong. To approach the group would be indiscreet if the reason for coming to Chester Square was innocent. All the same, he must let the Embassy know that Semonov had departed from her schedule. Such matters must always be reported at once.

He saw the four figures halt, saw the rising edge of the garage door, watched as they went inside and the door slid down again.

His position could have been worse. The mews was blind so when the car left it must come out the way it had entered. Now Kropotkin must find a telephone and report. After that... well, the fact that all four had entered the building suggested a stay of at least a few minutes. With luck, by the time they emerged again, reinforcements would have arrived from the Embassy.

Kropotkin hurried down the mews to where Semonov's group had entered the garage. There was no number but he noted that the garage door was black and he counted, as he ran back, how many other doors lay between it and the end of the mews. It took him three minutes to find a telephone and to his fury it was occupied. He waited, fuming, for another four minutes and spent two more using the telephone. He was assured that help would soon be on its way and instructed to return to his position and maintain observation. If Semonov and the others were to move before help arrived, he must be prepared to follow. It meant stealing a car. Perhaps the car would remain stolen for only a few minutes because the reinforcements would certainly arrive by Embassy car.

Kropotkin hurried along streets full of No Parking signs; naturally there were no parked cars. He was in a dilemma. He *must* return; equally he must have transport of some kind. A taxi was not the answer, even if he could repeat his luck outside the Albert Hall and find one quickly; if hard measures were needed, he didn't want a taxi driver as a witness.

Then he spotted the car, a dark green Morris 1300 shooting-brake parked half in a driveway. In front of it stood a Jaguar. Husband and wife, Kropotkin thought. He doubted whether they were in for the night because the gate was left open, but the Morris was perfect: mass-produced and quietly-coloured. He forced the quarter light swiftly and efficiently, climbed in and felt under the dash for the ignition wires. He swore to himself. The wires were boxed in and he'd have to raise the bonnet. He climbed out and fiddled for the catch. There was not one, but two, and it took him precious moments to find the second. He fixed the bonnet-stay and looked at the wiring, tore the wires clear and made the connections. The engine started softly with a clatter from tappets that needed adjustment. He lowered the bonnet, climbed into the Morris, found reverse and backed out, his foot gentle on the throttle for silence's sake. Now, the lights. He drove rapidly back to the mews entrance, hoping desperately that the Rover hadn't yet gone. Indicating left, he turned into the entrance just in time to see a car emerging from a garage halfway down. Almost certainly it was *the* garage. He had just time to notice two things before the headlights swung towards him: first that the Rover was still there; secondly that the new car was big and low-slung. He swung hard over to the right to force the oncoming car to pass him on his own left and flung himself across to the passenger seat, winding furiously at the window. The big blue car slid past him, a man driving, and Kropotkin saw the man turn his head and stare. The passenger seat was not visible, but he caught a glimpse of blonde hair just above the metal waist of the car. It was only a glimpse and it increased his dilemma. Assessing rapidly, Kropotkin decided he had two things to go on: the blonde hair and the reclining seat. Ordinary people, going out for the evening, would be unlikely to have a seat canted back like that. He must follow.

Behind him the car had stopped at the open end of the mews, left-hand indicator working. It was in the light now and Kropotkin could identify it: the car was a blue Jensen. He made a mental note of the number and, as the Jensen moved off, rammed the little Morris into reverse, backing it rapidly to the entrance, bringing it round on full lock. The Jensen was still in sight! He took the little Morris hard after it.

Once Budzinski had made his decision to leave Conan's flat, he acted quickly, putting together a mental list of necessary tasks, even as he was carrying out the first one. With another tie he secured the Russian girl's feet, then stuck the wide bands of sticking plaster he'd cut earlier in the evening across the mouths of Speight and the chauffeur and with two more of Conan's expensive ties, roped each man's ankles and hands together. Now, with the three of them secured he approached the girl, placed his hand over her jaw and pressed thumb and forefinger hard against the jaw hinge on each side. Her mouth opened protestingly and he could see she was going to scream. He said in Russian, 'Scream and I'll kill you!' Her eyes rolled up at him, wide now with fear, and he pushed four of the pheno-barbitone tablets into her open mouth and followed them with two of Ruth Conan's chocolate creams. Then he released the pressure on her jaw and quickly covered her mouth with his hand. 'Chew and swallow,' he ordered. She remained still. He pinched her nostrils together with the other hand. 'Chew and swallow!' With the air cut off, unable to breathe, she writhed in panic. Budzinski watched her unemotionally, then after a second felt her jaw begin to move. Her face reddened, but still he held the nostrils pinched until she was chewing and swallowing frantically. When he was satisfied he fetched a good-sized whisky from the tray and made her drink it to wash down the remaining contents of her mouth. The combination of pheno-barbitone and alcohol should knock her out quickly and effectively and keep her out for a few hours. He put the remaining pheno-barbitone tablets in his pocket, went into the study and began to look at the bookshelves. Conan had mentioned seeing Greenfield in Cambridge, but Budzinski was none too sure where Cambridge lay in relation to London. What he wanted was a road map, but he couldn't find one. He swore and reached for the telephone directory, looked up the number of *The Times* and began to dial.

Then he changed his mind and looked for a radio, found one and hunted round the dial for a newscast. Before he left he must at least know the situation. There was nothing on the medium wave; he switched to short wave and finally found a French broadcast. The hijack attempt was reported at fair length and there was new information, too. Budzinski listened carefully. There had been an unconfirmed report in Rome that the war criminal Joachim Schmidt had been on the hijacked airliner, travelling as a member of a Bulgarian orchestra. This had been vigorously denied by the Bulgarian Embassy in Rome. The members of the orchestra, meanwhile, were lodged in a villa in Rome belonging to the Soviet Embassy. Budzinski heard it through, as the announcer described the size of the crowd outside the villa; its demand that Schmidt be handed over for trial and the visit to the Embassy by members of the international press corps in Rome. The press men had been invited to meet the personnel of the orchestra and hear it play. It was understood that the press men had found nothing suspicious.

When the announcer moved to another topic, he switched off the radio, returned to the telephone and dialled.

'*Times* newspaper,' a man's voice said.

'News desk, please.'

He waited.

'News desk,' said a busy, get-on-with-it voice.

Budzinski said, 'Listen carefully. I have kidnapped the Russian woman gymnast Katya Semonov. When the Russians hand over Joachim Schmidt for trial, I shall release Katya Semonov. If they do not, she will be killed.'

'Would you mind,' the voice said gently, 'repeating that –?'

'You heard me,' Budzinski said.

'Yes, but just a min...'

Budzinski hung up quickly. They'd wanted to keep him talking in order to inform the police and let them trace the call, or at least to find a little more about the caller. He gave a grim little smile, returned to the drawing room and looked at Katya Semonov. Her eyelids were heavy already. He picked her up bodily and slung her over his shoulder. She weighed, he guessed, no more than ninety pounds.

He carried her down to the garage, put her in the passenger seat of Conan's Jensen and fastened the seat belt tight. It was then he noticed the lever operating the reclining seat. With the seat fully back, her head was almost below window level. Good! He switched off the garage light, opened the door and climbed into the Jensen. The rows of switches and dials looked as complicated as the controls of an aircraft, but after experimenting for a moment he had the engine going and the steering unlocked. He played with the switches until the headlights came on, put them on dip and put the car into gear.

He turned right into the mews, fully aware of the difficulties confronting him. He was as much on the run as he'd been two hours earlier, and this time he had nowhere to go except a faint possibility in Cambridge. Also he had the girl with him. And on top of that, once the British police became involved and got on to his link with Conan, the number of the Jensen would be known. He must get out of London quickly and change cars. Perhaps even make the change, if the opportunity arose, before leaving London. But first he had to find his route. At the top of the mews he turned left. A few minutes later a big roundabout loomed ahead, with traffic flashing knowledgeably round it. He moved among it carefully, glancing round for signs. One said *Piccadilly Circus* and he followed it. At Piccadilly, surely, there'd be better signs. But there weren't, or if there were he missed them; he was in the outside lane and several big red buses in a line blocked off the left hand pavement. He swung round Eros and followed the traffic stream. Still no signs, except one outside a cinema, announcing that this was the Leicester Square Theatre.

From time to time he glanced at Katya Semonov in the passenger seat. She seemed unconscious now and he wondered briefly whether he had overdone the drugs. The girl gymnast must be supremely healthy. It was probable that she had never taken a sleeping drug in her life, so she would have no tolerance of them; but he'd given her a dose of both pheno-barbitone and whisky. That was hefty for so small a body. If she dies... but no, he assured himself, four phenos and a good tot of whisky couldn't be fatal.

When an opportunity came, he moved into the left-hand stream and found himself virtually compelled to go left at a traffic-light then plunge, because he was in a one-way system, into gloomy side streets. Budzinski was now completely lost, with no idea whether he was heading north, south, east or west; he simply followed the arrows and concentrated on driving carefully enough not to touch any other vehicle. After several more turns he was at a traffic-light again and glancing up saw a street sign on a wall. Drury Lane, it said. He knew the name vaguely, but had no idea of where it lay. When the lights changed he went ahead, then bore right in the traffic. With relief he saw a sign, yellow lettering on green: *Bank and Stratford*. Bank, when he reached it, turned out to be another traffic maelstrom. He moved into it with caution again and saw men working in the road. A big blue and white sign said, *Diversion, eastbound traffic*. But did he want to go east? A van cut in front of him and he braked sharply, cursing, then noticed the lettering on the back of the van. Pye Radio. He blinked at his luck for underneath was the word Cambridge. The van took the eastbound diversion and Budzinski followed, greatly relieved. Then a thought struck him: at this time of night was it likely the van would be actually going to Cambridge? Was it not more likely the driver would be going home?

As things happened, by the time the van swung off and disappeared down what was obviously a side street, Budzinski had seen another sign that said A11, *Cambridge*. Breathing more easily, he let the Jensen move along a little faster. Beside him the girl was now clearly unconscious. He glanced at his watch. Half an hour since he'd left Conan's flat: it was time to change the car. To proceed with it became riskier with every moment.

CHAPTER FIVE

At the *Times* office, Harry Halliday, the assistant news editor, replaced the telephone with a little snort of exasperation, rose and went in to see his boss. 'We've had another,' he said. Earlier in the day, an anonymous caller had telephoned to say that the IRA had left a bomb in Harrods, but nothing had been found.

'Go on,' the news editor said.

'What he said was this...' The assistant news editor read from his shorthand note.

'Those words, eh?'

'Yes.'

'Okay, let them know.'

The assistant news editor reached for the telephone, dialled Scotland Yard, and asked for Assistant Commissioner Sellers. In the last few years, the number of calls of this kind made to newspapers had greatly increased and arrangements had been made between the Fleet Street editors and the Home Office that all such calls should be reported direct to A/C Sellers' office. Sellers was absent and Halliday spoke to his assistant, Chief Inspector Alastair McHugh of the Special Branch.

'That's all he said, eh?' McHugh asked.

'Those words. We tried to keep him on the line but he wasn't having any. Just spoke and hung up.'

'No idea where the call came from, I suppose.'

'No.'

'Had he an accent?'

'Not that I noticed,' Halliday said. 'He said what he had to say slowly and clearly and hung up. Standard English, more or less.'

'Did he *sound* like a joker?' McHugh asked.

'Well, they don't, do they, except occasionally? Sometimes you get some drunk phoning, but otherwise...'

'Okay. What was the precise time?'

'Eight-sixteen.'

'Thanks, Mr Halliday. Leave it with us.'

'You'll let us know?'

'As much as I can, *when* I can.'

Halliday replaced the phone and looked at the news editor. He said, 'If it's not a hoax, it's the Israelis, yes?'

'Could be. Get Matheson to re-nose the Rome story on this, will you, just in case. And get him to ring the Israeli Embassy. Let's see what we can come up with.'

'Okay.' Halliday turned to leave, then stopped. He said, 'If it's true, then the Rome thing wasn't the fiasco it seems, was it? I mean, it was a disaster, but they'd got the possibilities covered. One squad in Rome, the other in London. A real belt-and-braces job.'

The news editor grinned. 'More likely it was some disgruntled bank clerk. Still, you never know. If it's true, if the bloke in Rome *is* Joachim Schmidt, and if our Jewish friends *have* grabbed Katya, there's a good running story building up.'

At Scotland Yard, Chief Inspector McHugh recorded Halliday's call in his log, then picked up the telephone and dialled the special Israeli Embassy number for the duty officer. He listened to the ringing tone, counting as he always did, the number of rings. After twelve he broke the connection and redialled. When there was still no reply, he frowned and hung up. The Embassy duty officer could conceivably be in the lavatory or something. He'd wait five minutes, then telephone again. If there was still nothing doing, he'd have to act. He used the five minutes to tell A/C Sellers, at home, what was happening, then again telephoned the Embassy.

This time the phone was answered.

'Duty officer?' McHugh enquired crisply.

'No, sir. Commissionaire speaking.'

'Then may I speak to the duty officer, please. It's important.'

'I can't find him, sir. Not at the moment. Can I get him to ring you back?'

'Can't find him?' McHugh asked sharply.

'I expect he'll only be a few minutes.'

'Thank you.' McHugh hung up and thought for a moment. It was highly unusual for the duty officer in any embassy to be missing for long. He opened his desk, took out the list of diplomatic addresses. He spoke first to a servant and then to the Ambassador himself. 'I've been trying to reach the duty officer at the Embassy,' he said, after identifying himself. 'And I can't.'

'Can't?'

'No, sir.'

'Very well. You have something to tell us?'

McHugh scowled to himself. The Ambassador was audibly puzzled, but the matter was internal and he certainly wouldn't discuss it with policemen. He said, 'A few minutes ago *The*

Times had a phone call. A man says he's kidnapped a Russian girl gymnast called Katya Semonov and will release her only when the Russians hand over Joachim Schmidt in Rome.'

There was a pause. 'Where was this?'

McHugh said, 'Miss Semonov is in England, sir.'

'I see. Thank you, Chief Inspector.'

'Sir – you have no information, I suppose?' He couldn't push it, but the question was worth asking.

'My government strongly condemns such action,' the Ambassador said.

'I know that, sir. But as you know, it was reported in the press that one of the Rome hijackers had got away.'

'So I heard. I am grateful for this information. Is this girl in fact missing?'

'We're still checking, sir.'

'Thank you. Good night.'

'Good night, sir.'

McHugh knew he should have telephoned the Russian Embassy first, but talking to the Russians was a long, slow business and he'd hoped against hope that some small hint of the validity or otherwise of the call to *The Times* might have come from the Israelis. Now he must speak to the Russians, go through the endless routine, the passing on from one person to another, that the Russians always indulged in, the old Soviet runaround.

Tonight, however, there was no runaround. He was put through immediately to an unidentified second secretary who said Miss Semonov was at the Albert Hall, in the company of Sir Robert Speight, to present the awards in the British Junior Gymnastic Championships.

'Do you know whether she arrived, sir?'

'I have no information that she has not. Why do you ask?'

McHugh told him about the message given to *The Times* and the Russian said, 'If it is true, then we expect the fullest co-operation of the British police in tracking down the perpetrator of this heinous deed...' It went on and on, a couple of minutes of slogans.

'Naturally we'll do our best,' McHugh said.

His other phone rang. He excused himself to the Russian and answered it.

'Information Room, sir. We've had a report from the car we sent to the Albert Hall. Sir Robert Speight and Miss Semonov have not arrived.'

'Right.'

'The lads in the car have been checking the stage door, sir. There was a Russian there, waiting for the Semonov girl. He vanished in a hurry about forty minutes ago.'

'Where?'

'Not a clue, sir. Apparently he was standing there one minute, talking to the doorkeeper. Then he said something in Russian and went out.'

'Get a detective sergeant over there quick.'

McHugh hung up and went into the next room. 'What about Speight?'

His sergeant said, 'I've spoken to Lady Speight, sir. She's at home. She hasn't heard from him since before lunch.'

McHugh stood for a moment, thinking. The girl had been with Sir Robert Speight; both Speight and the girl were missing, but the supposed kidnapper had mentioned only the girl. So where was Speight?

He telephoned A/C Sellers at home. 'I think this one's real,' he said.

'I'll come in. Send my car over.'

'Right, sir.'

'And tell DI5 pronto. What about the Embassies?'

'Playing it very close, sir.'

'They always do. Don't bother with my car, McHugh. Send the nearest patrol car.'

The London house of the Israeli Ambassador to the Court of St James was a mere two hundred yards from the Embassy. After taking Chief Inspector McHugh's call, the Ambassador did not return to his dinner table; instead he put on his overcoat and hurried on foot to the Embassy, where he let himself into his private entrance and climbed the stairs to the office of Second Secretary Aaron Bloom. He was a badly worried man. Earlier in the afternoon, when the coded signal from Tel Aviv had informed him that it was virtually certain the fifth man in the Ciampino attack had been Josef Budzinski, the Ambassador had refreshed his memory by consulting Bloom's personal file and then sent for him. By that time everybody in the Embassy knew of the hijack and the Ambassador was aware that there was a great deal of private sympathy among the staff both for the hijackers and for their purposes.

The Ambassador had handed Bloom the Tel Aviv signal, watched him read it, and demanded, 'Do you know anything of this?'

'No, sir.'

'I have your complete assurance?'

'Yes.'

The Ambassador had been obliged to accept Bloom's assurance. He had asked Bloom where Budzinski might now go, assuming, as now seemed likely, that Budzinski had succeeded in escaping from Ciampino and must know he could not return to Israel.

Bloom had said he had no idea.

'He must have friends,' the Ambassador had insisted. 'You are one, are you not?'

Bloom shook his head. 'We worked together. I admired him. 'But he has only one real friend. Shimshon Talmon.'

'Killed today,' the Ambassador had said soberly. 'There is no-one else?'

'He has contacts all over the world,' Bloom had said. 'When the government stopped hunting war criminals you know that a lot of people disapproved. Those people will protect Josef Budzinski if he can reach them.'

'What about you,' the Ambassador remembered asking, 'did *you* disapprove?'

Bloom had been frank. 'At the time, yes. Very strongly. However now I believe the decision was correct.'

Thinking about it now as he approached Bloom's office door, the Ambassador found his suspicions growing.

If this Russian girl *had* been kidnapped here in London, it was a bold stroke, typical of Budzinski. It was also, diplomatically speaking, an extremely unpleasant incident. Was it coincidence that the kidnap, if there had been a kidnap, had occurred here, in London, where Budzinski's enterprising former lieutenant, Aaron Bloom, now lived? Could Bloom have lied?

He walked into the office and looked around. It was empty. There were papers still on the desk, not tidied away. That was odd in itself, since Bloom was a man of tidy habits. It looked to the Ambassador as though Bloom had been interrupted, while he was working. But where had he gone? It was forbidden for the duty officer to leave the Embassy during his duty period. He crossed to the wardrobe to see whether Bloom had taken his coat and found the door was locked and the key missing. The Ambassador turned to leave, thought better of it and crossed to the telephone. Before doing anything else, he must get somebody else on duty. It was then he thought he heard a sound. He stood still, listening. After a moment he heard it again, a faint whimper that seemed to come from the locked wardrobe. He tapped sharply on the door and heard the sound again. Still uncertain what it was, he hesitated briefly, then went to the head of the staircase and shouted loudly for the commissionaire. When the man appeared in the hall below, the Ambassador told him to bring a strong screwdriver – or better still some kind of lever – immediately to the Second Secretary's room.

When the man came, the Ambassador pointed to the wardrobe door. 'Prise it open,' he said. The built-in wardrobe was of heavy mahogany, old and very strong.

'It will be damaged,' the commissionaire warned him.

'So, damage it.'

As the wood round the lock splintered and the door swung open, Aaron Bloom rolled out on to the floor and for a moment the two men stared, the Ambassador grimly, the commissionaire wide-eyed.

'Wait outside,' the Ambassador ordered, then bent to unfasten the knots at Bloom's wrists and ankles. Even after the gag had been removed from his mouth, Bloom still whimpered. He was racked with cramp in both arms and legs. The Ambassador took each leg in turn and forced it straight, pushing against the ankle joints to stretch the spasmed muscles. After a couple of minutes when the cramps began to ease, he asked quietly, 'What happened?'

The answer came in one word. 'Budzinski.'

'When?'

'Soon after six.'

'Tell me,' the Ambassador said gently, and listened attentively as Bloom told him. He felt a little ashamed of his earlier suspicion.

'How did he get into the Embassy?'

Bloom shrugged. 'Or out again?'

The Ambassador shouted for the commissionaire. 'Did you let anybody out of the Embassy, anybody you didn't know, after the door was closed?'

'Yes, sir. Mr Bloom telephoned down, and –'

'Thank you. That's all.'

'You didn't telephone, of course?'

'No.'

Bloom said, 'He must have hit me with something. I woke up in there. I thought maybe I could get out, but as I stood up, I must have dislodged the loose shelf above. I fell, it fell on to me and after that I could not move. I thought I was going to die in there. There was no way to make anybody hear. I'm sorry, but he was just too quick. He's like that. One second we were talking, then...'

'Can you stand now?'

'I think so.' Bloom rose and stood shakily, flexing his limbs. 'I'm all right now.'

It was time to tell him. The Ambassador said, 'Budzinski's gone mad.'

Bloom frowned. 'Mad?'

'It seems he has kidnapped a Russian girl here in London. She is a famous gymnast apparently, and he wants to make the Soviets exchange Schmidt for her.'

Bloom did not, the Ambassador thought, look particularly surprised. He said as much. 'Budzinski is made like that. He thinks there is always a way.'

'Not this time,' the Ambassador said. 'The Soviets would never agree. It would be admitting they had sheltered Schmidt and only today that was formally denied. Where will Budzinski be?'

Bloom stretched. His face showed it was still painful to move, but he was recovering fast. He said, 'I don't know.'

'Can you find out?'

'I can try.'

The Ambassador nodded. 'You know him. You are experienced in these clandestine operations. Who better?'

'The British wouldn't like it,' Aaron Bloom said carefully.

'Do whatever you have to do. You can always be transferred later. But the British must expect us to look for him.'

'All right.'

'Good boy, Aaron. Find him. It's important. I'll stay here in the Embassy tonight. Let me know anything that turns up. Anything. Where will you start?'

'The telephone,' Bloom said.

'I'll leave you to it,' the Ambassador said. 'I must inform Tel Aviv what has happened and also arrange for somebody to take your place here tonight.'

After the Ambassador had gone, Bloom rubbed his aching calf and thigh muscles hard for a moment or two, then seated himself gingerly and picked up the telephone. A few weeks earlier he'd talked to a reporter from the *Jewish Chronicle* who had met Budzinski on a visit to Israel. He telephoned the reporter at home, warning himself to remember that he was talking to a journalist. The reporter, unfortunately, was out. Bloom sat and thought about Budzinski, reasoning that it would have been impossible for Budzinski to have set up the snatch without assistance and resources. Therefore somebody in Britain had helped him. Budzinski would have needed, at the very least, a car and some premises to which the girl could be taken, and somebody must have provided them. Who? Whoever it was must be Jewish, of course. Also, whoever it was must *know* Budzinski. He would probably be a refugee – that was another thing – not a second- or third-generation British. He frowned. He was narrowing the field a little, but nowhere near enough. There were plenty of well-to-do Jewish ex-refugees in London. Then a thought came from nowhere and he snapped his fingers in irritation as he tried to remember a name. He'd met the woman at some function or another, a widow who had lived three years on the kibbutz to which Budzinski had gone when he was put on the reserve list. Damn it, what was her name?

He had it suddenly. Meyer, that was her name, Lieselotte Meyer. Lived somewhere in Hampstead, if he remembered correctly. He fumbled with the pages of the telephone directory. *Meyer, Mrs L,* that would be her. He dialled quickly.

'Mrs Meyer? It's Aaron Bloom from the Embassy. We met once, you may remember.'

'I remember this.' She had a heavy mid-European accent.

Bloom said, 'When you were on the kibbutz, Joe Budzinski was there, wasn't he?'

'Budzinski! *Ja.* He is a fine man, that Budzinski.'

'I wonder,' Bloom said, 'if you remember any of the visitors to the kibbutz. Visitors from Britain.'

'Mr Bloom, there were hundreds. They came for holiday, to work.'

'I mean,' Bloom hesitated, wondering exactly what he did mean. 'People with money, especially from London.'

'Still many,' Mrs Meyer said.

'I wondered whether any of them came to see Joe Budzinski?'

'Why you ask me this?' Mrs Meyer's tone changed suddenly. 'It is this... today in Rome *nicht wahr?* Where the Israeli boys die? Was Budzinski one of these boys?'

Bloom said, 'Budzinski's very much alive, but I need to get in touch with some friend of his, here in Britain, if I can.'

'Why?'

'It's Embassy business, I'm afraid, Mrs Meyer. Can you help?'

'I don't know if I should.' Clearly she admired Budzinski; equally, it was likely she'd sympathise with the purpose of the hijack. Bloom said, 'Budzinski and I worked together, Mrs Meyer. For nearly ten years.'

'Aha! When they seek the criminals, *ja?*'

'That's right.'

'So let me think a moment. Hmm... we had many visitors to the kibbutz. Important men. Sieff, Wolfson, Cohen, Stein. Many of them.'

'Go on,' Bloom said encouragingly, 'do you remember seeing Budzinski with any of them?'

'Na. Except maybe in a group. Na, wait a minute. This I remember. Stein's daughter's husband, he was there. Once, maybe more than once.'

Sidney Conan! Bloom controlled his excitement. 'He talked to Joe, did he?'

'*Ja.* I remember this well. One day after dinner, they sit for hours in a corner of the dining room, while I wait to clear. I have to tell them at last to go.'

'Thanks, Mrs Meyer,' Bloom said. 'You've been a great help.'

'You are his friend,' she said. 'I would not want to make trouble.'

'I told you,' Bloom said obliquely, 'you're helping.'

He hung up and made a quick mental check. Conan filled all the requirements except one: he was British-born and so was his father. But Conan was rich, lived in London, had many well-placed friends. One thing puzzled him: how the hell had Conan and Budzinski established a relationship deep enough for this? They'd nothing in common; one was a barrister in London, the other a soldier in Israel.

Still, Conan was a good starting point. Bloom even knew where he lived, had once been to Conan's home for drinks. He reached again for the telephone, thought better of it, and rose. A phone call would only alert Conan, if Conan really was involved. Far better to arrive unannounced on his doorstep and watch his reactions.

He put on the raincoat Budzinski had used to tie him up, noting the heavy creasing with distaste, put his pistol in his pocket, and hurried downstairs telling the commissionaire to let the Ambassador know he'd gone out.

When Yuri Andropov and Alexei Kuznetzin, two officers of the KGB detachment at the Soviet Embassy in London, arrived at the entrance to the mews only five minutes after their colleague

Kropotkin had left in his stolen car, they knew only that Katya Semonov was not, as she should have been, at the Albert Hall. They had left the Embassy before the news had come from the British Special Branch that Semonov had been kidnapped. For a short while they waited in their car for Kropotkin to appear, as had been arranged. When he did not, they came to a reasonable conclusion that Kropotkin had had to leave to continue his surveillance. They discussed his report briefly and decided it was still necessary to investigate the house Kropotkin had identified. Four people had been seen to enter, but it was impossible to know how many might have emerged. Together the two men proceeded along the mews towards the car parked at the far end and identified it first by make and, as they came nearer, by number plate, as the car Kropotkin had followed to the mews. They then walked back towards the open garage door and there Kuznetzin took up his position. Andropov continued walking to the square proper to keep watch on the front of the house. They had agreed on three minutes before Kuznetzin entered. Kuznetzin kept his eyes on his watch as the second hand made three circuits of the face, then walked into the empty garage. He opened the door at the back, went up a short flight of stairs, and found himself in a small hallway, with the choice before him of a door and a stair. He knocked on the door and waited; nobody answered. He knocked again, to be certain, before forcing the door, quickly and expertly. He was in a flat and it was empty; was it the right flat? He looked round quickly, found some used envelopes in a waste basket addressed either to the Viscount Sudbury or Lady Sudbury, and made a provisional decision that he was probably in the wrong place, though he could not be sure. He returned to the stairs, climbed them, and knocked again. Once more he drew no response. He followed the procedure he had previously adopted, knocking again and waiting, before forcing the door. Kuznetzin took one look at the scene in the drawing room, then went to the window and gave a thumbs-up sign to Andropov. He pressed the electric lock-switch to release the front door. A moment later Andropov stood beside him.

'Who are they?' Andropov asked, nodding towards the two men who lay imprisoned beneath the heavy chesterfield.

Kuznetzin shrugged. 'Neither is Semonov. Look around.'

It took the two men almost no time to discover the name of the owner of the flat, and Conan's name was telephoned immediately to the Soviet Embassy. They then proceeded slowly and methodically with their search, ignoring the appeal in the eyes of the bound prisoners on the floor. Among the things they discovered were a copy of the *Evening Standard,* lying open on Conan's desk at the Londoner's Diary page and showing a photograph of Katya Semonov, and, in a desk drawer, the log books for Conan's and his wife's cars. They failed completely to discover any indication either of Conan's whereabouts or of Katya Semonov. Once that was clear, Kuznetzin made a further report to the Embassy. He was instructed that the two bound men on the floor should be released and interrogated.

A few minutes later, Sir Robert Speight and his chauffeur were offering dubious thanks for their belated release and Sir Robert was inquiring the identity of his benefactors. They declined to answer his question and instead asked some of their own. Speight, a fluent Russian speaker with two separate spells at the British Embassy in Moscow behind him, had no difficulty in placing the two men, and was accordingly cautious in his answers. He nevertheless told them what he thought their nationality entitled them to know: that he had been with Katya Semonov when an unknown man jumped into the car outside the Albert Hall and forced his chauffeur to drive away at gunpoint. All four had been brought here to the flat, and the man had left shortly afterwards with Miss Semonov. Deliberately he held back the information that the kidnapper had compelled Katya Semonov to swallow what looked like drugs; that information was for the British authorities. He insisted on using the telephone immediately, but was not allowed to.

When the two Russians, apparently dissatisfied with the volume of information he gave them, became threatening, Speight identified himself more precisely by telling them of his former position, and said that unless they intended actually to kill him, they should watch their manners since he was acquainted personally not only with the Soviet Ambassador in London, but also with Mr Gromyko, Mr Kosygin and Mr Brezhnev.

Kuznetzin again telephoned the Embassy and was given instructions that he and Andropov should return there immediately. They left, without another word, taking with them a silver-framed wedding photograph from the piano.

Sir Robert went immediately to the telephone, dialled Scotland Yard and asked to speak to the Assistant Commissioner on duty. He spoke, in fact, to A/C Sellers who had arrived minutes earlier. Tersely he informed Sellers of what had happened and where he was, and was asked to wait in the flat until Chief Inspector McHugh of the Special Branch arrived. Almost immediately after Speight had replaced the receiver, the doorbell rang.

Speight listened for a moment, wondering whether to answer. McHugh could scarcely be there yet, and in view of what had already happened that evening, heaven alone knew who might be at the door. On the other hand, whoever was there might throw a little more light into the dark corners. He crossed to the squawk box on legs still stiff from his bonds and depressed the switch. 'Who is it?'

A voice said, 'Sidney? It's Aaron Bloom.'

Never heard of him, Speight thought. He said, 'Come up,' pressed the release for the electric lock, and comforted himself with the thought that whoever Bloom might be, Chief Inspector McHugh would arrive within minutes.

Bloom and Speight eyed one another warily and in silence. Finally Speight said, 'May I ask who you are?'

'A friend of Sidney Conan,' Bloom replied crisply. 'Who are you?'

'Sir Robert Speight.'

'You're waiting for Sidney, too?'

'I'm waiting,' Speight said. 'Were you expecting him to be here?'

'I called,' Bloom said, 'on the offchance.'

They continued to eye one another, each by now half certain of the profession of the other. Both men had conducted too many oblique little diplomatic conversations not to be familiar with the convolutions. After a moment, Bloom said, 'Is Ruth Conan out, too?'

'To the best of my knowledge.'

'I was wondering who opened the door. To you, I mean.'

'So was I,' Speight replied equably as the doorbell rang again. He watched as Bloom's impassiveness was momentarily disturbed by a brief frown of speculation. 'That,' Speight said, 'will be the police.'

Bloom merely said, 'Police?'

McHugh came up the stairs, two at a time, followed by his sergeant. He looked at the three men and said, 'I'm Chief Inspector McHugh of the Metropolitan Police. Is one of you gentlemen Sir Robert Speight?'

'I am. That's my chauffeur over there.'

'And you, sir?'

'Aaron Bloom, Second Secretary at the Embassy of the State of Israel.'

'May I ask why you're here, sir?'

'I came to call on Mr Conan. What's all the mystery here?'

'Where is Mr Conan?' McHugh asked.

'I have no idea.'

'Nor,' said Speight, 'have I.'

McHugh turned to Bloom and said bluntly, 'I'm well aware of the privileged status of diplomats, sir. May I ask whether you're going to be able to help us?'

'With what?' Bloom asked innocently.

'In that case, I don't think I need detain you, sir. And perhaps you'll excuse us.' McHugh turned towards Speight.

Bloom, who by now wanted nothing more than to get away, said, 'I'm not sure I should. I come to a private flat and find it full of strangers, police all over the place, something unpleasant obviously happening. Perhaps I should stay, for Mr Conan's sake.'

McHugh said heavily, 'If you're in any doubt, sir, use the telephone. Ring Scotland Yard and ask for Assistant Commissioner Sellers. He'll put your mind at rest.'

Bloom shrugged and left. As the door closed behind him, McHugh went to the window and made two gestures, pointing with his finger at the as-yet-unopened front door below him, and then walking his first and second fingers along the sill. Below him, from an unmarked police car, a hand waved a quick acknowledgement.

Outside, Bloom paused on the steps to light a cigarette, noticed a car containing two men parked on a prohibited double yellow line, and walked away. What he needed now was a telephone. He walked for two minutes, then spotting the yellow sign of a cruising cab, flagged it down and asked to be taken to the Ritz Hotel. Turning in his seat he saw the car was following. At the Ritz, he took the street entrance to the downstairs bar, walked rapidly through it and up the interior stairs to the office of one of the assistant managers. Bloom had arranged several functions in the hotel and knew the man slightly. He knocked and entered quickly.

The assistant manager looked up. 'Good evening, Mr Bloom.'

'Good evening. I wonder if I might use your telephone?'

'There are public phones, sir, on –'

'But too public,' Bloom said. 'I have a message for the Ambassador.'

The assistant manager smiled. 'Of course, sir. Please use this office.'

'Very kind of you.'

He telephoned Joseph Stein's London home and was answered by the butler.

'Is Sir Joseph in?'

'Who's calling, sir?'

Bloom identified himself.

'No, sir. Sir Joseph is in Bournemouth.'

'I must reach him urgently. Have you the number?'

He hung up and telephoned Stein's Bournemouth house. There, too, he was answered by a servant, a woman. It must, Bloom thought briefly, be pleasant to be rich. When Sir Joseph came to the phone, Bloom said, 'Do you know where Sidney Conan is?'

'Why?'

'Can I just say it's urgent?'

Stein said, 'You a friend of Sidney's?'

'I certainly know him.'

'He'll be here tomorrow. What's all this about?'

Bloom said, 'I need to speak to him tonight.'

'Why?'

Bloom swore under his breath. 'About a case he's working on,' he lied.

'Oh. Well, I don't know. He's staying in Exeter somewhere tonight.'

'Do you know where?'

'Listen, we're having dinner!'

'Please,' Bloom said.

'All right, all right. I'll ask Ruth. Hang on.'

Bloom heard the phone put down and then picked up again. It was the woman servant who spoke now. 'Sir Joseph says Mr Sidney usually stays at the Rougemont Hotel, sir.'

Bloom thanked her and hung up. He asked directory enquiries for the hotel's number, and dialled. 'Is Mr Sidney Conan booked into the hotel tonight?'

'Yes, he is.'

'Has he arrived yet?'

'No, sir.'

'Will you give him a message, please. Will you tell him to talk to absolutely nobody until he's talked to me. My name is Bloom.'

'Yes, sir.' The girl's tone was mystified. Bloom wasn't surprised.

He said, 'It's extremely important.'

86

'Very good, sir.'

He left a pound on the assistant manager's desk and left, going downstairs to the bar again and leaving the hotel the way he'd entered it. A man, waiting a few yards away, beside a newsvendor's stand, gave him a hard glance. Bloom asked the commissionaire to get him a taxi and returned to the Embassy to report.

He told the Ambassador that Sidney Conan must be regarded as being involved to some degree in the Budzinski affair, even if all he had done was to allow Budzinski the use of the flat. It was possible that if Conan had gone to Exeter, so had Budzinski; but Bloom was not disposed to believe that. Conan was booked into a hotel and Bloom knew from his own experience that hotels were not the best of places in which to keep a prisoner.

Having reported, he tried the Exeter hotel again and was lucky. Conan had just arrived and was signing in. He came to the phone.

Bloom said, 'Can anybody hear what you say?'

'Yes. I'm at the reception desk.'

'You'd better take the call in your room, Mr Conan. I'll wait.'

'Okay. Hold on.' Conan's tone was neutral, but the fact that he raised no objection was in itself revealing, Bloom thought. He waited, tapping his fingers on his desk, until, with a click, the call was transferred. Conan said, 'Well, what *is* this all about? I got your mysterious message.'

Bloom plunged straight in. 'I know about Budzinski.'

There was a tiny pause, then Conan said, 'Budzinski? I don't quite follow.'

'I've just come from your flat, Mr Conan.'

'Oh, I see.' Another pause. Then Conan said, 'He's an old friend.'

'Hospitality is one thing, Mr Conan. Giving help in a criminal act is another.'

Conan said smoothly, 'Criminal act? What on earth are you talking about? Budzinski just arrived in England. He hadn't fixed up to stay anywhere. I told him he could use my flat.'

'You mean,' Bloom asked directly, 'that you don't know what he's done?'

'I know what he *is*, Mr Bloom. What he's been for many years. Are you saying he took part in the hijack in Rome today? I saw it in the paper on the train.'

Bloom thought for a moment. Conan either knew about Budzinski and Ciampino or had put two and two together. He was after all a lawyer. He'd be cautious. Or was it possible he didn't know about Semonov? He said, 'You sheltered a criminal. Not merely a criminal wanted in Italy, or a criminal according to Israeli law. The British also want Budzinski.'

'Why?'

'Don't you know?'

'No, I don't. Damn it, he only arrived earlier this evening! He's scarcely had time for –'

Bloom had had enough of question and answer. He said, 'Budzinski has kidnapped a Russian girl.'

'*What?*'

'He kidnapped a Russian girl, Mr Conan. Tonight. He says he'll kill her if the Russians in Rome don't hand over Joachim Schmidt.'

There was silence for a moment. Then, 'You *are* serious?'

'Absolutely serious.'

'And he's taken her to my flat?' There, Bloom thought wryly, spoke the man of property.

Bloom said, 'He may have. I think he did, but he's not there now.'

'Where is he, then?'

'I was hoping you could tell me. We've got to find him. Before this – well, it was bad enough, but *this!* You see, don't you?'

'I see very well.'

Bloom said, 'The girl's Russian. A famous gymnast. They'll want her back. They'll also want Budzinski. So do we. So do the British.'

Conan's tone still held a trace of disbelief. 'This isn't some kind of elaborate gambit you're making, Bloom?'

'Gambit?'

'To get him for the Rome business. I should tell you that when I spoke to him he was thinking of surrendering himself at the Embassy.'

'Then he changed his mind,' Bloom said sharply. 'The girl was with an Englishman called Speight, Sir Robert Speight, in a car. Budzinski must simply have got into the car with a gun or something. When I got to your flat, Speight was there. Then the police came. Conan, we know it was Budzinski. I doubt if the British do, but *we* know. I don't know about the Russians. Probably they don't. But Budzinski has to be found. And by us. Tell me where he might be.'

'I don't know,' Conan said.

'Who else does he know in England?'

'In England? He used to know quite a lot of people, of course. But that was a long time ago.'

'What did you say?'

'It was years ago.'

'Go on.'

'But he won't have stayed in touch. In fact, I know he hasn't.'

'Stayed in touch with whom?'

Conan said, 'Oh, I'm sorry. Didn't you know? He was at school here.'

Bloom felt himself stiffen. He'd worked ten years with Budzinski without knowing even *that*. 'Where?'

'Leefield. In Yorkshire.'

'So he may have gone to Leefield?'

'I suppose he may.'

Bloom asked sharply, 'When you talked, were any names mentioned?'

'We talked about Leefield, yes.'

'Names, Mr Conan, names!'

'I don't know. Let me see. Yes, Dörflinger was mentioned, I recall.'

'Who's Dörflinger?'

'He taught us German. He's Jewish. Refugee from Germany. He's over eighty now, though, and very frail. I hardly think –'

'Perhaps, perhaps not.' Bloom wrote down Dörflinger's name. 'Anybody else?'

'Hang on. Yes, there was Greenfield, too.'

'Is he in Leefield?'

'No. In Cambridge.'

'Jewish?'

'No. He's a priest. *Monsignor* Greenfield. He was a missionary. In India, I think. Now he lectures in Medieval History.'

'Greenfield, Cambridge,' Bloom wrote.

'Anyone else?'

'I don't *think* so. No. Not that I recall.'

'And you told Budzinski this man Greenfield was in Cambridge?'

'Yes.'

'Cambridge is nearer than Yorkshire. But he'd need a car.'

Conan said soberly, 'He has mine. I gave him my keys.'

Bloom groaned. 'So he's miles away.'

'If that's where he's gone. You're going after him?'

Bloom said, 'Somebody has to. The Russians will be after him. And the British. It's important we get there first. What's the make and number of the car?'

As Conan answered, he wrote it down. Then he said, 'If I were you, I'd go somewhere very quiet and have dinner. Make it last. When the police find you, and they will, be very innocent indeed. Don't mention Dörflinger. Don't mention Greenfield. Tell them you met Budzinski in Israel and invited him to stay with you when he was in London. If you can keep Leefield right out of it, so much the better. I need *time*, Conan. Israel needs to handle Budzinski herself, not to have him put on public trial here or in Moscow. You understand?'

'Of course.'

A few minutes later, the elder daughter of the Israeli Ambassador drove through the Embassy gate in her blue MGB GT. When, a short time later, she left, Bloom lay huddled in the tiny space behind the two front seats. To the policemen on discreet watch outside, she appeared to be alone in the car and they did not follow her, but half a mile away the girl stopped the car and Bloom climbed into the driving seat. As the girl set off to walk home, he drove off. His plan was first to go to Cambridge; it was, after all, more or less on the road to the north. If Budzinski turned out *not* to have gone to Cambridge, then the main highway of the A1 was not far away.

While Bloom threaded his way impatiently through the London traffic, the Israeli Ambassador was telling Tel Aviv what Bloom had learned, and demanding also to know why Tel Aviv had failed to inform him that Budzinski had gone to school in Britain.

CHAPTER SIX

'What we need,' said Chief Inspector McHugh to Assistant Commissioner Sellers, 'is to put a name to this so-and-so. And to know where he's gone. But with Conan missing...'

Sellers said, 'I've met this bloke, Conan, in my time. He does work for the Treasury. Home Office, too, I think.'

'So?'

'So he's briefed by their solicitors.'

'He's also Joe Stein's son-in-law. Stein might know.'

Sellers shook his head. 'This merchant is Jewish, right? So's Conan. So's Conan's pa-in-law. So we get on to him and we say, very politely, it's the Mets here, Sir Joseph. We want your daughter's husband and we want him fast. Let's suppose Joe Stein knows about this caper. He says he doesn't know a thing, doesn't he? Am I my son-in-law's keeper?'

'We can try.'

'Okay, try. But get somebody on to the Treasury solicitors and any other legal eagles who might brief Conan. They'll know who his clerk is. That'll be quicker.'

Sellers was right. When the police finally spoke to Sir Joseph Stein in Bournemouth, they learned nothing. After brooding for some time about the Israeli's urgent need to speak to Sidney, Stein had finally telephoned the Ambassador and been told in strict confidence precisely what had happened. He had then telephoned the Rougemont Hotel in Exeter, only to learn that Conan had arrived at the hotel, taken an urgent phone call, and gone out shortly afterwards. To Chief Inspector McHugh, when the police call came, Sir Joseph merely said he hadn't the faintest idea of his son-in-law's whereabouts, but expected to see him the next day.

'I warned you,' A/C Sellers said, a trifle smugly. 'What news about his clerk?'

'Playing bloody bridge somewhere,' McHugh said in exasperation. 'We've got an address. A patrol car's on its way.'

The Special Branch of the Metropolitan Police was not the only organisation searching for Conan. Nor, as things turned out, was it the most efficient. The Soviet Committee for State Security, the KGB, as a matter of policy had long made a point of having reliable contacts within the legal systems of every country in which it is active. In London, it had several, drawn mainly from the pre-war popular left of Spanish Civil War vintage. These men were telephoned forthwith and asked if they knew the whereabouts, or had any means of discovering the whereabouts, of Sidney Conan. It was here that the KGB had a huge stroke of luck. One of the tame solicitors had actually briefed Conan's rival for the following day's hearing in Exeter and knew, furthermore, that the case was second on the judge's list. 'It's more than likely,' he said, 'that Conan has gone down there tonight.'

As a result, three KGB men left immediately for Biggin Hill airport, where an air taxi had been chartered and stood ready to fly them west to Exeter. The KGB, in fact, had two men permanently in Plymouth, a mere forty miles from Exeter, but the Plymouth men had no photograph to work with. Before the light plane took off from Biggin Hill, Andropov's telephone call to KGB headquarters revealed that Conan was booked in at the Rougemont Hotel in Exeter. That information had been acquired by the simple process of telephoning all the Exeter hotels and asking for him. Within eighty minutes of leaving London, the three KGB men were in Exeter, heading by taxi for the Rougemont.

Yuri Andropov, who had been trained in the manner (though he hardly shared the attitudes) of the British middle class, went into the hotel and approached Reception.

'I should like to see Mr Sidney Conan,' he said.

The girl to whom he spoke said, 'I'm sorry, sir. He's not in.'

'Would you mind trying his room?'

'I did, sir. Just a moment ago.' She smiled. 'Everybody seems to want Mr Conan tonight.'

'Oh?'

'Yes, sir. We had the police here a few minutes ago. And –'

'Police?' Andropov smiled back at her. 'Mr Conan's a barrister, as you perhaps know. I'm a solicitor working with him. I expect the police want him for the same reason I do. Any idea where he is?'

'I'm afraid not. You could wait in the bar, sir.'

'I think not. I'll come back later.'

As he went out, Andropov asked the doorman if he knew where Conan might have gone.

'I don't, sir. He just went out. Matter of fact, the police asked me, too, sir. I told them the same.'

'Had he eaten?' Andropov slipped the doorman a fifty-pence piece.

'Thank you, sir. No, he couldn't have. Wasn't time, really. He'd hardly got here before he was out again. Maybe the gentleman's gone out to have dinner.'

'Perhaps he has,' Andropov agreed. Conan had been tipped off, that seemed clear enough, and was lying low to give Budzinski more time. 'I wonder where?'

'Well, there's several likely places, sir.' The doorman named two other Exeter hotels, the Imperial and the Royal Clarence, and added, 'or there's that new place, the Vieille Maison, by St David's Station. Very good, it's supposed to be.'

'Thanks.'

'But, sir, I expect the police'll find him. They seemed in a bit of a hurry and it's the restaurants and hotels they'll be looking in. Maybe if you wait a few minutes, he'll be back.'

'I think I'll look, all the same,' Andropov said. 'It's better than hanging about.'

Budzinski, heading eastward out of London some time earlier, found that he recognised almost none of the place names that kept coming up. All the same the signposting to Cambridge seemed efficient. A few minutes earlier a white police car had passed him going the other way and the driver had glanced idly at the blue Jensen, but only that. Budzinski, momentarily tense, had driven on with relief. All the same, it was becoming imperative that he get rid of the Jensen and find another car. He drove a couple more miles, thinking about the problem; he would need both luck and a suitably quiet place. And ideally the car he stole should be stolen from a place where it was unlikely to be missed before morning. A private house, then, or a factory. Best of all, perhaps, a hotel – the kind of place salesmen used in every country: fairly cheap and with a car park and a bar. He began to look out for such a hotel.

A few minutes later, almost before he noticed it, he passed one that looked suitable. It was screened by a wall and big, bare trees, so he hadn't seen it immediately. He drove on until he could turn, reversed the Jensen round, and drove back. The place looked ideal: old and a little seedy, but with a dozen or more medium-priced saloons drawn up in front. He drove in cautiously, stopped and looked round. The Jensen was so noticeable, parked among the humbler Fords and Austins. It would stand out like a jewel in a heap of coke. Then he noticed a sign, not illuminated, which read, 'More car parking at the rear.'

He slid the Jensen quietly across the hotel front and round the side. Perfect! There were three cars parked in a gloomy unlit yard. He drove the Jensen in beside a dark Cortina, switched off the engine, and waited silently. Nothing happened. The place was still and quiet. From the hotel kitchen he could hear pots and pans being moved about, but nobody appeared to be looking out. Such windows as were lit seemed all to be curtained.

Five minutes later, he was driving the dark brown Cortina out of the car park, turning left again on to the main road. He was reasonably sure that when he had lifted the unconscious girl out of the Jensen into the back of the Cortina, he had done so unobserved, hidden between the two cars. He rejoined the eastbound traffic stream and came, shortly afterwards, to a roundabout where he swung left on to the Cambridge road and began to pick up speed.

He failed to notice a dark green Morris 1300 which emerged from a side road by the hotel and followed the Cortina three or four cars behind. The traffic was still fairly heavy and the Morris 1300 one of the commonest of all cars. Also Kropotkin, long experienced in shadowing, had continued to vary his car lights, never driving for more than a minute or so without switching either to sidelights or back to dipped headlights. Kropotkin, however, remained alone. He had watched covertly as Budzinski changed cars, but had not dared to look for a telephone in case he lost his quarry.

But now Budzinski pushed the Cortina along the Cambridge road, he began almost automatically to carry out certain procedures he had been taught to detect surveillance. A mile at sixty, then down to forty. Now accelerate again to sixty. Did any of the cars behind follow the same pattern? He watched carefully through the rear-view window. There seemed to be one small car, though it was several hundred yards behind him and only visible in the straight stretches. He accelerated to seventy, then braked sharply to a halt at the roadside. A dozen cars slid by and as far as he could see, none had copied his own behaviour and stopped. He took off the handbrake and drove forward again, now watching the cars ahead and driving fast. After a couple of miles he passed a small Morris he thought had overtaken him earlier. It contained one man and was ambling along at a steady forty. Driving fast until he was beyond Epping, Budzinski then pulled sharply into the forecourt of a pub and waited. Seconds later the Morris flashed by. Budzinski swung after it and saw that the Morris had halted only a hundred yards or so farther along the road.

Relief at having identified the follower was mixed with anger and real fear. That he was being tailed was not in doubt. The questions were: who was trailing him? How had whoever it was got on to him? Was he alone? Above all, what should Budzinski do about it? He considered the questions as he drove, gradually fining them down. It was not, could not be, the British police. That police patrol car driver had seen the Jensen and done nothing. That left his own people, but it was surely unlikely the Israeli Embassy had managed to connect him with Conan's flat in time to put a tail on him. He gave a mental shrug; he'd thought he'd tied Aaron up securely enough, but Aaron was experienced and resourceful. Perhaps Aaron had got out of that damned cupboard almost immediately and been on his trail before he was even out of sight of the Embassy. But, no. That was impossible. It meant Aaron had stood idly by throughout the kidnap, and Aaron wouldn't have done that. At some point, seeing Budzinski was working entirely alone, Aaron would have stepped in. He'd have done it swiftly, with the maximum of surprise, and Aaron being Aaron, that would have been that.

So if it wasn't Aaron, and it wasn't the British, who the hell was it? The Russians? Budzinski knew how anxious the Russians would be to get him. After Ciampino they would have been keen enough; the kidnap would have vastly increased their determination. But he couldn't see how the Russians could have got on to him. Katya Semonov hadn't even had a Russian escort. Granted they could have had somebody at the Albert Hall, but if they had, if they'd followed Budzinski from the actual moment of the kidnap, they'd have struck before now, probably at the flat.

So who was it? One thing was certain: he'd have to get the man off his tail. It would be even better if he could discover who he was.

Beyond a town called Bishop's Stortford, Budzinski found what he'd been looking for. There had been other lay-bys, but there had been vehicles in them; this one was empty: a hundred-yard parking space just off the road and flanked on one side by a good, thick hedge. He swung off the road, braked sharply, climbed out of the car and forced his way through the hedge into the field beyond. From its shelter he watched as the headlights of passing cars swept by, waiting for the Morris, and glancing every few seconds at his watch. A full minute passed with no sign of the car. Carefully, Budzinski began to work his way back. Thirty yards brought him to the entrance to the lay-by. He moved on, peering through the bare, matted branches.

He was badly handicapped by the lack of visibility, but after another fifty yards, he caught a glimpse of the outline of a parked car. He came closer, hurrying. It was the Morris, and so far as he could tell, it was empty. He moved on, looking for a thinner part of the hedge, found one a short distance further on, brushed through it, shielding his face with his hands, and moved quietly, still in the shadow of the hedge, towards the parked car. Slipping in behind it, he peered inside. The car *was* empty, but its engine was still running. He ran softly towards the lay-by again, keeping to the grass verge, once scratching his face painfully on a trailing briar, suppressing the yelp of pain that rose automatically in his throat. When he looked cautiously round the bend in the hedge, he saw a man getting into the Cortina! *Hell!* He tore back towards the Morris, climbed in quickly, gunned the accelerator and let in the clutch brutally. The little car leapt forward as Budzinski wound down the window. To his left the Cortina was already moving off, heading for the exit from the lay-by. His pistol now in his right hand, Budzinski swung the wheel to the left, forcing the Morris off the road, over the narrow band of grass separating the road from the lay-by, aiming its bonnet at the Cortina's rear wheels. For a moment he thought he was going to miss. Correcting, he flattened his foot on the floorboards and hung on tight, diving to his left across the front seat as the smash came and the Morris spun off. The impact flung him helplessly into the space between seat and dashboard and his back was wrenched painfully. The engine stalled. Desperately he forced himself up again, swung his body so that his hand could come up and his pistol aim out of the window. The Cortina had been flung round by the impact, but was recovering now, swinging straight. Budzinski would have preferred not to shoot, but now he had no alternative. He put his second bullet through the driver and saw him slump, watched as the car swung uncontrollably round, and plunged into the hedge. He wrenched the door of the Morris open quickly and raced over to the Cortina. Its engine, too, had stalled. Keeping his pistol levelled at the limp man in the front seat, he pulled the door open. The driver did not move. Budzinski grabbed his collar and heaved him forward, watching the head loll, knowing instantly from the unnatural movement that he was dead.

Surely somebody must have seen; Budzinski looked round anxiously, but apparently nobody had stopped to investigate. All the same, it had been an appalling risk! He grabbed the dead man's collar and dragged him into the bottom of the hedge, then bent to search his pockets. There was nothing, nothing to identify him anyway. Some money, English cigarettes. And the man was wearing a dinner jacket. Why? He felt beneath the armpits and found a Czech-made gun! His eyes closed tightly in a quick spasm of fear as realisation went home that the *Russians* were on to him, actually on his tail.

He turned back to the Cortina, swore as the engine failed to start with the first contact of the loosened wires, heard its muted roar with relief, and backed it away from the hedge. The rear of the car was badly dented, but no metal scraped against the tyres. He could still drive it.

Leaving Kropotkin's body where it lay in the hedgerow, Budzinski drove on towards Cambridge.

The urgent signal from Israel's London Embassy arrived in Tel Aviv at almost exactly that moment. Copies of the signal went out immediately from the Foreign Ministry, both to the Mossad and to the office of the Prime Minister, who had demanded to be kept informed of every development. Her notorious anger exploded instantly. Why, she demanded, had this highly significant factor in Budzinski's background not been considered before?

The Mossad chief, sitting embarrassed at his desk, winced as her voice grated over the telephone.

'Budzinski's running,' she said harshly. 'Do we know where? No – that's what I'm told. We don't know. How *can* we know? That's what you say. He's a lone wolf, this Budzinski. I asked you, I asked *you* personally and you hadn't even looked at his file! Yet there it was. He went to school in England, so in England he has friends. The friends of his childhood. The best kind of friends. Why was this fact not given to me?'

The head of the Mossad gave her the only possible answer. 'Because he's Budzinski; because his record is well known, I suppose, Prime Minister. We had examined his contacts in recent years, but not so far back. Not yet.'

'Not *yet*!' the voice rasped angrily in his ear. 'When *would* you have looked?'

Defensively, the Mossad chief said, 'It would have happened.' His head was on the block and he knew it. He said, 'I'm having a check made. If there's anybody in the country who came here from the same town, from Leefield, I'll find them.'

'Be quick about it,' the Prime Minister said.

The Israeli Interior Ministry's immigrant files were well-organised and computer-controlled. A simple question punched into any one of a dozen terminals would have produced the information that Josef Budzinski, born Poznan, Poland in 1930, entered Israel 1949, had in fact attended a grammar school in the Yorkshire city of Leefield. But the Mossad man had been right when he told the Prime Minister why the terminal keys had not been tapped. It was because Budzinski was so widely known, particularly within the military/secret service apparatus. When they heard that Budzinski had been a member of the Ciampino group, nobody was especially surprised. He was so obvious a candidate, it was so clearly his type of operation, and they knew his past record of clandestine strikes so well that there had appeared no need to check such distant factors as his far-off schooldays.

The Interior Ministry computer ground on, working through immigrants from Britain, first by age, then by sex, then by point of origin. It was a big IBM 395, capable of many millions of calculations a minute and before long a name emerged chattering from the print-out. It was the promising name of Wilhelm Müller, German-born, two years older than Budzinski, who had actually attended the same school for five years and must presumably remember Budzinski. Müller was a doctor in Tel Aviv. Swiftly a Mossad man was sent to Dr Wilhelm Müller's home with instructions to check whether Müller did in fact know Budzinski and, if he did, to instruct him to pack a bag and be prepared to leave at once for Britain. A disappointment awaited the Mossad man. Like Chaim Lissak, who would have known about Budzinski's background but was unfortunately in France, Dr Müller was also away. Müller, the Mossad man learned, was on a two-month visit to a sister in Australia.

Meanwhile a second name had emerged from the computer; the name was that of a forty-two-year-old widow who practised as a dentist in Ashdod, less than twenty miles south of Tel Aviv, towards the Gaza Strip. The computer print-out read: WURZBURG, SUSAN RACHEL, BORN GEROLZHOFEN, MAINFRANKEN, GERMANY, 1931. PARENTS ENT BRITAIN 1937. EDUC: LEEFIELD GIRLS SCHOOL, LEEFIELD, YORKSHIRE, GB: DENTAL SURGEON: UNIV LIVERPOOL, QUAL 1953: IMMIG ISRAEL 1953: ARMY SERVICE 1953-5 SIX MONTHS COMP INF TRAINING, INF SUPPORT BATTN, 18 MONTHS LIEUT ISRAEL ARMY DENTAL SERVICE: MARR 1956 CAPT (LATER MAJ) LEVI WURZBURG (KILLED ACTIVE SERVICE SINAI 1966): DENTAL SURGEON BAR KOHAR KIBBUTZ 1956-66: PRIVATE PRACTICE, ASHDOD 1966---: CHILDREN: B (1) 1957, G (1) 1958 RESERVIST.

NOTES: DISPLAYED NOTABLE BRAVERY UNDER FIRE, TERRORIST RAIDS BAR KOHAR KIBBUTZ 1959, 62, 63, 64. WOUNDED (NOT DISABLED) 1962/64.

The Mossad man had no sooner reported Müller's absence abroad than he was sent driving south, fast. Roof-light blinking its warning, horn tooting almost continuously, his car made the eighteen miles to Ashdod in twenty minutes. Ten minutes after he arrived, Susan Würzburg's two teenage children were in the care of neighbours and the Mossad car was blasting north again, heading this time not for the Mossad headquarters in Tel Aviv, but for Lod Airport, where a Paris-bound El Al Boeing 707 was held for her. To the annoyance of the jet's passengers, it was delayed still longer while the Head of Mossad himself held a brief conference on the tarmac with her. The question had arisen of the wisdom of sending a woman in pursuit of Budzinski and the plane-side conference was, in part, to give the Mossad chief an opportunity to see her for himself. He had already decided, privately, that in the situation which faced him, any assistance from any source must be utilised. Meeting her now, he did not find her particularly impressive. On the other hand, her record spoke of commitment, intelligence and coolness. He could scarcely have hoped for much more and was grateful for what he had.

Susan Würzburg had been asked the same questions earlier by the man sent to fetch her. 'Yes,' she said again, 'I know Budzinski.'

'How recently have you seen him?'

'Five years, perhaps. By accident, in the street, in Tel Aviv.'

'And you'd know him?'

'I'd know him. I've known him since he was ten years old.'

'And his friends? His British friends?'

'Some of them were my friends, too.'

She was given the telephone number of the Israeli Embassy in London and the name of Aaron Bloom. 'Your task in Leefield,' she was told, 'is to find out whether Budzinski is there and report. If he is not, we want to know. If he *is* there, we need to know even more urgently. Report to nobody but Bloom or the Ambassador himself. Is that clear?'

'It's clear.'

'Good luck, Mrs Würzburg. This is important to Israel.'

'I know,' she said. She began to climb the staircase, but his voice stopped her.

'One more thing, Mrs Würzburg. Do not attempt to do anything yourself. If you find him, or find out where he is, inform the Embassy. Nothing more. Budzinski is dangerous.'

She nodded and boarded the plane. Minutes later it was airborne and Susan Würzburg was sipping coffee in evident calm. It was a calm she did not feel.

Like Budzinski, she was a member of the refugee generation. Her father had been a dentist in a small town in the Mainfranken district of Germany, not far from what is now the East German frontier. He had been, and was still in old age, a defiantly pessimistic man who always believed the worst was still to come and all his life had kept his eyes open for it. In many ways this trait had been difficult to live with, both for his family and his patients. For his family it had meant a constant brake on fun, on future plans, indeed on happiness. For his patients, it had meant additional minutes under the drill and the probe while the dentist made quite certain that he had blocked to the best of his considerable ability the further advance of dental degeneration.

But it had also saved his life, his wife's life and the lives of his two children. He had smelled trouble early and began, soon after the death of Hindenburg, to prepare to leave Germany. While many German Jewish families still hoped, despite all the mounting evidence, that Nazi anti-Semitism was a black cloud that would blow over, her father was arranging to sell his dental practice. His two brothers told him he was a fool, but he had made his decision. Before he left, in 1937, he tried to persuade them to join him. They refused, even though by then the cloud was darker still, and lower, and lightning in the shape of the ss was already striking unpredictably and often. Both brothers and their families died in Dachau. Nearly four decades later, after years of highly successful dental practice in Leefield, the old man still brooded, reproaching himself that he had not done more to persuade them.

Susan Würzburg, accordingly, had grown up in Leefield, a place which, like nearby Bradford and Leeds, had a long tradition of offering shelter to the dispossessed from Europe. She was six years old when she arrived there and within a year was effectively an English child, attending a local junior school, where the English she quickly learned had a Yorkshire accent. She was different from the other children only in her name, which was then Liebowitz, and the fact that from Friday evening until the Sabbath sunset she was not available to 'play out' with the other children.

At ten she won admission to Leefield Girls' Grammar School, a somewhat newer foundation than the boys' school, founded in the fifteenth century, but nonetheless the best school for girls in the area, and with a headmistress determined to fire her pupils into the male-dominated professions like so many bullets. Susan ultimately decided on dentistry, perhaps because her father pushed her gently in that direction, but more because of its familiarity. She had lived her life surrounded by instruments and knew how to use them, which was a good start.

But none of that mattered now, she reflected, as the airliner whistled westward towards Crete. What mattered now, and mattered greatly it seemed, was a two-year period between her sixteenth and eighteenth birthdays when, with the others of her age group, she had enjoyed the sudden freedom both of the immediate post-war years and of growing up. There had been a mob of them, thirty or forty altogether, boys and girls, who had played tennis and learned to dance, had walked the moors and 'gone to the pictures', had enjoyed flirtations and brief romances and generally begun the process of learning to live in a world now returning to normal. Josef Budzinski had been one of that group. She thought of him now and thought too what the years did to people. Into her mind came a sudden memory of Budzinski, in the hard winter of 1947, learning to skate on a frozen lake in Leefield Park. He had been clumsy and fallen endlessly, and been, as he always was, grimly determined to succeed. Afterwards he'd gone home again but not, like the rest of them, to parents. Her face softened. He'd been such a nice boy; her own mother had even said once: 'Josef is a nice Jewish boy, Susan,' like the Jewish mothers in jokes.

She'd said, 'But I don't want to get married for years and years and years. If ever!'

'I'm just pointing it out.'

Now she wondered just what had turned the young Joe she had known into Budzinski the man. Knowledge of his parents' fate? That was likeliest, but hardly the whole story; not every Jewish child who had escaped the holocaust had turned into an implacable hunter-down of war criminals. So why had Joe?

Of course, there was no single explanation. Part of it lay in Joe himself, part in the curious but natural mixture of fury and enthusiasm that had so characterised the early years of the new state of Israel. Joe had been part of that for so long, one of the avenging angels; for years she'd been rather proud of their childhood friendship. Yet now, here he was, a wanted man, a criminal, because he continued to do what he had always done. *Politics!* she thought.

Arrangements had been made for her to be met at Paris airport by the private plane of a French financier. In it she would fly on to the Leeds/Bradford airport and from there she would be on her own. Susan Würzburg closed her eyes and tried to decide where to begin her search. There were so many names and she couldn't talk to all of them at the same time. Nor could she go from person to person, asking, 'Have you seen Joe Budzinski?' because Joe would be staying well out of sight. No, the best thing would be to try to discover which friendships still existed after all these years, to try to find a chain and work along it. Women's gossip might be the most revealing thing of all, she decided. In the morning, she'd go to the coffee shop at Dewhurst's, Leefield's best-known meeting place. If no-one she knew was there, she'd have to start somewhere else. But in Dewhurst's, she felt instinctively, she could begin to look for the first link in the chain.

The story broke in Chicago, in the afternoon editions. It was datelined Rome and appeared under the by-line of Paul Giraud. It said:

Here today I listened as the Varna Chamber Orchestra played Mozart in a villa owned by the Soviet Government. I was one of a dozen reporters the Soviets were seeking to convince that one member of the orchestra, a man called Istvan Kodes, is not Joachim Schmidt, long-hunted top Nazi war criminal.

Schmidt, if he is now alive, is in his late sixties. The man Kodes is only twenty-six. So it was apparently an open and shut case. The Israeli commando which tried to kidnap Schmidt at Ciampino airport today had the wrong man and had paid a tragic price.

I asked Kodes how long he had played with the orchestra. The answer was: six years.

In this reporter's opinion, that is not the truth. For two reasons. Kodes plays the violin moderately well, but only marginally to professional orchestral standards. But the presence in an orchestra of one violinist worse than the others is not too unusual. Far more important, however, is the second reason: the violinists – there were five of them – did not play in unison.

Four did. The odd man out was Kodes. He tried. He tried very hard. But he couldn't do it.

Conclusion: the Istvan Kodes I saw is not Joachim Schmidt. But nor is the Istvan Kodes I saw a regular member of the orchestra.

So whose place has he taken? And why?

The Soviets, in seeking to dispose of a mystery, have merely created a greater one. What are they covering up?

Could it be that the Israelis were right? Could it be that Joachim Schmidt, the Butcher of Layerhausen, has been given sanctuary all these years behind the Iron Curtain?

If so, Schmidt is behind the Iron Curtain no longer. And outside a villa in Rome waits a crowd several thousand strong, determined that Schmidt will not get away again.

Giraud's story was promptly picked up by the international wire services and flashed round the world. It was too late for the evening papers in Europe, but timed perfectly for radio and TV news bulletins and for the morning newspapers already in production.

In the crowd outside the Rome Embassy were enough transistor radios for the news to be widely heard and rapidly spread. Instead of diminishing as nine o'clock, and then ten, came and went, the crowd continued to grow, in both numbers and determination. Chants began and continued. 'Istvan Kodes is a fraud,' the crowd shouted again and again. From somewhere an electric bullhorn was produced and an amplified voice kept demanding endlessly that Schmidt be surrendered to the Italian police.

Yet it was curious that the crowd, despite its evident determination, remained well-behaved. There was no violence; people simply stood and stared, or stood and shouted. The Italian police on its fringes watched as helplessly as the Russians and Bulgarians inside the villa.

It began to appear that the vigil would continue throughout the night.

At ten-thirty, Sidney Conan was still sitting at a quiet table at the back of the Vieille Maison restaurant in Exeter, drinking yet another cup of coffee. Twice already, in the course of the evening, policemen had come into the exclusive restaurant and spoken to the head waiter. Each time, the man had gone discreetly from table to table, asking whether Mr Sidney Conan was present. The first time, Conan had simply said no. Having said it, he was not approached a second time, and the policeman left.

As he toyed with his coffee cup, Conan was a badly worried man, torn between several duties and loyalties. He was a member of the English bar, with a plain duty to assist the police, especially in a situation like this. He was a strong, even a fervent Zionist, with a powerful, emotional attachment to the state and to the idea of Israel. Privately, too, he had disapproved when Israel finally called off the hunt for war criminals. With Schmidt, Bormann and Mengele still at large, it was to Conan absurd that justice should not be vigorously pursued. And lastly, Joe Budzinski was a friend. Not just a friend of thirty years. Joe Budzinski represented to Conan the qualities of courage, determination and action that had enabled the tiny state of Israel to survive and stay strong. Conan was sometimes privately ashamed of his own failure to go to Israel to share the hardships and dangers, to be ready to fight for what he believed. It was true, certainly, that in London he worked hard for the Zionist cause, and gave generously. But he was often deeply conscious of the softness of the life he led, and Joe Budzinski's life had been anything but soft. He filled the coffee cup again and sipped at it, thinking about his conversation with Budzinski a few hours earlier. The more he thought about it, the more certain he was that when Budzinski had arrived at Chester Square he had had no plan to kidnap this girl. Budzinski had seemed so beaten, so deeply sad, so nearly resigned. No, Conan reasoned, the idea had come after he himself had left, and its execution had been made possible only by the availability of his own flat and his own car. Unknowingly, *he* had provided the trigger that had fired off Budzinski's action. It was stretching things perhaps, but in a sense *he* had a share of responsibility. By failing to inform the Israeli Embassy of Budzinski's presence in London he had, in a sense, ranged himself alongside Budzinski. He felt a little proud of that.

Deliberately Conan had seated himself with his back to the door and refrained from making himself conspicuous by turning every time it opened. For that reason he was doubly unprepared when a man suddenly appeared at his table and sat down uninvited.

'What on...' Conan began, but something in the man's expression left the question uncompleted.

'You will pay your bill,' Yuri Andropov said quietly, 'and then you will leave the restaurant. If you do not, you will be killed, here at the table.'

104

'I *beg* your pardon!' Conan said angrily, but knew as he spoke that bluster was useless.

'Pay your bill and leave.' The man smiled pleasantly, as though conversing with a friend, but the smile went nowhere near his eyes.

Conan said, 'You'd never get out of the restaurant. You'd be stopped.'

'I have two friends outside, both armed. Now pay your bill.'

Conan felt cold all through, chillingly aware who the man must be. Not British or Israeli, Conan was sure of that, and it left only...

He swallowed as fear dredged bile up from his stomach. After a moment he made himself signal for the waiter. He paid, collected his coat and hat, and preceded his captor across the thick brown carpet.

The head waiter bowed as he left. 'Good night, sir. I hope you'll come again.'

Conan could not make himself speak. He nodded quickly as he went out and the head waiter, watching him, thought he looked unwell and wondered quickly whether something had gone wrong in the kitchen.

Outside a car was waiting, a Vauxhall. One man sat in the driving seat, another stood by the restaurant door. As Conan crossed the pavement and climbed into the car, he noticed a Hertz sticker on the rear window. The car drove swiftly out of Exeter, a few miles into open country where it turned off and drove bumpily along a track and halted. Conan was ordered to climb out, and did so, looking round instinctively for the help his mind told him could not exist. He stood on springy moorland grass and there was not a light in sight.

He also knew what was about to happen. Into his mind came an ironic recollection of his guilty thought so short a time ago, that his life had been soft. Well, now the softness was over. He straightened his back and made a private vow that whatever was done to him, he would protect Joe Budzinski. He was not the first of his people to face physical torture, or death, or both. Others had faced them bravely. So, he vowed to himself, would he.

He watched as the car's bonnet was lifted, as bulldog clips were fastened to the battery terminals.

'Now,' said Alexei Kuznetzin, 'you will tell us where Budzinski is.'

Conan braced himself. 'I don't know,' he said. Then it began.

Only five minutes later Conan was actually praying aloud for death. For him it had not been five minutes, but eternity, a seemingly endless intrusion into his body of pain in explosive and intolerable forms. He had never believed such agony could exist, but it mushroomed in him unspeakably, first in one part of his body, then in another. He whimpered for oblivion, but oblivion would not come near; he was almost praeternaturally conscious in the short intervals when the pain stopped and the questions came, but his lips moved only in prayer when they were not parted in the grunts and screams of agony.

Kuznetzin and Andropov looked at one another. Some men were like this, with minds so constructed that a mental door could be bolted even against pain of the kind Conan was suffering. Not many, but some, and even such people had an ultimate breaking point. The trouble was that time and subtlety were required and the prolonged application of pain that was almost, but not quite, beyond tolerance. It was becoming clear to Kuznetzin and Andropov that Conan was one of these. Therefore, they changed tactics. There were other techniques. The man who could withstand physical torture was often vulnerable to mental pressure. Sometimes it was a question of which took longest. Kuznetzin made a downward movement of his hand and the car's engine was switched off. He watched Conan's naked, writhing body until it became still again, listened to the gasps and whimpers that came involuntarily from the distorted mouth. He waited until Conan's eyes blinked open, then bent over him and said softly, 'You have a son and a daughter.' Kuznetzin let the thought sink in and watched as it did so, as the implications of the few words permeated Conan's mind.

Conan's eyes opened suddenly wide, staring up at him. After a moment he said something through puffed and stiffening lips. The word was almost indistinguishable, but Kuznetzin knew what it was.

'Yes, they are children,' he agreed, and turned the screw a little more: 'There is no way you can protect them.'

He said nothing more, letting the thought penetrate Conan's brain. It was always debatable whether threats to families would be effective. In many people personal survival overrode every other consideration. With such people, the kind of threat Kuznetzin had just made was entirely ineffective. You could murder their families before their eyes and they'd shriek and weep and protest, but they'd let it happen rather than die themselves.

He turned the screw a little more. 'Yes, we will torture them,' he said. He watched Conan's face carefully. The Jews had a deeply-embedded concept of family. 'Tonight, after you are dead, *they* will be punished for your stubbornness. Bournemouth is perhaps two hours from here. We will go there, take them from their beds...' Leaving the sentence hanging, he bent quickly to remind Conan of the feeling of agony, ramming the point of a small screwdriver behind his upper lip and upward excruciatingly into the acutely sensitive nerve centres behind the nose. Conan yelled.

'That,' said Kuznetzin, 'is how we will begin.' He noted the tears streaming from Conan's eyes. They were caused by the pain, of course, not real tears at all. But if they became real tears...

'Tell me,' he said, 'where this man Budzinski will go, the names of his friends. If you tell me, your children can sleep undisturbed. If not – ' Kuznetzin stamped his heel hard down on Conan's limp hand, and both heard and felt bones crunch under the impact. Conan's scream of agony was swallowed by night and distance. He rolled over, moaning, holding the smashed hand to his gut for a relief that did not exist. His shoulders began to move.

Ah! Kuznetzin exhaled with satisfaction. The sobbing had begun. The agony of the smashed hand would not fade quickly and now Conan's emotional stability had been breached and the mental door would gradually open. He bent low over Conan and began to describe in detail what would be done to the children. He watched Conan disintegrate. What a man could stand himself, he could not let others suffer. Sometimes it was a lover, a son, a daughter, in this case a father. Not always, of course, but if one technique failed, there were plenty of others.

It did not take long after that. A little more pain, a few more whispered descriptions, and the KGB men knew about Greenfield in Cambridge, about Leefield Grammar School where Budzinski had been educated, and the names of his friends there. It was all Conan knew, and it was little enough, but it might be helpful if Budzinski did, in fact, go there.

They left Sidney Conan in a ditch with a bullet in his brain. As he killed him, Kuznetzin felt he was being merciful.

CHAPTER SEVEN

The discovery of the body of an unidentified man in the bottom of a hedge on the main London-Cambridge road was made by a police patrol car whose driver had stopped because there was something odd about a Morris 1300 standing in a lay-by. The two policemen noted the bent front of the car and that it was empty. They swung torch beams about in case the driver had been injured and perhaps flung clear. For a moment, when they first saw Kropotkin's body, they thought that that was, in fact, what had happened.

Then they saw the bullet-hole.

Immediately they stepped back, away from the body, and one of the policemen returned to the white patrol car to radio his headquarters.

Budzinski, by this time, had just entered the city of Cambridge, and was wondering how he would find Trumpington Road. His car was parked beside a telephone box where he had just looked up in the directory the address of the Very Reverend Cyril Greenfield. The last thing he wanted was to ask the way. A moving car was totally anonymous, but a man who asked questions would be remembered later. A minute or so after he had driven away from the telephone box, he was halted at a traffic-light and saw with astonishment that he was actually *in* Trumpington Road. He stared at the street sign in near disbelief. His luck tonight had been almost flawless. From the moment he'd seen the girl's photograph, everything had gone right, with the single exception of the Russian who'd somehow contrived to be on his tail.

Budzinski was deeply concerned about that Russian; not about his death, which had been necessary and unavoidable, but about the fact that he had been there at all. He had encountered the Russians before and knew their thoroughness. KGB operatives bore no relation to James Bond, working brilliantly alone. They were *apparatchiks*, members of a system; the presence of one meant others nearby. He had to shake them off or he was finished.

He drove along slowly, looking at the house numbers. What he needed now was another change of car. The Cortina was stolen and would be missed. Perhaps it wouldn't be missed before morning, but he dared not chance that. Its owner could have gone out to it already, and have informed the police. Perhaps its registration number was even now being circulated. No, a change of car was essential. Would Greenfield help?

He came to the house, braked and looked at it. The house was quite large, and set back from the road, surprisingly prosperous-looking for a priest, just as it was surprising that Greenfield *was* a priest. Budzinski found the concept of the Very Reverend Cyril Greenfield difficult to grasp. In different circumstances, he would have found it amusing, but he was not amused now. He waited for a gap in the traffic, swung across the road into the drive and stopped just beyond the brick-pillared gateway, looking uncertainly at the house and remembering the boy who had become the priest who lived in it.

One year they had shared a double desk at school; the boys sat in alphabetical order and in that year there was a gap between B and G. After that, Farrell had joined the form. He was surprised how well he could remember it all. Farrell the rugby player, big and hefty but very agile. Fearless Farrell, who would tackle the side of a house. Budzinski screwed up his eyes tight, then blinked and shook his head. He was getting tired, naturally enough after the endless day (God, was Rome only this *morning?*) and it was Greenfield not Farrell who lived in this house. All the same, the memory of Farrell had stirred a memory of Greenfield. Greenfield had played rugby, too, and played quite well. He ran fast; yes, Greenfield had also been a fair athlete. But Greenfield didn't tackle. He liked to take the ball and run, liked to score; what he didn't like, and in fact avoided, was the hard physical contact and the risk of the tackle. Budzinski brooded. Lack of courage? *Did* it mean lack of courage? The question was important. Of course, a man did need courage of a sort to become a priest...

Beside him, for the first time since they had left London, Katya Semonov stirred. He turned his head to look at her and as he did so, she moved again and made a small sound of discomfort. She remained unconscious, but the drugged sleep must be shallower now. How long before she came to? And what then – more drugs? Or tie her up? He put the car into gear and moved up the short drive, turning the car across the front of the house until it was screened from the road. Then, with another glance at the sleeping girl, he climbed out and walked towards the door of the house.

He paused before knocking. From somewhere inside he could hear a piano and he wondered what it meant, how many people were in the house. Then came the orchestral sound. It was a

109

record. Budzinski raised the lion's-head knocker and rapped twice.

The door was opened a few moments later by Greenfield himself, tall, slightly stooped, hair greying now above the ears. Budzinski took in the picture quickly. Greenfield wore his clerical collar and his jacket. He might not be alone. On the other hand, the man was a priest, so there would be no wife, no children.

He smiled and said, 'Hello, Cyril.'

'Who is it?' Greenfield frowned and pulled a pair of glasses from the breast pocket of his jacket.

'It's Joe Budzinski.'

'Joe Budzinski! Bud? What on *earth* are you doing here?'

'I was passing. I thought I'd call and say hello.'

'Good heavens! Well, do come in.' There was no trace now of Leefield in Greenfield's speech. His tone was sonorous, the words almost sung rather than spoken. The door closed behind Budzinski. 'Come into my study, my dear fellow. There, on the right.'

Budzinski walked into the room. It was large and comfortable, stuffed with books. He turned and looked at Greenfield. The glasses were being put away again, folded with a practised flick.

'It's most remarkable,' Greenfield said. 'Of *all* people! But how did you know I was here? Do sit down. Would you like some coffee? Whisky, perhaps?'

'Coffee,' Budzinski said. 'Sidney Conan told me where you were. You're lecturing, I hear.'

Greenfield nodded. 'Medieval history. They were kind enough to offer me a fellowship at Peterhouse and the church is generous.' He went to the door. 'Excuse me. I'll order coffee.'

Budzinski watched him go, heard him speak and a woman's voice replying. How many people in the house?

Greenfield returned, almost beaming. 'Sidney, eh?' he said. 'He's a fine chap, Sidney. I do see him occasionally, you know.'

Not a word yet, Budzinski noted, about *him*. He nodded and waited, inviting Greenfield to go on. Greenfield did. 'I see hardly anybody, of course, these days. I'm the only one, I think, to find himself beached in an academic backwater, so... Still, it's a pleasant life. How *is* Sidney?'

'Very well.'

'Good, good. Well, now, it's certainly been a long time.'

'Twenty-five years,' Budzinski said. 'Yes, it's a long time.'

'A great flow of water 'neath the bridge of years, eh?'

Greenfield was pompous, Budzinski decided. Pompous and self-centred. A pompous self-centred priest who'd sloughed off his background and assumed a style. Conan had done the same, had developed a manner and affectations, but of the two he much preferred Conan. He always had. He said, 'Been here long?'

'Four years. I was an assistant priest for a while, then a missionary for some years. Then I went to the English College, you know, in Rome. Then the fellowship came up. That's the story, I'm afraid.'

Budzinski decided Greenfield was a climber. There was a knock at the door and a woman came in with a tray. 'Thank you, Mrs Everitt,' Greenfield said, 'that's all. You can go now. Good night.'

The woman smiled. Budzinski kept his hand over his mouth to minimise the possibility of future recognition. As the woman left, Greenfield said, 'One's calling forbids one a wife, but allows one domestic assistance.'

Leefield was now a very long way away, in time and distance, Budzinski realised, and Greenfield had deliberately made it so. Perhaps beneath the skin some traces of the old lazy but friendly Greenfield remained, but there wasn't time to find out. He could afford only rapid judgements and no additional risks. Outside in the car, the girl was moving towards wakefulness. His stomach felt hollow at the thought that the housekeeper might look into the car, see the girl. But no. As the front door closed, he heard her footsteps crunch steadily away across the gravel. He drank his coffee and went after information. 'You haven't seen anyone else we both know?'

'Indeed not, I fear. No, that's not true.'

'Oh?'

'I saw Theakstone, not too long ago in fact.'

'Where was that?' Budzinski remembered Theakstone well, small, very wiry, very tough.

'In Colchester. He's stationed there. You know he's a soldier, do you?'

Budzinski hadn't known; nor was he surprised. He said, 'I can imagine that. He'd be a good soldier.'

'Major now,' Greenfield said, 'in some regiment or other.'

Budzinski nodded. 'How far away is Colchester?' The word regiment was significant. In the British army, regiments did the fighting.

'Fifty miles or so?' Greenfield's eyes were raised in polite enquiry.

'I live abroad. In Israel. Rusty geography.'

'Oh, of *course*. I did hear.'

Budzinski said, 'You live alone?'

'Indeed I do. It provides me with tranquillity.'

'Well, you seem comfortable.'

'Too much so, sometimes. The hair shirt is occasionally difficult to assume, I do confess.'

I'll bet! Budzinski thought. He decided he couldn't afford to trust Greenfield an inch, man of faith or not, schoolmate or not.

He put his coffee cup down. 'Have you a car?'

Greenfield looked puzzled. 'Yes, of course. Why?'

'I wondered, that's all. Now I'm afraid I must go.' He made himself look regretful.

'So soon?'

'I'm only passing through. And it's late.'

'Yes. Well, if you're sure...' Budzinski noticed that there was no effort to dissuade him, no suggestion of further hospitality. They left the study and crossed the small hall and as Greenfield reached to turn the Yale latch, Budzinski hit him as he had hit Aaron Bloom: carefully hard and just behind and below the ear. Greenfield simply collapsed.

Budzinski bent, hoisted Greenfield across his shoulder in a fireman's lift, and climbed the stairs. It was a three-storey house and he wanted the attic. He was breathing hard by the time he reached it. He dumped Greenfield unceremoniously on the mattress of an unmade-up bed and set about finding the means of securing him. Finally he tore a sheet and tied him with it. He seemed to have spent half the day tying people up. The car keys were in Greenfield's pocket.

Budzinski hurried downstairs again, back into the study, looking for the telephone directory. On the front cover were the words Cambridge Area. Inside was a map showing the exchanges covered. Damn! Colchester wasn't among them.

He picked up the telephone and dialled the operator. 'I want to find out a number in Colchester.'

'You must get it from Directory Inquiries, caller.'

'How?'

'Dail one, nine, two.'

He dialled and waited, asked for Theakstone's number and was asked for the initials. Surprisingly they came readily into his mind. M.R. Michael Richard, or Michael Robert. M.R. certainly. He glanced at his watch. It was now after eleven.

How late did British majors stay in the officers' mess? He asked the operator to get the number. A woman's voice answered.

'Major Theakstone, please.'

'Who is it?' she asked, a little querulously.

Budzinski hesitated, wishing to avoid giving his name. What could he say? He tried to think about the British army. There was a big camp, somewhere. Yes, Catterick.

'Catterick adjutant,' he said.

'At this time?' The woman was clearly piqued.

'It's important,' Budzinski said. 'Sorry to disturb.'

'Well, he's asleep. He has to be up early –'

'It's important,' he repeated.

'Oh, very well.' The phone was put down.

He didn't have to wait long. 'Theakstone.'

Across the years Budzinski still recognised the thin, sharp voice, but now it had a snap of authority. He said, 'Remember me? Joe Budzinski?'

'Remember? Of course I bloody well remember. How are you? Thought you were in Israel!'

'Can I see you?'

''Course you can. Hey – you're a soldier, too, aren't you?'

'Yes.'

'Good man!' For the first time since Rome, almost twelve hours earlier, Budzinski found himself smiling naturally. He said, 'Tonight?'

'*Tonight?* Well it *is* a bit tricky. I'm off early tomorrow. But oh, look. Where are you?'

'Cambridge.'

'Hour and a half. Bit less at this hour. Well, all right. Be glad to see you. Joe, of all people.'

Budzinski found himself almost grinning. He said, 'Theaky, ha!' and heard Theakstone chuckle, then added, 'Will you take me on trust? Meet me quietly somewhere.'

'Eh?' Then Theakstone said unexpectedly, 'Were you by any chance in Rome today?'

Budzinski stared at the telephone in his hand, knowing that every passing second of hesitation made the question more significant.

'Never mind, eh?' Theakstone's voice came quickly, crisp, with a little undertone of excitement. No, not excitement, enthusiasm. 'Quiet, you say. All right. Got a car?'

'Yes.'

'Take the A604 from Cambridge to Colchester. Turn off it, a left-hander, right? at *Baythorne End* and go through Stoke by Clare, Clare, Cavendish to Long Melford. There's a hotel there. Can't miss it. Called the Bull. It's all ancient and timbered. See you in the car park there in an hour or so. Long Melford's nearer to you than Colchester. All right?'

'All right.' Budzinski repeated the instructions. He'd made no note. Then he was silent for a moment, considering. Theakstone had guessed so easily. This could easily be a trap and was certainly a hell of a risk.

'Joe! You there still?'

'Yes.'

'Don't worry. If I'm right you've had a bloody rough day. Had some myself in my time. So I won't make it any rougher. Clear?'

'It's clear.'

He wanted to believe Theakstone. He considered it. Perhaps it was because he'd always liked him as a boy; perhaps because Theakstone was a soldier; perhaps, and most likely, because he was tired and it was tempting to be optimistic. He went into Greenfield's kitchen, turned on the cold tap and put his head under it. His mind cleared and he made his decision: he *would* trust Theakstone.

Hurrying now he went to Greenfield's garage. The car was a Wolseley, leather upholstered, verging on opulence. It was also automatic, but that couldn't be helped. He went to the Cortina, unfastened the seat belt and lifted the girl out. She grunted a little as he did so, and he knew that soon he would have to do something: either give her more drugs, or find a sanctuary that offered a degree of security. The thought of more drugs worried him. She'd had four pheno-barbitones about three hours ago. Plus the whisky. How much more could he safely give her?

As he lifted her into the back of the Wolseley, he opened her mouth and placed another tablet under her tongue, hoping it would dissolve there slowly, that it wouldn't come loose in her mouth to be inhaled and possibly choke her. There was time for no more. He started the Wolseley and turned left out of the gate, glancing at the petrol gauge. Less than half full. Budzinski frowned. Still, it should be enough for an hour. After that – well, he had a sudden, confident feeling that Theakstone might come up with some answers.

At Exeter Airport, Andropov and Kuznetzin waited beside their air-taxi while their companion reported by telephone to a safe house from which the report would be passed to the Soviet Embassy in London. They had already told the pilot that they intended now to fly to Cambridge, instead of returning to London, and he had gone off to file his flight plan.

Within a few minutes the little plane was in the air. Flight time to Cambridge, the pilot said, was almost exactly an hour. Andropov and Kuznetzin exchanged glances. If Budzinski had gone to Cambridge, they would be perhaps an hour and a half behind him and the distance was closing. If not... well, if not, the search would be long and difficult.

Chief Inspector McHugh glanced at the slip of paper and whistled. A formal request was out to all forces that the Metropolitan Police be notified of untoward incidents which could conceivably be linked with the kidnapping of Katya Semonov. He'd put out the request reluctantly, knowing a leak to the press would inevitably follow. True, *The Times* had known already, but *The Times* would have kept quiet about its exclusive, perhaps until the last edition, and meanwhile McHugh and Assistant Commissioner Sellers had hoped to keep the news as well-contained as possible. At the Albert Hall, the audience watching the gymnastics championships had been told that Katya Semonov was unfortunately indisposed and could not attend. The few sports reporters there would have accepted that. But a nationwide call had let the cat out of the bag, squawking. All over the country, policemen would have given quiet tip-offs to press contacts. Even before the ten o'clock TV news, the growing flood of press phone calls to Scotland Yard's news room confirmed how widely the story had already been leaked. It was a pity; McHugh didn't enjoy working in a blaze of publicity. But still, the request had borne fruit.

Already beside him on his desk was a small pile of teleprinter tear-offs, each informing the Yard of a car theft. They came from all over the country, and one car had actually been stolen within a couple of hundred yards of Chester Square.

McHugh read the news slip again. It was from Hertfordshire Constabulary. A murder on the A11 road from London to Cambridge. A man in a dinner jacket killed, or so it appeared to the officers on the scene, with a gun. A single bullet-wound in the spine and a bullet-hole in a car the man had probably been driving. Make... number... McHugh pulled the stolen car slips towards him and looked for the one near Chester Square. *The numbers matched!*

He rose and went downstairs to Sellers' office, knocked and entered, and held out the two slips of paper in silence. Sellers read the brief messages quickly, and glanced up. He said, 'The detective sergeant who went to the Albert Hall. Didn't he say –'

'That the Russian who left in a hurry was wearing a dinner jacket,' McHugh interrupted. 'Yes, he did.'

'Well, well, well,' Sellers said mildly. 'They're at it again. Playing cops and robbers.'

'Do we tell them?' McHugh asked.

'The Russians? Why? It says here there's no means of identification. No, they'll only get cross and do something unpleasant. We'll tell 'em when we have to.'

'Meanwhile we think about Cambridge?'

'We do a damn sight more than think, my lad. This kidnapping is hot and getting hotter. We want to knock it over, quick. Tell me the tale as you see it now.'

McHugh said, 'I think this bloke probably saw the snatch happen, actually saw it, but he couldn't do much about it because he was solo. So he followed. And chummy found out he was being followed and *he* did something about it.'

'Fine minds coincide,' Sellers said. 'I think so, too. I also think chummy's a real bastard. Doesn't hesitate, knows what he's doing, and armed to the bloody teeth.'

'The other question is,' McHugh said, 'whether he's the one who got away in Rome. Or whether he's home-grown. Or what.'

'We'll only know that when we catch him,' Sellers said. 'Two things. We want a list of Israeli passport holders who've entered the country today, just in case. And *I* want to talk to the Chief Constable of Cambridgeshire.'

'Roadblocks?'

'You think of a better idea?'

McHugh left to talk to the Home Office. The request for Israeli passport holders wouldn't be popular. Still, it was nice sometimes to give other people a spot of night work.

Aaron Bloom, pushing the little MGB GT along the Cambridge road, saw the flashing blue light of the police car a couple of hundred yards ahead and braked quickly, then drove slowly ahead. The police car was in a lay-by and several other cars stood close by, plus a dozen or so uniformed men. He stopped and let his eyes take in the scene. Part of the lay-by had been roped off and under bright auxiliary lighting several men in plain clothes were bent over something on the ground.

A police sergeant walked towards him. 'Move along, sir, if you please.'

'What's going on?' Bloom asked pleasantly. 'It looks serious. All these ropes and lights. Has there been an accident?'

The sergeant fixed him with a hard eye. 'We need to keep the area clear, sir. Would you mind driving on.'

'All right. It's just that it looks like one of those pictures you see in the papers. Detectives at the scene of the murder.' Behind the sergeant's broad back he saw the flare of an electronic flash-bulb, then another.

The sergeant's mouth tightened. 'You realise you're causing an obstruction, contrary to the Road Traffic Acts, and also refusing to obey the reasonable request of an officer in uniform.'

'Oh, I'm sorry.' Another vehicle arrived, blue light flashing. An ambulance. 'Better go, then.'

'*Much* better, sir.'

'Then good night.' Bloom put the MGB into gear and drove away, thinking furiously, almost certain now that there was death in the lay-by. And on the Cambridge road, tonight, the coincidence was unpleasant. It was also, in a way, a signpost. In his own mind, Bloom was now sure that Budzinski's destination had been Cambridge. Of course, it *might* be Budzinski back there, in the lay-by. It might. Bloom doubted it, but there was no way of finding out. If it were Budzinski, then the whole thing was over anyway. No, what was far more significant was that Budzinski *had* driven to Cambridge. It meant that Budzinski was very thinly prepared. His old friend Conan had mentioned only one man, in one city, and that was where he'd gone. Budzinski was running without help, apart from what he'd been able to scrape from an old school friend. No, now it was *two* old school friends.

He did not know it, but the telephone box beside which he stopped soon after entering Cambridge was the one used by Budzinski. Like Budzinski, he looked up Greenfield's address. Then he drove on until he saw two pedestrians, a pair of students, boy and girl, walking hand in hand towards the city. He asked them where Trumpington Road was, and he too was startled to discover that was precisely where he was.

He arrived at Greenfield's home a little more than an hour after Budzinski had left. There was no reply to Bloom's knock. He circled the house slowly, checking whether there was a light on anywhere inside, but the place was in darkness. Bloom pursed his lips, facing the question that worried him squarely for the moment, and looking at it from a purely personal viewpoint. He was about to become a criminal. Diplomatic immunity was all very well. If he were caught breaking into the house, it was still extremely unlikely he would be charged and imprisoned. The British would declare him *persona non grata* and throw.him out. But they wouldn't stop there. They'd also let it be known in the diplomatic world why they'd done it; quietly, of course, but efficiently. After that there would be a lot of countries where Bloom would not be acceptable. His own foreign service would understand of course and he'd be given a job at home in Israel, but after a while he would become something of an embarrass-ment: a man who couldn't be moved around, who must be kept in Israel, who, as the years went by, would be thought too inexperienced for advancement.

Bloom stood looking at the house for several minutes and then made up his mind. He circled it again, looking for an open window or some other way of entering, but all the windows were closed and the two doors were locked. There was no alternative. The front door lock was of the Yale type. Bloom took a small oblong of strong plastic, a credit card, from his pocket, and pushed it firmly into the gap between door and frame. After a few minutes and one or two failures, he managed to slide the tenon back, turned the door handle and stepped inside. The offence, he thought grimly to himself, was breaking and enter-ing. Well, so be it. He found the light switch, closed the door behind him, and began to search the house. The ground floor was clean and tidy, with no sign of upset. In what was clearly a study lay two used cups and a tray with a half empty pot of coffee on it. Bloom touched the pot with his fingers. Was it *entirely* cold? In the middle of the desk blotter lay the Cambridge area telephone directory. He frowned, left the study and climbed the stairs. The first floor bathroom and three bedrooms were also empty, the beds unused. He went softly upstairs again. As he switched on the light in the small attic bedroom, angry eyes blinked at him from the bed.

Bloom stood looking at Greenfield, thinking hard. There was no doubt now that Budzinski had been here, but how long ago? The man on the bed, presumably Greenfield, made urgent grunting noises through a piece of the white cloth that had been used to gag him.

Bloom said, 'Budzinski? Joe Budzinski?'

The man nodded vigorously.

'He's gone?' More vigorous nodding. More angry grunts. Bloom nodded to himself. It could have been Budzinski back there in the lay-by, but he'd never believed it.

The next question was, where? But that question couldn't be answered without removing the gag, and if Greenfield was able to talk, he'd be able to shout too. Greenfield was an outraged British citizen of obvious respectability and had quite clearly not co-operated with Budzinski. Ergo, the first thing he'd probably want to do would be to call the police. The result of *that* would be to put the British police firmly on Budzinski's trail, the last thing Bloom wanted. Still, it wasn't really a problem. He left the room without a backward glance at the by now rather despairing, even frightened eyes, went down to the garage, then climbed the stairs again.

'Your car. Is it a Ford Cortina?'

Greenfield glared at him.

'Is it?'

An angry shake of the head. So Budzinski had stolen the priest's car, Bloom thought. And gone somewhere. There was now no alternative. He took his pistol from his pocket and saw the priest's eyes widen. 'If you shout or make a noise you will be hurt, understand?'

Greenfield nodded slowly. Bloom held the gun in his left hand and worked out the knot of the gag with his right. There was a wad of cotton in Greenfield's mouth, held in place by another strip tied behind the head.

At first Greenfield couldn't speak. The cotton had absorbed saliva to the point where the priest's mouth was lime-dry. Bloom waited, watching Greenfield's mouth and tongue working uncomfortably, then said again, 'You gave him a name, didn't you?'

'No.' Greenfield had difficulty even speaking the monosyllable.

'A name was mentioned,' Bloom said. 'What was the name?' There had to be a name. Conan had given Greenfield's name to Budzinski and if Bloom's theory was correct, if Budzinski was unprepared and improvising desperately, then he'd have demanded another name from Greenfield, almost certainly a Leefield name because it was Leefield the three men had in common. Had Greenfield passed him on?

He could hear the smacking of Greenfield's tongue and lips as saliva returned. Greenfield demanded to be released.

'Tell me the name.'

'We just talked, then he hit me. When I came round I was here. My head hurts.'

Bloom laid the pistol barrel on the bridge of Greenfield's nose and watched his eyes almost comically squint at it. 'What about Conan? Surely Sidney Conan was mentioned.'

Greenfield nodded. 'Oh yes. Budzinski said he'd seen him. I'm getting cramp in my legs. Please!'

'No-one else?'

Greenfield said, 'If I tell you?'

'Just tell me.'

'Then what's going to happen?'

'If you don't tell me, it will get unpleasant.' Bloom tapped the steel barrel very lightly against Greenfield's nose.

'Only if you untie all this –'

A harder tap. The priest's eyes widened.

'*Who?*'

'If I tell you, you won't let me go, will you? You'll leave me here all night?'

'I may even leave you dead,' Bloom said.

Greenfield's eyes closed tightly. He sweated. It was scarcely surprising, Bloom thought. A priest with a nice academic life suddenly interrupted by men who hit him and threatened him with guns.

'You talked about old friends. Friends at school,' he said quietly, 'you must have done!'

'Let me go, please. The cramp!'

'The name!'

Greenfield surrendered. 'We only mentioned one.'

'Who is he?'

'A man called Theakstone. He lives in Colchester. He's a soldier.'

'Soldier? What kind of soldier?'

'In the army,' Greenfield said sarcastically.

'Of course.' Bloom knew all about soldiers and didn't like the implication of this piece of news. Joe Budzinski was a soldier, too, and a kind of camaraderie often existed between soldiers even when they were on opposing sides. 'What kind of soldier?' he repeated.

'I don't know. An officer. Parachutes, I think. He was wearing a red beret.'

'And the number of your car?'

'Look, *please* let me go!'

'The number?'

When he'd got it, Bloom replaced the gag, tied the holding band tight, and left the room. He hesitated at the door, intending at first to leave the light on, but a glance at the flimsy curtains changed his mind. Better in every way if the house remained dark. He switched it off and went downstairs. Because he was a cautious man, he let himself out of the back door and moved quietly round the side of the house, keeping to the shadows and the grass. It was as well he did so. A small sound alerted him and he froze, looking quickly in the direction from which it had come. Two men stood at the front door of Greenfield's house. Bloom's scalp prickled. *Who else had got on to Greenfield?*

At Cambridge Airport at that time of night, the three KGB men had been unable to obtain a hire-car and had been compelled to telephone for a radio-cab and wait for it to arrive. They were unhappy about it. Taxis were unsatisfactory for obvious reasons and radio-cabs, with the driver's mouth permanently within inches of a live microphone, were especially unsatisfactory. But there was no other way of getting to this man Greenfield quickly and the need for speed was overriding.

Had the cab arrived more quickly, the three Russians would have been at the Trumpington Road house while Bloom was still questioning Greenfield. As it was, the taxi halted in the road outside just in time for them to see the single light in the house go out and they assumed Greenfield was just going to sleep.

CHAPTER EIGHT

The relationship between the Metropolitan Police and its sister forces up and down England is a complex one, reflecting on a smaller scale the relationship between the capital city and the rest of the country. The 'Mets' it is who control the Criminal Records Office; the 'Mets' who are inevitably first with every novelty from new traffic-handling methods to computers; it is the Mets, in the shape of Scotland Yard, who are called in when a particular case in the territory of a regional force turns out to be difficult of solution. Accordingly, the Metropolitan Police is respected, but hardly loved by the provincial forces, who believe, quite rightly, that the London policeman thinks of himself as a superior copper. They resent his belief that the rest of Britain's policemen are country cousins with straw in their hair. Accordingly there exists a kind of resentful neutrality. Provincial forces with, for example, a tricky murder case on their hands, often do not seek the Yard's help, not because help isn't needed, but because once the Yard is in, nothing will get them out.

The Chief Constable of Cambridgeshire had, of course, been informed of the finding of the body of an as yet unidentified man clothed in a dinner jacket, in a lay-by off the main A11 London-Cambridge road. Hertfordshire Constabulary had notified Cambridge at once as a matter of course, partly in case assistance became necessary, and partly as a courtesy. The formal message had included the words, 'we are investigating', which meant, murder or not, that for the time being, at any rate, the Mets were not invited to the party.

The Mets, however, in the person of Assistant Commissioner Sellers, levered their own way in, by way of a request for assistance. Sellers, a large road map of Eastern England on his desk, told the Chief Constable over the telephone that there was strong reason to suspect the man who had kidnapped Katya Semonov had headed for Cambridge by car and requested that police roadblocks be set up on the seven principal roads radiating from the city with the object of finding a car or other vehicle containing a girl who was nineteen but looked less; blonde hair, blue eyes, five feet two inches tall and of Russian nationality.

The working shift had recently changed. The Chief Constable

was short of men and said so. Nonetheless, he complied with the request. Not to have done so, on a matter of such conspicuous urgency, would have been to invite the intervention of the Home Office, at which point polite requests would have ended and firm orders would have been given in their stead.

'What's the man like?' asked the Chief Constable.

'No description. We don't even know if it's one or more,' Sellers said. 'The girl's the clue. She's tiny and she's blonde and she's Russian. Unless he's already gone to ground in some damned cellar, the girl *must* be identifiable.'

'I suppose,' the Chief Constable agreed, 'that there can't be too many small, blonde Russians on the road at the moment. Okay, we'll get cracking.'

'How long?' Sellers prodded gently.

'Minutes.'

'Good,' said Sellers approvingly. 'And thanks.'

The Chief Constable was as good as his word. Within eleven minutes, seven white Cambridgeshire police cars had radioed that they were in position. One, near Linton, on the A604 from Cambridge to Colchester, arrived at its roadblock point to see the rear lights of a large dark car vanishing over the county border into Suffolk.

One of the three policemen in the police car said cheerfully, 'There goes the one who got away.'

He was right. Budzinski had driven fast from Cambridge, foot heavy on the throttle, delighted with the way Greenfield's large comfortable car handled at speed. Beside him the girl lay still, her body moving only when the car body rolled on a bend. To Budzinski's mild irritation she was also snoring.

There had been an angry scene, a little earlier, in a medium-sized, modern, detached house which lay halfway between the garrison town of Colchester and the oyster-fisheries and sailing town of West Mersea. As Major Michael Theakstone put the phone down, his wife stopped glaring at the late night TV film and stamped into the hall.

'What,' she demanded to know, 'did *he* want?'

'Sorry, darling,' Theakstone said crisply. 'Afraid I have to go out.'

'At *this* time of night?'

''Fraid so.'

She stared at him, lips compressed in a tight line of exasperation. 'Have we declared a bloody war, or something?'

'No. It's just –'

'Jesus Christ!' she said. 'You're off on exercise tomorrow for three weeks and that's not enough. You have to play bloody soldiers tonight.'

'I'm sorry.' He was slipping on a raincoat.

'Well – when will you be back?'

'Not sure. Have you seen my cap?'

'Dress, SD, forage, dress forage, beret or tweed?' She was a brigadier's daughter and knew her army; the fact that it now seemed unlikely she would ever be a brigadier's *wife* contributed its quota to her savagery.

'Tweed,' he said, 'ah, here it is.'

'You *will* be back, I suppose? I mean some time before six, when you go off again?'

'I should imagine so.'

'I should bloody well hope so,' Marjorie Theakstone said.

Theakstone opened the door. 'I'll try not to waken you.'

She was angry and hurt; for years she had been growing steadily angrier and the hurt had intensified. She'd married a soldier, first because marrying a soldier came naturally, and second because in her youth there had still been some glamour: foreign postings, dress uniforms, riding, sunshine and the rest. She'd thought she could persuade Theakstone that *that* was the best part of army life. But he didn't agree; had never agreed. He was the kind of infantry officer happiest with mud all over him in a ditch, a dedicated soldier, the kind of man who actually volunteered for rigorous training courses. His men were inclined to call him 'that mad bastard Theakstone', in a tone that was half-contemptuous, half-awed.

'You don't give a bugger about me,' she called after her husband's retreating back. To herself she acknowledged occasionally, in moments of self-examination, that it was in large measure her own fault. All the same, there he was, marching unconcernedly out to his blasted car!

She raised her voice. 'You needn't bother coming back at all, damn you! I'm going across to mother's. At least there's somebody there to talk to.'

'Right,' he called. 'See you when I get back.'

Marjorie Theakstone slammed the door hard and went to their bedroom to throw some things into a case. Come to think of it, she could spend a few days, even a week, with her mother. Why should two lonely women sit in two separate lonely houses, when they could share a roof? Tomorrow she could pick up the rest of her things, but tonight she'd better be quick, or mother would have gone to bed. It would, she thought crossly as she fastened the case, serve Major Michael Bloody Theakstone, DSO, M bloody C, bloody well right if she never bloody well came back again.

She went out to the double garage and tossed the bag on to the passenger seat of her five-year-old Mini. Other people had nice cars; she had an old Mini! She slammed it into gear and set off for her mother's house a few miles away. In doing so she saved herself from very serious trouble indeed.

Her husband, meanwhile, was driving rapidly round Colchester's one-way system, and turning off to make for the Sudbury road. His car was a Triumph: an elderly, somewhat rusty TR4 which he liked to drive hard and fast. He hammered it along the winding country road, quiet at this time of night, enjoying the application of his skill with one part of his mind and thinking about Joe Budzinski with the other.

It must be twenty-five years since they'd met, but Theakstone had heard about him once or twice, just odd pieces of information. There had, for example, been a night at the Small Arms School at Hythe when he'd had dinner with a couple of visiting Israeli officers. They'd talked commando tactics and out of nowhere Budzinski's name had come up. That had been years earlier, soon after the Eichmann snatch. Then later, at the School of Infantry in Warminster, he'd again met some Israelis, had mentioned Joe, and heard about a daring and brutal strike Budzinski had led against a rocket site in Sinai, in the Six Day War. It was the kind of soldiering Theakstone admired; he'd done some himself, in Sarawate and one or two other places, though his medals had come elsewhere, the MC after some orthodox hand-to-hand fighting in Korea when he was only a boy, and the DSO in Kenya, when it was his turn, 'Buggins' turn' as the saying went.

Tonight, after he'd seen the TV news and the pictures of the broken Bulgarian plane at Ciampino, he'd wondered idly about Budzinski; he often did when the Israelis made one of their swift and tricky strikes. Later, in an uncanny way, he hadn't really surprised to hear Joe's voice.

At Sudbury he took the Long Melford road, feeling the old, happy excitement concentrating inside him, and remembering. What year would it have been? Forty-five? No, it must have been forty-six. The business with the rifle. They'd stolen it, three of them, from the school's Army Cadet armoury, to monkey with in the summer holidays. It had been crazy, of course, absolutely crazy, but they'd taken the Lee Enfield and five hundred rounds and blazed away in a disused stone quarry, just for the hell of it. They'd thought the rifle wouldn't be missed, but old Weasel, the master in charge, *had* missed it and all hell inevitably broke loose. The headmaster, naturally enough, hadn't wanted to call the police; theft charges and publicity about stolen rifles would be bad for the school. But he'd said... what was it? Yes, he'd said if the rifle was returned, only the guilty would be punished; if not, then he'd punish the school. Games and holidays cancelled. Theakstone grinned as he recalled it: dire threats indeed! Joe, though, had actually *done* something. He'd quietly let it be known that he was willing to be the go-between. So they'd told him, the three of them – Farrell, Blamires and Theakstone – that they had the rifle. Budzinski had gone promptly to the headmaster to say he was in a position to arrange for its return.

The headmaster had been a fool about it. Instead of accepting Budzinski's mature and sensible offer, he'd actually picked on Budzinski. If he could get the rifle back he must know who had it. It was his duty to give the headmaster names. And so on. Budzinski had said, straightforwardly and with notable courage considering his youth and position, that a war had just been fought so that people did not have to inform on their friends. Did he know the names? He was honest. Yes, he knew.

In a fit of pique, the headmaster had expelled Budzinski and there had been nothing the three miscreants could do to help. Miserably, they'd owned up, and been thrashed painfully on successive days for a whole week. They were not expelled, but the expulsion of Budzinski had stood. Theakstone wondered whether it had been merely defiance the headmaster hadn't been prepared to tolerate, or if there'd been a touch of anti-Semitism in it.

As he entered the long, thin Suffolk town, Theakstone slowed. It was a notorious speed trap, so he drove along the main street at a meticulous thirty miles an hour until the timbered front of the Bull Hotel showed up. Then he turned into the car park. There were six other cars, all empty; they would almost certainly belong, since it was now after closing time, to people staying the night. Theakstone glanced at his watch: twenty minutes to wait, maybe a little less. Would he know Joe after all this time? Physical characteristics changed. It would be interesting to see...

There wasn't much traffic; just the occasional car floating down the hill from Bury St Edmunds and continuing on into Melford. Theakstone wondered again why Joe was coming from Cambridge, of all places, and how he'd got there? Cambridge was a long way, worlds removed, from Ciampino Airport, Rome. He glanced at his watch. Any time now. Two or three minutes later he watched a car approach and slow, then move slowly forward and halt. Theakstone flashed his headlights twice, then climbed out of his car and walked over. Somebody was getting out of the other car. He saw the thick quiff of dark hair, still low on the forehead and recognised across the years the set of the features.

'Hello, Joe,' he said quietly.

'Curly Theakstone,' Budzinski said.

Theakstone grinned. 'Not any more.' He took off his cap to show the bald pate. 'Is this place quiet enough?'

Budzinski looked round. 'No.'

'Then follow me.'

Theakstone drove off towards the village of Acton, turned down a quiet lane that led ultimately back to Sudbury, stopped the car and got out again. The Wolseley pulled in behind him. Theakstone rested his bottom on the back of his own car, waited for Budzinski and examined Joe's face in the moonlight as he walked towards him. Older, much older, but essentially the same face; harder and tougher certainly, but then so was his own. They'd both seen enough to account for *that*. He said, 'Tell me, Joe.'

Budzinski didn't reply for a full minute. Instead he turned his body carefully, looking all round, taking in the full three hundred and sixty degrees. Theakstone waited until the survey was over, then said, 'Foxes, rabbits, cows and us. That's the lot.' Budzinski was staring at him, and Theakstone stood still, understanding why, allowing it. 'You need help?' he said quietly, making it a question.

Again the stare. Finally Budzinski said, 'Yes. I need help.'

'The police know you're here? In England, I mean?'

'Perhaps. No – by now they *must* know.'

'What do you want to do? Hide for a bit?'

Budzinski said, 'It's not that simple.' Still he hesitated.

Theakstone said, 'Tell me just what I need to know. No more unless you want to.'

'It could be dangerous for you.'

'Could it now?'

'If they find out you wouldn't be forgiven.'

'Perhaps,' Theakstone said, 'that would be because I wouldn't forgive myself. I'll do all in my power, Joe. So tell me.'

Budzinski told him.

Theakstone was first startled, then quickly almost amused, listening with a half-smile. When Budzinski had finished, he said, 'She's here?'

'In the car.'

'You,' Theakstone said, 'are a caution.'

Suddenly the awkwardness was gone and they stood looking at one another with a kind of appreciation.

'So it's not just the police, you see. It's my own people *and* the Russians.'

Theakstone chuckled shortly. 'A little intelligence exercise, gentlemen. You're alone in a car with a Russian girl you've kidnapped and three forces are looking for you: A, B and C. Jesus Christ!'

'That's right,' Budzinski said.

'Well, I have my limitations. I've about four hours. I'm off on exercises in Wales in the morning and there's no way of avoiding it. What can I do? You need an efficient hiding place. Good cover, communications, okay? You could have my house, but my wife – well, she's not exactly... er, cut out for this kind of caper.'

'No.' Budzinski looked at him, not doubting Theakstone's willingness, but suddenly doubtful of his capacity to do much in a few hours.

Theakstone grinned suddenly. 'Leefield.'

'I'm leaving a trail,' Budzinski said soberly. 'Conan is from Leefield. Greenfield, too. And you. They'll look for me in Leefield, sooner or later, when they realise the connection.'

'Big place, Yorkshire,' Theakstone said. 'You've friends there.'

'I had.'

'*Have*. Farrell for one. Hey, Freddie Farrell's an estate agent! Christ, he'll have keys for empty houses all over the bloody place.'

They looked at one another. Budzinski said, 'Freddie? But would he –?'

'The only thing is,' Theakstone went on, ignoring the question, 'how you get up there. It's two hundred miles. You know that, of course, but... ' He looked up, suddenly boyishly gleeful. 'Unless,' he said slowly, 'I can talk Jackie Chandler into... '

'Do I know him?'

'No, but I bloody well do. Come along, my old lad, we need a telephone.'

From a call box, in Acton, Theakstone dialled a number. 'Wattisham? Good. I want to talk to Captain Chandler. I don't care if he *is* asleep. Tell him it's about Exercise Wanderer. Yes, Colchester Garrison.' As he waited he half-covered the mouthpiece with his hand and winked at Budzinski. Suddenly the Israeli felt like a schoolboy, fifteen years old and up to mischief.

'Jackie? Mike Theakstone. Hope I dragged you out of your pit. No? Pity. What time d'you leave in the morning? Yes, well how about leaving a couple of hours earlier and sliding off north a bit first? No I won't tell you why. Not now, anyhow. Can you do it?'

He listened for a moment. 'It depends what you mean by fun, Jackie. Anything to stop you? Good. Yes I *am* collecting my bloody debts. That's right. In dead earnest.' Budzinski saw him glance at his watch. 'Half an hour or so. Yes. Good on yer.'

Theakstone hung up the phone and slapped Budzinski's shoulder delightedly. 'We've got a chopper, old lad!'

Budzinski looked at him in amazement. 'Chopper? Helicopter?'

'Precisely that. One of those whirly things. Jack Chandler will slip you up to Yorkshire.'

Budzinski felt his knees sag momentarily. This kind of luck was unbelievable. He'd had break after break, each one better than the last –

'Got any change, Joe? No, never mind. We'll reverse the charges. Freddie can pay.' Theakstone vanished again into the phone box, leaving Budzinski almost in a daze on the pavement outside. It couldn't possibly last. Everything had been too smooth; even killing the Russian had not been difficult. Troublesome, certainly, but only an interruption in an incredible run of luck. Perhaps Fate was making up, in Britain, for the retribution she had exacted in Rome. He realised suddenly that it was half an hour or more since he'd even thought about Rome. Momentarily he saw the scene again in his mind and felt the chill crawl across his scalp and down his back. For a little while, with Theakstone, it had become almost an adventure; now, suddenly, the feeling had gone again. His chances of getting away with this madness were almost nil; his danger acute. He must accept the good luck as his due, but be icily prepared when it changed, as change it would.

Theakstone emerged from the phone box rubbing his hands. 'All's well. Freddie'll meet you.'

So the luck continued! Budzinski merely nodded, and Theakstone looked at him sharply. 'You all right?'

'I'm all right.'

'Reaction, old boy. Familiar signs. Don't worry, you're as good as there. Now look – I'll lead, right? You follow. When I stop, I'll get out of my car into yours and we'll go into RAF Wattisham, straight to the chopper park. Jack'll be waiting there. After that I'll ditch your car and take my own.'

From the shadows, Aaron Bloom peered through the heavy screen of bushes and over the low wall which separated Greenfield's garden from Trumpington Road. A taxi stood half-blocking the drive, its driver sitting patiently at the wheel. He wondered for a moment what a taxi was doing there, then answered his own question. Ordinary life continued and it was scarcely uncommon for a Catholic priest to be called out late at night. He glanced back at the two men at Greenfield's door. They'd knocked twice and seemed to be waiting patiently... no, wait a minute! They had separated and were going in opposite directions round the house. Bloom waited and after a moment heard a faint tinkle of glass. He swallowed then; whoever the men were they were emphatically *not* part of ordinary life. They also weren't Israelis, and police would hardly arrive by taxi. That left only –

He moved towards the pillared gateway, silently, on the edge of the lawn, then stopped as he saw a man standing near the taxi. His eye measured distances. It should be possible, just possible, but if he was wrong... Rapidly he returned to the MGB and slid into the driving seat. When the engine started, they'd be alerted. For the moment he left the door open. Bloom took a deep breath, turned the ignition key, rammed the gear lever into reverse and spun the little car back. The door slammed but now the sound no longer mattered. He engaged first gear and accelerated sharply, listening to the harsh spatter of gravel on the car's wings, and roared towards the gateway with his headlamps full on. The space was narrow: he moved the steering to widen his angle of approach and tore into the narrow gap. He might make it. No, a sharp bang against the rear wing told him he'd hit the cab. He braked. Now the MGB was moving by, metal scraping on metal. He spun the wheel, swinging left, out to the middle of the road, glancing in the mirror, but the angle was wrong and he could see nothing.

Suddenly the windscreen in front of him went opaque. A tiny hole had appeared and round it the laminated glass was crazed. Bloom punched at it furiously, driving his fist through as he gunned the MGB forward. Behind him there was a squeal of brakes as some unfortunate driver came up fast. Fist hammering at the shattered glass, Bloom slowly improved his vision, changing gear, roaring forward. Cold night air streamed into his face and not far along the road he saw a red traffic-light. It wasn't even a choice, he thought grimly, using his lights and horn as he went through; not with the Russians behind! Another light controlled the Colchester turn-off, green this time. He swung sharply left and blazed along the road, then sharp right at the end. Glancing in the mirror he could see nobody following; not that it was any comfort. If those men were Russians, and the bullet-hole left no doubt in Bloom's mind that they were, they'd find out about Budzinski's friend Theakstone in ten seconds flat. Greenfield couldn't hold out longer than that. He felt sorry for Greenfield.

The signs directed him on to the Colchester road and in minutes Cambridge lay behind him. He settled into his seat and concentrated hard, using the MGB to the limit. When he reached Colchester, he'd need every second he could now gain. Thinking about the Russians as he drove, he remembered the taxi. *That* might be a bit of luck for him: if it was the only transport they had, it certainly couldn't match the MGB's performance, and the driver wouldn't want to risk his licence and livelihood in a high-speed cross-country chase. Not that the Russians would worry about a cab driver.

He roared up the hill, on to a piece of dual carriageway where the needle went easily over the hundred mark, and flashed on. A roundabout slowed him briefly, but then he was off again, pounding along the Colchester road. A few miles further on, quite suddenly, he saw a white car with its blue rooflight flashing and a policeman holding a torch waved him down. Momentarily uncertain, Bloom swore. He had to stop, anything else would be stupid. He braked sharply, listening to the tyres protest, and wound down the window impatiently.

The policeman's torch shone into his face, dazzling him for a moment, then it was shone into the back of the MGB.

'Going a bit fast there, sir.'

'I'm sorry,' Bloom said.

'In a hurry, were you?'

'Rather a hurry, yes.' The policeman could do nothing; not, at least, unless there had been a radar trap back along the road. But no, there *was* something the policeman could do: he could delay him.

'Your car, sir?'

Bloom gritted his teeth. 'No.'

'I see. May I see your licence, please?... Hm, so you're a diplomat are you, sir?'

'I'm Second Secretary at the Israeli Embassy,' Bloom said. 'The car belongs to the Ambassador's daughter, as a matter of fact.'

With relief Bloom saw the licence was being handed straight back. 'All right, sir,' the policeman said. 'You're free to proceed. But not so fast, if you don't mind, you're not chasing Arabs now.'

Bloom made himself smile, moved into gear and the MGB slid away. Seconds later he was up to sixty, exhaust noise booming off the walls of a small sleeping village.

Behind him the policeman said to his mate, 'Israeli diplomat, that one. In a hell of a bloody hurry.'

'No little blondes, though?'

'No such luck.' He thought for a moment. 'Reckon I'll radio in.'

'Why?'

'Dunno. But I will, all the same. Something in the geezer's face, maybe. Watch the road for a sec, will you?'

'You're barmy.'

The policeman grinned. 'Always was. Still, it breaks the monotony. AD to control. Listen, we've just had a bloke through here going like smoke. Israeli diplomat, name of Bloom. Aaron Bloom. No, no girl. Just thought I'd let you know.'

It was the word Israeli that caused the message to be fed back and up. It reached Chief Inspector McHugh only a few minutes later. Anything Israeli and untoward was high now on all priority lists. McHugh lifted his phone and rang first West Suffolk Constabulary at Bury St Edmunds and then Essex Constabulary at Colchester. In each case the message was the same: 'Request surveillance only, repeat surveillance only, of blue MGB car heading your direction. Driver Israeli diplomat named Aaron Bloom. Request car be followed discreetly and self informed of its destination. Repeat discretion essential. Car number...'

An Essex County police car picked Bloom up as he worked his way through the old town of Halstead and it radioed news of the contact. By the time Bloom reached Colchester, an unmarked car manned by two plain-clothes detectives was waiting for him. As the road to West Mersea swung off from a roundabout, the detectives handed him over again, this time to a policewoman in a little Sprite sports car. He had some trouble finding the house, and when he finally did so, he discovered that it was in darkness.

Bloom scowled to himself, disliking the situation intensely. He could hardly keep on breaking into private houses forever, if only because sooner or later he would be seen and the British police were efficient. He was deeply conscious, too, that if for some reason his own pursuit of Budzinski came to a halt, the Russian pursuit would not. He was alone, but the Russians had had three men, *at least three*, in Cambridge. If he were to drop out of the chase, it would then be between the Russians and the British, and the Russians had a good start.

He stared at the house. There was no gleam of light, no sign of movement; nothing to tell him whether anybody was inside. Unlike Greenfield's house in Cambridge, which had been private, well screened by trees, and surrounded by a large garden, this house was raw and almost new, one of many on a modern estate. It lacked privacy. Irritated with himself, Bloom halted that line of thought abruptly. He had simply been finding reasons for inaction. The fact was that Budzinski and the girl might be in the house and that he had very little time before the Russians got here.

'He's getting out of his car,' the policewoman reported back to her headquarters. 'He's outside a house in Cornwall Close. The number will be... ten, twelve... will be fourteen...'

'Get the voters' list, quick,' said the duty inspector at Colchester to the PC standing beside him. 'Find out who lives at 14 Cornwall Close.'

'He's gone to the front door,' the policewoman reported. 'He's just waiting now. I think he's rung the bell. Now... he's looking in the windows... he's going round the back...' She had the window down and was listening, but could hear nothing. 'He's still round the back. Should I investigate?'

'No. Stay where you are.'

'He's been there two minutes... Three... sir, a light's gone on inside!'

'The house is occupied by Michael Robert Theakstone and Fiona Marjorie Theakstone,' the inspector was told. He ordered the PC to inform London immediately.

'The light's just gone out, sir. Now he's walking back to his car. He *must* have got inside.'

'Stay on his tail. We'll fix a change of following car as soon as possible.'

'Yes, sir.'

Chief Inspector McHugh, in his office in Scotland Yard's new skyscraper block, was talking again to *The Times*. 'I'm sorry,' he said. 'At the moment I can neither confirm nor deny. No.' The news editor of *The Times* said they could no longer hold the story. McHugh said, 'You can say we're investigating.'

'But you're not getting very far, is that it?'

'Investigating, I said,' McHugh snapped. 'No further comment.' He hung up knowing the story would be in the next edition of *The Times* and the others would pick it up. Both the *Express* and the *Mail* could get new material into the final London editions until four am. It was going to be a frustrating night.

He looked again at the notes on his pad. The man Bloom, who'd been in Sidney Conan's flat earlier, was now in Colchester. Furthermore, he'd gone there via Cambridge, driving like a maniac, it seemed. Meanwhile there was the murder on the Cambridge road. Had Bloom done that? The embassies were being characteristically stolid, too. When he'd told the Soviet Embassy about the dead man, they'd simply said none of their people was missing, and the Israelis had told him nobody was available, for the moment, to talk.

Anyway, who the hell was Michael Robert Theakstone? He'd asked Colchester police to knock on neighbours' doors and find out, but they couldn't do that until the man Bloom had moved away, and Bloom apparently was still sitting in his bloody car outside the house.

His phone rang again. He snatched up the receiver. 'McHugh.'

'Cambridgeshire Constabulary. Chief Constable speaking.'

'Yes, sir?' Something was badly wrong. He could tell from the tone of voice.

'Two of my men have been attacked on the A604 by three men who got out of a Cambridge taxi.'

'The roadblock, sir?'

'I've just got it by radio. They were knocked over the head.'

'Was the cab reported stolen, sir?'

'Not yet, but I think we must assume that it was stolen and that it's heading east. Don't you, Chief Inspector?'

McHugh said, 'I'm in contact with West Suffolk and with Essex, sir. I'll get them to pick 'em up if they're going that way.'

'I have already made exactly that request. Surveillance is no longer enough.'

McHugh rose tiredly to go and report to the Assistant Commissioner. He had not reached the door before his telephone rang again. He went back to his desk and picked it up.

'McHugh.'

'Colchester, sir. We've had one bit of luck. One of the lads here knows Theakstone.'

'And?'

'Michael Robert Theakstone is an army major. We've been on to Eastern Command. He's a company commander in the Parachute Regiment.'

'Where is he now?' McHugh asked quickly.

'That's not such good news, sir. They're off to Wales on manoeuvres or something, at six o'clock.'

'*This morning?*'

'Yes, sir. Eastern Command say it's possible Theakstone's gone down there already.'

'Whereabouts in Wales?'

'The Brecon Beacons.'

'Jesus Christ!' McHugh said disgustedly. 'No. Hang on. Ask Eastern Command for details of Theakstone's record. Tell them it's a formal Special Branch request, direct from Assistant Commissioner Sellers. I know the army doesn't like giving these things out, but do your best to make it quick.'

The police roadblock outside the village of Linton had come as an unpleasant surprise to the three Russians pursuing Bloom and its consequences were hampering them considerably. They had dealt with the initial situation with the awareness of overall priorities. To have burst through the barrier and gone on would merely have been to invite every police car for miles to join in the pursuit. They would have been stopped at some point, and duly identified, even if the identification took some time. Accordingly the taxi had stopped and the two policemen had been attacked and left helpless in their own police car, while the Russians drove on. No word had been spoken; there was nothing to give the policemen, when finally they were released, any reason to say they had been attacked by Russians. They had merely been attacked. However, there was no way of knowing how soon they would be found and released, and immediately that happened, the hunt would be up. They must abandon the taxi as soon as possible, report what had happened, and then stay off the road until London decided on the next step. A few miles further on, at the town of Haverhill, they found both a telephone and the perfect place to abandon the stolen car: a vast new estate of small houses where cars by the dozen were parked in the streets. Instructions from KGB headquarters were forthcoming immediately: the three men were to make themselves inconspicuous and wait through the hours of darkness and then return separately to London by public transport. Other arrangements would be made for any further action necessary in Colchester.

In a way the fact that it was to Colchester that Budzinski seemed to have gone, made the KGB task easier. Their spy system in Britain was, naturally enough, centred on specific targets and the principal army, navy and air force establishments were subject to continuous observation. In Portsmouth, Plymouth, Aldershot, Catterick, Colchester and so on, KGB organisation was resident and permanent and it was the operatives' business to be familiar with the local service establishment. The local senior resident was therefore able to say immediately first that he knew who Major Theakstone was and secondly that Theakstone's battalion was leaving that morning for exercises in the Brecon Beacons. The information about the exercise had not been difficult to come by: it had, in fact, been reported in the local paper.

'Observe his house,' the agent was told. He was a local doctor, Lithuanian-born, with a long-established practice in the town. For him there was never any difficulty in moving almost anywhere: there were always a few seriously-ill patients on his list and it was his duty to visit them. He got out his car, drove to Cornwall Close and saw that a man was sitting in a blue MGB in the road outside number fourteen. He also noticed, just round the corner, that one of the little police Sprites was parked. He even knew the policewoman in it, and gave her a friendly wave as he drove past.

Shortly afterwards he duly reported what he had seen, offering his opinion that the house must be supposed empty since Bloom, who could not know he was under observation, was apparently content to sit and wait.

At that moment, the chief London resident of the KGB was thinking the same thing as Aaron Bloom. Both men felt angry and frustrated.

The trail of Josef Budzinski was, for the moment, lost. It might reappear a hundred and fifty miles away, but that was only speculation. And how, in any case, could Budzinski travel those miles?

CHAPTER NINE

Katya Semonov began to regain consciousness shortly before four am as an army Whirlwind helicopter sped northward from Wattisham in Suffolk towards Yorkshire. Joe Budzinski, crouching beside her in the troop-carrying space, first noticed in her a kind of restlessness. Ever since he'd forced her to swallow the pheno-barbitone, hours earlier in Conan's flat, she had been as immobile and as limp as a doll. Now her legs began to stretch and her facial muscles formed involuntary grimaces. He looked at his watch, estimating quickly. In twenty minutes, no more, the helicopter would reach the rendezvous Theakstone had made for him.

He looked forward, to where the pilot sat alone at the controls, Theakstone's friend Chandler who was paying off a debt of some kind and not enjoying it. To Budzinski Chandler was a familiar type, the kind of man to be found in the armed forces of every country, high-spirited and adventurous yet somehow at the same time dedicated and responsible. He'd been game for fun, grinning welcome at Theakstone, but his face and manner had changed abruptly when the purpose of the flight had been explained. A point-blank refusal had followed.

'Leave us, Joe,' Theakstone had said, and Budzinski had moved away out of earshot searching his mind for other possibilities and finding it sterile. Glancing back at the two men who stood dwarfed by the black silhouette of the big helicopter, he had read in the stiffness of their postures the end of an easy relationship, perhaps the end of a friendship. It had been several minutes before Theakstone had joined him, face set, to say, 'It's okay. He's on.'

Budzinski said, 'If he's unwilling –'

Theakstone said quietly, 'Don't be bloody stupid! Get in and go. Chandler's taking you.' He explained then about the rendezvous: Freddie Farrell would be waiting with a car and from that moment on, it was up to Farrell and Budzinski. Budzinski listened in silence, then went over to the car, lifted Katya out and began to carry her towards the helicopter. Once inside, he extended his hand down towards Theakstone.

'Thanks.'

Theakstone didn't smile, but he took the hand and shook it firmly. 'It's all I can do, Joe. Good luck.' Then he turned and walked rapidly towards the car.

Shortly afterwards the Whirlwind had lifted away. There had been not a word from Chandler, nor did Budzinski now expect one. Chandler clearly had some kind of duty to friendship strong enough to make him accede to Theakstone's demand; it was now evident that it was a once-and-for-all duty and that it was being discharged totally. Whatever had existed between the two men was now over.

He wondered what to do about the girl. There were more sleeping pills in his pocket, but he was hesitant about using them. Looking down at her now, a pale, almost frail figure on the hard floor, he saw her clearly almost for the first time. She was young, fragile and a victim. His victim. Earlier she had been merely a target, after that no more than a quantity of goods to be transported. She turned her body, groaning a little, and Budzinski found himself staring at the red silk bow in her hair. She was almost a child, of an age to be *his* child... He put a sharp brake to the train of thought. She was Russian; think of it one way and she was just a part of the Soviet propaganda barrage with the important difference that she could be used against them in a proper cause. She had been one of *their* weapons; now she was *his* weapon. Very well, then. She was secured, she couldn't run. Chandler, however much he might dislike it, was transporting them and would not interfere. At the other end, Freddie Farrell would be waiting. It didn't matter a damn if she woke; she could be kept still and quiet until they reached whatever cover Farrell could provide.

He sensed the Whirlwind was descending and looked briefly out of the window at the dark landscape below. He'd walked this country a hundred times as a boy, but recognised nothing now; it was strange and, until he was safely in Farrell's car, hostile country. The helicopter's motion changed perceptibly and in a pattern Budzinski knew well. It was hovering, coming down slowly, motor roaring. He wrenched back the door and looked out. Fifty feet below lay moorland.

Moments later it touched. He dragged the girl to the open doorway and jumped down, then pulled her after him, bending low to avoid the whirling rotors. He need not have bothered; the helicopter was big and the rotors spun high over his head, but the action was instinctive. He reached upward to close the door, but even as he did so it vanished, lifting away from him. There was no wave from Chandler, no opportunity of thanks, just the big chopper clattering off noisily into the night sky, becoming in a few seconds no more than a noise and a regular flashing of lights.

As the engine note faded, Budzinski straightened and looked around, feeling solitary and exposed. On the high moorland the wind was cold and he shivered briefly. Where was Farrell? He waited, eyes searching the darkness for the lights of a car, but nothing seemed to be moving.

He felt suddenly deeply depressed as realisation came to him that by himself he was wholly helpless, that he was entirely dependent upon somebody else. If Farrell, for any reason, failed to turn up, Budzinski knew his escapade was finished. He himself might escape, if only for a while, but the girl would have to be abandoned. Around him the wind stirred heather and moorland grass in a continuous low rustle. Budzinski watched and listened and waited. He heard the girl make a small sound and bent to look at her, and suddenly the night exploded into a flaring light of pain that turned instantly into total dark...

The edition of *The Times* carrying the news that a man who had refused to identify himself claimed to have kidnapped the Russian gymnast Katya Semonov, and would release her only when the Russians themselves handed over Joachim Schmidt to face trial for his crimes against humanity, naturally triggered a great deal of activity. Within minutes of the appearance of *The Times* in London newspaper offices, half the reporters in Fleet Street seemed to be on the telephone to Scotland Yard. McHugh left his own telephone off the hook and instructed the switchboard that all press inquiries were to be handled by the press department for whom, half an hour earlier, he had prepared a statement. It said simply that Scotland Yard was making inquiries.

The lateness of the hour prevented the reporters from pursuing their inquiries to any great effect, though they dragged the general manager of the Royal Albert Hall from his bed and forced a reluctant Soviet Embassy to issue a statement. The statement confirmed the disappearance of Katya Semonov, deplored this new manifestation of imperialist, Zionist piracy, and repeated the assertion of the Soviet Embassy in Rome that Joachim Schmidt was not and never had been a member of the Varna Orchestra.

By this time, however, the press had several pieces of information upon which to build stories. The wire services had duly distributed the *Chicago Tribune* reporter's opinion that the man purporting to be Istvan Kodes was almost certainly not a regular member of the orchestra. Additionally, and as McHugh had known it would, the call for assistance he had issued had been leaked, up and down the country, to various newspapermen. The press knew that this was a major story, indeed it was a major man hunt, and they were infuriated by Scotland Yard's refusal to go beyond its initial, and bald, statement. However, though facts might, according to the celebrated dictum of a long-ago editor of the *Guardian*, be sacred, comment was certainly free, and already leader-writers were working briskly on advice to be offered in final editions to the Russians. Here was a situation in which everybody could be condemned: the Israelis, who complained of piracy while still practising it vigorously; the Russians, who had apparently offered shelter to the vilest of war criminals; the police, who apparently preferred to remain silent when the best chance of apprehending the man who had abducted a young girl admired by millions, was to ask for the public's help. All were duly torn to shreds.

In Rome, news of *The Times*'s story was hastily crammed into the stop press boxes of the daily newspapers. At three am newsvendors on foot approached the crowd around the Soviet Embassy's villa, crying their wares.

By that time, inevitably, the crowd had thinned. Many Italians, faced with the prospect of a new working day within a few hours, had been slowly drifting away since soon after midnight. Nevertheless, the crowd remained sizeable, and the tourists, particularly the youngsters among them, had stayed on. The news in the Rome papers now fed both their enthusiasm and their determination, and, instead of quietening further as the night wore on, the chanting became louder, demanding that the exchange be made. This crowd was now noticeably younger and the idea of swapping the elderly criminal for the youthful gymnast had an almost incendiary appeal. New placards began to appear. *SAVE KATYA!* they demanded, and a couple of thousand voices repeated the slogan endlessly in a variety of languages.

The ambassador of the Bulgarian Soviet Socialist Republic watched the crowd from a window, thankful that for the moment it remained peaceful. He found himself thinking of Eisenstein's film sequence of the storming of the Winter Palace in St Petersburg. The villa was no Winter Palace, and two floors below him was a man who might or might not be Joachim Schmidt.

In London the Minister of State at the Foreign Office telephoned the ambassadors of the Soviet Union and Israel, apologised for disturbing their sleep, and assured both that every effort was being made by the British police to find the man who had kidnapped Katya Semonov. He told both men that the police were now acting under Home Office instructions and that he was confident police resources were such that they would be swiftly successful. He was aware that it was so much hot air, but was determined that the implicit message should be clear: we can do it, so don't start any nonsense on our territory.

Both men thanked him. And ignored him.

Two pieces of information, meanwhile, had arrived on the desk of Chief Inspector McHugh. The first lay there for some time, its importance unrecognised not because McHugh was tired, though he was, but because it was, by itself, unrevealing. It was a brief biography of Sidney Conan, barrister-at-law with chambers in the Temple. Shortly after three am, however, the War Department produced the confidential record of Major Michael Robert Theakstone. McHugh took the sheets of paper brought by a police motor-cyclist from the Ministry of Defence and began to read through them carefully. He frowned suddenly and reached for the biography of Conan, eyes flicking from one to the other.

'Jesus Christ!' he exclaimed softly. He read no more, instead leaving his office to report to Sellers.

The Assistant Commissioner, informal at that hour in braces and shirt-sleeves, working moodily through the contents of his in-tray, looked up as McHugh came in and saw from the expression on his face that something had happened.

'Well?'

McHugh placed the papers on Sellers' desk. 'Read those, sir.'

'Just tell me.'

'There's a connection between Conan and Theakstone, sir.'

'You mean *another* connection. What?'

'They went to the same school.'

'They did, did they?' Sellers exhaled slowly.

'In Yorkshire, sir. Leefield Grammar School.'

'At the same time?'

'They're the same age.'

Sellers' fingers tapped ruminatively on his desk top. After a moment, he asked, 'What does that tell you?'

McHugh hesitated. 'We need to talk to one or the other pretty damn quick.'

'That all? Conan's Jewish. How about this bloke Theakstone?'

'No mention of it in his record.'

'When did he join up?' Sellers picked up the War Department file. 'Late in 1947. If he'd been Jewish the army'd have known. That was Irgun and Haganah time, British troops in Israel. They weren't damn well sending any Jews out there, not then. Let's see. Mother was called Helen Ollerenshaw. Doesn't sound very Jewish to me. Okay. That's probably not the link. The school's the link. Old school pals, eh?'

McHugh said, 'So's somebody in Cambridge.'

'True enough.' Sellers bent an eyebrow in acknowledgement. 'But who?'

'He goes to Conan's flat, right, sir? Then there's shenanigans of various kinds on the Cambridge road. The bloke's vanished, but the other fellow, Bloom, suddenly he's going like smoke from Cambridge to Colchester, where he drives direct to the home of Theakstone. Bloom's waiting outside the house, still waiting, right this minute.'

'What do we know about Bloom?'

'Not much, sir. We never do, do we? Not with diplomats. But it's bloody peculiar, isn't it, that he goes from the home of one Leefield man to another!'

Sellers said, 'Get on to Leefield police. Tell them I want a list of contemporaries, the other people who were at school with these two. Okay?'

'It's damn near thirty years,' McHugh said. 'D'you think the school will still have records?'

'There's a record somewhere. An old photograph on a wall, something like that. And somebody in Leefield will remember. Thirty years is nothing in the Old Boys' world.'

McHugh checked the time on his watch and looked up to find Sellers looking at him sardonically. 'Listen, get on to the headmaster yourself. Yes, I know the time. Think of it as a little *lèse majesté* on behalf of his boys.'

'Right away, sir.' McHugh made for the door, but there was a quick knock and it was opened before he reached it.

'Well?'

'Sorry to interrupt, sir,' said a breathless constable. 'Message from Colchester force. Major Theakstone's returned to his home. They're asking what action–'

'Pull him in,' Sellers ordered sharply.

'Arrest, sir?'

'Help with inquiries, damn it. If he's cagey get his CO to make it a direct order.'

McHugh said, 'I think I'll go myself. At this time of day, Colchester's not much more than an hour and a half. Have I your permission?'

Sellers frowned. 'I suppose so. He's the direct link.'

'The only link, sir.'

'Okay. Go.'

Aaron Bloom had waited a long time in his car outside the Theakstones' house. He was both cold and depressed. Occasionally he switched on the car's engine and the heater fan to warm himself a little, but the depression remained; he felt increasingly that the continued wait was futile, that wherever Budzinski might be, he was clearly not in Colchester. But he had no other lead of any kind and his only hope lay in meeting Theakstone. As time went on, however, he was becoming convinced that Theakstone was not coming back, that he was away somewhere and would stay away. Bloom was also concerned that he had made no progress report to the Embassy for several hours, but was unwilling to leave to find a telephone in case Theakstone should return while he was away.

Once, an hour or so earlier, a pair of headlights had alerted him, but the car had simply cruised slowly by and Bloom's long vigil had continued. He was staring moodily at the darkened house when light reflected from his driving mirror flashed abruptly in his eyes.

Bloom sat up sharply. A car was approaching! As he watched it turned in through the gates and halted. The lights were switched off and a man got out. Bloom opened the door of the MGB and got out quickly. Softly he called Theakstone's name.

Theakstone, by that time, had reached the front door and was putting his key in the lock. He turned.

'Are you Major Theakstone?'

'Who the devil are you?'

Bloom hurried closer. 'I want to talk to you. It's very important.'

'At this hour it would need to be. What's your name?'

'Bloom. Aaron Bloom.'

He felt Theakstone's eyes boring into him, a stony gaze from a small, square face. The man was very hard, he thought. Quite small, but tough mentally and physically.

'State your business.'

Bloom said simply, 'I'm from the Israeli Embassy. May I come in?'

Theakstone's eyes widened a fraction. Bloom pressed on the tiny lever of surprise. 'I know Joe Budzinski's a friend of yours.'

'Better come in.' Theakstone's eyes didn't leave Bloom's face as he turned the key, pushed the door open and signalled Bloom to precede him. He closed the door behind them, switched on a light in the hall and faced Bloom. 'You mentioned Joe Budzinski.'

'He's been here tonight.' Bloom made it a statement, not a question.

Theakstone shook his head.

'Very well. But you've seen him.'

'With the greatest respect, Mr Bloom, I should expect you to know more about Budzinski than I. He left this country twenty-five years ago. *My* country, that is. He now lives, to the best of my knowledge, in *yours.*'

Bloom said, 'You've seen him tonight. Where is he now?'

Theakstone looked at his watch. 'I've no doubt you're aware of the time, Mr Bloom. I was prepared to be courteous, but I see no point at all in continuing this nonsense. You have no right to question me and I do not care to continue this conversation.'

Bloom eyed the small, tense figure. He said, 'If you are aware of what he's done, and I believe you are, you must also be aware that the consequences will be drastic. I can understand personal loyalty, Major Theakstone, and I'm sure you can understand that other factors sometimes overwhelm it. I need to see Budzinski. If you won't help me do that, then at least get a message to him.'

'I can't help you. Now will you please leave my house.'

Bloom said quickly, almost pleadingly, 'Joe is my friend, too. We worked ten years together. He's throwing a great deal away, including, probably, his life.'

Theakstone looked back at him stonily. 'Even if I knew what you were talking about, Mr Bloom, I can only say that Joe Budzinski's life is his own affair. Will you please leave.'

'At least let's discuss –' But the telephone rang, interrupting him.

Theakstone picked it up. 'Hello.' He listened, eyes on Bloom. 'Very well, sir. Yes. What about the exercise? Yes, sir, as soon as I can.' He hung up. 'Get out, will you.' He opened the door in silence and as he did so the headlights of a car swept round the corner.

144

Bloom watched the police car come to a halt in front of the house. Two men got out and hurried up the path and one of them said, 'Major Theakstone?'

'Yes.'

'May I ask who *you* are, sir?'

'My name is Bloom. I'm an official of the Israeli Embassy.'

'I see, sir. Well, I must ask you both to come with us to the station.'

Bloom said, 'You understand my diplomatic status?'

'We can clear that up at the station, sir. No doubt, if you can prove your identity, then –'

'I can prove it now.'

'At the station, please, sir. It won't take long, I'm sure.'

Bloom shrugged and walked towards the car. The short journey to Colchester police station was made in silence and once there, the two men were separated. Bloom found himself being shown politely but firmly into an interview room, where he was left alone with a constable whose clear and only duty it was to ensure that Bloom did not leave.

Theakstone was accorded precisely the same treatment. He sat on a plain chair with his elbows on a small, deal table and began quite deliberately to reconcile himself to the knowledge that his world was now in ruins. Within two years he would have been able, though he had had no such intention, to retire on pension. Now he would either be court-martialled or, if his superiors were merciful, be allowed to resign his commission. In either case, his soldiering days were over. The thought, to his astonishment, brought a brief prickle of tears to his eyes and he blew his nose hard, scotching them, determined to look ahead, not back. The situation must be assessed, not regretted; he was lucky to be alive anyway, after Korea, Malaya, Kenya, Sarawate, Cyprus, Aden and Northern Ireland. All right, then. It was over for him now. But Chandler must be kept out of it and he must try, too, to keep the dogs off Budzinski. That meant silence. Refusal to answer questions would mean no mercy, no quiet resignation of Her Majesty's commission. Silence would mean court martial. Then so be it. He recalled suddenly an offer, two years earlier, of well-paid service in one of the Gulf sheikdoms. Maybe that would still be open. If not – well, he had some money and his health. It was all perfectly clear, even if the future was more than a trifle uncertain.

He straightened in his chair and said to the constable, 'If it can be arranged, I should like some coffee.' Quite soon now Budzinski would be landing and Freddie Farrell would meet him. Chandler would immediately fly off to complete his supposed night navigation exercise. There was no immediate likelihood of the police putting two and two together there. Quite suddenly part of his mind asked a question and for a moment he allowed himself to think about the answer. He decided he did not regret offering help to Joe Budzinski. The impulse had been sound, well-rooted in respect for the man and what he stood for. He'd decided and had known the risks. All his life he'd made decisions, knowing the risks and always prepared to accept them. This was no different. But what the devil was causing the delay?

Two hundred miles to the north, the telephone at the bedside of the Headmaster of Leefield Grammar School gave a muted chirrup. The telephone was his wife's choice, a small and rather effeminate thing in pink plastic, and for a moment or two it failed to awaken him, but finally he sat up, switched on his bedside lamp and put on his spectacles before lifting the receiver.

'Yes?'

'Am I speaking to the Reverend H. R. Sampson?' a voice enquired.

'You are.'

'I'm sorry to disturb you, sir, at this hour...'

Sampson glanced at the clock, saw that it was almost four o'clock and said, 'So I should hope.'

'... It's the Special Branch of the Metropolitan Police, Assistant Commissioner Sellers speaking.'

Sampson said angrily, 'Is this some kind of joke?'

'No, sir. Call me back if you like, at New Scotland Yard. I'm sure you know the number.'

'I think I'll do that,' Sampson said. It was not the first time in forty years' schoolmastering that he'd been telephoned in the middle of the night. Sometimes the school was on fire; at others the caller would ask when the pubs opened. It was one of the small hazards of the profession. He put down the telephone and prepared to go back to sleep. Within five minutes, the instrument chirped again. Sampson stretched out a weary hand.

'Assistant Commissioner Sellers again, sir. I take it you thought... well, you said you were going to call me back. Would you mind doing so now, sir. Immediately, if you please.'

Sampson sighed. Usually when some hare-brained boy made such a call it was kept short for fear of recognition and retribution. He said, 'The traffic in Piccadilly. Which way does it flow?'

He heard a soft laugh. 'One way east, sir, from St James' Street. Two way west to Hyde Park Corner. But there's been a new adjustment for buses outside Fortnum and Mason. I'm genuine. Now please call me back.' Sampson heard a click as Sellers hung up.

His wife stirred beside him. 'What is it, dear?'

'Some nonsense. Go back to sleep.'

'Boys again?' She was smiling tiredly.

'I expect so.' Sampson dialled, asked for Assistant Commissioner Sellers and was surprised a moment later to hear the same voice.

'Satisfied, sir?'

'I suppose so. I'm sorry. Usually this kind of call is from a boy.'

'I can imagine,' Sellers said. 'What I'm after is your school records.'

'Somebody in trouble? Look here, *did* you say Special Branch?'

'I did. It's nobody at the school now. In fact it goes back a long time.'

'Well, so do the records. Hold on a moment. I'll take the call in my study.'

Dressing-gowned, he sat at his desk. 'Specifically who?'

'Specifically the school contemporaries of two men called Sidney Conan and Michael Theakstone. They're both now forty-three years old.'

'Before my time, I'm afraid.'

'The records, sir?'

'Well, they're at the school. It will all be there, of course. But we have a thousand boys. Rather a lot of contemporaries.'

'I'm thinking of classmates, sir. Could you go to the school now?'

'Is it necessary?'

'It's very important, sir. I'll arrange for a senior man from the local force to be present.'

'Oh, very well. I'll set off straight away.'

Sampson was mildly ashamed of the tiny pleasure he felt at awakening the school secretary and demanding his immediate presence at the school. He shaved, dressed and told his wife the police wanted some assistance from him. It wasn't the first time and she took it quite calmly.

Two policemen were waiting when he arrived, one of them a Detective Superintendent named Hutchinson whom he'd met a few times socially. Sampson nodded, opened the door of the administrative block and led them to his study. A few minutes later the school secretary arrived.

Seven years' records were stored in filing cabinets in the secretary's office, the rest were under lock and key in a basement room. 'What year?' the secretary asked.

'If they're forty-three now, it would be nineteen thirty-nine, forty or forty-one,' Sampson said crisply. 'That's nearly four hundred boys. We've a yearly intake of a hundred and thirty.'

The secretary took a small, thin blue-bound book from a shelf. 'Be quicker to try the form lists first.' He blew dust off the little book and looked quickly at an index of names. 'Yes, here we are. Conan and Theakstone were in the same form. At least, they were in forty-one.'

'That's a list of the form they were in?' asked Detective Superintendent Hutchinson. 'May I have it?'

'Of course.'

'And I'd like the files on all the boys in the same year.' He stood for a moment, running his eye down the list, then turned to Sampson. 'This one, a lad called Ellis, B. N. Ellis, is he ours?'

Sampson looked puzzled. 'I'm sorry, I don't –'

'We've a Detective Sergeant Ellis. Brian Norman, I think it is, off hand.'

'Don't know, I'm afraid.'

'No, well I can check fast enough. One other thing, sir. Do you know any of these people?'

'I may.' Sampson took the book and glanced down the list. 'Yes, I know this chap. Anfield. He was president of the Old Boys Association last year, or maybe the year before.'

'Mr Gilbert Anfield, sir? Solicitor?'

'Yes.'

'In that case I know him too. Thanks very much. We'll just get this little lot down to headquarters, then.'

'That's all you want?' Sampson asked.

'For the moment, sir.'

'Why the Special Branch, Mr Hutchinson?'

Hutchinson said, 'I really don't know, sir. These things happen sometimes. Good night and thank you.' By now he was in a hurry. Brian Norman Ellis was a stroke of luck; nothing special as a copper, but he had a memory and by God he was going to use it!

In a room at the rear of the Embassy of the Soviet Union in Kensington, the London *rezident* of the KGB was also in a hurry. He was thinking hard and anxiously about the trail that had been lost and where it might once again be picked up.

He had written the word Leefield on a sheet of paper and his eyes kept moving from it to the big map of the British Isles which hung on his wall. The man Conan came from Leefield. So did the priest, Greenfield, in Cambridge. And Budzinski had been to school there with them – a piece of information the Great Index had failed to produce. There was also this army officer, Theakstone. Had this man, too, attended the same provincial school? He would know in the morning, when the British records could be quietly inspected, but morning was hours away.

Looking at the map, he followed the route Budzinski had taken. London to Cambridge; from Cambridge almost certainly east to Colchester. Perhaps he hadn't gone to Colchester, but if he had, where after that? He could be hiding in Colchester, of course. It was a garrison town and it was likely the soldier Theakstone would have friends there. All the same, the *rezident* doubted it. He looked from the map to his pad and back again. Leefield was a long way away, two hundred miles, and the British police were searching for Semonov. That journey would be a tremendous risk for Budzinski, but when he got there – well, *what*? Roots. Friends from childhood. Familiar territory. The KGB *rezident* knew very well how attractive familiar territory was to a fugitive. But to *this* man? Budzinski was experienced and wily; he'd know they'd look for him in Leefield once the connection was discovered. Would that encourage him to go there, in a kind of double bluff? Or would it make him avoid the place?

To his left lay a file, as yet unopened. It was labelled Leefield and contained a detailed rundown of all available sources of information within the town. Such a file existed for every administrative area of Britain. It included such information as membership lists of local Communist Party and Anglo-Soviet Friendship Society branches, names of known sympathisers who were members of neither and lists of refugees from countries now within the Communist bloc who were known still to have relatives in the countries they had left. The *rezident* opened the file and began to examine its contents. He knew roughly what he would find, but the extent of the information pleased him. In the years immediately following the war, several thousand Poles, Latvians, Estonians and Lithuanians, displaced from their own

149

countries, had gone to Leefield to work in the then-thriving textile industry. Societies existed in which each national group attempted in exile to maintain its own cultural traditions. It had never been difficult to use such organisations, simply because so many of the refugees had left families and friends behind. The only problem lay in keeping the information up to date and a good deal of time, trouble and cash was expended on that.

The *resident* spent some time extracting from the file a short list of names. When he had finished, he was moved to reflect that however much the system might be criticised as wasteful and expensive – and such criticism came frequently – its usefulness in times of emergency was not to be doubted.

In Moscow, too, and in Sofia and in Varna also, agents of the KGB had been hard at work. The news that the violinist Istvan Kodes was believed, by the Israelis at any rate, to be in reality Joachim Schmidt, former commandant of the extermination camp at Layerhausen, had come as a nasty shock. In the immediate post-war years, Soviet war crime investigators had concluded, from such evidence as they could find, that Schmidt was either dead or had been smuggled, like so many others, along the Odessa route to South America. The file at 2 Dzerzhinsky Square had not been closed, but it remained only technically open. Russian pursuit of war criminals had been directed principally against those men whose crimes had been against Soviet citizens. One thing was certain. Schmidt had not deliberately been given asylum. If Kodes *were* Schmidt, then he had disappeared from view by his own efforts. Now, however, the KGB knew where to look. It was one thing to search a continent for a man who might or might not be alive, quite another to run a swift and detailed check on a single, named individual. The outline of the story emerged with surprising swiftness considering the length of time that had elapsed. Schmidt's file revealed immediately that his mother had been Bulgarian, a fact previously of no apparent importance but now highly significant in itself. A search of records of births and deaths in Varna showed that Istvan Kodes was apparently the last surviving member of his family. Old Secret Police records, compiled in the days of King Boris and continuously maintained after the Soviet invasion of 1944, revealed that one Istvan Kodes, listed as coming from nearby Constanza, had been among the Bulgarian partisans who resisted after German tanks rolled into Bulgaria in 1941. He had been captured. *And handed over!* The scenario was far from complete, but it was not difficult to imagine what might have happened. Kodes had already been in the hands of the RSHD, of which Schmidt was a senior officer. After the Allied invasion of Europe and the Soviet invasion of Eastern Europe, when to the discerning the writing was already on the wall, it would have been simple for Schmidt to make preparations to assume another identity. Many like him were doing so at the time. Accordingly, when the time came to run, he would run to Bulgaria, his mother's country, where he knew the language and had another man's ready-made background. In an attempt to turn surmise into proof, Kodes' one-room flat in Varna was microscopically searched. Nothing, however, was found… nothing, that is, until a KGB man inspecting Kodes' collection of gramophone records noticed that the label was missing from one record. Intrigued, he played it and found himself listening to the *Horst Wessel Lied*, marching song of the ss. It was perhaps not conclusive, but it was enough. A detailed report of the investigation went immediately to both Sofia and Moscow.

CHAPTER TEN

Two and a half miles from where he stood the carillon on the Town Hall clock banged through *Ilkla Moor Baht 'At*. The late January morning was still and damp; there had been no night frost, but a chill was deep in Budzinski's body as he contemplated the speckling lights in the valley below through an open wooden shutter. It was seven o'clock and dawn could not be far away, but Budzinski had no idea just when useful dark would go and unfriendly light begin to spread. He was hollow-eyed with weariness; his body felt like some marionette's, the response of his limbs unpredictable and imprecise. His head seemed empty of everything but depression, almost despair. The distant bells stopped their celebration leaving an emptiness in the air to match the emptiness inside him.

Leefield. It was Leefield out there.

He must be mad! Why the *hell* had he let Theakstone shunt him up here? But he knew why... weariness, reaction, the momentary leap of hope when of all things a helicopter had been whistled up so magically, had blinded him. The advantage had seemed so enormous, offering instant escape and the seeming certainty of sanctuary. Now, staring out as the lights on the hillsides flicked on, he recognised his delusion. This was not a place of sanctuary; with the morning light the hunt would come: when he needed anonymity above all, he was trapped in the one city outside Israel where literally dozens of people knew him. The hunt would concentrate on Leefield, too; he did not doubt that. The signposts pointed there, all of them, Greenfield most dangerously. Even if Greenfield had not been found already, he would be found soon. And his first words would be the names of the city and of the men: Budzinski, Theakstone, Leefield.

Luck had turned with a vengeance.

He shook his head angrily, but it would not clear; his mind refused to concentrate; it was as though a death-wish had surfaced within it and demanded inaction.

Behind him, on the scarred wooden floor, the girl wriggled uncomfortably. He glanced down at her without sympathy. His mind advised him treacherously to abandon her now, to get away while he could. Alone, he might have a chance, even a good chance. With her, he had no chance at all. She could not be kept tied up forever, yet it was impossible to free her, impossible even to move her, tied up as she was, through the streets. An hour ago it had seemed important only to get here; to get out of sight. After her kick had briefly smashed away his consciousness, he'd been lucky to find her again, crouched in a dark cleft in the moorland. Had her ankles not been tied, he'd never have found her. He'd realised then that in kidnapping Katya Semonov, he'd seized trouble. Small and young she might be, but she was also fit, strong and dangerous; above all she had nerve. That kick had come while she was feigning unconsciousness and feigning it successfully; it had been timed well and delivered with precision, tied ankles or no.

His mind limped sluggishly round possibilities that seemed increasingly non-existent. Because two of his boyhood friends had taken risks to help, he had thought others might do the same. Now it seemed much likelier that they wouldn't. Conan and Theakstone had had their reasons. The one held within him the eternity of Jewish hope and struggle, the other the curious bond that can exist between soldiers, even sometimes in opposing armies and on battlefields. If Farrell had been there as arranged, he might now be in some temporarily safe house in Leefield, but Farrell had *not* been at the rendezvous. And Farrell was probably typical.

His ears caught something and he stiffened before he recognised the sound: a tap dripping somewhere. He bent and picked up the girl, slinging her body over his shoulder, and carried her through to the shower room. Even in the dark, he could find his way round this place: the baths down one side, the showers in the middle, the lavatories in a row against the far wall. He crossed the room, checked that the window was secure and pushed the girl into one of the cubicles. She'd just have to manage. For him a cold shower might, just *might* knit together the shreds of concentration. He turned on the shower, allowed her three minutes, then opened the cubicle door. She stood glowering at him. He knotted the lavatory chain round her wrist binding and took his shower with deliberate brutality to his body, stepping into the icy jet without hesitation to ensure the maximum shock. Instantly he felt stronger. It wouldn't last, but it was there. He stepped out, pulled a ragged old towel from one of the wall hooks, and dried himself perfunctorily and dressed, his brain working again.

He needed to make decisions: they must be correct, and he must make them quickly, with very little to go on but memories a quarter of a century old. He asked questions of himself and answered them. Would this sports pavilion be in use today? He'd no way of knowing. Wednesday *had* been the sports afternoon, but that could easily have been changed. To remain in the pavilion beyond noon would therefore be risky, so he must move before noon. Should he move alone, or seek help? If Farrell was anything to go by, he couldn't expect much assistance. Or even take the chance. Budzinski frowned and checked himself. If there *was* help available, he certainly needed it. His danger lay in the fact that boys had become men and changed accordingly; himself more than most. He remembered his conversation with Conan and the mention of Doctor Dörflinger. It was unlikely Dörflinger would have changed much; a man of strong character remained just that, unless old age had drained him. Dörflinger was the best possibility available, but Dörflinger must be approached with care; sympathy from him was probable, but approval far from certain. Dörflinger believed in the rule of law, and had left Germany for ever when he saw it disappearing. The whole idea of the kidnap would certainly be repellent to Dörflinger *unless* the old man shared his own eye-for-an-eye view of the need for revenge.

All right. It was tenuous, but it *was* a move forward, a glimpse of a path to follow. He must reach Dörflinger, preferably not by telephone; better to stand on the old man's doorstep and to do that meant moving through Leefield. The girl would have to be left, so she must be totally immobilised, the hell with her discomfort!

As he unfastened the chain, she tried to knee him and swung off balance. He let her tumble on to the hard, tiled floor and heard her grunt with pain, then picked her up like a sack and carried her up the stairs to the first floor. Outside the dark sky was beginning to lighten and he could see dimly the wooden rungs that led into the scorer's box in the pavilion gable. It was the rugby season now; no reason why the box should be used until the cricket season began. He slung her over his shoulder and climbed to the box, pushing away the manhole cover, then clambering awkwardly through. It was here he'd smoked his first cigarette with furtive excitement, and been sick in the corner over there. Strange to think... he forced his mind back to the present. The girl must be secured, so effectively she could be left safely, and if necessary, for a number of hours. He left the box and went hunting for the means to accomplish it. The groundsman's shed beside the pavilion, with its grass-cutters and rollers and tractor was a treasure trove. There was a big canvas covering one of the mowers. He took it and a rope and struggled up to the scorer's box again. The girl had wriggled towards the manhole, but been unable to climb through. He rolled her in the canvas and knotted the rope round it several times. In the burgeoning daylight she watched him, unable to speak because of the gag in her mouth. There was no plea in her eyes, though; they reflected only anger and defiance. She'd try. But could she get out? Budzinski doubted it. Could she make a noise? She'd find it difficult, but this one would work at it and find a way if there was a way. He found the means to prevent it by raising her off the ground and suspending the whole canvas cocoon from the rafters. Get out of *that*, madam!

He climbed down again, replacing the trapdoor. There were working clothes in the groundsman's shed. He put on a pair of workman's bib-and-brace overalls and a greasy old tweed cap and looked at the tractor. Tempting. He was in the driving seat when he remembered something and checked. The tractor had no number plates. So no. He let himself out through the big green gates of the sports ground and walked down the hill towards the main road. Address first, then either a bus, or walk. There had once been a phone box by the cemetery gate; would it still be there? It was. *Dörflinger, Dr Helmut,* still lived at 8 Glentop Drive. Fine, he knew it. He set off on the two-mile walk, but changed his mind when he saw the bus stop at Hall Grove Road. When the bus finally halted at the bottom of Wharfe Lane, he walked briskly up the once familiar road.

There was a light in the kitchen of number eight. Budzinski walked through the gate and round to the back door of the plain semi-detached house. Maybe it was Mrs Dörflinger, if she were still alive, or a housekeeper if she were not. But it was a man who stood in the kitchen, a white-haired old man whose hand shook a little as he held a kettle under the tap. Budzinski stood still, watching. If Dörflinger had become too old, then he would go away. A couple of minutes sufficed. The hands might shake a little, but Dörflinger moved neatly as he prepared his breakfast.

Budzinski took a step forward and knocked on the door. A moment later, Dörflinger was looking at him, frowning. Budzinski did not speak. If the old man failed to recognise him he would simply leave.

'Come,' Dörflinger said abruptly, turning away from the door.

The slight tremble of Dörflinger's hands and a noticeable decrease in height, were scars age had made on the body. There were no comparable frailties in his mind, or none that Budzinski could discover. Dörflinger knew instantly why he was there. But Dörflinger was a schoolmaster, a scholar. He began, first, to philosophise about rights and wrongs. Predictably, all the wrongs were Budzinski's; all the rights, in every sense, were the girl's. Budzinski tried to be patient, and found it increasingly difficult.

Finally he said, 'Understand this. I *demand* your help!'

'Demand? By what right?'

'Blood. Jewish blood. Yours and mine and six million more.'

Dörflinger's mouth tightened in anger. 'Always blood! Do you wonder I stayed with the young?'

Budzinski said brutally, 'What have you ever done for your people?'

'You're Israel, are you, Budzinski?'

'I'm the nearest thing you'll ever meet.' It was cruel to play on the guilt felt by expatriate Jews. But pressure was needed and he applied it. 'The world isn't innocent for Jews. While you taught, Jews were dying and Schmidt was murdering them. While you were teaching, I was fighting. It's come to your doorstep now.'

His reward was a visible mistiness in Dörflinger's eyes. He pressed on. 'I need a hiding place that's safe. I need protection while the negotiations go on. That means I need people I can trust. Here, in this town. You know who they are and you're going to find them for me.'

Dörflinger said, almost with contempt, 'And help to save your skin.'

Budzinski said, 'It's Schmidt's hide I want. When this is over they can make mine into lampshades. Stand by and watch *then*, if you want to.'

Dörflinger turned his back and stood for a moment, rigid with anger.

'Well?' Budzinski demanded harshly.

The old man turned, and when he spoke his voice trembled. 'You put your case badly, Budzinski. You always did. But then I feel guilty and always have.'

'You'll help!'

Dörflinger nodded. 'But try not to harm the girl.'

'It's not in my interests!'

On the long drive from Colchester, Chief Inspector Alastair McHugh had tried hard to rest in the back of the speeding white police Jaguar. He had, in fact, managed a few minutes' fitful doze, but his mind was too busy to let him relax enough for real

156

sleep. His conversation with the man Theakstone at Colchester police station – it could scarcely be described as interrogation – baffled him. McHugh was not unaccustomed to people who kept their mouths shut and damn-the-consequences, but as a rule their motives were at least comprehensible. Theakstone was something entirely new to him: a soldier of ability, almost of distinction, whose record showed not only courage but patriotism. Theakstone must have known his army career was wrecked from the moment he refused co-operation. In case he hadn't understood, the fact had been explained to him forcefully; yet he had said nothing, admitting only two things: first that he had been out for a drive. He would not say where, would not say whom he had met, would not say whether anybody had telephoned him. Secondly he had agreed he knew Sidney Conan. They had been at school together, but Theakstone said he had not seen or had any communication with Conan for at least twenty years. This latter point baffled McHugh. The man who had kidnapped Katya Semonov was known to Conan, was known to Theakstone and was known to somebody else too, in Cambridge. The link was the school at Leefield. There was unquestionably a conspiracy of some kind and Theakstone was in it up to his neck. Yet McHugh had believed Theakstone when Theakstone said it was twenty years since he'd had any contact of any kind with Conan. Now Conan had vanished – Exeter police had been able to find no trace of him – and Theakstone was apparently prepared to sacrifice his whole career. Why? McHugh had tried for an hour and got nowhere. Theakstone had, in effect, given him name, rank and number and told him to go to hell. Finally, McHugh had admitted defeat, told Colchester police that Major Theakstone was to be detained to assist with inquiries and allowed no outside communication at all, and had gone out to his car. Everything pointed in the direction of Leefield Grammar School, so he'd damn well go there.

He arrived at Leefield police headquarters just before eight am to be greeted by Detective Superintendent Hutchinson.

'Any news?' McHugh asked, dry-mouthed.

'Dunno about news,' Hutchinson said. 'We've a fair amount of information. We've been in direct contact with Mr Sellers and acting on his requests.'

'Go on.'

Hutchinson picked up the phone. 'Ask Detective Sergeant Ellis to come in, please.' He passed McHugh a typewritten list, headed: *Leefield Grammar School, Form IVA, 1941-42.* 'He's on

157

there, Ellis, B.N. Some of the other names'll interest you, too. I could tell you myself, but Ellis'll do it better and you'll want to ask him questions.'

McHugh didn't bother to count. 'How many?'

'Twenty-seven.'

'Do we know where they all live now?'

'Some. Not all. We're fairly certain about the ones who live locally.'

'Go on.'

There was a knock at the door and a man entered. Hutchinson said, 'Ellis, this is Chief Inspector McHugh, Special Branch.'

'Yes, sir.' Ellis waited.

'Tell him about your mates.'

Ellis nodded. 'Of the twenty-seven on the list, I think fourteen are still in this area, sir. But there's a problem. There were five forms in each year's intake. After a couple of years the intake was divided and they had about thirty boys on the classical side. The rest did modern studies, which included languages and sciences, and they were swapped about a bit.'

'How?'

'Well, a lad who didn't do well might go down from an A form to a B form. One who did well would go up. C to B and so on. The usual thing. So I don't think this list's a complete guide, sir. The list would change each year.'

McHugh said, 'Conan and Theakstone. Were they in the same class all the time?'

'I'm relying on memory, sir, and it's not easy, but I think so.'

Hutchinson broke in. 'I've sent to the school for later form lists. It shouldn't take long.'

'Right. So start with Conan and Theakstone. Who were their mates?'

Ellis said, 'I don't think Conan and Theakstone *were* friends, particularly.'

'Oh?' McHugh frowned. 'Well, maybe they got together later. Take them one at once. Who were Conan's friends?'

Ellis shrugged. 'That's what I've been trying to remember. Conan was quiet, like. Kept to himself, except he had a pal called Harrison. But Harrison was killed a long time ago. Car crash, I think.'

'Nobody else?'

'Well, he's Jewish, you know that, sir. I think his family was orthodox. They sort of stayed out of school things. If he had any close friends apart from Harrison, they'd be lads who lived near, if you see.'

158

'I see very well. What about Theakstone?'

'He was a lot… well, a lot more free. He was a sportsman, you see. Gregarious, if that's the word. But there was a fellow called Blamires and another called Farrell. They used to knock about together.'

'Where are they now?'

'Farrell's an estate agent, sir. Here in the town. Inherited his father's business.'

'Still in touch?'

'I don't know. I'm *not* in touch, if you see…'

'And this other one. This bloke Blamires.'

Hutchinson said, 'We know Mr Blamires, don't we, Ellis?'

'Yes, sir. Blamires is a wrong 'un. He's done time.'

McHugh sat up. 'For what?'

'He's a funny 'un,' Hutchinson said. 'Qualified man. Chartered accountant.'

'Money fiddles?'

'No. That's the strange thing. Petty theft. Bits of breaking and entering. Ellis reckons there was some kind of personality change when he was about thirty. That right, Ellis?'

'Something of the kind, sir. He got TB and was in a sanatorium about two years. Three maybe. Then it started. He went in straight and came out bent.'

'Where is he now? Inside?'

'Out, sir. I checked. He came out of Armley about eight weeks ago. Eighteen months for breaking and entering. Maximum remission.'

'He used to be visited inside by this bloke Farrell,' Hutchinson said. 'Hang on.' The telephone on his desk had rung. 'Speaking. Yes. What? Well I'll be damned!' He replaced the receiver and turned to Ellis. 'Does the name Budzinski mean anything to you?'

'Yes, sir. He's on the list.'

'Hang on a minute,' McHugh said. 'Who's this Budzinski?'

'That was Cambridgeshire Constabulary,' Hutchinson said. 'A fellow called Greenfield was found not long ago by his housekeeper, bound and gagged.'

'In Cambridge?'

'He's a priest. Catholic. Lectures at the university. He said this man Budzinski came to see him last night, thumped him and tied him up. Then some other people came. No names, but one was a man on his own, then two others. He got the impression the man on his own knew Budzinski and that the other two were foreign. This chap Greenfield had a rough night.'

'He's not the only one,' McHugh said sourly. 'Who's Budzinski?'

'Joe Budzinski,' Ellis said promptly. 'He's Jewish.'

'And?'

'Refugee from Poland, I think. I'd forgotten him. He emigrated to Israel way back. While I was in the army, or about then.'

'You've never heard of him since?'

'No,' Ellis said. 'Not a word.'

'Use your phone?' McHugh reached for it and asked for the Yard. A few moments later he was speaking to Assistant Commissioner Sellers. 'I've just heard about Budzinski.'

Sellers said, 'Cambridge told me, too. I've just been having him checked.'

'And?'

Sellers' tone was deliberately measured. 'He's a very hard case indeed. Not too much known officially, but DI6 have a file of sorts. Mostly hearsay. He's been years in the Israeli action squads. Kidnapping, executions. He was even on the Eichmann thing in Buenos Aires.'

'Bloody hell!' McHugh exploded.

'Yes. Well we know the story now, don't we? We can pretty well take it for granted he was in Rome yesterday, trying to snatch this bloke Schmidt. It looks to me as though he did this Semonov thing on the spur of the moment. He got to England somehow and just grabbed her and started running. First to Conan's flat, then to Cambridge. The man Greenfield wasn't any help so he put him out of action and headed for Theakstone in Colchester. After that, Christ knows. So where does that leave you, McHugh, all the way up there?'

McHugh said, 'In just the right bloody place. Budzinski went to Leefield Grammar School.'

Maria Rowan was a British citizen, as were her father and husband. Her mother, however, was not and it was through her mother that Maria Rowan was vulnerable. Her mother had been married twice. First, in Warsaw, to a young officer in a Polish infantry regiment in early August of 1939. They had been on honeymoon in Sweden when Hitler attacked Poland and the campaign was effectively over before her husband could get back. Together they had gone to England, where the young officer served with the Polish forces until he was killed, in 1944, in France. In 1946 his widow had married again; her second husband was British, a soldier she had met in London. He was a wool sorter, and when he was demobilised a few months later, she had gone with him to Leefield, where Maria was born. For thirty years she did not return to Poland, though she maintained a correspondence with her two sisters. In 1972, when Maria was married, she was finally able to accept the latest of a long series of pressing invitations to visit them, largely because her husband had been lucky in a foofball sweepstake. She took Maria and her new husband with her as a kind of second honeymoon trip.

Maria Rowan had met her husband at work; she was a secretary at Leefield police headquarters. David Rowan was a police constable. That information was entered on their visa applications when they visited Poland, and was routinely noted by the Polish authorities and equally routinely added to the Great Index maintained in Moscow by the *Komitat Gosudarstvennoi Bezopastnosti*. Thence, in the normal course of abstraction, the information became available to the *rezident* in London.

Had Maria Rowan been seeking to join either the civil service or the armed forces, her mother's Polish birth would have emerged and almost certainly have prevented her, despite her own British birth and citizenship, from being employed in any security-sensitive area. But she was simply a secretary and the police service in Leefield was not a security-sensitive area. Her references were good, even her name was English; there was no problem.

That morning, however, as Maria Rowan rode on the bus towards the town centre, a car followed. When she alighted from the bus, she had walked a mere twenty yards when a man's voice behind her said, 'Mrs Rowan?'

She turned. 'Yes?' The man was no-one she knew.

He took a piece of paper from his pocket and read from it two names. Maria blinked at him, puzzled and beginning to be afraid.

'They are sisters of your mother?'

'Yes they are. What – ?'

The man told her what. He described what would happen to them, and to their husbands and children, unless Maria was prepared to co-operate. She felt tears start in her eyes. She had heard of this kind of thing; there had always been gossip about it in the immigrant community, stories of people suddenly and unexpectedly put under pressure. In a few cases, it was said, people had actually been compelled to return to Poland, or Lithuania or Latvia.

The conversation did not last long, and when it was over, Maria Rowan had been given precise instructions and a telephone number. She had also been given a name. Anything, anything at all, that might be said about a man named Josef Budzinski must be reported at once.

She went on her way in a daze. The man had known all about her, even that she was secretary to the Deputy Chief Constable, and he'd also said they had somebody else at police headquarters, some other contact, who would know whether or not she was obeying his instructions. She walked very slowly, frantically trying to find some way out, but whichever way her mind darted, there was a wall. She could tell her boss, perhaps, and pretend to co-operate; she could ignore the instructions altogether; but either way, if there was another contact within police headquarters, she might be found out, with the threatened consequences to her relatives in Poland. No, she decided, she must do as she had been told. It was the only safe way.

From a call box at Yeadon Airport Susan Würzburg telephoned the Israeli Embassy in London, identified herself, and asked to speak to the Ambassador personally. Her call was transferred through the internal switchboard to his house and she reported her arrival. She was told that a member of the Embassy staff was at that moment on his way north to Leefield to join her. Where, the Ambassador asked, did she suggest that the rendezvous should be? She thought for a moment, then suggested the restaurant of Dewhurst's department store. She said she would tell the head waiter her name and that she was expecting a guest. Bloom would be shown to her table.

On the flight from Tel Aviv to Paris, she had slept, well aware that rest was necessary. Flying in the little executive jet from Paris to Leeds/Bradford airport at Yeadon, she had tried to think how, once in Leefield, she should try to locate Budzinski. She had found that the more she considered the problem, the more difficult it became. Leefield was not a great city, but neither was it merely a small town. Within it, Budzinski was likely to go to ground, and he'd have, almost certainly, the assistance of local people who knew the place far better, now, than she did. It would be no use tramping the streets, and she had changed her mind about listening to gossip in Dewhurst's, because she wouldn't see him and there would *be* no gossip. She decided that if Budzinski's strength lay in his friends, his weakness lay in the fact that he was Jewish. Her own strength also lay in her Jewishness and in the fact that no-one in Leefield knew she was coming, or would know the purpose of her trip. In the taxi from the airport into the town, she made a mental list of names, considering each in turn. Freddie Farrell seemed a likely contact; Budzinski and Farrell had been fairly close. But it would be difficult to approach Farrell. She hadn't seen him in years, even on her own occasional holiday visits to Leefield; in those circumstances, she could hardly just telephone and say hello, what about a drink? The same applied to Blamires, *if* he was not in gaol. And to all the others. What she needed above all was a starting point. She thought about it and decided that their mutual Jewishness virtually dictated that as a point. The rabbi, then? She rejected the idea quickly. If Rabbi Hirsch had still been alive, it would have been different, but this was a new man and Budzinski wouldn't know him. She herself had only met the man a couple of times. Who, then? Mentally she ticked off names. Sidney Conan apart, there had been one or two other Jewish boys about that time. Michael Aber was in America somewhere, had been for years. Willie Hauser... Where was *he*? She'd heard, somewhere... Yes, she remembered now, he was a doctor in London. Was that the lot? She believed it was and that brought her back to Farrell and Blamires. No; she'd better stick to her own people, at least in the beginning. The Edelmans, who'd given the orphaned Budzinski a home, were both long-dead and in any case were the wrong generation. Or was it the wrong generation? Might Budzinski not expect to find greater sympathy among the people who had actually fled from Hitler, the people whose relatives had been murdered? People like her own father? Or Dörflinger! *He'd* been a kind of unofficial father to all the refugee boys, Budzinski included. More important, she could call on Dörflinger quite easily and naturally; on her visits to Leefield she had always visited the old man, and with Dörflinger she might be able to gossip to some purpose.

She glanced at her watch. It was nine-thirty. Should she go to Dewhurst's first and wait for Bloom? She decided against it. Bloom was not in Leefield yet, and would, in any case, wait for her. She leaned forward and gave the taxi driver Dörflinger's address.

CHAPTER ELEVEN

'Want to talk to Farrell yourself?' Detective Superintendent Hutchinson asked.

McHugh shook his head. 'I've been thinking. Fourteen of 'em we know, right? Fourteen still in this area. If we start questioning them, *they* start chatting among themselves.'

'Yes they do,' Hutchinson said. 'But there's not much alternative. Start trying to tail fourteen men in a town this size and everybody'll be falling over everybody else like the Marx Brothers.'

McHugh smiled faintly and nodded, conceding. 'All the same, no serried ranks. This bloke Blamires interests me. We'll hoik him in for starters. Have him picked up, Ellis.'

'What about Farrell? He's candidate number one, sir.'

'Blamires first, Ellis.'

As Ellis left the room McHugh said, 'Is he any good?'

'Ellis? Not much. Wouldn't be a detective sergeant at forty-odd, would he?'

'What's his weakness?'

'He's a bit savage, is Ellis. A bit savage and a lot lazy. Still can't see why he's always passed over – you know the kind.'

'Too well. I was thinking of leaning on brother Blamires.'

'Well Ellis can lean hard enough. Might lean a bit too hard, that's all.'

'All right. I'll listen while he does it. But not in the room.'

'You'd better tell Ellis,' Hutchinson said, 'exactly what you want. Don't give him discretion; he hasn't any. What about the others?'

McHugh shook his head. 'I don't like this thing. There's too many and they're all respectable. Businesses, premises, motor cars, Christ knows what!'

'And one magistrate and two solicitors.'

'Jesus God. All the same, Farrell's very likely the key. Do you know him?'

'A bit. Not well. Met him here and there.'

'Tell me.'

'Estate agent, you know that. Fairly prosperous. Inherited his father's business. He's a widower with one girl away at university.'

'Personally?'

'Nice bloke. Decent golfer, plays off six or seven.'

'Tough?'

'Fairly fit for a man his age, I'd say.'

'I mean mentally. Put yourself in his place. You're a nice bloke, local estate agent, Jaguars and golf clubs, fair-size fish in your own pond. Then this hairy-arsed commando-type you knew when you were a kid comes out of nowhere after twenty-odd years –'

'We don't know he did. Not yet.'

'We're imagining, right? This Farrell, he may have done a fiddle or two here and there – wouldn't be an estate agent otherwise, would he? – but suddenly, right on his doorstep, there's everything he's read about in the papers. Plane hijack, terrorists, kidnapping, murder. You name it. What does he do? I'll tell you what ninety-nine out of a hundred would do. They'd say *bugger-off, old friend!* Can you think of any of *your* old mates you'd take on in those circumstances?'

Hutchinson thought for a moment. Then he said seriously, 'Yes. There's one. It's a long story.'

McHugh stared at him. 'All right, don't bother with the story, the point's made. But you're a hard case yourself. You know the ins and outs. How tough is Farrell?'

Hutchinson said, 'We'll have to find out, won't we?'

Twenty minutes later, McHugh watched as Ellis led Blamires through to an interview room at the rear of the building. He followed them, entered the room next door and slid back a grille through which he could watch unseen. He'd briefed Ellis thoroughly while a squad car picked up Blamires from his lodgings.

Blamires was tall, pale and fair; slightly sickly in appearance. Rather to McHugh's surprise, he wore a suit, collar and tie.

Ellis said, 'Sit down, Colin.'

Blamires obeyed and waited, blank-faced. McHugh read the signs easily. Blamires was scared and fatalistic in a scene and setting that had become familiar. No protests, nothing; Blamires simply sat and waited.

'Next time,' Ellis said, 'you know what it'll be. Five anyway. That's for certain, five is. But on top of that you know what judges think of you. They think you should know better, so they're liable to talk about sharp lessons. Ten years, maybe.'

McHugh watched Blamires' face. Nothing moved.

Ellis said, 'You understand?'

Blamires nodded.

'I said, do you understand?'

'Yes. But I've been straight since I came out.' Blamires spoke for the first time, voice soft and not uncultured. It wasn't protest, just a statement. McHugh wondered what had bent him: hatred of the whole wide world because he'd had TB? Unlikely, but you never knew; stranger things came his way.

'It goes like this,' Ellis said conversationally. 'In a town like this, there's only a certain number of regulars. When something happens, we usually have a fair idea where to start looking. And you, well you're a regular, aren't you, Colin?'

Blamires said nothing.

'Bloody well answer!' Ellis said.

'I suppose so. But I haven't done anything.'

'So you say. Let me put it this way. A few jobs have been done. Little tickles. Your kind of rubbish. Where were *you* three weeks ago last Thursday at half-past nine?'

Blamires said, 'I didn't do it.' He tried to say it quietly, but there was a tremor in his voice.

'Got an alibi, have you?'

'I didn't do it. Whatever it was.' Blamires sat very still, his face pale, sweat on his brow. McHugh decided the man was unbalanced in some strange, even masochistic way. Blamires knew exactly what was coming and hated it but was accepting it.

'I've three I could load on you,' Ellis said. 'Maybe more if I really try.'

'Why?'

'A ten-stretch, Colin. Fancy it?'

'No.'

'Pay you to be friendly, wouldn't it?'

For the first time reaction showed on Blamires' face. He was and looked puzzled. 'How d'you mean?'

'Favours. Grassing.'

Blamires said, 'I've nobody to grass *on*.'

'No? Well, let's try it another way. You've been working, have you?'

'Yes.'

'For Fred Farrell again?'

'I do some of his accounts. You know that.'

Ellis laughed. 'But he doesn't let you near his petty cash! Dear old Freddie. How much have you nicked off *him* over the years? Bear some investigation, would that.'

Blamires said nothing.

'Well?'

'I've never robbed Freddie. Not a cent.'

'You wouldn't, of course,' Ellis sneered. 'You're both decent fellows!'

'Freddie is.'

'Aye, Freddie. Freddie doesn't forget his old friends, does he?'

'He's been generous to me,' Blamires said.

'Freddie Farrell.' Ellis repeated the name thoughtfully. 'Funny if the boot was on the other foot, eh? If you were visiting *him* inside?'

Blamires looked puzzled again. 'It's hardly likely.'

'Not as likely,' Ellis said, 'as a ten-stretch for you, Colin. That's a near certainty. And it's a promise too. I'm going to fit you up, Colin.'

Blamires was trembling and McHugh now was fairly sure he understood the reason. Blamires' body had let him down and in this weird way he punished it. When Blamires got TB he hadn't gone bent, McHugh decided, he'd gone round the twist. The prison sentences, the constant humiliation in his native city, were some nutty kind of deliberate mortification of the flesh. In which case, the threat was unlikely –

McHugh said sharply, 'Get Ellis out of there!'

In the corridor outside, he thought about it quickly, then turned to the waiting Ellis. 'Think he'll do it your way?'

'If I press a bit longer, sir.'

'Well, he won't,' McHugh said. 'He's a nutter and only out to punish himself.' He told Ellis how to proceed and returned to the grille to watch.

Ellis said, 'Hear the news this morning? On the radio?'

Blamires frowned and nodded.

'That hijack in Rome, know who did it?'

'No.'

'Joe Budzinski.'

'*What!*' Blamires was not merely surprised, McHugh thought, he was flabbergasted. At least he could be sure Budzinski hadn't been in touch with Blamires.

Ellis pressed on hard. 'And the Russian girl. The gymnast. She's missing. Well, Budzinski's got her!'

Blamires said, voice pitched high with surprise, 'I don't believe you!'

'Well, it's true. So now let's get down to cases. If Joe Budzinski comes here, who'd he come to see? Freddie and you, wouldn't he?'

'Has he –?'

'Don't interrupt. We think he has. Budzinski's bad news, Colin. The worst kind. He's a terrorist. He was a terrorist before they got fashionable. And if you, or Freddie Farrell or anybody else helps him, it's the high jump. Right?'

'I don't believe...' Blamires said softly. 'Not Joe. I mean, for God's sake!'

Ellis said, 'There's a Special Branch dossier a mile long on Budzinski. You'd better believe it. It's true. And you can't help him, nobody can. But Freddie Farrell might try, mightn't he? Because Freddie stays loyal, doesn't he, even to bloody idiots like you! So he might just be daft enough.'

'I don't understand,' Blamires said. 'What do you want me to do? You could warn Freddie yourselves.'

'That's right. We could. But we want better. We want Budzinski and the girl. The girl especially, before he does her a mischief. So here's what you do, Colin. You stick close to Farrell today. You keep your eyes and ears open. If he does anything ususual, you let me know, and fast. If he even looks unusual, the same. And you don't say a word to him about it. Right?'

Blamires hesitated. Then he said, 'He ought to know.'

'I told you – just watch.'

Blamires thought about it. 'What'll you do to Freddie?'

'If we get Budzinski, nothing. Otherwise, God help him, and you! Now go to his office.'

Blamires rose. He said, 'I'd do anything for Freddie.' It was, McHugh thought, a curiously childlike statement. He thought there was very little malice in Blamires, and what there was was directed inward, against himself. Twenty minutes later, McHugh realised something else, and with a sudden shudder: Blamires would certainly seek to protect Farrell. But he might also try to help Budzinski; that, too, would be to protect Farrell, but in a different way. And it would also match up with his self-punishment complex, if McHugh had diagnosed *that* correctly.

But by that time, Blamires had reached the offices of Farrell and Son.

McHugh considered this new problem quietly for a few moments, and decided he'd been wrong. What was needed, after all, was some old-fashioned bobbying.

Through the night, the crowd in Rome had thinned and quietened, as both the police outside and the Russians marooned inside the Embassy villa had known it must. Night always had the same predictable effect on a crowd. Hunger intervened, and in the chill of the early hours, emotional kettles boiled less fiercely. All the same, there were still a lot of people.

The assistant cultural attaché at the Rome Embassy of the USSR (he was also KGB *resident* in the city) stood at an attic window and watched them in silence through binoculars. Fourteen hours earlier, when the crowd was still building, its composition had been different; then there had been many older people. But for hours now it had been predominantly young and international: idealistic youth. To the youngsters it had been one more all-night session; for the older people, the night had been long and there were few above forty left. But from his fourth floor vantage-point the Rome *resident* could see what people at ground level could not. From several directions on the fringes of the crowd, people were moving through it, in ones and twos, converging on a point twenty yards or so away from the villa's big wrought-iron gates. Once they reached that point, they simply stopped and stood still. The *resident* allowed himself a small smile of satisfaction, but the smile was tinged at the edges with tension. The ploy had been conceived, was being put into action and ought to work... *Ought* to work...

At five in the morning, a decision, accompanied by the instructions which followed from the decision, had come from Moscow. Moscow was embarrassed and angry and Moscow wished to be rid of the embarrassment. The *resident* well knew that the anger would continue and have consequences for other people; he hoped there would be none for him.

The embarrassment was named Joachim Schmidt and the nature of the problem he presented had been analysed. Schmidt was on Soviet diplomatic premises and there was no way of getting him out, alive or dead, unobserved. The crowd had not stopped anybody entering the villa, but nobody had been allowed to leave. The *resident* would have been tempted to kill Schmidt and hide the corpse somewhere, but Moscow had ruled that out. Attacks on embassies were almost commonplace in those days and the possibility certainly existed here. Moscow had, accordingly, decided on a suitable strategy... After receiving his instructions, the *resident* had busied himself in organising the means to carry out his orders; the people unobtrusively gathering into a group to the left of the gates were the fruit of that organisation. He watched as more people filtered slowly towards the specified position. Gradually the pattern of movement stopped. They were ready, waiting for his signal. The *rezident* reached for a lace curtain covering the window, opened it, closed it again, and continued to watch.

Below him forty men moved with startling suddenness, boosting one another up and over the ten-foot wall. Most were young, but among them were men of middle age and one or two in their sixties. That, too, was part of the plan. The *rezident* noted with satisfaction that others moved to follow. The more the merrier, he thought. At the moment, confusion was a friend.

The smashing of the villa's big door echoed through the house. A sledgehammer and two pickaxes had been left handily beside it. The *rezident* watched the wall as a few more youths climbed over and ran towards the villa. He left the room and stood looking down the well of the staircase as men poured on to the black and white marble floor four floors below.

He counted slowly to twenty, lit a cigarette, and strolled down the staircase. As he reached the ground floor, he saw a group of men emerge from the kitchens, four or five more came out of the reception suite, several from the cellars. The cellar group included Schmidt.

A brawny Italian in his thirties tore over to the *rezident*, seized him by the lapels and roared, 'Where is the bastard? We know you have him. Where is he?'

'No,' the *rezident* answered, quaveringly, in well-simulated fear. 'We haven't. He's not here. Never has been here.'

The man flung him against the wall and shouted, 'Let's search the place!'

The *rezident*, pretending to cower against the wall, watched them rush by up the staircase. The villa's occupants had been instructed to offer no resistance and presumably did not, because in a few minutes, the men began to reappear, asking one another in loud voices whether Schmidt had been found and shouting that he had not.

Meanwhile a captain of police, unable to enter Embassy territory without invitation or permission, had been banging ineffectually on the gate. Fifteen minutes after they had climbed the gate, the mob had rushed out of the Embassy door to climb the wall and shout to the crowd: 'He's not there!' A few invaders remained, however, somewhat sheepish now. They were not invited guests at the party, and the *rezident* was glad to hand them over to the police who, by this time, had been invited on to Embassy territory to mop up. The Ambassador addressed an Italian police captain in stinging terms and promised strong and immediate protest to the Foreign Ministry, a protest, he said,

170

which would certainly cost the captain his job. When he made the protest by telephone a few minutes later, he also informed the Foreign Minister icily that, since half Rome had searched the villa, it must now be abundantly clear to all that Joachim Schmidt was not and never had been there.

A little while later, the Ambassador and the KGB *rezident* stood together on the steps of the villa beside the shattered door and watched the crowd begin to melt away.

As the additional class lists were brought in to Leefield police from the grammar school archives, the original list of fourteen names was revised. Five more were added, two removed. One was that of a university lecturer spending a year in Canada, the other that of an insurance man transferred a few months earlier to his company's London office. There were now seventeen of Budzinski's contemporaries to be considered and they formed a nice cross-section of Leefield's lower-middle and middle-classes. To the police they formed an unusual problem, for they were ordinary and respectable citizens engaged in the life of the town. Of the whole group only Blamires had ever run foul of the law. Police files recorded a few speeding offences, but nothing more serious.

McHugh's 'old-fashioned bobbying' was consequently polite and careful. Each of the men was visited by Leefield detectives at his place of work; each was told what Budzinski had done, and that it was believed Budzinski was either in, or heading for, Leefield; each was warned that offering assistance of any kind to this particular fugitive would constitute an offence of great gravity. Each was then asked whether Budzinski had made any attempt to get in touch. All the men reacted in the same way: initial surprise, understanding of the warning, denial that Budzinski had been in contact. All promised to inform the police immediately if any information came his way.

Farrell, however, was not interviewed. McHugh had decided that Farrell should, for a couple of hours, only be watched. The interview could come later, by which time one of the others would almost certainly have spoken to Farrell anyway. McHugh reasoned that since Budzinski's need was urgent, Farrell would act either quickly or not at all. An unmarked police car followed Farrell from his home to his office, where surveillance was taken over by plain-clothes men in the street outside. By that time, too, a wire-tap operation had been arranged with the telephone service; all Farrell's calls would, from that moment, be monitored. And Blamires was in Farrell's office. By now McHugh had done all he could. Foot and car patrols had been warned to keep a sharp watch for Budzinski and had been issued with the only available picture of him, a blow-up from a twenty-five-year-old school photograph. The picture was regarded as unsatisfactory but was in fact still a fair likeness. All the police could now do was to wait for somebody to make a move. The machinery for a massive police operation was already in existence, but there was little point in setting up roadblocks, for example, until police were certain Budzinski was actually *in* Leefield. It remained possible that he had not headed north at all, or if he had, had not yet arrived, and in the latter case, roadblocks might even be a handicap. The police purpose remained: to recover Katya Semonov: and to capture Budzinski.

Frederick Stewart Farrell was trying hard to behave normally in spite of a sense of failure that made his stomach feel queasy. He had failed to keep the rendezvous with Budzinski for the most mundane of reasons and was guiltily conscious that Joe had, as a result, been left stranded on the moors. After receiving Theakstone's telephone call the previous evening and digesting his astonishment, he had dressed and thinking about Joe's predicament and his own, had come up with what seemed the perfect answer, an answer his profession allowed him to provide. Among the properties handled by his firm was a holiday cottage on the fringes of Wharfedale, owned by a Yorkshireman who now lived in the south, and let by Farrell to summer visitors when its owner was not using it. The cottage was isolated and screened by trees, stood on the low slope of a fell side and would provide a near-perfect hiding place. There was no need for Budzinski even to come into Leefield; the rendezvous lay just off one of the roads to the Dales, and after picking up Budzinski he could simply keep on driving and install him there before daylight.

He had decided it would be foolish to arrive too soon at the rendezvous and had waited until half an hour before the time arranged before going out to his car. Half an hour would give him plenty of time. He climbed into the car, started the engine and began to back out of his garage and the squishing sound and the lightness of the steering told him immediately what had happened: the offside-near tyre was flat. For a couple of miles, he might have chanced it, but he had nearly seventy miles to drive, much of it on winding, hilly Dales roads. Therefore the wheel would have to be changed. Stripping off his jacket, he set to work, jacking up the car, knocking off the hubcap – then tried to unfasten the wheel nuts. The spanner provided with the car proved ludicrously ineffective. As he wrenched and heaved and sweated, the nuts failed to move. The inept leverage he could apply did not compare with the leverage applied by a strong mechanic using a spider spanner two-handed. For half an hour he had struggled frantically, and had succeeded in loosening only one of the wheel nuts. The others had simply refused to budge. He had tried muffling the spanner handle with cloth and using a hammer, but the two careful blows had seemed to echo down the quiet road and he had not dared to hammer more.

As the time for the rendezvous came, Farrell was in despair. There were two all-night taxi firms in Leefield, but he daren't use a taxi. Nor was there any possible way to warn Budzinski. He wrestled on, to no effect, and finally, after a further half-hour, went back indoors to sit by the phone in the hope that Budzinski would telephone. There was a garage nearby which opened at eight where he could get the wheel changed; he would tell Budzinski to wait quietly until he could get to the rendezvous.

But Budzinski had not phoned. Farrell had listened to the radio news every half-hour, and assumed since Budzinski did not appear to have been caught, that he must have hidden himself successfully. But where? And what should Farrell do? He could go looking, but risks were attached to that, and Budzinski would probably have had to move some distance from the rendezvous. He would simply have to wait and hope.

He had debated staying at home for the day, but decided against it. The two Farrell entries in the phone book were together and Budzinski could as easily telephone one place as the other.

Now, at his desk, he stared at the telephone, willing it to ring. Once or twice it did, but the caller was not Budzinski. He wished desperately that there was something he could do.

Shortly after ten o'clock, the direct telephone rang on his desk. It did not go through the firm's little switchboard and was ex-directory. Farrell answered, knowing it could not be Budzinski.

A noisy voice with a deliberately exaggerated Yorkshire accent said, 'Fluked any more putts in lately, lad?' He knew the voice. John Wainwright in humorous mood.

'I don't fluke 'em in,' Farrell said. 'It's delicacy of touch.' He didn't want to talk to Wainwright now, so he'd keep it short. 'All right for Sunday?'

'Aye, lad. Half-past eight, first tee. Got any good houses?'

'For you?'

'Nay. My sister's getting wed and not before time, all things considered.'

'Good for her,' Farrell said. 'Yes, I've one or two.'

'No rubbish. No pretty views of mill backs. By the second green at Fairholme'd be nice. Handy, too.'

'All right, I'll bring the lists and details Sunday.'

'Nay, lad. Not Sunday. How about a coffee in Dewhurst's now? You're doin' nowt, I'll bet.'

Farrell scowled to himself. He said, 'I can't at this second. What area are you thinking of?'

'Fairfield Lane.'

Farrell's scalp tingled. Budzinski had lived in Fairfield Lane. It was in an old part of the town, much of it now flats and offices. He said carefully, 'Well, it's convenient, I suppose.'

'Aye, lad. Dewhurst's in twenty minutes, eh?'

'All right.'

'Who's he meeting?' McHugh asked.

'Dunno, sir,' the constable said. 'They didn't use names. Seemed to know each other's voices.'

'Play it over again.'

McHugh heard the conversation through as the tape recorder turned, then said to Hutchinson, 'All this "aye, lad" stuff. How natural is it?'

Hutchinson said, 'Local character, it's called.'

'Genuine conversation, then?'

'Probably. I wouldn't want to live in Fairfield Lane myself. Big old houses, but I'll admit there are some natty conversions.'

'Well just make sure you don't lose him,' McHugh said. 'I want him tailed into the coffee place.' A thought struck him. 'Get a plain-clothes policewoman at the next table.'

Hutchinson grinned. 'No use. There's a men-only coffee shop. They'll use that. We haven't got women's lib up here, yet.'

'A man, then. But no blue collars and raincoats.'

Farrell glanced quickly round the carpeted interior of Dewhurst's coffee shop. There was no sigh of Wainwright.

Mavis, a fat, motherly waitress who'd been there almost as long as he could remember, said, 'Who are you sitting with, Mr Farrell?'

'By myself.'

'Very good. Somebody left a note for you.'

He took the envelope and opened it quickly. The note inside said simply, 'Ring me at 74105.'

'Thanks, Mavis. I'll make a call first.' He went out quickly through the door that led to the barber's shop, entered one of the phone booths and dialled 74105. Wainwright answered.

'What the hell *is* all this?' Farrell demanded.

'I had the coppers round this morning,' Wainwright said. 'Did you?'

Farrell's heart thudded. 'No.'

'Well, they're outside your office, I'll tell you that.'

'How d'you know?'

'I bloody looked. Two of 'em, one at each end of Royd Street.'

Farrell said, 'What did they want?'

'They want Joe.'

'Joe who?' Farrell asked rather desperately.

'Don't play silly buggers. You should know. You of all people.'

'What did they say?'

'High jump for anybody who lends comfort or whatever it's called. Now listen, I'll be at the golf club lunch time. Otherwise you can leave a message here. Okay?'

Farrell said, 'I don't quite understand...'

'All right, lad. Play it that way. But if you want anything, you know where I'll be. This is the biggest thing in this town since Tottenham Hotspur. I'm not going to be left out!'

He hung up.

Farrell replaced the receiver and went back into the coffee shop. He drank a cup of coffee and quietly inspected the other customers, most of whom he knew, at least by sight. The news that he was being watched had shaken him and he wondered if he'd been followed here. If so, it was important to appear normal. Finishing his coffee, he rose, stopped at an alcove occupied by four wool merchants he knew, and exchanged a few words. Then he left and returned to his office, thinking hard about John Wainwright. He was glad to know he wasn't entirely alone, but Wainwright bothered him, and always had. Wainwright was tough, shrewd and successful, with a good-sized business he'd built by himself from scratch. The trouble with Wainwright was that he was obsessed by his own supposed cleverness, always out to prove himself the better man. And there was a phrase he'd used which worried Farrell. Wainwright had said, 'I'm not going to be left out!'

'And that's all he did?' Hutchinson said into the telephone. 'He didn't sell any houses?'

'Didn't have time, sir. At least, he didn't seem to have.'

'And you didn't lose him? Even for a minute?'

'Yes I did, sir. For three minutes.'

'Good Christ, man! What happened?'

'He'd gone through into the barber's shop.'

Hutchinson scowled. 'The phones are on the other side! Didn't you know?'

'No, sir. I thought he was in one of the alcoves. By the time I'd found out he wasn't, he'd come back again. And the gents is by the barber's shop, too, sir.'

'Where is he now?'

'Back in his office, sir.'

'Right. Stay outside. And don't let him go again!'

Hutchinson hung up, shrugging irritatedly.

McHugh said, 'How long?'

'Three minutes.'

'You can say a lot in three minutes,' McHugh said. 'I wonder who the *hell* he was talking to!'

Helmut Artur Dörflinger had taught German at Leefield Grammar School for precisely thirty years. He had remained healthy and had been allowed to continue teaching until he was seventy-four, partly because he did not want to retire and partly to build up his pension. In those thirty years, as he had once calculated, he had taught somewhere between four and five thousand boys. Many, upon leaving, never thought about him again; others did, for Dörflinger had been a popular figure, just eccentric enough to be a character, also notably fair-minded, and good at getting boys through examinations. By some, particularly by boys who had musical abilities, he was particularly remembered, for Dörflinger was an accomplished cellist. His years in Leefield had also included a long and devoted attachment to the reform synagogue whose congregation, though nowadays perhaps a little smaller than it once had been, was still the envy of the other churches in the town. He knew a great many people. He also now knew where Katya Semonov was and understood very well the difficulty of moving her. As Budzinski ate, Dörflinger went carefully over names in his mind, looking not only for people who could be trusted, but for those whose occupations might also be useful. Had he merely been seeking assistance with some private business, there were literally dozens of people he could have called upon; this, however, was very different. The man who gave assistance to Budzinski was placing himself at very considerable hazard. If the man happened to be married, the hazard was extended to his family. The list of names shrank steadily.

The telephone rang and Dörflinger went to answer it. When he returned, he said, 'The police believe you're in Leefield.'

'Who was that?'

Dörflinger said, 'John Wainwright. The police have questioned him.'

'Wainwright,' Budzinski said. 'I'd forgotten him. Why did he telephone you?'

'Just to inform me. That's all.'

'To inform you...?' Budzinski thought about it. 'The police have been to see Wainwright, so they'll see the others. Probably you, too. I'll leave now. What's in your garage?'

'My garage?' Dörflinger frowned. 'I have no car.'

'Paint, buckets, ladders?'

'Yes.'

'Good.'

Budzinski went out quickly and re-appeared at the kitchen door a minute or so later with a stepladder and two gallon-tins of paint. He said, 'Wainwright suspects you'll be involved with me. He can think straight. What does he do?'

'He's a wool merchant.'

'Name of his company?'

'His own name, I think. Why?'

'Check it, quickly, in the phone book.'

A few minutes later, Budzinski was ambling down Glentop Drive, the stepladder on his shoulder, the paint tins swinging from his hand. He had told Dörflinger to forget him. If he needed Dörflinger later he'd try to reach him, but the old man was now too risky.

It was necessary to take blind chances now. The police would come to Dörflinger soon and would already have seen Freddie Farrell. He glanced at his watch and cursed himself for lodging the girl in the pavilion. By this time the school groundsman would be at work and the chances of getting her out unobserved would be slender, at least without violence. Dörflinger had been told the police *believed* Budzinski was in Leefield and that was a long way from *knowing*. Any violence and they'd *know*. They might also know from Farrell and might con something out of Dörflinger, but Budzinski was inclined to think the police could not yet be certain. The moment they became certain, everything would clamp down.

What about Wainwright? As he reached the foot of Glentop Drive he glanced round before crossing the main road towards Roundway Road. He could cut through the estate towards the park. As he did so, a car approached, indicator winking, and turned up Glentop Drive. It was a taxi and he glimpsed a face in the back. A woman, familiar, somehow. Recognition hit him like a blow. Sue Würzburg! He lowered the ladder, put down the paint and bent to retie a shoelace, watching the taxi move up the road and stop, if not outside Dörflinger's house, then very close. No, it *must* be outside! What on earth was Sue Würzburg doing at Dörflinger's? A casual visit? Home to see her parents? Probably. But the coincidence was powerful. He straightened and crossed the road, walking away, thinking furiously. Accept the coincidence, he told himself. Then rule it out and think of the other possibilities. If the timing was not merely coincidental, then it was deliberate. Why, then, would she have gone to Dörflinger's? Perhaps because the police had called on her parents. Maybe. Perhaps because she'd thought it through and concluded that he himself would go to Dörflinger. Also possible. He had a probability and two possibilities. Any others? Yes, there was certainly one. He thought about it grimly; he'd known and worked with the Mossad too long to ignore it. The Mossad would know about him from Bloom and it would be typically Mossad thinking to send Sue Würzburg to sniff him out. But could they have got her to Britain so quickly? He'd left Bloom early last evening. He tried to work out a timetable that would have got Sue Würzburg from Israel to Leefield so quickly. On the face of it, it was impossible. Other factors? Other factors! Come on, *think,* he urged himself. She was in a taxi yet her parents' old house was no more than a quarter of a mile away and she had not come from that direction. Maybe they'd moved, though. All right, which direction *had* she come from? He turned and retraced his steps quickly. The taxi was coming down Glentop Drive, empty now. He watched it stop at the road junction, then move into the flow of traffic. The lettering read: *Yeadon Taxi Service.* Yeadon! The airport! That clinched it: Sue might not be working for the Mossad, but he must assume she was. And if she was, there was something else: Bloom would be here too.

Police and Mossad. Both in Leefield. Well, he'd known they'd find him, but they'd been fast. Turning again, he hurried down the steep slope of Roundway Road.

CHAPTER TWELVE

Sue Würzburg rang the doorbell, waited for it to open, and found herself watching the play of expressions across the old man's face. Surprise came first, then puzzlement. The welcoming smile was far behind – weak, almost forced. She had intended to talk quietly with him; gossip a little, sip her coffee and pick Dörflinger's brain for possibilities. Watching what was happening on his face she realised, suddenly, that Dörflinger actually *knew*.

She said urgently, 'Where is he, Uncle Heini?'

He blinked at her. 'Who, Susan?'

'Josef. Where is he?'

'I saw your father yesterday, Susan. He didn't say –'

'He doesn't know,' she said. 'I'm here to – to help Joe.' She almost tripped over the lie and rushed on. 'He's in terrible danger. You know that. He needs help badly. Tell me, Uncle Heini, please!'

Dörflinger gave a helpless little shrug and glanced past her down the road.

'He was *here*?' she said, interpreting the glance. 'How long ago? Where's he gone now? Uncle Heini, the *Russians* are after him. Everybody. I've *got* to find him!'

Dörflinger said, a little helplessly, 'He's at Kirkhall.'

'Kirkhall? Where?'

'The playing field,' Dörflinger said. 'In the pavilion.'

'Thank you, Uncle Heini.' Her tone was gentler now that he had told her. 'And don't worry. You were right to tell me.' She turned to go, wishing she hadn't paid off the taxi, then faced him again. 'Is there anything else? Any other information at all!'

'The police are looking for him,' Dörflinger said sadly. He seemed to be ageing before her eyes.

'How do you know? Have they been here?'

'I was told.'

'By whom?'

'Wainwright. John Wainwright. The police talked to him.'

'And that's all?'

'It's enough, *nicht wahr?*'

Susan Würzburg said, 'Yes, Uncle Heini, it's enough. They'll come to you, too. Do you know what to tell them?'

Dörflinger's hands moved in a little hopeless gesture. He said, 'I know nothing.'

'That's right. Keep saying it. You knew him as a boy. Nothing else.'

She hurried away, out of the gate, into Glentop Drive and began to run, cursing because there was no taxi and no bus that went there directly. And Kirkhall was at least a mile and a half... and Bloom ought to be told... and she'd been told not to act on her own... and she'd lied to Heini Dörflinger... and, oh *God!* She tried to close her mind, to think of nothing but reaching Kirkhall. She couldn't run *all* the way, but at least it was downhill the whole way, down the valley slope until the last hundred yards or so. But what would she do when she got there? Speak to him? Follow him? She became sharply aware of an abrupt conflict of loyalties within herself, and was surprised because the conflict was unexpected. She hadn't felt it when she left Israel, nor in the planes. She had started out simply as a good Israeli citizen whose clear duty it was to seek to curb another, one whose actions and loyalties were... *were what?* Out of date? Criminal? But how could they be when Budzinski's own *parents* had died in Layerhausen?

She crossed the road at the bottom of Glentop Drive and ran on, taking the same quick route Budzinski had taken, but panting now and increasingly confused. It was Leefield that had started the confusion: the familiar roads, part of her life, part of a childhood of which Joe had also been a part.

Susan Würzburg slowed to a walk, inhaling deeply to regain control of her breath. Memories surfaced in her mind: tennis, swimming, the Saturday night hops at St Peter's Church Hall, bonfire night and treacle-toffee and parkin pigs, animals cut out of gingerbread with a currant for an eye. Eating and laughing. Walking for two minutes, trying to bring her mind under control along with her breathing, she recognised her dilemma and its seriousness, the clear choice it now represented for her. Either she tried to stop Budzinski and hand him over to Bloom, or she helped him, in every way she could.

Twice more, down the length of Roundway Road, she had to slow again. A few people looked at her curiously and she was acutely conscious of the odd sight she must present: a middle-aged woman, red in the face from exertion, running as fast as she could down the long curved road. Crossing over at the next junction, she was in the park. It was years since she'd been here, but there was the bandstand and below it the lake where she'd learned to skate in the hard winter of 1940. Where Joe had learned, too, with Freddie Farrell and Blamires and Patricia Scott and Kathleen Hardie and the rest. Where *did* her loyalties lie? To the state, the abstract concept of the state? But it wasn't *just* the state. It was Israel, whose creation she had left Leefield to join; Israel which had been her home for a quarter of a century. The Jewish homeland – yes, but the Jewish homeland for which Budzinski had fought, too. Had it not been for the soldiers, the men like Budzinski, Israel would have ceased to exist, long ago.

The slope was steeper here. Her feet pounded metronomically, and blood pounded in her head. She swung off the asphalt path on to the main park road and saw, ahead of her, a man walking swiftly. He was carrying something and after a moment he must have heard her running footsteps, because he half-turned to look back over his shoulder, broke into an awkward run and a moment later was round the bend in the road and out of sight. Susan Würzburg forced herself on, near exhaustion, now, her body aching with the strain. It *was* Budzinski, she was sure of it! She must get closer, reach him somehow! Only the slope kept her going, only gravity and her own momentum maintained her forward movement on legs rubbery and almost beyond her control. She staggered to the bend and stopped. The road ahead ran down to the wrought-iron gates of Roundway Park – and it was empty: he'd vanished!

Wearily she moved on, walking now, slowly, her lungs dragging gaspingly at air they could not hold. She thought her heart might fail; it was hammering frighteningly, and her head was full of pressure. Where had he gone? The playing field lay ahead, beyond the gates and a little way up the hill, and Budzinski must go there sooner or later. She'd go there, then, and wait. And perhaps find herself able to decide, too.

Sixty yards down the hill, she suddenly knew where he'd gone. A short, broken concrete path led through the shrubbery to a squat stone building and at the start of the path stood a green wooden sign whose peeling paint gave the clue. On it was one word: *Gentlemen*. Despite her physical distress, she laughed, heard that the laugh shaded towards hysteria and caught it quickly. She'd known this park so well, and not realised the place was even there! But why should she, since it had never been any use to her…? She moved on aching feet and leaden legs towards the little path, and even then she hesitated as the humour became momentarily irresistible. To go into the Gents! In Leefield! What's a nice Jewish girl like you doing, going into…

181

She felt light-headed; hysteria a real danger – she clenched her fists in anger at herself and walked determinedly along the little path.

The space inside the entrance was unoccupied, though a stepladder and a couple of paint cans stood beside the wall. But one of the cubicle doors was closed.

She said softly, 'Joe.'

No response.

She stepped forward and tapped on the door. 'Joe!'

It flew open suddenly, inward, away from her, and Budzinski stood glaring at her. He said, slowly and distinctly, 'If you're Mossad, I'll kill you.'

She felt the tremble begin at her knees and spread until her whole body was shaking. She heard herself say, 'Oh, Joe!' in a voice that trembled, too, and then the weeping began uncontrollably and she stood, still gasping for breath, head bowed, arms limp by her sides, and let the tears flow down her face.

The blow was hard, the harder for being utterly unexpected: the flat of his hand came stingingly against her cheek.

'Mossad!' he said. 'Where's Bloom?'

Her senses were restored suddenly in the numbing aftermath of the blow. She looked at Budzinski's face and saw his eyes and read in them the implacable nature of the man, the determination. Her mind clicked to a decision and her confusion fled. This was no longer the boy she'd known. She was here to do a job. To do it she'd already lied. She must lie again.

She said, 'They sent me, Joe. The Mossad sent me. But they don't understand, do they?'

'Understand what?' Budzinski demanded harshly.

'Anything, Joe. Anything at all. How can I help you?'

He put his hand beneath her chin and raised it, searching her face. 'How did you get here?'

She told him.

'And to Dörflinger?'

She told him that, too.

'Where's Bloom?'

'We meet at Dewhurst's. In the restaurant.'

He gave a sharp bark of laughter. 'Of course. Dewhurst's. In Leefield, where else?'

'Can I help, Joe?'

He stood looking at her. The imprint of his fingers was white on her cheek. Finally he said, 'I must have transport and a place to go. Yes, you *can* help. You can drive?'

'Yes.'

'Then telephone Hertz. If they're not in the book, try Avis. But rent a van and bring it to the gate by the pavilion. Understand?'

'Yes.'

'Then go.'

He watched her hurry down the road. He was far from convinced. By the time he reached the telephone box, she was already leaving it. She glanced at him and nodded, then hurried towards the bus stop. Budzinski went into the box, found a coin, looked in the directory and found Wainwright and Co. Dörflinger had said Wainwright was a wool merchant. He hesitated a few seconds before dialling. He was already taking a chance with Sue Würzburg. Wainwright was a worse one. A girl answered. Mr Wainwright wasn't there, she said, and asked who was speaking. Budzinski said, 'My name is Farrell.'

'Oh, Mr Farrell. He told me to tell you that you can reach him at 74105.'

'Thanks.' Budzinski hung up and dialled again.

'John Wainwright.'

Budzinski said, 'How are you, John?'

'Who's that?'

'I'm a friend of Mr Farrell's,' Budzinski said.

'Oh?' There was a pause. Then, slightly breathless, Wainwright said, 'Do I know you?'

'I think you'll remember.'

'From abroad?'

'Yes.'

Wainwright, surprisingly, chuckled. 'You're a bugger, you are.'

Budzinski said nothing, waiting. It was up to the other man.

Wainwright said suddenly, 'Are you mobile?'

'I will be.'

'All right. Remember Hardy Street?'

'No?'

'Behind the Town Hall. Off Leeds Street.'

'I remember.'

'There's a little warehouse. Number twenty-three.'

'No good,' Budzinski said.

Wainwright said, 'Don't worry. It's not mine. Mine's two doors away, but I rent this sometimes. The sign on the door says Robinson's.'

'Who'll be there?'

'Nobody.'

'You?'

'If you like.'

'Be there,' Budzinski said.

He hung up, frowning. It was too neat, too convenient. Wainwright had never been a friend. Now Budzinski was faced with two unknown quantities; either Würzburg or Wainwright or both might be out to betray him and he was almost defenceless against them. Unless, he thought, he could find a way to defend himself.

Maria Rowan made her report at ten forty-five. Instead of going to the police canteen for her morning coffee, she put on her coat and slipped out to the post office to telephone the number she had been given earlier.

A man's voice answered and she gave her name.

'Well?' the voice said.

'There are... well, there are several things. I don't know quite where to begin.'

'It doesn't matter. Just tell me.'

She said, 'This man Budzinski. They believe he's here.'

'Go on.'

'He went to Leefield Grammar School when he was young.'

'Did he? What are the police doing?'

'They've interviewed a lot of his school friends, to see if they've seen him.'

'And?'

'And nobody has, apparently. But there's one man, he's called Farrell and they think he was Budzinski's best friend –'

The voice cut in sharply. 'Who is Farrell?'

'He's an estate agent.'

'Go on.'

'Well, there's also a man called Bloom. I think he's a diplomat or something.'

'What about Bloom?'

'They think he's trying to find Budzinski, too.'

'Where is Bloom?'

'Nobody knows. He was interviewed by the police down south, somewhere, and they had to release him because he works for an embassy. They think he might come here.'

'Anything else?'

'Yes. All sorts of things. That's what I mean. I don't know where to begin.'

'Just tell me.'

She said, 'Well, a man's been found dead. Murdered. He's a man called Conan and he was at the same school. Then there was another one, called Greenfield, and he was attacked in Cambridge by this man Budzinski. And there's still another man, called Blamires. He's here. He's got a criminal record, but he's a friend of Farrell and he was at school with them both.'

'Go on,' the voice said. 'What else?'

'Well, there was a milk van stolen this morning, quite early, near Otley, and it was found in Leefield. They think this man Budzinski may have used it to get here, but they're not sure.'

'Very good. That's the lot?'

'I think so.'

'Be *sure*.'

She swallowed. 'It's all I've been able to get.'

The voice said, 'Continue to listen, and report anything you hear.'

'The ladies in Poland...' Maria began, but the man had hung up before she could ask him whether they would now be safe.

Miserably she hurried back to her desk.

Two floors up from his own office, Freddie Farrell entered the premises of a firm of accountants. He knew both partners well. He explained that his telephone was out of order and asked if he could use theirs for a couple of urgent calls. The junior partner was away and Farrell used his office to telephone Wainwright.

'Heard anything?'

Wainwright seemed to hesitate.

'Well, have you? Look, don't worry. This is somebody else's phone.'

'Yes, I have. He rang me up.'

Farrell's heart thumped. 'What did he say?'

'He needs a hiding place. He's coming to the warehouse.'

'Where is he now? Has he got transport?'

'He says so. I don't know where he is.'

'You don't know –! How did he get your number?'

Wainwright said, 'Phone book, I expect. I got on to old Dörflinger a while ago, just in case.'

'You think he's talked to Dörflinger?'

'Seems like it.'

'Thanks. I'll call you later.'

'I'm going to the warehouse. But don't *you* come there, Freddie, for God's sake!'

'I won't. Don't worry. But I'll be at the golf club at lunch time.'

'Okay.'

'And if there's anything…'

'I'll let you know.'

Farrell hung up, hesitated, then telephoned Dörflinger. The old man sounded relieved to hear his voice and a minute or two later Farrell knew where Budzinski was, and that Sue Würzburg had gone to find him. He looked out of the window. Two men were hanging about unobtrusively; one in the doorway of Boots, the other on Exchange Street corner. The mention of Sue Würzburg bothered him, as did the idea of Wainwright's warehouse. Without knowing why, he felt an urgent need to go to Kirkhall himself. The trouble was that he'd be followed. Unless, he thought, he could somehow give the watchers the slip. People were always doing it in films and books, but was it *really* possible? Farrell sat down at the desk and thought about the geography of Leefield, about one-way streets and buildings with more than one entrance, about the small carriers whose vans waited twice a week outside his sale room to remove the sold auction lots. He made another call.

A few minutes later he left his office walking fast, and went into Dewhurst's, downstairs to the toy department, upstairs again, out of the other entrance, up the hill to the market, past the fish stalls and through the archway into the general section, then out again and into the Co-operative. He went up one flight of stairs and down two – the shop was on a steep hill – and left by the basement door, plunging directly into the web of narrow streets behind Bradford Road. There, he risked glancing over his shoulder and saw no-one following. Relieved, he hurried on, turning at last into a cobbled yard.

The van was a big old Commer and its owner, who depended to some extent upon Farrell for his livelihood, handed him the keys. Farrell slipped into the driving seat, headed out of the centre of Leefield and cut south, avoiding the ring road, but driving parallel to it. In twelve minutes, he reached Kirkhall, parked the van and entered the sports grounds taking care to close the big, green gate quietly. Once inside, he looked round carefully. The groundsman was two football fields away, pushing the little paint trolley that marked white lines on the turf. Farrell waited until the man was walking away from him then slipped quickly round the front of the wooden building.

'Joe!' he called, softly and urgently. He waited a moment, then called again.

'You stupid berks!' Superintendent Hutchinson snarled into the telephone. 'No, I *don't* want you to stay there. Not much point now, is there? Get back here!'

He hung up and turned to McHugh. 'They've lost Farrell!'

'What happened?' McHugh asked quickly.

'Farrell came scampering out of his office and played upstairs and downstairs through the stores and markets. They hadn't a chance, really, just the two of 'em.'

'It was deliberate, then,' McHugh said. 'Okay, that settles it. He's involved. He's involved and Budzinski's here. We can be sure of *that* as well.'

'So?'

'Roadblocks. Right? Every road out of the town. Quick!'

The roadblock plan already existed; it had merely to be implemented. Hutchinson gave the order, then said, 'We can't very well do a house-to-house. Town's too bloody big.'

'Get Blamires here. No, on second thoughts, don't bother. I'm going to see him. That's if *he's* still at Farrell's office. Is he?'

'I don't know.'

'We'll go anyway. Get somebody to ring and let him know we're on our way.'

A few minutes later, Blamires was gesturing at a filing cabinet.

'How many properties?' McHugh demanded.

'About a hundred and eighty.'

'Christ!' McHugh said. 'And all over Leefield, naturally.'

'Leefield and beyond,' Blamires replied. 'You may be having a property boom in London, but Leefield isn't. There're a lot of unsold houses in this town.'

'You're telling me. Right – how many people leave you the keys?'

'The ones who've moved out.'

'I said, how many?' McHugh said dangerously.

'They're here.' Blamires pointed to a wooden rack. Dozens of door keys hung from it, each with a label attached.

Hutchinson said, 'Let's rule out semi-detached and estates for the time being. Concentrate on the ones with possibilities. Any of these keys missing?'

Blamires said, 'I've no way of knowing.'

'Right. We start matching up.'

Forty minutes later, they stared at each other in frustration. Apart from six sets of keys which had been duly signed out to prospective purchasers, none was missing.

'What about rentings?' McHugh demanded.

'I don't think so.'

'Let's be bloody sure, shall we?'

The telephone rang. Blamires answered and handed it to Hutchinson. 'For you.'

Hutchinson listened and hung up. He said, 'The crowd finally broke into that place in Rome, that embassy villa, or whatever it is. Apparently they didn't find Schmidt.'

'Or else the Russians got him away,' McHugh said.

'One or the other. Anyway he's not there.'

'Which leaves chummy with a girl on his hands,' McHugh said. 'Come on, what about these bloody rentals?'

Blamires said, 'Only commercial property.'

'Keys?'

'All there. But I've been thinking. Some of them have more than one key.'

'And you don't know which?'

'No.'

The phone rang again. Hutchinson said, 'I'll save you the bother,' and reached for it. 'Yes, Ellis, speaking.'

He listened. 'Oh, you have have you? What's his name? And the address? Right. You're a blithering bloody idiot, Ellis. No, I *don't* want you to go. Sit tight and think some more and get those wheels going round a bit faster!' He hung up. 'Christ on a pogo stick! He'd *forgotten!*'

'Forgotten what?'

'There's an old master at the school. German-Jewish refugee called Dörflinger. He was a sort of unofficial father to the Jewish boys. You know him, Blamires?'

'Yes.'

'True, is it?'

'I suppose he was.'

'And Budzinski. Would he go there?'

Blamires said, 'Dörflinger must be eighty.'

'Aye, and Budzinski must be desperate!'

'Will you go see him,' Hutchinson asked McHugh, 'or should I?'

McHugh said, 'We've got all these premises to search, remember.'

Hutchinson gave a bitter grin. 'Okay, but I don't think they matter.'

'Why not?'

'Because if Ellis forgot something, then it's important. I can feel it in my water!'

'All the same…' McHugh was cautious.

'Okay. I'll get somebody over to organise the search. Come on.' Hutchinson turned to Blamires. 'Wait here, right? I'll radio HQ from the car.'

Blamires watched them go. He, too, had forgotten about Dörflinger. But Dörflinger was surely too old, and Budzinski would realise it. He'd thought of something else; he went into Farrell's office and looked for the key to Dale Cottage. Dale Cottage was rather special and rather private and Farrell let it only to people he was certain about. Farrell also used it himself sometimes.

The key was missing.

Blamires came out of the office, and leaned on the counter. His tightly-closed eyes reflected the pain within him. Either he betrayed his friends, or he betrayed himself, totally and finally, without any possibility of…

The door opened and two men entered. Blamires looked up.

'Mr Farrell?' one man asked.

'Mr Farrell's out.' Blamires stared at them, wishing they'd go away and leave him to his misery.

'Mr Blamires, then,' the man said pleasantly.

'I'm Blamires.'

'Police officers,' the man said. 'Come with us, please.'

He went. He climbed obediently, almost blindly, into the waiting car. It was several minutes before he understood that he should, by now, be at the police station. He looked out of the window and realised where he was; the car was in the middle of the Old Church district: a twenty-acre demolition area where almost nothing remained of the long terraces of back-to-back hovels, except a few whose gaping windows and wrecked roofs awaited the pick and the bulldozer.

The car stopped and Blamires was bundled quickly inside one of the few remaining houses. The two men stood easily before him, and Blamires backed away from them, to the wall. He said, tremulously, 'What is this?'

One of the men stepped towards him. 'You're going to tell us what you know about Josef Budzinski,' he said, then drove his fist into Blamires' gut.

CHAPTER THIRTEEN

Had Budzinski stayed to watch Sue Würzburg, he would have seen that she let the bus go by and, as soon as he was out of sight, returned to the telephone box. She rang Dewhurst's restaurant, said she had been intending to meet somebody there and was unable to keep the appointment. Her name was Würzburg. Had anybody been asking for her? A gentleman? Oh, good. Could she speak to him, please?

Bloom had a little difficulty in finding his way round the one-way system, but it was still only twenty minutes before the blue MGB drew up beside the telephone box on the low side of the park. A woman stood waiting, looking anxious and slightly dishevelled. He wound down the window. 'Mrs Würzburg?'

She got in beside him. 'You're Bloom?'

'Yes.'

She pointed up the hill. 'He's up there. It's a school playing field.'

'Alone?'

'No. A van came. I didn't see who was driving it, but it's parked up there by the gates. A man went inside.'

'Know him?'

'I only got a glimpse. I didn't see his face.'

'But?' Bloom said.

'No. I didn't get the chance.'

Bloom climbed out of the car, walked to the corner and looked up the hill, then returned. 'What's on the other side of the gate?'

Sue Würzburg said, 'The pavilion. That's all. Rugby fields, running track. What will you do?'

Bloom thought for a moment. 'Wait, then follow.'

'You can't tackle them here?'

'No,' Bloom said shortly. 'Here, I could kill them, but that's all. And we don't want them dead. We want them *out*!'

'If we follow, they'll see us. We might lose them.'

'So?'

She told him. He thought for a moment, then leaned forward and started the engine.

* * *

'Citizenship is not an inalienable right,' McHugh said harshly. 'Especially not for you. It can be revoked and you can be deported, all quick and quiet. You'd be surprised what the Home Office can do if it's pushed. And we can push bloody hard. Understand?'

Dörflinger sat in an armchair, looking up at Hutchinson and McHugh. At seven that morning he had been still brisk; old but in possession of himself and proud of it. The morning's events had diminished him. He felt small and frail, almost lost in the chair, and there was a film of moisture over his eyes that would not seem to clear.

'You won't know many people in Germany now, I don't suppose?' Hutchinson said.

'Imagine it,' McHugh went on. 'Hunting round Dortmund or Düsseldorf or somewhere looking for a flat you can afford on your pension. And all this stuff in crates' – his gesture took in the room and its furniture – 'packed and coming after you.'

'He *was* here, wasn't he?' Hutchinson demanded.

'Why else,' McHugh added, 'would there be two of everything on the kitchen table. Eggs for two, coffee cups for two.'

'Where is he?' Hutchinson asked crisply.

'You any idea what the exchange rate is against the Deutschmark?' Hutchinson said.

'Or look at it this way.' McHugh made his voice suddenly gentle. 'He may have been one of your lads. Nice boy, maybe. But he isn't now. He's a killer and a kidnapper and he's got hold of a girl. Hard luck on her, isn't it? Poor kid; how do you think she feels?'

Dörflinger's head moved slowly from side to side. 'I –' He sighed heavily, raised a hand and let it fall.

Hutchinson said, 'You're a right-thinking man, sir. Why protect him? I know he's Jewish, but that's not a real reason to protect him. Not now, not when he's a killer.'

'So tell us. For the girl's sake,' McHugh said. 'Let's at least protect the innocent.'

Dörflinger's face moved and he straightened in the chair. He said, 'Joachim Schmidt is not innocent.'

It was a small, final flaring of spirit.

'Budzinski was wrong there, too,' McHugh said flatly. 'Schmidt wasn't in Rome yesterday.'

'But the radio…'

'The place was searched. No sign of him,' McHugh said. 'So it's just the girl, now. We've got to protect *her*. Don't you see?'

'Is that the truth?' Dörflinger asked. 'About Schmidt?'

'Absolute truth. So, you see...'

Dörflinger seemed to grow visibly smaller. He muttered, almost to himself, 'I told him to take care of the girl.'

'Quite right, too, sir. Do you think he will?'

'I don't know.'

'Better be sure, then,' McHugh said, encouragingly. 'Where did he go? After he left here, I mean?'

Dörflinger said something, but neither man caught the words. 'What was that, sir?'

'What happens... to *him*?'

'Well, what would happen, sir? He'll be apprehended. Proper trial. That's all. There's no death penalty, you know. Not nowadays. You'd even be able to go see him.'

Dörflinger nodded slowly. '*Is gut.*'

'Where is he, sir?' McHugh's tone was very soft.

'The playing field,' Dörflinger said. 'In the pavilion.'

The two policemen exchanged glances. They left quickly; McHugh did not look back, but Hutchinson did. The old man sat very still, looking straight ahead, and tears were streaming down his cheeks. When he reached the car, McHugh was already on the radio, and scowling.

Hutchinson said, 'Don't tell me!'

'Over and out,' McHugh said. Then, turning to Hutchinson, 'Blamires has vanished. When the lads got there, he'd gone.'

Hutchinson winced. 'We shouldn't have left him!'

'It's not that. The typist there said he'd left with two police officers. Only they weren't.'

Budzinski had remained inside the wooden building and they had talked quickly through the shutter.

Budzinski said at last, 'You'll have to distract the groundsman. If you do, I can get the girl out.'

'Okay.' Farrell set off across the grass. The groundsman was already turning his little machine to mark the dead-ball line. When he turned to mark the next line, he'd face the pavilion.

'Good day to you,' Farrell called, more cheerfully than he felt.

The groundsman heard, stopped walking, and waited. As Farrell came close, he said, 'Help you?' He had turned and was facing the pavilion and the gate.

'I want some advice,' Farrell said.

'Oh?' The groundsman took off his cap and ran his hand across his forehead, not sorry to be interrupted.

'I used to go to this school, you see. And I've been thinking for a while now that I'd like to give something. Present something to the school. You know?'

The groundsman nodded. 'It's the Headmaster you want, sir.'

'No.' Farrell took a couple of steps past him. 'I know what he'd say – he'd tell me to put a few quid in the building fund and I don't want to do that. I'd like to give something the boys will enjoy. Something to do with games. See what I mean?'

'Yes, sir. I do. A nice cup for the athletics. Or rugby maybe. How about that?'

Farrell affected to consider. The groundsman had had to turn to face him and behind his back the pavilion door had opened. 'Cigarette?'

'Thank you, sir.'

Farrell held the match and watched over the man's shoulder as Budzinski, carrying a long bundle over his back, moved quickly across the front of the building.

'No, not a cup,' he said. 'But I wondered about some springboards for the pool. What do you think?'

'Be popular, sir. That's true. But there's regulations. Water has to be a certain depth, for safety and that.'

Farrell again glanced past him. Budzinski had the gate open. He said, 'Any idea what the regulations say?'

'No, sir. Not my line, you see. But I expect they'd tell you at the council offices. They'll know because they've pools of their own.'

'Of course. Thanks. What do you think of the idea?' Budzinski was through and the gate was swinging to.

'Me? I like it, sir. But whether the Head will...' he shrugged.

'I'll try him when I have the facts,' Farrell said. 'Many thanks.'

'Right, sir.'

Farrell had to prevent himself breaking into a run. Instead he marched briskly off towards the gate. The walk seemed to take forever. He got there at last, tense and breathing hard. The road was quiet and the van's back doors were closed. He hurried to the driver's door, swung himself in and turned his head to look over his shoulder into the back. 'All ri –?' he began, but shock full-pointed his question as he found himself looking into the muzzle of a pistol. The man holding it said, 'Face the front and drive.'

'Who – ?'

'Do as you're told.'

Farrell turned the key, put the car into gear, and took off the handbrake. His hands trembled. 'Where?' he asked. 'Where do you want to go?'

Aaron Bloom said, 'Take us where you were taking Budzinski.'

'Why should I?'

'The same considerations apply. Budzinski mustn't be caught.' Farrell swallowed, his throat dry, and moved away from the kerb. Behind him, Budzinski said, 'They were in the van, waiting for me.'

'How?... I mean...'

'My fault,' Budzinski said. 'If you look in the mirror, you'll see Sue in here, too. Sue Würzburg.'

'Be quiet,' Bloom ordered.

'He may as well know,' Budzinski said.

'I said, be quiet!' And, to Farrell, 'You had arranged something. What is it?'

Farrell asked, helplessly, 'What do I do, Joe?'

'Tell him.'

He told him. 'There's a cottage, up the dale. It's quiet. I was going to take him there.'

'Up what dale?' the voice behind him demanded.

'Wharfedale.'

'How far?'

'Thirty miles. A bit more.'

'This cottage, is it yours?'

'No. I rent it out for somebody.'

'Are there records in your office?'

'No.'

'Who else knows about it?'

'Just the owner, and he's in Bournemouth.'

Budzinski's voice said angrily, 'What the hell do you think you're doing?'

'I'm untying her,' Sue Würzburg said.

'Don't!'

'We can't leave her like this! Look at her face, she's in pain.'

Bloom said, 'Leave her.' And then, a moment later, as the van slowed, 'What's the matter?'

'Traffic hold-up,' Farrell said. 'Long queue. Look at it.' He pulled up at the tail of the line, peering ahead.

Bloom said, 'Are there traffic-lights?'

'Not for a couple of miles. Why?'

Budzinski said, 'It could be a roadblock. That's why.'

Susan Würzburg climbed over the back of the passenger seat, opened the door and got out. She walked briskly ahead beside the line of traffic. A couple of minutes later, she returned.

'Police roadblock,' she said briefly. 'They're checking all vehicles.'

'There's a side road there,' Bloom said. 'Turn into it.'

Farrell obeyed.

'Now turn round. Back the way we've come.'

'What good will that do?' Farrell demanded. 'If this road's blocked, they'll all be blocked.'

'Do it.'

Two minutes later he was heading back towards Leefield, glancing in the mirror. The van was not apparently being followed.

Farrell said, 'What now?' He was sweating.

'Is there a side road? Something they won't have covered?' Bloom demanded.

'No,' Farrell said. 'Main roads run out from Leefield in all directions, but they're all *main* roads.'

'*All*? Think!'

'Yes,' Farrell said, 'I'm afraid so.'

Sue Würzburg said suddenly, 'What about Morton's Farm? Does it still exist?'

'Yes.'

'And the quarry? The stone quarry beside it?'

'The gate!' Farrell said. 'Yes, by God.'

Sue Würzburg said, 'There's a track leads up to the farm. It was a riding school once, that's how I know it. But the track doesn't stop at the farm. It goes past, and the farm adjoins a stone quarry. It comes out on the Maston road.'

'Try it,' Bloom ordered.

The track was bumpy and exposed, snake-like on the steep hillside. As the van climbed, Farrell could see, glancing down, the queue of traffic on the road below. The van reached the top, rolled past the old stone farmhouse and came to the gate. Again it was Sue Würzburg who got out to open it.

They breasted the slope of the hillside, and began the bumpy, potholed descent. At the bottom, where the track joined the main road, traffic swished freely past. The roadblock must be further back. Farrell slid the van into the traffic stream with a feeling of relief, and turned off for Guiseley and up on to the Ilkley road.

Susan Würzburg said suddenly, 'I'm going to untie her.'

'No!' Bloom said.

'She's in agony, look at her face – how long has she been like this?'

195

'A while,' Budzinski said.

'You're cruel!'

Budzinski said, 'She's Russian. Leave her.'

'No, I won't leave her.'

There was a scuffle and a sharp slap and Farrell, glancing in the mirror, saw Budzinski holding his cheek in surprise. Sue Würzburg said sharply, '*You're* Jewish, Budzinski. So show some decency!'

'Not the gag,' Bloom said. 'Leave that. Screams we can do without.'

Farrell drove steadily north west, through Ilkley and then, following the line of the Wharfe, past Bolton Abbey, Appletreewick, Burnsall and Kilnsey to the little village of Arncliffe. Now, from beside the road, the high fells climbed away. They were no longer in Wharfedale, but in Littondale. He took the tiny road west, up the steep hill, with Fountains Fell rising to two thousand feet dead ahead.

Behind him Bloom said impatiently, 'How much farther?'

'Couple of miles.'

'This cottage. You're sure it's secure?'

'It's remote enough,' Farrell said. 'We'd take some finding.'

The cottage stood on a low slope, screened by trees; a strange building in this setting. Once it had been a chapel, built by one of the extreme non-conformist sects in the eighteen-nineties and intended as the centre-piece of a small self-governing community. The Dales had several times attracted such groups, but the hard beauty of the landscape was matched by the harshness of a winter climate that made for unremitting labour and precarious rewards. The chapel alone now remained. It was perhaps fifty feet long and twenty wide, with a sharply-pitched roof of split sandstone slabs. Inside an upper floor had been constructed along half its length, with two bedrooms and a rough bathroom. The rest of it was as it had always been, a big stone-flagged room with no ceiling but the roof and beneath it the lattice work of timber and metal supports. A wooden stair ran upward from the big room to the upper floor.

Farrell ran the van in among the trees, parked it and unlocked the heavy oak door. Inside, the cottage was cold and rough, a place of no great comfort.

Bloom said, 'Watch them,' and went up the stairs. Doors opened and closed. While he was away, Susan Würzburg's pistol remained steady on Budzinski. When Bloom returned, apparently satisfied, Budzinski said quietly, 'You'll take me back to Israel?'

'What do you expect?'

'And the girl?'

'We release her,' Bloom said.

'Like that? You just forget about Schmidt?'

'I make myself forget.'

They were in the high room and the girl lay on a couch, Sue Würzburg sitting beside her. Farrell, watching spasms of cramp strike repeatedly at the girl's limbs, found himself sharing the pity that showed in Sue's face. The child must be about the same age as his own daughter; even a bit younger. He said, 'Can't you help her?'

'Yes, I can. Help me carry her upstairs.'

'Make Joe carry her,' Bloom said. 'And watch him. No, wait a minute!' He turned to Farrell. 'Is there a cellar?'

'No.'

'I don't believe you. Watch them, Mrs Würzburg.' He left the room and returned a few moments later, smiling faintly. 'Over here, Budzinski.'

Budzinski shrugged and preceded him. They all heard a door open and close, a bolt slide home. Bloom said, 'Now he can carry her.'

Upstairs, Farrell placed Katya Semonov on the bed and turned. Sue Würzburg, following him with a gun, had now placed herself well clear. 'Back to the stairs,' she ordered.

From the top of the staircase, he was covered by Bloom. He walked down slowly and turned, as directed, towards the cellar door. 'Unfasten the bolt and go down,' Bloom said curtly. Farrell obeyed and the door slammed behind him. The darkness was total and he almost fell. He felt his way carefully down the stone staircase.

With the door safely bolted, Bloom allowed himself to relax a little. They'd done better than he'd believed possible: they'd caught Budzinski without either bloodshed or public commotion and now held him in a place where it was highly unlikely they'd be discovered. The problem, now, was to get Budzinski safely on to Israeli soil – and initially that meant the soil of the Embassy. The Embassy had resources and would arrange things, but first the Embassy must be informed and here there was no telephone. Either he or Sue Würzburg must drive off to find one and tell the Embassy what to do. Bloom found himself a chair and positioned it where he could watch the cellar door, then sat down and began to think of the best means of transporting Budzinski.

Above his head Susan Würzburg, her sleeves rolled up, worked with strong, neat hands on Katya's muscles, feeling painful knots beneath her fingers and trying to knead them away. The girl's feet and hands were pale and bloodless, her wrists and ankles deeply marked from the way she had been tied. Every few seconds Katya's body arched in the agony of cramps which seemed to hit her everywhere, arms, legs, back and stomach. Budzinski, she thought angrily, had been stupidly, needlessly brutal. Bloom, too, for that matter; Bloom had insisted the girl remained gagged. Well, now the gag could come out. This place was remote and the gag was wholly unnecessary. She touched the gag and was appalled at its dryness: a cloth stuffed in the child's mouth for hours! It would be stuck to her tongue and the membranes of her mouth. Even to pull it out would be painful. She found the bathroom but there was no running water, so she went downstairs.

Bloom said, 'Don't leave her alone!'

'She's doubled up with cramp,' Susan Würzburg said angrily. 'She couldn't take two steps. I want water.'

There was an old-fashioned hand pump in the kitchen and she filled a small jug, took it back upstairs and poured a few drops at a time on to the gag, enough only to moisten it, careful not to let water flood into the throat. A few moments later, she began to ease the gag out. Then she proffered the jug, holding it herself and the girl took a few sips, nearly choking once as a vicious cramp knotted her stomach.

'Now lie still,' Susan Würzburg said. 'I'll try to ease the cramp a bit more.'

The girl looked at her uncomprehendingly. Sue Würzburg spoke again, in German this time, and the girl nodded and rolled on to her stomach. She worked on, massaging firmly, watching colour return as circulation came back to feet and hands.

Once or twice the girl gave a sudden grunt of pain, but there were also small, inadvertent sounds of ease. The cramps were going. 'Better, now?' she asked.

Katya turned her head. 'They will kill me?' She spoke in German, a little ragged, but fluent enough.

Susan Würzburg said gently, 'Nobody's going to hurt you. Not now. I'd better explain what happened...'

The two agents of the KBG who had taken Blamires from the estate agent's office to a demolition site and there had beaten him until he told them all about Dale Cottage, were now on distinctly unfamiliar territory. Blamires had known the name of the cottage, but not its precise location; nor did he have its formal post office address. The two agents thought at first that he was concealing information from them, and made him suffer a good deal more as a result. When it became clear that he had told them all he knew, they abandoned him, semi-conscious and bleeding badly from the mouth, on the rat-run floor of the derelict house, and left quickly. Their car contained the Automobile Association handbook, but the AA maps were too skeletal to show in detail the complex pattern of winding roads in the Yorkshire Dales. A better map was therefore an urgent necessity. One of the agents got out of the car in Exchange Street and bought a Bartholomew's half-inch-to-the-mile sheet at W. H. Smith's, and the two men then drove hurriedly out of Leefield, following the Ilkley signposts. Their car spent almost twenty nervous minutes in a police roadblock, but when it was inspected a constable merely glanced inside, asked that the boot be opened, and then waved them through. He did not ask for driving licences and even if he had, would have been satisfied by the documents the men carried. They had arrived in Leefield earlier that morning, each summoned urgently from his normal area of operations because the London-based KGB operatives could not reach Leefield quickly enough. The two were Stanislas Bers, whose normal duty it was to report on activities at Catterick, the huge army camp on the Yorkshire-Durham border, sixty miles away, and Andrej Sakharov, whose assignment was the city and port of Manchester. Both were, in theory, refugees from the Ukraine and British citizens.

Each man knew his own area: each had a carefully-constructed cover which included both a job and leisure activities; neither, however, was a walker or an admirer of scenery, so this big area of mountains and fells, of little valleys and stone-built villages, was strange to both.

All the same, the road to the Dales country was well signposted. They drove easily and fast to Ilkley and up the Wharfe valley, until gradually the big yellow-on-green road signs began to be infrequent and were replaced by white posts and pointing arms bearing strange village names. 'Somewhere between Arncliffe and Malham,' Blamires had told them, speaking with difficulty from a badly-bleeding, swollen mouth and through smashed teeth. Bers, navigating in the passenger seat, found Malham on the half-inch map, and they drove there. All they now had, by way of guidance, was the name of the owner of Dale

Cottage. After some discussion, Bers climbed out of the car and went across to the post office. The door was closed and locked and a sign said, *Open at 2.15 pm.* Bers swore, walked round to the side door, and knocked.

A woman opened the door, plainly displeased, her mouth full of food.

'I'm looking,' Bers said, 'for Dale Cottage.'

'Two-fifteen,' the woman said. 'Can't you read.'

He wanted to hit her, but made himself smile. 'Please. I have come a long way.'

'Oh! Have you?' she said. 'Can't even let a busy woman have her dinner!'

'Please,' he repeated.

The woman relented slightly. 'Dale what?'

'Dale Cottage.'

'What, here? In Malham?' She had a broad accent and Bers found difficulty in understanding.

'Not here,' he said carefully. 'Otherwise I should not have worried you. I understand the cottage lies between Malham and Arncliffe.'

'Dale Cottage,' she said, chewing. 'There's about ten I know of. Dale Cottage, Dale House, Dale Bank. Over by Arncliffe, you say?'

'Arncliffe, yes. The owner is a man called Priestley.'

She laughed sharply. 'You've a choice of three, then. Happen more. There's Priestleys up off Mastiles. Mastiles Lane. Priestleys by Litton. Priestleys Darnbrook way. All related.'

'Dale Cottage,' Bers persisted.

'Stiff wi' Priestleys here,' the woman said. 'My husband'd know.'

'Is he here?'

'Nay, he's i' Skipton.' She'd stopped chewing now. 'See, it won't be Mastiles. It's Dale Farm is Mastiles. You'd happen better try t'others.'

'Where were they, please?'

'Darnbrook,' she said, 'and Litton. Mind if I have my dinner now!' The door closed firmly, and Bers hurried back to the car. Darnbrook and Litton, he found, were on the same road. The car swung out of Malham up the steep hill where a sign pointed the way to Litton. Twice more, Bers climbed out of the car, to ask directions at isolated farmhouses. The accents were universally broad, the replies not easily comprehensible. They found themselves in Litton, nearly ten miles away, still not having found Dale Cottage.

In Litton, however, they were luckier. 'Tha maun mean t'owd church,' an old man told them. 'Abaht fower mile back on t'Malham road.'

From that Bers had absorbed the important words: 'church' and 'four miles back'. The car turned again and they headed back the way they'd come.

In the darkness of the cellar, Budzinski said quietly to Farrell, 'I'm not going back.'

'Where then?'

'Nowhere.' Budzinski gave a small, bitter laugh. 'No, a good Jew shouldn't say that. Jehova's bosom – or hell. Hell seems likely.'

'Don't be bloody daft!' Farrell said.

'I'm a sad story now, Freddie. I failed.'

'You tried. You bloody well made an effort.'

'Sounds like a school report. Budzinski made an effort, *but...!* Takes you back, doesn't it?'

Farrell said soberly, 'Don't. Don't think it, even.'

Budzinski said, 'I've had some practice.'

'Eh?'

'I was Brutus, wasn't I? End of the last act, Brutus runs on sword and dies. You should remember. You were Strato.'

Farrell strove to answer brightly. 'It was a rubber sword.'

'But there's a friend up there with a real pistol.'

'Friend?'

'Aaron. Aaron Bloom.'

'He wouldn't do it, surely...?'

'I know Aaron. I could force him.'

Farrell said, 'You must get *out* of here.'

At the top of the staircase the door opened. Bloom's voice said, 'Josef!'

'Well?'

'Schmidt wasn't even there!'

'He was in Rome.'

'I've just heard the radio. The crowd broke in. He wasn't there.' The door closed again.

'He was there.' Budzinski's voice grated angrily. 'They got him out!'

Farrell didn't care whether Schmidt was in Rome or Timbuctoo. He said, 'You've got to get away, Joe. Just concentrate on that. The girl doesn't matter. It's just you!'

'Just me,' Budzinski agreed. 'That's the whole trouble, Freddie.'

The boy was dawdling on his way back to school, strongly tempted to play truant. Half a day wasn't much, and his mother might never find out. It was maths this afternoon, and he hated maths. But if his mother *did* hear about it! He winced at the thought. He'd be late anyway; he knew that. But the bus money in his pocket would buy a Milky Way. He weighed the equation in his mind, balancing Mum and arithmetic, bus fare and a 'late' mark. If he ran, he'd only be a minute or two late and he'd have the Milky Way. That was best... or was it? He scuffed his toes in the dirt and tried to decide.

Suddenly he stopped. He'd heard something. He listened, but the sound didn't come again until he was turning to go on. Then he heard the groan. The boy frowned, unsure what the sound meant, but a little frightened. The *frisson* of fear decided him. He'd run to school and endure the maths. Then he remembered another boy, who'd found somebody drowning in the canal and been given five pounds. Five *pounds!* Anyway, he'd have an excuse to be late.

Hesitantly, he glanced around him. The whole area was deserted. What if it were a ghost? He didn't really *believe* in ghosts, but... the sound came again; it came from one of the derelict houses, too, and Mum had forbidden him to go near them. Still, it *was* a groan, and...

He tiptoed closer to the house and peered furtively past the broken door. He felt his hair tingle and he turned and ran, as fast as he could, for the safety of his classroom, where he arrived breathless and wide-eyed.

His teacher was elderly, experienced in the ways of small boys, and this child was badly frightened. In two minutes she had it out of him. In three she was in the headmaster's office, telephoning Leefield Police.

Katya Semonov listened as the woman explained; she asked questions and received answers. Why had *she* been kidnapped? Why had Susan Würzburg and Bloom, if they were Israeli, intervened to stop another Israeli at gunpoint? The reasons were explained. And what now? She would be released. The woman said she was sorry, deeply sorry, that Katya had been put through this ordeal, but the man Budzinski was a kind of rogue elephant. Israel had once been proud of Budzinski; now, she, at least, was ashamed.

Katya saw that the woman meant what she said, and found herself, in spite of everything, drawn to her. She was angry, more than angry. But it was impossible to be angry with Susan Würz-

202

burg, whose face radiated concern for her and who so clearly shared her anger at the treatment Katya had received.

She said, 'Don't worry, I'm all right.'

'Until you're back with your own people, I worry. Until a doctor has seen you, I worry. Those knots he tied! You could have lost a foot.'

Katya swung her legs off the bed. It was some time, now, since the last seizure of cramp. She stood and stretched, pivoted her torso from the waist, reached high then swung to touch her toes, right and left.

'You see. I'm fine.'

Susan Würzburg smiled. 'I'm very glad. Please understand that not all Israelis are like Budzinski.'

Katya gave a little jump to grasp the wooden beam above her head and pulled herself up, chinning the beam. Then she repeated it. It was so good to have limbs free again, to know she was physically undamaged! She said, 'The Israelis... I don't understand. You are imperialists. You attack the Arabs and force them into wars. Why is that?'

Susan Würzburg tried to explain. Israel was the Jewish homeland. After two thousand years of the Diaspora, the Jews had at last come together...

Katya Semonov dropped lightly to the floor. 'I was in Munich for the Olympic Games. It was very sad.'

'There have been many tragedies for us.'

'For us, too, in the People's War, when the Germans held the Ukraine.'

'I know.'

Katya jumped again for the beam. 'My grandfather, the Germans took him away. He was gassed.' She chinned herself again, then looked down and smiled. 'I do not remember, of course.'

Susan Würzburg smiled back. 'Of course.'

'When the whole world is Socialist, it will not happen.'

'Perhaps.'

'It will not,' Katya said. 'Socialism means peace. We must all work together.'

'We have places in Israel where it happens already,' Susan Würzburg said. She described the kibbutzim.

'Like collective farms.'

'Quite like them.'

They talked as Katya went steadily through a repertoire of exercises. Susan Würzburg watched with admiration. The girl's suppleness and balance were astounding; she was graceful, pretty and above all, *young*. 'I should like, one day, to see you in a competition,' she said.

'I do not think,' Katya replied gravely, 'that it will be possible.'

'Why not?'

'After this, I shall not be able, I think, to leave the Soviet Union again.'

'That's a shame!'

'A pity, yes. I should have liked to see the kibbutzim. That's right, kibbutzim? When can I leave?'

'Quite soon. We just have to arrange things. You're not frightened now?'

Katya smiled. 'Not now. You – *you* I can trust!'

Susan Würzburg smiled back. 'You must be hungry. I'll see if there's any food.' She picked up the pistol that had been Budzinski's and left the room.

CHAPTER FOURTEEN

'Where's that bloody doctor?' McHugh said savagely, glancing again at his watch.

'On his way. Just minutes now, I expect.'

'In London we'd have had him here by now!'

'In London,' Hutchinson said, 'doctors have wings. I know. There's the bell now.'

The white Daimler ambulance came fast along the hard-packed rubble-strewn ground, and stopped. The two policemen followed the doctor inside and watched him bend to examine Blamires. 'How did this happen?'

'We don't know,' Hutchinson said. 'And I'm not going to guess. But we've got to talk to him.'

'Not now,' said the doctor briefly. He rose and called for a stretcher.

'Now,' McHugh said harshly.

The doctor shook his head. 'He's too ill. Christ, man, *look* at him!'

'All the same. He's got to talk. Can't you get him conscious, just for a few minutes? After that he's all yours.'

The doctor hesitated. He'd encountered the police before, as every casualty officer was bound to. But these two men were bigger guns, far more authoritative than the pencil-licking coppers who waited at the hospital to take details of road accidents.

'Why the urgency?'

Hutchinson said, 'Lives depend on it. Several, perhaps. Will he die?'

'Impossible to say. I doubt it, but he might. He's had one hell of a beating. God knows how much internal damage!'

'Smelling salts, or adrenalin?' McHugh insisted quietly. 'You'll be quick?'

'Very quick.'

'I'll see what I can do.' The doctor opened his emergency bag...

Minutes later, Blamires was blinking up at them, whimpering with pain.

McHugh said, 'Who did this?'

Blamires' reply bubbled through a mouthful of blood and was distorted by brutally swollen lips, but it was at least understandable: he did not know.

'What did you tell them?'

His eyes closed in pain and the doctor said, 'He isn't up to it. Really, he's not. I'm certain his jaw is shattered.'

'You told them something,' McHugh said. 'What was it? Somebody's after your pal Budzinski, right?'

Blamires' head nodded weakly. His lips tried to frame words, but failed. His right hand made movements in the dirt on the floor.

Hutchinson said, 'He's trying to write!' He tore a leaf from a note-book and put his ball-point pen carefully in Blamires' fingers. They watched as letters came slowly. Blamires could not see the paper and the pen straggled wildly over it.

'Day?' Hutchinson asked. The word was indecipherable. Blamires' head moved weakly from side to side. He made a capital *L*.

'Dal…? No? Da… *Dale?*' A nod. 'Dale what, lad? Looks like "cabbage". No?' Blamires' swollen tongue clicked across ruined teeth, producing a faint 'tut'. Hutchinson experimented with the sound… 'cabbet… cattage… *cottage!* Is it cottage?'

The nod was scarcely a movement at all.

'Dale cottage,' Hutchinson repeated. 'There's a million of 'em. Where is it, lad?'

The fingers moved painfully. Another *L*. A straight stroke… *I*… the painful 'tut'… then a kind of spastic groan.

'Litt…? Little something, lad? No?' Hutchinson looked into Blamires' mouth as the agonised spastic groan was repeated. Lips open, keeping his tongue low, he tried to reproduce the sound.

McHugh said, 'An *M?*' A tiny movement of the head gave a negative answer.

'*N*, then.'

A nod.

'Litt…*N?*' McHugh said.

Another nod, almost imperceptible now; Blamires' consciousness was going.

'*Litton!*' Hutchinson said suddenly. 'Up in the Dales? Dale Cottage, Litton? Right, lad?'

A tiny, final nod. Blamires, who had been clinging desperately to consciousness, had now let go.

'How far?' McHugh demanded.

'Thirty miles plus.'

'An hour?'

'More than that,' Hutchinson said. He nodded to the doctor. 'Take him. And thanks.'

'Helicopter,' McHugh said crisply. 'How near's the RAF?'

In the cellar beneath the chapel, Farrell was growing increasingly angry. Budzinski's spirit seemed to have been evaporating steadily since their capture, and he now stood against the cellar wall, disconsolate and unresponsive.

Farrell attacked him with uncharacteristic harshness. 'Think, Joe, bloody well think! How many men died in Rome? They were *your* friends, Joe, and there were four of them! And I'm not going to get out of this scot-free, either, am I? Aiding and abetting, if nothing worse. Yet now you just want to back out. What the hell has it all been *for?*'

He got no reply.

'Do me the favour of answering, for Christ's sake! What *for?*'

Budzinski said dully, 'Schmidt. Just for Schmidt.'

'Schmidt! You want him for years and now, suddenly, all you want is to give up! Four men dead and you want to give up!'

'What else can I do, Freddie?'

'I'll bloody well tell you what else: it may sound pompous but you keep the faith, Joe! Do you think your friends died so you could commit suicide in some bloody corner? If you're so determined to die, do the job properly. Die *trying!*'

'Trying what?' Budzinski said.

'Trying to find Schmidt. That's what you want isn't it?'

'From a cell in Israel?'

'They still have to get you there,' Farrell said. 'Now listen. I'll tell you about this place. The bloke who owns it is a potholer, understand? And the whole area round here is riddled with caves. Get out of here and you can go to ground, right? I can tell you exactly where and how.'

Budzinski said with a sudden spurt of anger, 'You've spent your life sitting on your fat behind, Freddie. You know nothing. I've had years of this –'

'You have, haven't you! So now you don't care. Joe Budzinski gets an idea and drags people into it and they die. Does he care, does he *hell!*'

'Careful,' Budzinski said threateningly.

'Or you'll kill me, too? Friends or enemies, it doesn't matter any more – is that it? Easier to threaten me than Schmidt. Is *that* it? But as long as you're walking, Joe, you're a threat to Schmidt. Don't you see?'

'You know what's going to happen now,' Budzinski said. 'The Israeli Embassy has contacts in Britain. It has, believe me. Aaron will whistle up some kind of transport – probably a container truck – and I'll be marched out of here and into it at gunpoint. After that, Israel.'

Farrell said, 'If the chance came, the chance to break, would you take it?'

There was a moment's hesitation. Then Budzinski said, 'It won't come.'

'If – would you?'

'I suppose so.'

'Does that mean yes?'

'Yes.'

'Well, listen. Three quarters of a mile from here there's a hole in the ground. From the chapel steps you can see a little limestone outcrop. It's about ten feet high and on the far side there's a chunk of rock. Under that rock there's the entrance. It's narrow and it's difficult and they keep it covered in small boulders to stop idiots getting in. But inside it expands. They call it Beer Bottle Pot and it's a new one, only found last autumn. Not even properly explored, yet.'

'How do you know all this?'

'Because my daughter crawls down holes. It's a nasty, dangerous pastime and I wish she wouldn't, but she does. A bunch of Leeds University students discovered Beer Bottle Pot. They were staying here, and Ann drew the diagram afterwards.'

Budzinski said, 'If it happened... if I did get there, then what? They'd just wait for me to come out.'

'Yes. If they saw you go in.'

'It's crazy!'

'It's *there.*'

'Okay, it's there. Aaron Bloom's upstairs. And Sue. And they're both armed. How do you suggest –'

Farrell said, 'Well, you won't do it leaning against the bloody wall! Let's find out what's in this cellar, for a start. There may be something useful...'

The two KGB men had at last found Dale Cottage, and now stood beside their car on the metalled surface of the road, gazing down the fellside to where the steeply-pitched roof of the former

208

chapel rose clear of the wind-whipped, stunted trees that surrounded it. They looked over the terrain, examining the approach from the shelter of a high dry-stone wall that bordered the road. Finally, with their attack plan decided, they moved briskly down the hill in the lee of the wall, to a point where they could climb it unseen and make their approach through the trees.

Inside Dale Cottage, Aaron Bloom paced impatiently across the stone floor of the big downstairs room. A few minutes earlier, unable to find a news programme, he had switched off the transistor radio and now listened in irritation to the sounds that came to him. Upstairs there was the occasional thump as Katya Semonov exercised herself, apparently interminably. From the kitchen came the subdued rattle of cups and plates as Susan Würzburg prepared food. From the cellar he heard nothing. Every few seconds his eyes twitched towards the cellar door, checking the bolt.

This almost domestic hiatus irked Bloom. He had reached the edge point of success and his instincts demanded that the momentum which had carried him so far be maintained. On the other hand, food and drink – a snack of some kind – was an urgent and logical need and would not take long either to prepare or to consume. After that, either Bloom himself or Susan Würzburg would have to get quickly to a telephone and seek the Embassy's assistance. He had already decided – as Budzinski had predicted – to ask for a truck. There were several major Jewish industrialists in Leeds who could be relied upon to give maximum assistance and once the Embassy had been contacted, it was probable that assistance could actually be on hand in little more than an hour. A truck could reach London, down the M1 Motorway, in less than four hours. Add on the hour needed to reach the motorway and they could actually be safe in London by early evening.

But the telephone came first. Bloom would have preferred to go himself, but it was wiser, he decided, to send Susan Würzburg. The police might possibly have circulated a description of Bloom himself and even up here he might be stopped and the operation hazarded or seriously delayed. She, on the other hand, could move about freely.

Impatiently he took a few paces towards the kitchen door. 'Be quick with the food,' he called, 'we *must* move!'

'Two minutes,' Susan Würzburg called cheerfully. 'I'm just waiting for water to boil.'

He heard the low whistle of the kettle climb in pitch, then stop, and a moment later the smell of fresh-brewed coffee wafted towards him.

'Sugar, Mr Bloom?' Susan Würzburg called.

He was instantly irritated. It was like a damned café! No urgency, and none of the tautness that operational work unfailingly demanded. But he made himself reply, then turned and walked slowly back into the big room, now with a sense of unease. There was something wrong; experience and instinct told him so – and over the years he had learned to trust the warnings that came occasionally and inexplicably into his mind. He glanced at the cellar door as he passed. Still bolted. Putting his ear to the wood, he listened. Silence. What were they *doing* down there? He moved to the middle of the room and looked about him, his sense of unease growing.

Behind him there was a sudden sharp tap and the crash of falling glass. Bloom spun towards the direction of the sound and saw a head and shoulders framed where the window had been, and a pistol aimed at him through the shattered glass. He dived fast to his left, full-length, hand already groping for the pistol in its holster beneath his left armpit.

'No!' The order came sharply, but Bloom ignored it; he'd made an angle, made the shot more difficult, and his hand had closed over the pistol's butt. He was still trying to draw it clear when the first bullet smashed into his thigh, spinning his body across the floor. But the pistol was in his hand now, and despite the shattering pain he snapped one frantic round in the direction of the window. It was the last thing he did. The second bullet, perfectly aimed, destroyed his heart an instant later.

Susan Würzburg was in the kitchen, about to pick up a loaded tray, when she heard the sound of the window smashing. Two steps took her to the kitchen door. From there she could see nothing, but the three fast raps of pistol fire told her instantly what was happening. She moved swiftly along the corridor and almost halted in shock as she saw Bloom's body motionless against the far wall of the big room. Then a movement at the window caught her eye. Instantly she thought of Budzinski. Had he...? But no, a glance told her the cellar door was still firmly bolted. Quickly she wrenched the bolt back from its socket, then hurried across to Bloom, ignoring the falling glass as a man began to climb in through the window. She knelt swiftly beside him, realising as she did so that Bloom was dead, that the eyes staring up towards the roof were already sightless. His pistol lay

210

beside him and she reached and slid it hard across the floor towards the corridor.

The man was almost through the window now, clambering clumsily down to the stone floor, but though his movements were awkward, his pistol pointed directly at her. Behind him stood another man, also armed.

She watched helplessly as the first approached her. With his pistol barrel, he indicated Bloom's body. 'Budzinski?' he demanded softly.

She shook her head.

He moved closer, the gun now pointing unwaveringly at her face...

In the timber-walled bedroom above, Katya Semonov had also heard the crash of glass and the rapid exchange of shots. She moved quickly out of the door and nervously approached the head of the wooden staircase. First, she saw Bloom's body and Susan Würzburg on her knees beside it, then, as more of the big room became visible, she could look down on the whole scene and absorb its significance and what it meant to her. Two people had saved her. Of those two, one now lay dead and the other, crouched helplessly on her knees, seemed about to be shot. Her nightmare had seemed over; now it was beginning again and the woman who had been her only ally now stared wide-eyed into the barrel of a pistol.

Katya Semonov was suddenly, desperately afraid. She felt her skin tighten across her scalp, a swift tension in her body. Below her the man stepped towards the kneeling woman.

She acted almost without further thought, believing deep within her that without the protection of the Israeli woman, she was finished. Her eyes flickered across the room towards the roof supports, taking in distances, computing instinctively. Then, knees bent, her upper body tilted smoothly forward, she dived outward towards one steel bar she had selected among the roof supports. Her hands closed expertly upon it and she let her legs swing pendulum-like through the arc of impetus and into control again, then with knees drawn up, she was swinging over the bar again, gaining momentum. Athletic instinct, the long years of work and practice, gave her the timing; her hands relaxed her grip and her body hurtled forward and down, almost rigid in flight, her feet driving at the man's back.

He had sensed, perhaps heard, the movement and half-turned, but too late. Her feet smashed against his shoulder, hurling him ahead of her against the stone wall, and then she was concentrating on landing without injury in a twisting, slapping breakfall against the stone floor that sent swift agony up her arm. She yelled aloud at a pain so sharp it was like a shot, but rolled swiftly away and rose cat-like to her feet, realising only slowly that it had truly been a shot and that the man she had smashed to the wall had fallen on his gun; that his finger must have triggered it as he fell; that he, too, was dead or dangerously wounded.

'Semonov!' a voice snapped. She turned and saw a man at the shattered window. He, too, had a gun.

She blinked at him, feeling despair spread like a kind of paralysis through her body, despair that weighted both limbs and spirit. A bullet would come. That, now, would be the end.

'Semonov!' The word snapped at her again. 'This way – and quickly!' She saw that he was gesturing to her and she moved slowly towards him. One obeyed a man with a gun.

As she moved, she pleaded with him: 'Please, no, please! Don't shoot, *please!*' She came close, with tears running down her cheeks. Impassively, recognising growing hysteria, he slapped her hard.

She gaped at the man as he ordered: 'Climb out here. Move, girl!'

At that moment she realised suddenly that he had spoken in Russian. With a vast surge of relief she took his proffered hand. A moment's easy agility and she was through the glassless window, dropping to the ground outside...

Even muffled as they were by the heavy cellar door, the three sharp cracks of the shots were unmistakable, to Budzinski if not to Farrell.

'Attack,' he said softly.

'Who –?'

'Quiet!' Budzinski whispered. He groped his way across the cellar, found the foot of the steps and went up quickly. He was halfway when he heard the bolt snap back; a moment later he was pulling cautiously at the door, cursing softly at the sudden dazzle of light and screwing up his eyes against it until his pupils had the chance to narrow. As the door swung inward he heard quick, running footsteps and a moment later a metallic scraping as something slid across the stone floor to his left and bumped against the wall. Keeping low, his head only just above floor-level, he risked a glance round the door frame. The little corridor was empty, but in the big room a man was clambering through the shattered window, gun in hand. Still half-blinded by the light, Budzinski saw the man move out of sight and then heard a moment later, a quick scramble of sound: bumps and grunts, a slapping noise and the sharp crack of a pistol shot. He tried to understand what was going on: an attack, certainly, but by *whom*? Not the British police, he thought grimly. They at least didn't shoot first and ask questions later. That left who –? The Russians? He'd have sworn he'd lost the Russians completely the night before. But...

Simultaneously two things happened. As his vision improved a little, a vague object lying against the wall ten feet away was suddenly recognisable as a gun. Then he heard a voice, sharp and peremptory, say a single word. 'Semonov!' and say it, furthermore, in the Russian way. A moment later other words came to him, sobbing and almost hysterical: the girl's voice saying repeatedly, 'No, please, no!' It *was* the Russians! And the despair was unmistakable in the sound that came from Katya Semonov. Why? Why *despair*?

Behind him, Farrell whispered: 'What's happening?' There was a quaver in his voice. Budzinski half-turned, held his finger warningly to his lips, then went silently up the three remaining stairs and cautiously into the corridor. Flat to the wall, he edged towards the gun, listening hard, eyes flicking from the floor to the rectangular doorway into the big room. There was no movement now; no sound except the girl's pleas, nothing to indicate what had gone on in the room, or what was happening now...

'Semonov!' The voice came once more, harshly, commandingly. Budzinski glanced again at the gun. He'd have to grab and go, take the chance that his reflexes would be fast enough. One more pace... As he moved forward, the angle of his vision widened. He tensed himself, flung himself towards the gun and grabbed it accurately, feeling the butt come neatly to his hand, his right index finger curling slickly to the trigger. From flat on the floor, he could now see most of the big room. His eyes searched rapidly for a target and failed to find one. He frowned and once more looked round the room. Four people: two men dead or wounded; two women, Sue Würzburg on her knees beside one man, and the girl at the window, taking an extended hand and jumping quickly to climb out.

He watched Sue Würzburg's eyes swing towards him. She called quickly, 'Joe, watch out!'

He nodded and wriggled backwards on knees and elbows, grazing skin on the hard stone. In a few seconds he was approaching the kitchen door. He wondered how many men were in the attack? One was dead or wounded: how many left? He glanced quickly round the kitchen door. Nobody was at the big kitchen window, anyway. Briefly Budzinski attempted to consider the situation, but there was nothing to consider and he knew it. Only surprise stood a chance. He glanced towards the main door and rejected it instantly. If there were two men left, one would be watching that door. He must hope there were not more than two.

A deal table stood beneath the kitchen window. Budzinski climbed on to it, risked a quick look outside, then wrapped his arms round his face and hurled himself through the glass. He crashed grunting to the hard-packed earth beneath and rolled quickly into the shelter of the wall. Nobody had shot at him. Raindrops picked at his face as he looked carefully round the hundred and eighty degree arc of available vision. Still nobody.

He rose to a crouch and crept forward to the corner of the building, snapped a quick look round it, then inched forward again, still low against the grey wall. The door was unguarded. Only *one* man left, then, almost certainly, and round the next corner *he* would come in sight. Budzinski inched forward, feet silent on the dark earth and keeping tight to what cover he had. At the corner he again bent low, taking his first, fast glimpse from close to ground-level. A pistol cracked and the bullet sang past him, badly aimed at a target unexpectedly low.

To go round the corner now would be suicidal. *Suicidal!* He grinned mirthlessly as his mind assessed the possibilities. Withdrawing three paces, he sprinted suddenly for the trees and zig-zagged into them, running in a low crouch until he was out of range of all but an exceptionally lucky shot. He dived flat on to the springy moorland grass at the foot of the dry-stone wall and looked back at the cottage, then kitten-crawled forward along the base of the wall until he could see the whole side of the cottage. Nobody there. The man had gone, either behind the far end of the building or through the window or... *no!* Two figures were hurrying up the slope, away from Budzinski, towards a step in the hillside eighty or a hundred yards higher.

He watched the figures become dimmer in the now-drenching rain that plastered his hair to his forehead and streamed down his face into his eyes. His clothes were already soaked and the raindrops spattered against them noisily.

From the cottage, Farrell's voice called suddenly. Still prone in the shelter of the wall, Budzinski shouted back. 'Any others?'

'I don't think so.'

'What's the situation in there?'

'I'm not sure. I –'

'Find out!' Budzinski watched bitterly as the dim figures vanished. He heard Farrell shout a sudden *'Don't'*, and turned his head quickly.

Sue Würzburg was running towards him. 'Get down!' Budzinski yelled, but she ran on and flung herself down behind him.

'Bloom's dead,' she gasped. 'And one of the men who –'

'I saw,' Budzinski spoke shortly, but the hurt arrowed deep inside him. They'd all gone; Shimshon and Moise, Manfred and Guyon, all dead. And now Aaron, who for so long had lived dangerously, had died in spite of a deliberate choice against violence.

He stiffened suddenly, raising his hand for silence, turning his head as he listened. He'd heard the brief, distant muted noise only for an instant and then it had vanished.

'Joe...'

'Quiet.' A moment later he heard it again, more clearly this time; somewhere not far off was an unmistakable clattering roar. 'Helicopter,' he said. His face was lifted to the sky as he listened and his whole concentration was on the sound. Her movement was too unexpected, too swift. He found himself staring in disbelief at his own pistol, suddenly in Sue Würzburg's hand.

She said, 'It can only be the British.'

He said nothing, his eyes fixed on the muzzle of the familiar Uzi pistol that had been Aaron's and then briefly his, and now... now... He sighed deeply and shudderingly as weariness and defeat destroyed his concentration. A drop of rain grew on the end of the pistol barrel and he watched it, waiting for it to fall, no longer caring...

'The *British,* Joe.'

Wearily he said, 'Let them come. It's over. I don't ca –'

'You have a few seconds,' she said.

'For what?'

'To be decent again.'

He gave a short laugh at the incongruity. The raindrop fell, but already another was gathering. How many before the helicopter came, or before she shot him?

'Yes, Joe. *Decent.*'

He looked at her now, weirdly amused at her intensity. All the failure... all the dead ... and she prated about decency!

She watched him sadly, near to tears. Budzinski was burdened by too much guilt and too many deaths. The boy she had liked, the man she had admired, the fanatic he had become, all reduced suddenly to an uncaring nothing waiting for an end on a wet hillside miles from anywhere.

She said, 'So many destroyed.'

His eyes closed and she watched the swift wince of pain on his face.

'And there will be another.'

A moment passed, then he blinked up at her. 'Who?'

'The girl. Katya Semonov.'

He shook his head slowly. 'She's Russian.'

Sue Würzburg said fiercely, 'She's a child. Just a child. And she's innocent.'

'Well she's up there.' Budzinski's wave took in the whole hillside. 'She's free as –'

She interrupted him – 'She's Russian. She killed a Russian.'

'So?'

'So another Russian saw it happen. And now he's got her.'

The helicopter roared nearer, circling in the murk. 'Don't you see what it means?' She watched him carefully. He no longer wanted to comprehend, wanted no more involvement. She said, 'That girl killed *him* to help us.'

The words began to get through then, and their implications. She could see it in his eyes. She had his attention and now she went on urgently, 'She can't even go home. Not like that. They'll know what she did. They'll never forgive her!'

'So *I* kill again, is that it? *I* go after them and *I* kill him?'

'Yes, Joe. *You* kill him.'

They were shouting now because the helicopter was swinging closer, blasting its noise down at them.

His eyes held her for a moment. For a little time they had been slack-focused, almost unseeing, but now the glazed look was going. He still looked weary beyond bearing, with a sadness in him that went to the depths of his soul; but somehow, in a tiny miracle of strength, whatever had broken in him was coming together.

He gave her one small slow nod and held out his hand. She gave him the Uzi pistol without hesitation. Then she rose, turned, and hurried back towards the cottage.

It had taken time to lay on the brand-new Westland Gazelle helicopter; time to reach it, even though the machine flew to its rendezvous with their police car; and more time to search the

Dales folds for a cottage that was not, after all, in Litton itself. Time had been lost in landing in the village; more time lost trying to discover where Dale Cottage lay.

But now, in the diminishing daylight, as heavy rain and low cloud hurried the dusk, they were on to it at last, two angry and impatient men. As the helicopter swung down through the rain's thickness, Hutchinson and McHugh stared down, picking out only with some difficulty the line of the road; just succeeding in discerning the shape of a slate roof and the dark trees around it.

'As close as you can,' McHugh shouted. The pilot waved and the helicopter came lower. As it touched, McHugh took out the pistol he had signed for at Leefield police headquarters, jumped down and ran, crouching beneath the whirling blades, towards the door of the cottage.

As he ran, the door opened and a woman appeared. 'Who are you?' McHugh demanded breathlessly. Budzinski watched the running figure, then his eyes switched back to the helicopter. Another man, older and bulkier but also conspicuously armed, was climbing heavily out of the machine and lumbering after the first man.

He swore under his breath. They hadn't seen him yet but he'd be seen the moment he ventured far from the sheltering wall and unless he moved fast the Russians would be clear. There'd be a car, or some form of transport nearby and ... he glanced at the van but dismissed it instantly. It was too old and too slow. He needed –

He was running on the instant, still bent low, relying on the rain and the thin trees to give him his moment of surprise. Twenty yards and he heard a shout and a pistol shot behind him, but by then he was close to the tail of the helicopter and flinging himself towards its still-open door in the buffeting force of the rotors' downdraught. As he scrambled inside, the pilot's face swung towards him with a look of inquiry that turned swiftly to a gape of dismay as he saw the Uzi in Budzinski's hand.

'Up!' Budzinski shouted, underlining the command with a movement of the pistol. The pilot simply stared at him. Budzinski moved close and jammed the muzzle against the man's head. 'Up!' he repeated.

This time the pilot reacted. A quick pitch adjustment and the rotors bit at the air, then the helicopter tilted slowly forward and lifted.

Budzinski pointed to the step in the fellside where the running couple had disappeared. 'Up there!'

The chopper clattered forward and Budzinski peered anxiously through the armoured glass windscreen, waiting for the flat ground beyond the step in the slope to come into view. When it did, it was deserted and his sideways vision was badly limited by the extent of the blade-wiper's stroke across the windscreen. Beyond the clear quadrant it created, the glass, speckled with water, might as well have been totally opaque.

'Turn through three-sixty degrees clockwise,' he demanded. The pilot hesitated and momentarily Budzinski debated taking the controls himself. He rejected the idea immediately: the machine was unfamiliar and the parameters of height and visibility too demanding. 'A circle,' he snarled.

The nose came round, obediently but slowly, and it was some seconds before he glimpsed the couple, running hard towards the wall. 'Head them off!' As the chopper slid low over the ground towards them, he waited tensely, unsure for the moment whether the gap would close quickly enough. They got there with feet to spare and Budzinski turned quickly to the open door, flicking off the safety catch of the Uzi. He watched the ground flowing past beneath, saw the Russian and Katya crouching low as the helicopter tore over them, and snapped off a shot at the man.

The shot missed. Not because it was a difficult shot, though it was; not because the Russian himself fired upward at the same moment, but because the floor of the helicopter tilted abruptly and viciously beneath his feet as the pilot tried desperately to tip him out of the machine. Hurled off balance, Budzinski grabbed desperately at the door frame, clutched it with a frantic hand and wrestled to retain his grip. But the chopper seemed to have gone mad, waggling in the air like a thing demented as the pilot bent all his skill to finishing the job he had begun. Three times he banked the helicopter steeply and each time Budzinski's grip almost failed. He was being given no chance to recover, and in a few seconds he would be flung clear and dashed against the hillside. Then, quite suddenly, instead of open space beside him and the ground looming below, he was hurled back into the rear of the helicopter's tiny cabin as the pilot had to take violent evasive action to avoid crashing into the steep hillside.

Bruised and aching, Budzinski struggled to his feet. But he was safe now. Three quick steps brought him to the pilot's side and the man's face turned to him, white-faced and apprehensive.

'Once more and you're dead,' Budzinski shouted above the roar of the engine.

218

'You'll die too,' the pilot shouted back.

Budzinski's grin was like nothing the pilot had seen before.

'But I don't *care,*' he roared. 'Now swing it round!' In the lost seconds the Russians could have reached the wall. He watched anxiously for them, now taking care to hold tightly to the winchman's special grip by the open door. Had they?

But they'd backed away from the whirling monster above, and as the chopper roared nearer, they turned and ran, back the way they'd come.

'After them!' Budzinski shouted.

From the cottage door, the helicopter was no more than a dark silhouette, topped by flashing lights, moving slowly across the vastness of the fell's dark face. McHugh and Hutchinson watched it in helpless anger and beside them Farrell and Sue Würzburg stood tensely. There was nothing to see except the slow, inexorable movement of the dark machine; nothing to hear except the hissing rain and the helicopter's clattering roar. Alone among them, Sue Würzburg understood what was happening and her whole being was tensed as she waited for the shots she knew she could not hope to hear.

Suddenly, they saw the helicopter lift and climb fast up the face of the fell. They saw it briefly as it reached the summit a thousand feet above, a black insect shape faint against the leaden dark of the sky. Then it vanished from view.

'All right,' McHugh said grimly. 'Let's have it and let's have it fast. Where's Miss Semonov?'

Sue Würzburg faced him calmly and in silence. Then her eyes moved from his face to look past him, up the face of the fell. McHugh, watching her in fury, saw her eyes widen fractionally and what could have been a tiny smile of satisfaction flickered briefly at the corner of her mouth.

'Damn you, *where* – ?' His face was inches from hers. Then he realised that she was raising her arm and pointing.

Beside him, the phlegmatic Hutchinson said quietly, 'Look behind you.'

McHugh whirled and stared. Dimly he could see a small figure, just below the glacier-scraped step, stumbling slowly down the slope towards the cottage. He ran towards her, up the slope. Before he was halfway his feet in their city shoes were sliding and slipping on the steep and sodden slope and he was gasping for breath. But the figure came on and as they neared each other, he saw the crown of fair hair, the face pale in the darkness. He stopped, waiting.

'Miss Semonov,' he began.

He got no further, for high on top of the fell the night flashed suddenly; a ball of flame began to form and to climb slowly in the dark sky.

Hutchinson puffed up beside him. He said in sudden astonishment, 'Christ, the helicopter!'

McHugh tore his attention away from the flame to catch the girl as she stumbled exhausted towards him. 'Miss Semonov?' With an effort he made himself speak quietly and gently.

She nodded, too tired to speak, and almost fell into his arms.

'Take her,' McHugh snapped to Hutchinson. 'I'm going up there.' He pointed through the drenching rain to the glow on the fell top. Already the fireball had gone, but something still burned up there.

As Hutchinson picked her up, turned and began to pick his way carefully back down towards the cottage, McHugh flung himself at the slope. It was highly unlikely anybody could have survived the explosion, but he had to see.

By the time he reached the slope, sweat was streaming down his body. He stopped to fling off his coat and something caught his attention a few yards to his left: a dark shape lay flat on a kind of step on the slope. He hesitated, then moved towards it, but a second's examination of the body told him that it was beyond his or anybody's help. There seemed to be two bullet-holes, one well below the shoulder, the other cleanly through the head. He left it and moved upward again; the dead would have to wait – there just might be someone injured up at the top.

He'd forced himself up almost seven hundred feet and was close to complete exhaustion when he lifted his eyes from the slope for a weary glance upward and lurched to a halt. He'd glimpsed another figure briefly against the sky, heading down the slope towards him.

McHugh grabbed for his police revolver and flung himself to the ground. He heard the man's grunting, slipping downward progress and strained to see him clearly through the mixed rain and sweat that ran down over his eyes. The man remained out of view, hidden again by some fold of the slope. But McHugh could hear him and he waited, gasping, as the man came closer, only yards away now, an indistinct figure stumbling downward. Listening to the racket of his own breathing, McHugh knew the man must already have heard him: but he came on, apparently oblivious. McHugh's heart was thumping, and not only from the physical strain it had undergone. This must be Budzinski!

'All right. Stop. Raise your arms above your head,' McHugh ordered. The figure stopped and turned and McHugh looked at him incredulously and with relief.

The man who stood before him, swaying dazedly was not Budzinski but the helicopter pilot. As McHugh came nearer, the man collapsed in a heap on the slope.

McHugh knelt beside him. 'Where's the other man?'

The pilot blinked up at him and McHugh slapped his face sharply. 'Where?'

His hand at his cheek the pilot looked resentfully up at him. 'He blew up the bloody chopper. Brand-new bloody Gazelle, it was. Knocked me out and shot up the petrol tank.'

'But where did he *go?*' McHugh demanded.

The pilot groaned and pressed his aching head against the wet grass. 'How the bloody hell would I know?'

McHugh was never entirely sure, but he thought at that moment that he heard, faintly, the sound of a car's engine starting.

Hutchinson had left them, driving in the old van to find a telephone to spread the alarm that would restart the hunt for Budzinski. In the cottage, McHugh faced Sue Würzburg and Farrell. The pilot sat in a chair holding a cold compress against the back of his head. Katya Semonov was upstairs, tucked into bed and well wrapped in blankets.

'We'll get him,' McHugh said.

'I think it would be best,' Susan Würzburg agreed mildly.

He looked at her grimly. 'Don't play the bloody innocent with me, madam. We're going to get to the bottom of all this.'

The explanation, when it came, was simple. McHugh and Hutchinson later agreed privately that it was also believable. But it was not believed. There were holes in the explanation; unfortunately they were not holes that could easily be exploited. Budzinski had been there, certainly; the helicopter pilot recognised him from the old photograph and the Würzburg woman admitted it freely. Budzinski had kidnapped the girl, yes, and he *had* sought their assistance. But they had persuaded him of the stupidity of the whole action and persuaded him to leave the girl in their care. Where was he now? They said they did not know. He had simply gone.

Why, McHugh wanted to know, had the girl been brought *here?* Why had they not got in touch with the police immediately?

There was an answer to that, too. Budzinski had said he was being hunted; and begged them to see that the girl was safe before the police were contacted.

'Safe!' McHugh snorted. 'Safe! – this has been a blood bath! The miracle is that she survived at all. Who are those two?' He indicated the two bodies, still not moved because the murder investigation teams had yet to arrive to take measurements and fingerprints and photographs.

Susan Würzburg said, 'I know only one of them.'

'I know him too. His name's Bloom. Tell me how he died?'

She shook her head. 'It was very sudden. The window was smashed and a shot – no, two shots, were fired. Then that man must have climbed in. I wasn't here – I was in the kitchen. There were other shots. When I got into the room... well, it was like this.'

'And you've really no idea,' McHugh said sarcastically, 'who the other man is?'

'None.'

'You, Mr Farrell?'

'No.'

'I'll go ask Miss Semonov.'

Susan Würzburg said, 'She speaks no English. I'll translate her German if you like.'

He stared at her hard. 'There's more. A lot more. And I'll get it.'

'There are only two really important things,' Susan Würzburg said. 'First that the child is safe. Secondly that while it was admittedly an Israeli who took her, it was also an Israeli who *kept* her safe.'

CHAPTER FIFTEEN

It would be convenient if, when a series of events ended, there were no loose strands. Sometimes it happens and the records can be filed away neatly, with all the ends tied round the parcel. But that is rare.

The end of the Budzinski affair left several separate and unexplained strands, and no connection between them was successfully established. They were directly related, of course, to the Budzinski affair; that much was abundantly clear.

But how?

A body had been found near Exeter and subsequently identified as that of Sidney Conan, barrister-at-law and former schoolfellow of Josef Budzinski. But the body was near Exeter and Budzinski had, at what was estimated to have been the time of death, been in East Anglia, two hundred miles away. And while it was acknowledged that Budzinski was both fast and dangerous, he was neither as fast nor as dangerous as the time and distance involved would require. It was surmised, perfectly correctly, that Conan had been first tortured and then murdered by agents of a foreign power – almost certainly the USSR operating clandestinely on British soil.

Bloom's death was easily, even facilely disposed of by Susan Würzburg, and her story, because it was simple and true, was unshakeable. She had not been present, so she could not know precisely how Bloom had met his death, except that he had been shot.

The other body, found by McHugh on his frantic chase up the hill, was identified later as that of a British citizen and former refugee from the Ukraine, who lived and worked in Manchester. Oddly enough, the man who lay dead with Aaron Bloom in the big room at Dale Cottage was also a Ukrainian refugee. He, however, was resident in Darlington, near the Yorkshire-Durham border. Both men, when their homes were subsequently examined, were found to have possessed various objects which indicated that they were engaged in very dubious activities indeed. However, neither could be traced in any way to Exeter. The question of how they had reached Dale Cottage also remained unanswered and the finding, a few days later, of a car belonging to one of the men, in the port of Hull, did not answer the question to official satisfaction.

Major Theakstone, still detained in the police station at Colchester, had still not spoken. At last, however, he volunteered a statement. In it he admitted that he had had a telephone call from Josef Budzinski and had driven out to meet him. He agreed that such a meeting was somewhat odd, but insisted that they had merely talked for a little while and then parted. Certainly he knew nothing of the girl. Theakstone could have been court-martialled on two counts: for impeding the police and for failing to obey the orders of a superior, but it was officially regarded as unwise to rekindle the affair by submitting him to trial. All the same, Theakstone was punished. In the army there is always the matter of promotion and seniority and certain notes were added to Major Theakstone's career records which ensured that in spite of his undoubted qualities, the major would never become a lieutenant-colonel.

It was never officially known how Josef Budzinski got out of Britain, if indeed he *had* got out of Britain. Eventually, of course, it was assumed he must have done so, and perhaps the car found in Hull gave some clue as to the means? In fact only two people ever knew about Budzinski, and neither spoke of it. But about a month after the affair had ended, picture postcards were delivered at two addresses more than two thousand miles apart. Both bore pictures of the composer Mozart's house at Salzburg in Austria. The first, addressed to Mrs Susan Würzburg at her house in Ashdod, read, 'One hunt successful. The other goes on.' It bore no signature: nor did it require one.

The other card, delivered at the premises of Farrell and Son, auctioneers and estate agents, and addressed to Mr Frederick Farrell, said simply 'Keeping the faith.' It was extracted from the morning mail and delivered to Farrell's small office by a man who still limped and whose shattered jaw was now wired together.

Coincidentally, Colin Blamires had received, by the same post, a formal letter from the Institute of Chartered Accountants informing him that under no circumstances could a man convicted of a criminal offence involving theft ever again be considered for re-election to membership of the Institute.